THE KING'S SHADOW

Gate of Myth and Power Book 2

K. M. SHEA

A huge thank you to the amazing Taylor Goldhardt for her help with my portrayal of Aristide. Her diligence and thoughtfulness over Aristide's blindness made his character possible. Thank you, Taylor, for your patience and expertise!

THE KING'S SHADOW

Cover Art by Trif Book Design
Edited by Deborah Grace White

ISBN: 978-1-950635-21-4

www.kmshea.com

CHAPTER ONE

Chloe

There were only a few times in my life when things felt so out of control, none of it seemed real. Previously, I would have said the time the Curia Cloisters told me I was on my own in terms of protection from other supernaturals was undoubtedly the worst memory I had.

However, I was pretty sure Noctus—the *King* of the Mors elves—informing me I was something called a shadow, which was the only natural enemy of elves, just shattered that experience.

I tried to form words—thoughts, even. But my brain had chosen to take a holiday in an attempt to reject the vital information I had just learned.

"I...*what?*" I tried to say more, but my tongue was thick and numb, and I couldn't move my mouth.

Noctus ignored my reaction and pushed open the door we'd stopped in front of. "This will be your room."

I couldn't even turn to look at it, I was too stunned.

I'd been lying to Noctus, leading him to believe I was a mere cat. That alone was a big enough sin to inspire an elf to kill me, but to add to my iniquities it turned out I was basically his *nemesis?*

The world had it out for me. That was the only reasonable explanation.

This is beyond worst-case scenario. This is catastrophic.

Noctus watched me, tilting his head slightly so the flickering lights from the hanging lanterns caught the glints of gold in his hair.

"Wait, I'm sorry. I apologize. Please. I think there's been a mistake." I clasped my hands in front of me as I tried to kick my brain into high gear—I couldn't afford to further insult him. "I'm not...I can't be what you think I am."

"There's no mistaking it," Noctus said. "The shadows are the only supernaturals who have the powers you possess."

I shook my head. "Except the Curia Cloisters don't even know what I am. If I was a shadow, they'd know."

"Not necessarily," Noctus said.

A door creaked open, and Aristide swaggered into the hallway. "Noctus," he called. "Who are you talking to? And where's Ama? I have a tuna treat one of your people gave me for her last night, and it's stinking my room up." He seemingly gazed past us, his eyes unseeing as he tried to size me up—he was probably listening to my heartbeat.

Vampires didn't have as good of hearing as werewolves, but they had a special affinity for heartbeats, given what they were.

"Aristide," Noctus said. "This is Chloe."

"Ah—the Book Nookery clerk?"

"Yes. And Ama."

"*What?*" A candle in one of the lanterns hanging over our heads flickered, casting shadows across Aristide's slackened jaw.

Another door farther down the hallway opened. "Hey, what's all the yelling about? I thought we were done for the night." Ker yawned widely as she poked her head into the hallway, then retreated a step when she saw me. "What—who?"

I nervously peered up at Noctus—I was going to follow him on *all* of this. I didn't have a hope of escaping this place, and there wasn't a point as long as I wore my collar that let Noctus track my location. Unfortunately, that collar could only be removed by Noctus, and I had a feeling he wasn't going to do that anytime soon.

Noctus shut the bedroom door. "We'll meet you two in the library."

"The library? Not your study?" I hurried after Noctus, following him back down the spiral staircase.

He silently led me to a different part of the house—one I had never ventured to because I didn't want to see any skeletons in his closets.

Unfortunately, it seems like I'm one of those skeletons.

When Noctus opened a set of double doors, I obediently followed him, then froze when the sensation of magic surrounded me, inspiring me to finally look up.

Noctus's library was immense. It was easily the size of three or four Book Nookeries put together—complete with a second floor that stretched high over my head.

The ceiling was mostly glass, which showed the night sky outside the villa, and the edge of the mountain the building was nestled against, but every inch of the walls was either decorated with a fresco painting, mosaic, or stone carving—most of which were statue-like carvings of winged, rearing horses or burning phoenixes.

At the center of the room a glass globe that was as large as I was tall spun in the air. I could feel magic radiating off it, and something swirled in its depths.

A flowering tree surrounded by a moat of aqua water grew at the far end of the library, and enormous lanterns that twinkled with soft light gave the room a warm feeling.

On the second story, walkways with wood railings led from platform to platform, and as I watched, the platforms themselves *moved*, going to a new set of staircases that connected to a different part of the library.

But the most impressive part was the endless rows and shelves of books. Ranging from pixie size to troll appropriate, books lined the shelves—some sparkling as if they were recently purchased, while others were torn and tattered.

Library wasn't a strong enough word. This place almost felt like a monument to books and knowledge...and magic.

"Chloe," Noctus snapped, breaking me out of my reverie.

Oh gosh, did I just make him madder? I need to avoid that. The best possible scenario I can hope for right now is that he throws me in a dungeon or something instead of killing me.

The optimistic part of me dared to hope he might be less severe than that, but rarely was the optimistic part of me brave enough to hope since it was *never right*, so I brutally kicked those thoughts down.

"Sorry." I scurried after him, following him to a small circle of chairs.

I gingerly sat down on one as I struggled to sort through all the magic in the place.

I could feel the magic in the books—there was elvish magic in them to be sure. I'd recognize that sharp magic that poked me in the ribs anywhere. But the buzzing feeling in my fingers marked out wizard magic, and the silky brush of fae magic tickled my elbow.

If I'd known this place existed, this is where I would have come when I was trying to figure out how to get my collar off. Not that it would have been much help. The collar Noctus put on me was undoubtedly elvish, and while surely one of the elvish books in here could help me, I wouldn't be able to read it.

The doors opened again, revealing Ker and Aristide. "What's going on?" Ker asked.

Aristide settled himself in an armchair covered with embroidered flowers and vines. "Yes, what do you mean by...this?"

Noctus glanced at me.

I shrank in my chair. *I should have to explain—I'm the one that lied to them. But...hopefully I survive this.*

"My name is Chloe," I said. "And I can transform into a cat. A black cat."

"You're Ama," Aristide said. "That's what Noctus meant, isn't it?"

"Yes," I said.

Ker narrowed her eyes, and I could feel her warm and bubbly personality instantly cool. "Explain."

"I moved to Magiford because I want to get a job at the Curia Cloisters. The Cloisters have never been able to successfully sort out what I am, which means I haven't ever been allowed to join a House or a Court. Working at the Cloisters was my safest option," I said.

"What does that have to do with pretending to be Ama?" Aristide asked. His voice wasn't hard, but I felt it like a blade at my throat.

"I don't have anyone," I said. "So the Unseelie and Seelie Courts like to pick on me since I can't fight back. I was getting chased the night I came here, and the Seelie fae took me. They planned to rough me up, but their king had ordered them to speak to Noctus, so they brought me with."

Ker had opted to stand, and she paced back and forth like a prowling wolf. "And you tricked Noctus into taking you in."

"No—no, no." I wildly shook my head. "I don't have any powers like that!"

"Then what magic *do* you have?" Aristide pressed.

"Very little that I can actively use. My blood tests say I'm human, but I can change into a cat like a shifter, except I don't have a shift time, it's instant. I'm also immune to most types of magic, and I can go unnoticed. My senses are a little better, particularly my night vision, but that's about it."

"We know what you are," Aristide said. "Isn't that right, Charon?"

I twisted in my chair, peering at Charon as he slipped through the library door. He approached us, bowing briefly to Noctus. "The trash has been relocated, Your Majesty."

Noctus nodded, but he didn't take his eyes off me. "You heard, Charon?"

Charon glanced at me. "Yes."

"Then you agree?" Aristide asked.

"That she's a shadow? Certainly."

Aristide smiled, showing his pronounced fang teeth. "That's what I thought. It's the only explanation—you're a poster child for them, Chloe. I'd say we should have thought of it sooner, except I thought all the shadows were slain."

"It seems not," Ker said, her voice still cold.

"Given that elves exist in secret, I don't think it's all that farfetched that some shadows escaped the hunt," Noctus said. When he looked at me, the spiral in his eyes swirled. Even with the shackles on his wrists containing his magic, I could still feel it waft off him in his anger.

When I hugged him to snap him out of his magical fit, he didn't seem to mind. He was gentle. But...I guess that was before he realized the full extent of what it all meant.

His reaction wasn't the only one that worried me. Ker's cold eyes were like a knife in the heart. I'd been certain she would be the first to forgive me, but her frown was chilling.

"I didn't mean any harm." I could feel my heartbeat speeding up, but I couldn't keep calm with all of them looking at me like that—well, everyone except for Aristide. He seemed remarkably relaxed as he tucked his hands behind his head. "I had no idea about any of you—I just wanted to escape and keep living my life."

Noctus sat in his chair in a way that made me feel like I was kneeling before him on a throne. "Ama did leave the first opportunity she had."

"Yes." I scooted to the edge of my chair. "I thought that would be the end of it. I had no idea you'd put a tracking spell on me."

Wait, that makes it sound like I'm blaming him for the situation.

"I should have told you when I realized you were looking for me," I rushed to add. "But I was scared. I thought..." I trailed off.

There isn't a nice way to say "I thought you'd kill me," is there?

"And now you know about Noctus, about the city, about everything," Ker said.

"Oh, I'm sure not everything," I nervously laughed. "I tried *not* to learn more, because I knew I could be a risk to you all. Just as I wanted to leave and go back to living my life, I also wanted to make sure no one was harmed because of me." I paused, the words tasting like sand.

I need to tell them, about the tracker.

I braced myself for even more anger. "Which is why I need to tell you what made me look for you guys at Magiford Donuts. Someone is trying to kill me. I don't know why, or who—but he's a supernatural and he uses magic."

Noctus steepled his fingers together, his eyes lowering to half-mast as he watched me. The pressure that radiated from him went up a notch, and I was finding it hard to breathe.

Was this really the guy who had crooned to me in Elvish? *It doesn't matter. I need to warn him.*

I took a shaky breath of air and made myself continue. "He came here last night and tried to break through the protective barriers you have on the Cape Cod house—to get to me." I nervously rubbed my hands together. "I thought the barrier would hold, but I didn't want to risk it. I was trying to figure out if I could alert someone to contact you when I saw the lights come on in Shiloh's house, so I ran out to lure him away and came to you because he won't bother me if I'm with you."

The muscles on Noctus's face hardened. "Charon."

"I'll check, Your Majesty." Charon bowed, then slipped out of the library—most likely to check the barrier.

"Is that why whenever Noctus found you, you were forever running around town?" Aristide asked.

"Yes," I said. "I was running from him. He chased me into the Seelie fae, who grabbed me in my cat form the night I, um, met you all. I hadn't tried to get away from them because I wasn't sure if he was still following me at the time."

Ker folded her arms across her chest. "It seems...convenient, but she's not lying. Or if she is, she's excellent at covering it up."

"I doubt that," Aristide dryly said. "I now understand why Ama frequently sounded like her heart was going to explode."

Ker shifted from foot to foot. "Should I check, Noctus? If this supernatural was outside the house tonight, I'll be able to smell him."

Noctus nodded.

"He was by the fence," I said. "He put some things on the ground—I didn't see them when we got home—I mean, back—so he either took them when he was chasing after me, or he came back for them." I nervously bit my lip. "If you go down a few blocks you'll find my backpack—I flung it onto someone's yard while I was running."

Ker nodded to me—not with anger, but with a stiffness I'd never seen in her. She left, leaving me alone with the elf king and the vampire.

"Well. In the meantime, I might as well tell you why you have a stalker." Aristide clapped his hands twice. Out of everyone, his conduct surprised me the most—I thought he'd be icy like the others, but he seemed to still be his open self.

Is he acting this way to try to gain my confidence because he thinks I'm somehow lying and he wants to trip me up?

"It's probably because you're a shadow," Aristide blithely continued.

"I don't know what that is," I said miserably.

Aristide rested his hands on the textured arms of his chair. "Your family didn't teach you?"

"I'm adopted," I said. "When I turned into a kitten as a toddler, my parents realized I was a supernatural. They got me tested, but the Curia Cloisters were never able to accurately sort me."

"Ah, yes. That would explain a number of things," Aristide said. "But then, you mean to say you know nothing of your heritage?"

I shook my head. "I know I'm a human, but that's it."

"I see." Aristide drummed his fingers on his chair. "Then it seems you are in for quite the education. Noctus, would you like to explain, or shall I?"

Noctus stood up. "You can."

"Goodie, I do love a good history lesson." The vampire wriggled in his chair, then pointed his head in my direction—though his gaze went beyond me. "Simply put, shadows were a subset of wizards that were so gifted by magic, there isn't a supernatural that can compare to them."

I'd been somewhat distracted watching Noctus stride deeper into the library, but Aristide's declaration got my attention back. I stared at the vampire for a heartbeat, trying to sense if he was being serious. Come on, I was among the *weakest* of all supernaturals. "What?"

"Immune to all negative types of magic, but still able to benefit from things like healing magic and portals to the fae realm, shadows were magically impossible to beat. If that wasn't enough, the ability to instantly swap from their human to cat body and back was a magnificent boon in battle."

Now I know he must be kidding. How would turning into a housecat make a difference in a fight?

"Do shadows turn into big cats? Because I can only turn into a housecat, and I can't say I've ever felt anything but desperate when facing off against anyone," I said.

"Shadows only have housecat forms." Aristide tsked, and his forehead wrinkled, as if he was concerned I was stupid. "Anything bigger would be a shifter."

"And a housecat would be a *boon*? In a *fight*?" My voice was squeaky with my disbelief.

"Yes, it was very helpful," Aristide said. "The cat form made shadows particularly skilled at subterfuge and...hmm...that is to say...assassin work."

"*Assassins*?"

"Your natural magic makes it very hard for anyone—human, supernatural, or even elves—to notice you in your cat form," Aristide pointed out.

That, I knew. I frequently took advantage of it when I didn't want to be noticed, and I could ditch just about any supernatural when I turned into a cat—except for the tracker, that was.

Aristide sat patiently, waiting for some kind of response from me.

"I guess," I finally said.

He nodded. "While shadows didn't have the increased healing rate elves and vampires have, they benefitted from increased physical abilities: jumping, speed, stamina, and falling."

"Wait, *falling*?" I asked.

Aristide ignored me and continued. "Given all of that, shadows were uniquely positioned to fight the elves as they could walk through any defense spell, watch without notice, and choose when to attack using techniques that would unbalance any elf."

This is not looking good—no wonder Ker is so reserved. If I really am a shadow, me hiding here could be interpreted as looking for a way to attack Noctus—wait...

"Earlier you said you thought that all the shadows were killed," I said.

For the first time since we'd started chatting, Aristide hesitated.

Was that rude to point out? I shifted nervously in my seat.

"That's because...it was believed all shadows had been wiped out. Before the elven wars, as Noctus said," Aristide finally said. "Which is likely why the Curia Cloisters couldn't tell what you are. The only supernaturals alive who would remember them are the oldest of vampires—and almost all of them are now hiding in coffins—and...the elves."

"What happened?" I asked.

Aristide puffed his cheeks, then blew out hard. "It, that is to say...hrm."

"We elves killed them." Noctus emerged from the shadows of the shelves, tall and imposing.

"W-what?" I stammered.

"Shadows were the one predator that could take out elves," Noctus said. "Elves are immortal in the same way vampires are—age, disease, and most wounds can't touch us, but there are specific methods of execution that can end us. Shadows excelled at those tactics, and as such elven assassinations were common."

Noctus rejoined Aristide and me, though the relative dimness of the room cast shadows on his face that made it hard to judge how he felt about what he was saying.

"In the end, the ruling elven families decided they posed too great a threat, and they needed to be eliminated." Noctus stared at me, his expression stony. "The Mors family was tasked with the job, and they carried out a mass execution."

I sank deeper into my seat and started sweating.

Logically, I knew Noctus wasn't going to kill me right this moment. In fact, I was hopeful that his telling me this was proof he was going to let me live. But hearing about it...it was still frightening.

If the Mors killed them...did Noctus go out and hunt shadows? Was he part of it?

"If the shadows had any weaknesses, it was that there were never very many of them," Noctus continued. "And they were known to congregate in family groups, which made targeting them much easier. It took decades, but eventually it was believed they were eliminated." Noctus glanced at Aristide. "Though it seems we were wrong."

Aristide clasped his hands together and rested them on his lap. "And the proof of that does sit before us."

I had to bite my tongue to keep my jaw from chattering in fear as I looked from Aristide to Noctus.

My heart felt like it was going to explode, and it must have been pretty close, because Aristide offered me a sad smile. "It all happened long before the war between elves and supernaturals," he explained. "But it was one of the reasons why the vampires sided with the other supernaturals. The vampire elders, then, were not so old that they spent their time shut up underground, but fought in the war...because they remembered what had happened to the shadows, and understood the elves could and would do it again."

"So...what are you going to do with me?" I asked.

Aristide cocked his head. "That depends, I imagine."

As if on cue, the door opened. Charon and Ker entered together. Both of them studied me with guarded but thoughtful expressions as they marched across the library—blind to its beauty—stopping short of the circle of armchairs.

Charon bowed to Noctus. "The barriers were disturbed, Your Majesty. There is evidence that magic was used to try to tamper with them, but to no avail. They are not damaged in any way."

Noctus nodded. "Did the porch camera pick anything up?"

Wait—there's a porch camera? Suddenly, I was very grateful that

I'd always been paranoid and had changed from cat to human in a bush several houses down.

"Some." Charon's lips tightened, and the spirals of his eyes swirled in a brief show of anger. "Only enough to show someone standing on the sidewalk used magic. It picked up Ama—that is, Chloe—running out of the house, and the person chasing after her."

"I smelled the guy—he's a supernatural all right." Ker snapped her head in a nod that made the two braids her dark hair was pulled into fall over her shoulders. "But he's not a full blood. I can't say for certain, but I think he might be part elf—though probably only half."

"Anything memorable about him, Chloe?" Aristide asked.

"He has blue hair, but it's very obviously dyed that shade. He doesn't even use magic to color it." I scrunched my nose as I tried to remember details from our unfortunate meetings—I mostly just registered the overwhelming sense of fear that always accompanied him. "He's tall—I think nearly Charon's height, although he's built lankier. Oh, and he's got a neck tattoo."

"Definitely an elf—or half elf, at least," Ker said.

Charon blinked. "A devotee of Auron I assume."

Wait, Auron, I recognize that name. He sent a supernatural here to the Cape Cod, and Noctus thrashed him.

"Auron is another elven royal family," Aristide said for my benefit. "They were summoners and used tattoos for their magic."

"Oh," I said, confused. Noctus had definitely been referring to a single person—unless, did that mean someone from the Auron family had survived?

Before I could further mull it over, Aristide raised his voice as he turned his head in Noctus' direction. "It makes sense her stalker would be an elf. He's likely a lunatic and thinks shadows still need to be eliminated, an easier battle to delude yourself over and win instead of attempting to beat the rest of supernatural society. Shadows are his scapegoat."

"Possibly." Noctus rested his hands on his belt, where I knew he had at least one hidden dagger, then looked at me. "A clerk from Book Nookery is unlikely to have any true enemies."

"None." I violently shook my head, making my teeth rattle. "And I thought all the elves were gone until I was brought here."

Noctus didn't react, so I wasn't sure if he believed me or not.

But there's no way he can think I was planning to assassinate him, right? I mean, I slept in the sink because I was too shy to be in his bedroom when he was sleeping!

"I found Chloe's backpack—a few blocks up just like she said it was," Ker added. "I searched it, but she only packed clothes, a wallet, her phone, and keys. Charon searched her phone. There's nothing on the phone that mentions us. She's only got texts of cat pictures from a 'Pat' and 'Joy' and has a text message from her boss. I left the backpack by the base of the staircase."

"Thank you," I said.

Ker shrugged, her shoulders jolting. She didn't look at me with anger, but something worse—disappointment, with a touch of jadedness I didn't know she was capable of.

Aristide tapped his fingers on his chair, a hint of a smile tugging at his mouth. Charon stood at attention with his hands behind his back, while Ker scratched her jaw, then reluctantly lowered herself into a chair.

"What do we do?" she asked.

Noctus was silent.

"If there is any takeaway from this, I believe it is that we need more cameras," Charon dully said.

"Human technology can be dead useful—particularly since supernaturals frequently fail to realize it exists," Aristide cheerfully said.

Something caught in my throat—fear and hope, probably, with each struggling to rip free and kill me first. I swallowed, then dared to speak. "I, I could leave if you're concerned about the tracker finding you."

I don't really want to stay, but I'm not sure leaving is a great idea, either. The tracker could tear me to bits. I'd have to hotfoot it to the Curia Cloisters, and then how do I convince them the tracker is a half elf?

"If the tracker is an elf, I don't think we'd have to be too concerned that he'll out you, Noctus," Ker said. "He wouldn't betray his own kind."

"This is the wrong house to declare elves can't turn on each other, Ker." Noctus's voice was sharp.

Ker winced. "Sorry, I didn't think."

Noctus shrugged, then swiveled his attention to me. "You will remain here until I decide what to do with you."

I cowered a little under the intensity of his eyes. "Here as in the library?"

"No. The villa," Noctus said.

"What do you mean 'until you decide what to do'?" Aristide asked. "Are you plotting plots without telling us again?"

Noctus blinked. "Chloe's knowledge of the area is troubling because—due to her powers as a shadow—she cannot be spelled to forget. Conversely, if she runs it doesn't matter due to the tracking spell on her. As such, the tracker is the most immediate problem."

"Why?" I asked. "He never actually saw inside the house. I don't even think he knows you're an elf."

Noctus's magic scraped at my ribs as he narrowed his eyes. "Whoever is tracking you obviously knows you're a shadow. I am inclined to think Aristide is correct, and they're a lunatic. If such a person discovered the city, their lunacy might *grow* and hatch impossible ideas."

"Ah, you're saying if he's a nut, he might reveal everything because of his belief in elf superiority and all of that rot your parents used to spout," Aristide asked.

"Exactly."

"That would be dangerous," Ker agreed. "Which means Aristide and I should probably face him—so he never knows elves are involved."

"That's only if we can find him," Aristide said. "Chloe said he just emerges whenever she's out in Magiford. We don't know how to flush him out—unless you think you can track his trail through downtown?"

Ker made a face. "Not likely. The scents are too strong in the inner city where we were. I could give it a shot, though."

"Perhaps we could use Chloe to draw him out?" Charon suggested.

My eyes bulged in their sockets as I stared at Charon, but he seemed apathetic to me.

Ker turned to study Noctus, and even Aristide peered in his general direction as they waited to hear his response.

Noctus rolled his shoulders back. "No." The word was final and hardened.

I let out the breath I'd been holding and my head lolled on my neck in my relief.

"Charon, take Ker downtown to see if you can pick up his scent. The night is still long enough that most Magiford residents won't be up, so the trail might not be covered up yet," Noctus said.

"You got it," Ker said.

"If you find the corner where Noctus picked me up, the tracker should be a block down from there," I rushed to add.

Charon nodded to me—which was something. Ker just glanced at me, then Noctus. Her eyes briefly pinched—almost as if she was sad—then she headed for the door.

"Charon, is there a leash in the car?" Ker asked.

"No, only your guiding harness."

"Then could you grab a leash?"

"If you wish."

Charon closed the door behind them, once again leaving me alone with Aristide and Noctus.

Aristide slapped his thighs. "Well, I am beat. I need to turn in."

"You're a vampire," Noctus said. "You don't need much sleep. And you're nocturnal."

"Fine." Aristide sighed and tapped his cane on the ground with obvious impatience. "I was trying to spare your feelings, but a new episode of my favorite true crime podcast dropped at midnight, and I'd rather listen to it than you. Satisfied?"

"Far be it from me to keep you from your podcast," Noctus dryly said.

"That's what I thought. Good night, Noctus." Aristide strode confidently across the library, using his cane as a guide. When he reached the door he paused momentarily. "Oh, and Chloe?"

"Y-yes?" I jumped to my feet and nervously wiped my hands on the sides of my exercise pants.

Aristide's fang teeth flashed when he smiled. "Welcome home."

He was out the door before I could respond, leaving me gaping like a fish.

Welcome home? That was a loaded phrase, particularly given the elf city and the villa itself.

Does that mean...he accepts me, and he isn't suspicious of me? But why wouldn't he be? My entire situation sounds shady at best and ridiculously fake at worst.

I was grateful—I'd need every ally I could get to survive... whatever this was. But out of everyone, Aristide was the last member of the household who I would have expected to welcome me.

"Hide the collar," Noctus said, shaking me from my thoughts.

I turned on my heel so I faced him again. "I'm sorry, what?"

Noctus's eyes went to my neck. "The collar. Don't let anyone —including Charon, Ker, and Aristide—know you still wear it. Your natural magic that helps you avoid notice will work for it, just make sure you don't draw any attention to it."

Why would he want me to hide it from them? Does it have something to do with the magic he used?

The collar was the least of my problems tonight, so it didn't matter to me, though it struck me as odd that he wanted to keep it on me when I knew from my conversation with Ms. Booker that it must have some unique magic on it.

I rubbed at the three gems sewn into the collar. "You're not going to take it off?"

"And lose the best way to track you? Not a chance," Noctus scoffed.

Well, at least he specified not to tell any of his *friends about it, because, sorry Your Majesty, but Ms. Booker already knows!*

Noctus continued, "You may return to your room. I assume you know the way?"

"Yes, thank you." I stared at Noctus's boots, then reluctantly raised my eyes. "But, tomorrow, could I maybe go to my apartment? I'd like to pick up some more clothes. I only packed one spare set."

Noctus studied me for a moment, his hazel eyes so dark they were closer to a deep umber color. Then, without answering my question, he left the library, leaving me alone.

I rubbed my forearms and peered around the library.

Normally I found the presence of books reassuring. But the library was too grand, and the books were too old and full of magic. It felt...cold, and unwelcoming despite the beauty.

I shivered a little as I left the library, entering the hallway. I headed back in the direction of the spiral staircase, and despite everything—my worry for the wellbeing of my life, the dangerous situation, and the very worst happening—there was a part of me that was...*sad.*

I was used to Ker's pep talks, Charon offering me toys, Aristide's teasing, and Noctus carrying me everywhere.

They'd been happy to see me, and would take me everywhere. I hadn't had that since I'd moved away from my family.

Shadow or not, no one in Magiford greeted me like that, except maybe French Fry.

It's better this way. As a cat, I wasn't really me, but a pet. The worst has happened, and I'm still alive, and I didn't get thrown in a dungeon. That's the best I can ask for.

CHAPTER TWO

Noctus

I stepped out onto the front porch of the human house that served as the connection point from my villa to Magiford. Everything was still and silent. It was four in the morning, and the sky hadn't started lightening yet, but soon it would.

I need to do this fast, before the street starts to wake up and someone notices.

I tugged on the thin trickle of my magic that got through the shackle I'd agreed to let the tea-toting Paragon put on me. It answered, wrapping around my fingers. I waited another moment, then used that tiny bit of magic to poke the vast oceans of my power that were dammed behind the shackle.

The shackle fractured, then broke, letting my power gush back into me.

I glanced at the fragmented shackle, and my magic held it midair, floating in a metallic cloud. I'd need to put it back on after I finished here.

Thus far, I've managed to hide it from the Paragon that I can take his ridiculous safeguard on and off at will. Hopefully, he isn't anywhere nearby, or he'll realize the truth.

But if I was going to blow my rules, tonight was the night to do so, considering I'd already blown the shackles to bits when the Unseelie fae had threatened Amalourne—that is...Chloe.

My eyebrow ticked in my irritation as I strode down the sidewalk.

I extended my right hand, reaching into the realm that held my magical weapons.

I felt various weapons brush my hands, emitting different notes in my mind as they plucked at my magic, but I was looking for a specific one. When I felt the halberd that I wanted strike a thrumming chord in my chest, I wrapped my hand around it and pulled it from the realm, bringing it into the human world.

The halberd, Furor, glittered in the light shed by the flickering streetlight. I adjusted my grip on it, confirming it had attuned to me, then pulled wild magic through it, kick-starting the weapon's abilities.

Magic wrapped around me, hardening into an armor set. This one had a heavy cape that draped across my shoulders, and a full crusader helm that covered my head.

Power pulsed through the halberd, and the edge glowed as I left my property and strode to the cul-de-sac entrance.

The wild magic present in the very air stirred. I couldn't see it like certain elves could, but I could hear the noises it made when it moved—like a breeze.

However, as soon as it sensed my general ire, it fled.

Being at full power does have its uses.

My footsteps were silent despite the armor—well-made elven armor never made a noise. It was lighter, too, and could stand up to a great deal more damage than anything human or fae made.

When I reached the top of the street I turned around, surveying the area one last time to ensure no one was around.

Satisfied, I slammed the butt of the halberd on the ground, sending out a ripple of magic.

I tilted my head as I heard the chorus of the various spells I'd put on the neighborhood respond.

They were whole and unharmed, despite the attempted break-in by Chloe's stalker.

I was displeased he had found the cul-de-sac despite the layers of spells I'd placed on it to make it avoid notice from nearly every supernatural, but it was unsurprising. Once the Paragon found me, I'd had to dismantle the most obvious spells, or he'd realize just how determined I was to hide the area.

Unfortunately, that had made room for the Seelie and Unseelie fae to start hounding me.

They're nothing but pests, but even a pest can bring down an army if they're underestimated.

I tuned the spells and glanced down the street, my gaze lingering on Shiloh's house before shifting to my own.

If Chloe intends to visit Shiloh, I should invest in another barrier spell —even if it perturbs the Paragon.

Although Amalourne—Chloe—was not what I expected, I'd still have to protect her.

She was another loose end that could cause great damage—though on the scale of irritation from the Seelie/Unseelie Courts all the way up to the Paragon, she was less annoying but far more dangerous.

I was irritated that she'd managed to deceive *me*. Shadow or not, that took a level of skill I had never seen, and I'd lived through the mass executions when her ancestors were in their heyday.

Did I hate her? No.

I'd known Amalourne wasn't a normal cat; I'd even figured out she was connected to supernaturals somehow. From a strategy viewpoint, I could even understand why she'd done what she had.

Chloe had no idea about her parentage. Her fright and disbelief had been real—Aristide and Ker would have been able to tell if they weren't. Besides, I doubted that a shadow who was so shy of sleeping with me that she chose to instead nap in my bathroom sink was harboring a secret plot to avenge her people and assassinate me.

I'd never had a quarrel with shadows. It was fear and greed that had driven the ruling elven families to stomp them out, and such emotions were weaknesses I would never indulge in.

What I was infuriated with was wild magic.

I'd given Chloe, a shadow, a part of *me* with her collar, because magic itself had stirred at the idea.

Chloe's arrival as Amalourne had been the first time magic had sung for me since I'd slain my family during the war. I'd assumed that meant it supported the idea. What I hadn't thought to ponder was *who* it supported the idea for.

A sigh that was veined with so much irritation it was almost a growl escaped from me. "Shadows always were the favorites."

All humans were, really. Magic played favorites with who it affected, and humans were undoubtedly at the top of that list, with shadows being the most over-powered imaginable.

That wizards and their various subsets hadn't ever realized this had always been puzzling to me, but even if they were magic's favorites, nobody ever said they were particularly intelligent.

And I was the dolt who listened to the favorite-picking magic.

I could take the collar off Chloe, but if she wore it, I'd be able to tell where she was. I could even feel her to a certain extent. It was a good insurance plan, as long as she never figured out what the collar really was.

And if Ker and Aristide don't notice.

Charon wouldn't question me. But if my werewolf and vampire friends noticed, I'd never hear the end of it.

I ripped my magic from the neighborhood spells, and concentrated my power into Furor. It hummed, then disappeared back into the fae realm, waiting for the next time I would call it.

My armor faded, dissolving like fog, as I strode back down the sidewalk.

I slipped my cellphone out of my pocket, glancing at it as I strolled across my lawn. As I reached for the front door, I felt wild magic curl around me again, warm and decadent in a way that I knew was a lie.

I don't hate Chloe, but the situation is...regrettable.

The revelation was an unwanted one that I attempted to savagely push down, but it was too persistent.

Amalourne was a kind of peace I hadn't experienced in ages. And now...that's gone.

"Gone," I repeated out loud, more as a reminder to my weak conscience. "It's finished."

I needed to remember, Amalourne had been a mere cat. She was safe. Chloe was a shadow. Whatever Amalourne had been to me, Chloe couldn't be.

CHAPTER THREE

Chloe

After my nightmare of an evening, I didn't think I'd be able to sleep, but I must have, because I woke up to a sunbeam dancing on my face.

I yawned, stretched, then promptly had a heart attack when I realized I was in my human form. As I lay, paralyzed, the events of the previous night slammed into me.

I'm in a spare bedroom in Noctus's villa. He knows I'm Ama, and says I'm a shadow.

I still wasn't wholly convinced I was. Shadows sounded like warriors. I was as frightening as the cat I'd pretended to be.

I burrowed out from underneath my blankets and got my first good look around my room, since last night I'd tip-toed in and defeatedly crawled into my bed.

It had a similar light blue and white scheme to Noctus's, but instead of the large, dubious reflective pond, the center of my room had a vaulted, circular skylight that let in rays of the sun, which warmed three rose bushes planted into a mossy square beneath it.

Two of the bushes bloomed white roses, snowy and impossibly perfect. The last bush—the largest of the trio—had beautiful flowers that were a crimson orange at the center and bloomed into a fiery pink, so they almost looked like little balls of flames.

They gave the room a floral scent and a looser feeling as the thorny branches swayed in a breeze I couldn't feel.

The stone fireplace looked similar to Noctus's, except it was at the opposite end of the room. My bed was technically put head-to-head with Noctus's with the wall between us.

Was that done on purpose? Does that mean he can hear me through walls?

I hadn't seen proof he could do that, but how well did I really know the Mors King and his friends?

I padded up to the floor to ceiling windows, tucking myself behind the heavy, velvet draperies as I watched the elven city that sprawled outside.

Citizens zig zagged from store to store, and I watched as a truck rumbled down the top tier of the city.

Apparently I have the same view as Noctus.

I watched for a few moments longer, then I puffed out my cheeks and exhaled. "What now?" I asked my empty room.

For the last few weeks, my goal had been to suck up to Noctus as his cat and to find a way to free myself of the collar that tied me to him.

I felt for the fabric at my throat, and my nails scraped across the three, pomegranate red jewels affixed to it. Yep. It was still there.

Ms. Booker, my boss, had told me it was most likely part of a rare elven bonding magic, which was why I couldn't take it off and Noctus could track me across the city.

I didn't know for certain about the magic. Maybe Ms. Booker was wrong? Not likely, but I'd rather hope for that than bring it up to Noctus after he warned me not to reveal it to Ker and Aristide.

I sighed and turned away from the window, slumping my way across my luxurious room to the bathroom.

I frowned at my reflection.

With my brown hair and brown eyes, I liked to think I could pass for a common kind of cute. The only feature of mine that stuck out was the beauty mark by my left eye, which gave my round chin and nose a little more sophistication. I usually covered it up because it made me a tiny bit more memorable, but I didn't have any makeup. Not that it mattered. Now—with morning breath and flyaway hair that made me look like I'd played with an electrical socket—rough was the only appropriate description for me.

Oh, yeah. I can totally see, now, how I'm a shadow. It's in my style, 'chic slob.' I grimaced. *Yuck. I would beg on my knees for a toothbrush and toothpaste.*

I poked around the bathroom with caution—not because I thought I'd find something I didn't want to see, but because I was ninety percent sure the gold frames on the two oversized mirrors were *real* and not painted, and there was no telling what other useless opulence the elves had invested in. I didn't find toothpaste, or even lotion or shampoo and conditioner. I glanced at the shower—a massive thing with three shower heads—but there weren't any hygiene products there.

Maybe that should be my next goal: find ways to make myself look less like a stray cat.

I licked my dried lips, warming to the idea. *It seems like Noctus intends to keep me around for the foreseeable future, and thankfully*—miraculously—*it seems like he doesn't plan for typical, dungeon-style imprisonment. Last night he brushed it off when I asked, but I really need to go back to my apartment to get more clothes—and toiletries.*

I certainly wasn't going to buy any—I hadn't been to work in weeks, which meant no paycheck. I'd have to tap into my emergency fund to pay for my apartment for the next month or two.

Okay, new short term goal: get the tools necessary to look presentable. Let's go!

I tried to comb my fingers through my wild hair, but it only made the snarls worse, so in the end I patted it down with water, then headed for the door. Maybe my appearance would help drive my case—I couldn't see Charon putting up with me looking like a slob in the luxurious villa.

I wrestled with my backpack for a minute, searching its various pouches until I found my wallet and cellphone. Next, I reclaimed my shoes where I'd shed them by the door, picked them up—as a Wisconsin native it was unforgivable to wear shoes in someone's house—and slipped outside.

I started down the staircase and wasn't all that surprised when I saw Charon waiting at the bottom of the stairs. Today the butler—or steward? I'd never figured out his role—was wearing gray slacks with his usual gray cloak and hood, which drooped from his shoulders. If it wasn't for his tapered ears, spiral swirled eyes, and elf build that was a little too lean and limber, he could have passed for a human.

"Good morning," I said.

Charon studied me just long enough to make my cat senses prickle. "Good morning."

I nervously clutched the staircase railing as I cleared the last step. "Did you and Ker find anything downtown last night?"

"No," Charon said. "Ker picked up his scent, but lost it when he got into a vehicle on main street."

"Oh." I blinked in surprise—I hadn't thought he'd tell me anything.

Lest I think Charon had forgiven me or something, he narrowed his eyes at me and started to turn away.

Wait—my shower!

"Sorry, one more thing, Charon." I scrambled so I stood in

front of him. "I was wondering, could I go to my apartment to pick up some more clothes and some personal hygiene products?" I asked.

Charon drew his shoulders back like he was going to refuse, until I mentioned the word "hygiene" and he glanced at my hair. "I will ask His Majesty." He pulled his cellphone out and tapped away on it.

I awkwardly clasped my hands behind my back, juggling my cellphone and wallet as I waited.

After a minute, Charon bowed his head to his cellphone—as if Noctus could sense the show of respect through it—tapped out a reply, then put it away. "His Majesty has indicated it is acceptable for you to do so, but directed me to remind you of the tracking spell placed upon your person. If you go near the Curia Cloisters you will be forcibly brought back to the villa."

"I won't—my apartment is north of here and is nowhere near the Cloisters," I said.

"Then it won't be a problem."

"Okay, but could I have your number?" I waggled my phone for emphasis. "In case something happens?"

Charon tipped his head. "The tracker?"

I grimaced. "Yes. And the Seelie and Unseelie fae."

Charon frowned. "The fae shouldn't be a problem."

For you, maybe.

"I'd still like to have your number," I said.

Charon shook his head in a gesture that was so slight I almost missed it. "You are not very shadow-like."

"I'm sorry I'm disappointing?" I timidly laughed.

Charon took my phone and added himself as a contact. "I was referring to the idea that you requested the phone number of an elf for reinforcements, but your physical abilities are lacking, too." Using my phone, he called himself, then recorded my number.

I kept my mouth shut because I didn't think I'd be able to say anything that wasn't dripping in sarcasm.

Charon started to turn away from me, then he paused and looked back at me. "Elven memory charms won't work on a shadow, but they will work on every other supernatural being. Do not even *think* to speak of us to any other person. Not only will it not work, but you will be punished."

It's a little late for that! Ms. Booker already knows about Noctus—but at least she doesn't know about the city or Charon and the others. It doesn't matter, though; she's not going to tell anyone.

I debated telling Charon that, but wilted under his steely gaze. "I won't say anything," I said—carefully choosing my wording.

I can't bring trouble to Ms. Booker. She's helped me too much.

"Thank you, Charon." I bowed a little to him since he was a stickler for shows of respect, then headed off to the magical gate that served as the doorway to the human neighborhood.

Everything will be okay. They haven't killed me. I can survive this. And I'll certainly feel better about it once I've brushed my teeth and washed my face.

FRESHLY SHOWERED and dragging a small suitcase of clothes, my laptop, and necessary products, I was feeling a lot better about my situation.

I just need to rebuild trust with everyone. If they realize I'm not a threat—not even a seed of a threat—I bet they'll let me go rather than bother with keeping me.

I was so confident in this idea, I texted Charon to ask if I could go to Book Nookery to talk to Ms. Booker about my work schedule.

He didn't text me back, so I chose to interpret that as permission. I set off down the sidewalk, pulling my rolling suitcase.

Trekking across the city with luggage wasn't going to be buckets of fun, but it was nice to be back in my human shape, so I didn't mind.

I was so happy I was humming as I checked my phone. It was a Saturday, so Joy wouldn't be working. On a whim, I dialed her up.

"*Hey little sis*," she answered in a sing-song tone. "*What's up?*"

"Not too much. I'm just outside enjoying our spring weather."

"*Enjoy it while you can—it's supposed to rain later today.*"

"Good to know. How are you? How's Pat, and our parents?"

"*Mom and Dad want you to call them. They said they've tried calling you but only get your answering machine, which you don't want to keep up much longer, because they told Pat, and now he's been mentioning he wants to come down and check on you.*"

I stifled a groan. I needed to avoid seeing Pat or Joy. My siblings were some of the smartest people I knew, and I was a supernatural.

If they came to Magiford, there was no way I'd be able to hide Noctus from them. He'd have to use magic on them, which I wanted to avoid at all costs. Magic was inherently dangerous. It wasn't something I wanted frequently cast on *my* family.

My luggage clattered as a wheel rolled over a stone. "I'll call them," I said. "How's the boyfriend?"

"*Marco? I broke up with him two weeks ago. He turned out to be such a creep.*"

"Did he do something to you?"

"*Yeah, he enraged me. He went on this anti-supernatural rant, which means he was even less intelligent than Pat said he was.*"

I laughed as I turned a corner, reaching the downtown Magiford area. "Nice. But that's pretty surprising—most humans are cool with supernaturals."

Most of the hate I'd encountered in my life had come from other supernaturals, not humans. But I did have a protective adopted family.

"*Yeah. I'm pretty sure he's just upset that werewolves are better built than him, and he couldn't pass as a gorgeous fae if his life depended on it. Idiots hate what they can't compete with.*"

I smiled at the disdain in Joy's voice. "Thanks, Joy."

"*For what?*"

"For always accepting that I'm a supernatural."

"*Of course. Though I still wish you would have let me bring you to the college pet show when you were small and cute. We could have cleaned up and made a ton of money.*"

"Love you, sis."

"*Love you, too. Take care, Chloe.*"

"I will. Bye."

My spirits bolstered even further, I was grinning when I hung up.

My smile dimmed a little when I peered up and down the streets around me. I couldn't feel the deep dread the tracker's presence brought, but that didn't mean he wasn't nearby.

I craned my neck as I looked, my attention so narrowed I almost lost my chance to avoid a stale french fry that was tossed at my forehead.

I stopped and immediately looked up, spotting a trash griffin precariously perched on a street sign. "French Fry," I called. "What are you doing?"

The trash griffin whipped his striped raccoon tail and cooed at me as he industriously shredded a greasy paper pouch that had at one point held french fries.

"French Fry, don't litter," I said. "That's rude. Give it here." I held my hand out, carefully watching him—not because I was afraid he would hurt me, but because he was an idiot, and he'd fallen off more high places than I could remember.

French Fry jerked his head back and forth, twisting it so he looked at me with first his left orangey-red eye, and then his right. He abruptly opened his front feet—which were pigeon feet—and the french fry bag floated down toward me.

I caught the bag and trotted ahead to toss it in a trash can, grimacing at the grease it left on my fingers.

French Fry launched himself off the sign. It took him a few

precarious moments to get the momentum to propel his furry rear end upwards, but then he circled over my head, cooing at me, until he almost smacked into a stop light.

Trash griffins were not the smartest of fae creatures.

His little display, unfortunately, got the attention of some of the humans who were out and about. A few cars stopped in the middle of the street, and I could see the drivers and passengers gaping at the little guy.

"French Fry," I hissed. "Come on, you're getting too much attention!"

I hustled down a side street, relaxing when I heard French Fry follow me, loudly beating his wings and cooing some more.

It wasn't that supernaturals weren't allowed out in public, but the Curia Cloisters made it clear that using magic in public was banned unless in case of emergency. Additionally, besides the fae kings and queens who had unique animals—like the night mares of the Night Court and the spring stags of the Spring Court—fae animals weren't supposed to be out in public.

Now, creatures like French Fry were rules unto themselves, and just because the Curia Cloisters made the rule it didn't mean they would follow it. But fae animals typically stuck to their fae realm. I'd always been a bit confused by French Fry's presence, but I didn't want him to get in trouble, so I tried to keep him out of danger.

I squinted up at French Fry as he drunkenly zoomed overhead. "You better not poop on me again."

French Fry ignored me and landed on the rim of a trash barrel, balancing precariously on it so he could peer in at its contents.

I shook my head as I power-walked past him. *I guess he has to get his french fries somewhere.*

When I reached the end of the block French Fry nearly smacked into me as he flew past. He tried to land on a lamp post, but the surface was too slanted so he slid off it and lost a few feathers in the scuffle.

I craned my neck—looking around for the tracker—but I didn't see or sense anything suspicious. Even so, by the time we reached Book Nookery I was sweaty from the power-walking and had bruised my heels from banging my luggage into them.

French Fry landed on Book Nookery's sign, as was his custom, and cooed at me as I headed up the stairs of the front porch, wrestling my luggage the whole way.

When I reached the front door of the twenty-four-hour bookstore, I cautiously slipped inside.

I half expected to see one of my coworkers behind the desk, but Ms. Booker herself was there.

She was wearing a yellow dress with a bright flower print, and her customary string of pearls and pearl earrings. When she looked down her button nose at me it gave her a sharper look, but it was softened by her gentle smile.

"Chloe, dear, I didn't expect to see you today."

"Hello, Ms. Booker." I took another step into the store, and the overwhelming sense of comfort swamped me. I didn't know if it was the papery smell of books or the familiar scent of the wood polish Ms. Booker had us use to obsessively clean the shelves, but whatever it was, my shoulders relaxed.

This is what books should feel like. Comforting. Not judgmental.

Ms. Booker folded her hands and rested them on the desk—as proper and elegant as always. "You look like you could use a cup of tea."

"Maybe," I agreed. "A lot has happened."

"Oh? Then why don't you tell me in the kitchen?"

"Thank you."

"Of course, dear. It's only proper."

"I hope you still think so after everything I need to tell you..."

TWO CUPS OF TEA, a trayful of cucumber sandwiches, and a flood of words later, I clutched my empty china teacup and rubbed my thumb across the lavender sprig design.

Ms. Booker sat in silence for several long moments, contemplating everything I'd told her. I'd kept my story to Noctus discovering me and telling me I was a shadow, and me telling him about the tracker. Ms. Booker didn't know about Charon, Aristide, Ker, and the elven city, and I meant to keep it that way for her own safety.

"That is quite the adventure," Ms. Booker said.

"Adventure?" I squeaked. "If Noctus realizes I've told you about him, he's going to bespell you."

Ms. Booker patted my hand. "That is for me to worry about, Chloe, dear."

"He knows I work here," I said. "He's going to get suspicious sooner or later."

Ms. Booker pointedly gazed at my collar. "I do not share your certainty."

I almost dropped my teacup before I recovered and set it on the matching saucer with a delicate clack. "He didn't leave the collar on me because he has any kind of positive emotion for me."

"Did he say that?"

"No, but he confirmed that the collar lets him track me, and that it's no use trying to run as long as I'm wearing it."

"And yet, even though you were discovered just last night," Ms. Booker said, "you are allowed to wander around Magiford?"

"Because of the collar."

Ms. Booker took a delicate sip of her tea. "If you say so."

I rubbed the sides of my head, trying to ward off the brewing headache. "What do I do?"

"Wait for them to settle on what to do with you, I imagine," Ms. Booker helpfully said. "If they are willing to let you wander around—collar or not—it seems His Majesty will be lax with you. Perhaps you could return to your usual patterns."

I chewed on my lip. "Maybe they'd let me come back to work."

Ms. Booker raised her drawn-on eyebrows, but said nothing of the matter. She gently set her teacup down, then poured herself some more tea from a white teapot decorated with an ivy pattern. "What I am concerned about, however, is this tracker you mentioned. It seems foolish to let you wander about when that blackguard has proven most persistent."

"He hasn't found me yet today," I said. "But maybe that's why Noctus decided to let me out, to see if the tracker will pop out."

"Is he that interested in finding him?" Ms. Booker took another sip of tea.

"Yes," I said, dragging out the vowels.

I hadn't told Ms. Booker about the elven city—to protect her, and the elves themselves. The truth was, Noctus would absolutely use my life as bait for the tracker if it meant capturing the guy. The tracker's focus on me was probably a good thing. If he'd shown any interest in breaking into Noctus's house when I wasn't there, I didn't know what would have happened.

I hope he didn't realize what Noctus is, and that's why he's now missing.

I was a jumble of emotions from this mess, but I knew myself well enough to predict that I'd feel unbearably guilty if Noctus was outed because of me.

Which is kind of crazy considering he's the King of the Mors—the epitome of death for elves, and possibly the most dangerous individual I could ever meet in my entire lifetime. Then again, no one ever said emotions were logical.

"Then perhaps you are right that you are allowed to move about so this tracker can be caught. Regardless I believe you would be best off waiting for King Noctus to make the first move," Ms. Booker said.

"First move for the tracker? I'll kind of need to. I can't take him out on my own, unless maybe I try the pepper spray Joy got me."

"No, I was referring to your relationship with King Noctus," Ms. Booker said. "Discretion is an excellent start. It will give you the chance to read the room, so to speak, and judge how you are being received. Based on what you observe, you can better decide how you should move forward with things like the collar and your general freedom."

"Oh, yeah." I started to slump in my chair, but I corrected my posture when Ms. Booker primly pressed her lips together in silent disapproval. "Then you think I shouldn't try to make a break for the Curia Cloisters?"

"Not at this point," Ms. Booker said. "There are too many unknown variables. It would be too easy to make a mistake. Besides, it seems to me you have no reason to resort to that desperate measure yet."

"I don't know about that. Things feel pretty desperate."

"And yet, you sit here with me drinking tea," Ms. Booker said. "Your leash is not as tight as you seem to believe."

It might seem that way, but that's only because you don't know how seriously Noctus takes the security of his city.

I cleared my throat and slapped a smile on my face. "Maybe," I evasively said. I glanced at the clock, and stood up. "I should probably go—they might get suspicious if I'm here too long."

"In that case, I bid you a fond farewell." Ms. Booker daintily pushed her chair back and stood, smoothing the wrinkles out of her floral dress. "Be careful—the Seelie and Unseelie Courts have been squabbling more than usual."

I'd been carrying my teacup to the sink, but I turned around with a frown. "They aren't hanging around the neighborhood, are they?"

"No, no, nothing of the sort." Ms. Booker dryly chuckled. "There are too many wizard Houses nearby for them to risk these parts of Magiford. But they have been more active in the human residential areas. There was a fight downtown—which was fair stupid of them given it's supposed to be a neutral zone. If they keep this silliness up the Curia Cloisters will be forced to act."

I started washing my teacup. "I hope they resolve their problems quickly."

"Unfortunately, I doubt they will. If magic keeps fading away, I imagine things will only get worse," Ms. Booker said.

I rinsed the cup, then set it on the soft towel Ms. Booker had laid out. "I guess. It's just one more thing to worry about, then. But thank you, for everything, Ms. Booker. And I'm sorry for endangering you with all of this." I grabbed my suitcase—taking care to pick it up, because Ms. Booker wouldn't like it if the wheels scratched her floor.

"Of course, Chloe dear. Call me if you have need."

"I will—goodbye!" I called as I opened the back employee door. I hauled my suitcase down the stairs and lugged it around the house, setting it down when I reached the sidewalk.

French Fry popped out of a lilac bush that was starting to flower, showering tiny purple flowers everywhere and taking the fragrant scent of lilacs with him as he flapped down the street.

I followed him, heading back to Noctus's cul-de-sac.

So I have to wait? That's understandable, and smart now that I'm not necessarily pressed for time. I mean, I am, but that's mostly from a financial standpoint. I can't make Noctus change his mind on anything, and something tells me I won't be able to butter him up since I'm no longer Amalourne. I guess the big thing is to keep Pat and Joy from visiting, and to try to be as helpful as possible so eventually I get released.

I sighed as I pulled my luggage along, the handle jostling as I ran over a crack in the cement.

Spring hadn't quite turned into summer yet, but the air was warmer than it had been even a week ago, and there were more flowers blooming, so it was a pleasant walk.

I was maybe ten minutes away from Noctus's house when my magical senses kicked in.

I paused mid step and looked around the seemingly normal neighborhood.

Something's wrong. It was a gut instinct; one I'd learned to trust over the years.

A scan of the street revealed nothing.

French Fry was farther up the road, sitting on a small bird feeder that was attached to a sapling tree that was bending heavily under his weight.

Beyond the joyful trash griffin, I didn't see or hear anyone else.

No kids were playing, no one was out walking in the lovely weather. In fact, the longer I listened the quieter the chatter of squirrels and chirps of birds became.

They're leaving. I twisted in a circle, my guard coming up. Was it the tracker? But I didn't feel that horrible sense of dread, and surely that would have hit me by now.

It doesn't matter what it is. If the prey animals are leaving, I need to get out of here too.

I jogged down the street, my luggage swerving wildly behind me. "French Fry—come on. We need to go." I motioned to the trash griffin.

French Fry looked at me with his left eye, then the right. He weighed down the feeder so much, it was only about two feet off the ground. When he hopped off it, the feeder walloped him as it sprang upright.

The trash griffin made a scolding noise, but he followed me as I jogged.

My instincts were riding me so hard I considered abandoning the suitcase—I could come back with Aristide the blind but dangerous dagger thrower and maybe Ker for backup—when the silken sensation of fae magic tickled my elbow.

You've got to be kidding me. Now?!

I was halfway down the block when a roar so loud it shook the ground sounded behind me.

CHAPTER FOUR

Chloe

I darted behind a bush and turned into a cat. Safely hidden, I peered back down the street.

Two trolls stood at the top of the street. Both were shirtless, but wearing pants that looked like they were made of burlap bags stitched together.

How did they even find *burlap in this age?*

A screech that sounded like the hiss of a snake combined with the call of a hawk thrummed, and a shadow passed across the street.

My fur puffed up as the shadow slunk around the corner of the road, and I didn't know whether to laugh or cry.

I have the worst luck ever.

The creature—made of muscle, scales, and fur and easily the size of a truck—roared as it extended its clawed paws. When it turned in a circle, it revealed a faun perched on the back of its rat-like body, cooing to it—its handler, most likely. Its long, scaled tail ended in a snake head that hovered over its back, testing the air with its forked tongue, while its head was a bare lion skull. A mane puffed around the white skull, and its eye sockets glowed red, testifying that the creature was still alive despite its terrible appearance.

Looks like a variation of a chimera. Chimera were one of the many dark creatures that roamed the fae realms. Fae could sometimes tame wild creatures, so it wasn't unheard of to have a pet chimera, though its owner must have paid dearly for it since I was presumably looking at a Seelie/Unseelie face off, and neither of those Courts had access to the fae realm.

The Unseelie black teardrop on the rider's blanket marked it as Queen Darina's pet. Which meant the trolls were likely Harel's minions.

I turned back into a human long enough to frantically wake up my phone and swipe open my messages.

"Help, fae."

I fired the text message off to Charon, trusting the competent elf would realize what I meant.

I need to get out of here. But first, I better warn someone. If these fae go too far, they'll hurt humans. And then we'll all pay.

I did the fastest saved-contact search of my life, looking for the Curia Cloisters emergency number, all while I collapsed the handle of my suitcase and kicked it into the front yard of a cute, two-story home.

The fighters were thankfully too busy posturing for the moment—the trolls smashed their fists on their chests, and the faun rider had flung herself off the chimera and was fluffing up its mane.

The dial tone died as my call picked up. "*Curia Cloisters emergency line—*"

"Fae turf war," I interrupted. "At this address." I rattled off the street name while I inched toward the human house.

I'd turn into a cat and flee through the backyard. Once I had at least a two-block buffer zone, I'd turn human again and see if Charon had gotten back to me.

"*What's your name?*" the Curia Cloisters caller asked me.

I furrowed my brow as I watched the trolls exchange fist bumps before they started jogging down the street. "What?"

"*Who is reporting the—*"

I tapped the end call button—I didn't have time for specifics, and I was pretty sure Noctus wouldn't like it if I brought *any* extra attention to myself.

I turned back into a cat and frantically looked around for French Fry. I spotted him, sitting calmly on the roof of the next-door house, watching me.

Good, he's out of the way.

The trolls reached the chimera, who rammed its skull into the belly of the first troll—knocking it three house lots down the street. It tried to strike the second troll with its snake tail, but the troll caught the snake head, holding it back.

And that's my cue to leave. I slunk along the side of the house, nosing my way through several flowering bushes of bleeding hearts. There was a wooden fence, but I jumped it, landing on the top where I balanced for a moment.

I was about to hop down to the other side, when—over the roar of the trolls and the screech of the chimera—I heard a bell jingle.

I looked back. Across the street, standing in the front yard, was a petite, orange tabby cat with a bright purple collar and bell.

She flattened her ears when a troll thundered past her house and attempted to throw himself on the chimera's back, but then perked her ears and meowed when she saw I was looking at her.

Oh...no...

Part of my magic was that I was universally liked by cats. This worked in my favor, because if I stuck around in an area long enough as a cat, one or two local felines would naturally come to see what I was up to. It was perfect camouflage.

Except now, when danger roamed the street.

If she doesn't head back inside, she's going to get hurt, even if she stays on her front lawn.

The chimera bucked off the troll, sending it hurtling backwards. It landed on a large lilac bush planted on the curb space, flattening it all the way to the roots.

The cat crouched lower to the ground, but she didn't move from her house's front sidewalk, and kept watching me.

If I leave, she'll run home.

I jumped down, landing on top of the recycling container tucked against the fence. Standing on top of it, I could peer over the side of the fence.

The cat didn't move. No, it actually got worse.

As I watched, the front door opened, and an elderly man stepped out, calling to the orange cat. The man glanced at the trolls and chimera with obvious fear, but he shuffled down his porch anyway, heading for his pet.

My heart jumped into my throat, and before I knew what I was doing, I sprang back over the fence and scrambled onto the lower roof of the two-story home.

I ran to the edge, turning myself into a human at the last moment for the jump. As soon as I cleared the roof I turned back into a cat and let the momentum carry me farther than I could have leaped as a cat.

I let my instincts guide me so I twisted in the air and landed in the road, on my paws, without any pain at all. The perks of being a cat.

The chimera rammed into the troll that was still holding its tail, trying to flatten it. The troll braced himself, but he was shoved several feet back across the pavement.

I stayed in my feline form as I put on a burst of speed and skittered across the road, barely avoiding the troll when it stepped backwards, trying to keep the chimera from overwhelming it.

This is insane—how can the Courts possibly think this is okay? There's no way the humans will miss all this property damage! Harel and Darina are crazy!

The orange tabby hadn't returned to her owner. Instead, she puffed up to twice her size and hissed at the monsters.

As soon as I cleared the old man's front sidewalk I turned into a human. "Get inside!" I shouted.

Still clutching my cellphone—Charon had better get back to me after all of this—I scooped up the orange cat.

Thankfully, she didn't fight me or claw me. I raced across the lawn, the cat bouncing in my arms, as the little old man hurriedly opened his front door.

As soon as he made it inside, I jumped in after him, dumping the cat into his arms.

"Cheesecake!" the old man cried as he cuddled the still puffed up cat.

I stepped out onto the porch. "Head to the back of your house," I said. "They should stay on the road, but just in case. And lock the door."

"Wait, miss," the old man called.

I pulled the door shut behind me. As I listened for the lock to click into place, my instincts grabbed my heart and shook it.

I swung around, my mouth turning dry as I realized the chimera snake head was watching *me*.

The chimera had one troll pinned under its front paws, and the other was wrestling with its lion skull head.

The trolls rocked the chimera from side to side as they struggled to get free. The chimera's snake head curled into a striking position, but it kept its eyes on me.

How—with two trolls struggling against it—did it decide that I *was interesting?!*

I turned into a cat—for the superior, if temporary, speed, and in the hope I'd be harder to see—and zipped back across the road.

I'd made it to the other side, avoiding pebbles and grit that got tossed when the pinned troll finally succeeded in getting itself free.

The newly freed troll kicked the chimera's stomach.

The chimera body slammed him, rolling him head over feet down the street. The second troll roared, but was silenced when the chimera headbutted him with a painful crack that tossed him after his friend.

I tried to track its snake tail, but I couldn't see it from this side of the street. I jumped on top of the white picket fence again, then clambered onto the first floor of the two-story house.

When I finally realized what was happening, the tingling in my whiskers turned into a knife of fear.

The chimera lumbered down the street, not to close in on the trolls, but to halt when it was standing on the sidewalk just outside the old man's house.

The snake tail wasn't pointed at me, but at the old man's *front door*.

It's not after me, it's after the old guy.

The urge to run away shook me, but I couldn't leave the old man to get attacked, just because his cat had sensed me.

What to do, what to do, what to do?

For some silly, senseless reason, I pitifully meowed in a way that used to bring Noctus to my side in an instant.

But I wasn't his beloved pet. He didn't care about me—in fact, if I got myself killed in this turf war, he'd probably be happy. It would certainly make his life easier.

I'm on my own. I need to figure out how to take care of this.

I crouched on the roof and watched as the trolls attacked the chimera head on again. The chimera headbutted them again, tossing them like they were dolls.

Obviously, attacking it straight on isn't going to work.

I glanced down the street where I saw the rider—the faun—smirking as she leaned against a mailbox.

Bingo—I've got it.

I jumped off the roof in my cat form and streaked across lawns—taking care to hide whenever I could.

I heard an ominous crunch, and when I looked back the snake head was clamped around the old man's mailbox like a boa constrictor. As it tightened the coils of its body, it ripped the wooden post out of the ground.

...I need to hurry.

I passed the faun, then skittered across the street behind her back.

This is such a bad idea. It's the worst. But it's the only option.

Fleetingly, I thought of Noctus again, before I shook my head, aimed myself at the faun's back, then sprinted at her.

I waited until the last second to turn into a human, springing into existence behind her.

I was taller than the slight fae, so it was easy to knock her to the ground with a good kick to the back.

I was on her before she could cry out, my arm wrapped around her throat as I pinned my knee against her lower back.

"As soon as I release you, call the monster off, end the fight, and immediately go back to your Court." I half growled the words out—I was trying hard to keep her pinned and scared but not actually hurt her. I didn't need the Unseelie Court paying me any special attention, or doing mental gymnastics to turn this into a slight.

The faun made a whining noise, and she tried to wriggle out of my grasp, but as a certifiable escape artist—and having been trained by my paranoid brother—I knew just how to hold someone so they *couldn't* escape. She couldn't even try to bite my arm or headbutt me—I had my arm tight under her chin so her head was pulled against my shoulder and she couldn't get any kind of ramming motion.

But holding her would only work until the chimera noticed she was in distress.

"*Vow it*!" I said, as I scrambled for a threat. "Or I'll hand you straight over to the Cloisters."

Hah, as if I could hold her that long!

"Let me go," the faun cried.

"*Vow it.*"

Fae couldn't lie, which also meant they couldn't betray any vows they made. If she said it, she'd have to do it.

She clawed at my arm with her blunt nails, so I increased the pressure on her neck.

"Fine!" she cried, going slack in my arms. "I vow upon the Unseelie Court that, once you let me go, I'll call my chimera off, end the fight, and immediately go back to my Court."

I stood up, hauling her up with me. "Then do it." I pushed her in front of me, then dove behind a bush, turning into a cat before she turned around.

She looked up and down the street, and didn't seem to notice me where I crouched. "Queen Darina is going to be mad," she whined as she turned back to the chimera. "Dew Drop! Enough—we're going home."

The chimera flung both of the trolls again so they hit the road with a painful thud, then it turned around and ambled toward its handler.

The faun's lower lip jutted out in a pout as she retrieved her rider blanket from the sidewalk where she'd dropped it.

The trolls stirred on the street.

Without turning around, the chimera slammed its tail into them, tossing them back to the ground and cracking the pavement.

Oof, yeah, glad I didn't have to face the chimera.

As if it could sense my thoughts, the chimera's skull head swiveled in my direction, its glowing red eyes staring right at me.

The faun didn't seem to notice. She threw the blanket on the creature's shoulders and climbed on.

The chimera's snake tail hissed, but when the faun thumped

the monster's sides with her heels—as if it were a mischievous pony—it finally turned away from me, ambling up the street.

I relaxed, and for the first time since all of this "fun" had started, my black fur started to settle back into place.

I hunkered down as the trolls rolled to their feet, speaking to one another in lowered, growly tones.

I'll just wait until they leave, then I can grab my luggage and head out. The Curia Cloisters will show up soon, anyway, and—what are they doing?

My brief moment of relaxation evaporated as the trolls strode down the road, heading in my direction.

My fur puffed up again, and I hastily backed deeper into the bush, crouching at the very base, where I'd be best screened by all the low branches and foliage.

"It was looking over here before its rider led it off." The troll stopped directly in front of my bush. "Wonder what interested it..."

Go away, go away, go away. Come on magic, WORK!

I curled up, making myself as small as possible.

I held my breath when one of the trolls crouched down and broke a large branch off my shrub.

I'll have to run—hiding in landscaping is my best bet. If I swap between human and cat a few times that should flash my magic enough to confuse them.

I was so scared that the tingling of my whiskers made my face feel numb. I tensed ready to run.

The troll yanked another branch off, and the late morning sunlight crept deeper into the bush. "What's this?" The troll leaned closer, peering in. "There's a cat." He reached for me, his giant, sausage-like fingers grasping.

This is terrible. My magic will keep them from realizing I'm me, but it won't keep them from being curious about a cat!

I clambered toward the back of the shrub, freezing when the shrub groaned under the sudden weight of an unconscious troll.

He slid off the branch, landing on the ground with a thump. Peering through the leaves, I could see the equally unconscious form of his friend, splayed out in the middle of the road.

W-what?

"Amalourne."

Noctus.

CHAPTER FIVE

Chloe

I cautiously crawled out of the bush, poking my black nose out first. Noctus stood a few feet away, leaning over the trolls.

Something in me—probably the silly part that had been hoping he'd somehow find me—buckled in relief.

He came after all.

His hair looked more golden than usual in the sparkling sunlight, and his utilitarian clothes were boldly dark among the green of the watered lawns and the brightly colored flowers.

There was something decidedly wrong about his presence on the street. Not that he didn't belong—like the trolls and the chimera hadn't. But it felt like he was...too much to be limited to the small, picture-perfect street. Too strong, too powerful, too overwhelming.

Noctus glanced at me as he sheathed his sword. He started to bend down, and I automatically trotted up to him, leaning against his legs. Noctus slid his hands underneath my belly, presumably to scoop me up.

We froze at the same time, our minds finally catching up to our habitually ingrained movements.

Oh. I'm not Amalourne anymore.

Noctus broke away first, stepping back. He pivoted, pointing down the street where Charon stood with the car.

Ker was present. For the first time I'd ever seen, she was *not* in her wolf form while outside the house, but had remained in her human body. Every other time she had ventured outside the villa she'd been careful to come as a wolf.

I hadn't managed to put together why, but I suspected it had something to do with her being incredibly long lived.

I watched for a moment, before I retreated to the bush to transform into my human form.

I wasn't worried about being discovered—I was the only one of my kind that I knew of, after all—but the Curia Cloisters didn't like magic getting flashed around in public, and even if two trolls and a chimera had just wrestled in the streets, I was nothing if not a rule follower.

Human again, I cleared my throat, hoping to get Noctus's attention.

He didn't stop watching Ker as she tossed my luggage in the SUV's trunk. "What?"

"Thanks—for coming," I said. "I meant to run away after I messaged Charon, but there were...complications."

Ker shut the trunk, then weaved back and forth across the street. Judging by the way her nose twitched, she was scenting the area out.

Noctus gestured at me with two fingers, motioning for me to follow, then started down the street, heading for the car. "What happened?"

"I think it was a turf war between the Seelie and Unseelie," I said. "I don't know what else would bring the fae to a human neighborhood. It started out of nowhere. Thankfully it doesn't seem like there's too much property damage. Oh—I did call the Curia Cloisters to warn them."

Noctus nodded, and we were close enough that Charon must have heard.

"Shall I start the car, sir?" Charon asked.

"In a moment," Noctus said. "I'd like to give Ker a little more time. What kept you from running, Chloe?"

I cringed. "There was a cat." I explained the situation, pointing out the old man's house. His mailbox was done for, but otherwise the property was unscathed.

Around the time I finished, Ker looped back to us, having heard my explanation with her superior wolf senses. "Who did the Unseelie send?" she asked, tilting her head back and forth.

"A chimera and its handler," I said. "They left maybe two minutes before you arrived."

"That explains the odd smell." Ker sneezed, then shook her head, disrupting the two dark braids her hair was pulled into. "Fae creatures always smell weird."

"We should go, I imagine the Curia Cloisters will show up shortly," Noctus said.

"Indeed." Charon opened the front door for Noctus, and Ker piled into the back bench seat.

I paused, tilting my head as I felt my gut instinct tug at me.

Magic incoming. Must be the Curia Cloisters team.

I heard the purr of a car engine, and could feel the buzzing in my fingertips that marked human magic. They had a wizard among their ranks. It felt like a vamp, too, and maybe a...

"Ker!" I threw myself into the car, closing the door behind me.

"What?" Ker frowned and lowered her eyebrows over her eyes when I grabbed her by the shoulders, but she didn't struggle when I shoved her in the foot space between the front seats and the bench seat.

I don't know where the Curia Cloisters task force parked, but they were suddenly *there*, on the street, mapping out the fight.

The supernatural I'd been most nervous about—a werewolf—was busy scenting the mailbox, tracing the chimera's path.

A woman with red hair and a dusting of freckles trotted up to the car, holding her hand up in a request for us to stop.

"It seems our exit is too late," Noctus cryptically said. He started to push down the button for the window, but I was faster than him.

"Hello. I'm the one who called the turf fight in," I called. My window was already halfway rolled down. I popped my head out of my window, using my body to fill the space and block out Ker.

It went against everything in my instincts to call attention to myself, but if Noctus was designed to draw people in, I was meant to deflect attention away.

If they keep their attention on me, they'll be more dismissive, which is what we need.

"Ahh, yes. Thanks for the tip." The woman—she looked roughly my age—smiled at me, positioning herself so she was in front of my window and ignoring Noctus, exactly what I wanted. "Could you tell me what happened?"

I recited the events—including the little old man and his cat. (The Curia Cloisters already had a record on me, and they had my phone number from the numerous job applications I'd turned in, so I'd be easy to trace anyway.)

The woman nodded and asked a few questions as she took notes on her phone.

One of the other task force members, a tall, curious fae, watched me with interest.

"Really. You can turn into a cat?" he asked.

The red-haired woman—who had to be a wizard—elbowed him sharply, all while keeping a smile on her face. "Thank you for your cooperation."

"Of course. Um, but if you choose to go after the Courts for the damage...could you..." I trailed off, wondering how to phrase it.

"Your involvement will be kept for Cloisters records," the wizard said. "We won't share any information with the Courts."

"We pinky promise," the fae smirked.

The wizard—moving so fast she was a blur—smacked him in the gut, batting some of the typical fae smugness out of him.

Oh, she's not a wizard. She's a vampire slayer.

Vampire slayers were a fellow subset of humans, except their magic typically came in the flavor of increased speed, increased healing times, etc.

Behind the pair, the wolf started to pad in our direction.

I could tell by the puzzled frown, he'd likely picked up Ker's scent.

Come on, magic. Work. Please, work!

"Thanks. Since my friends swung by to pick me up, can we go?" I rested my hands on the edge of the window.

"Hmm?" My magic must have been working, because the vampire slayer looked away from me and peered back at the team. "Sure. You can go. Thank you for reporting the matter."

I sucked my head in and rolled the window up. "Go!" I hissed.

The vampire slayer strode off, intercepting the wolf —thankfully.

The fae stayed behind for a moment longer, his expression flickering between confusion and complete apathy.

Charon didn't give him enough time to fight off my magic. He calmly pulled out and started down the road, driving away from the street that now swarmed with Curia Cloisters task force members.

I collapsed in my seat, belatedly remembering to buckle myself in. My t-shirt stuck to me like a second skin from my anxiety sweat, and I finally exhaled once we made a turn, and the task force members were no longer visible.

"That was close," I said.

"It could have been handled," Noctus said with a deceptive amount of mildness.

I slumped in my seat. "I know you're not opposed to flinging memory charms around like they're candy, but please allow me to assure you, as the lowest supernatural in the city hierarchy, that we're better off if we can escape notice altogether. It decreases the chance of an accident."

Noctus snorted. "That you truly believe you are—to quote you —the lowest supernatural in the city hierarchy, does not recommend your ideas given how far that statement is from the truth."

"Ouch, that was a little hurtful, Noctus," Ker piped up as she flopped into her seat and also buckled herself in. She gave me a thoughtful expression—one that included just the slightest upturn of her lips, which was the warmest she'd looked at me since realizing what I was. "Why did you push me down?"

"I could tell they were coming," I said. "And that they had a werewolf."

"So?"

"You're trying to avoid being seen in your human form, right?" I asked.

Ker stared at me.

My shoulder tapped the car's expensive leather interior when Charon took a turn a little sharply. "I mean...you're very careful to only go out into Magiford as a wolf. I assumed there must be a reason. I figured you wouldn't want any of them to see you."

A fully formed smile bloomed on Ker's face, and her regular sunny temperament returned. "You're a smart one. Noctus is right, you need to recognize your power. I should teach you how to use words of affirmation. If you say it to your reflection in the pond in Noctus's room, you'll get better results, because it's magic."

"It is *not* magic," Noctus said, exasperation lining his voice. "I wish you and Aristide would stop saying it is."

"Aristide only says that to get a rise out of you," Ker said. "I say it because it's true. You all would benefit from affirmations spoken to your reflection in the pond. Except Charon is happy the way his life is—which I respect—you, Noctus, are too *busy*, and Aristide is too self-conscious to try self-affirming or any kind of confidence boosting exercises," she concluded.

"I see," I said when Ker looked at me, expecting some kind of reaction.

Ker nodded, and her eyes turned gleeful. "But you, Chloe! You're plenty smart! Have you read the book, *How to Win Friends and Influence People*? If you haven't, I'll lend you a copy!"

"Ker, stop acting like a cultist," Noctus said.

Ker rolled her eyes. "The first thing you'll need to learn, Chloe, is how to deal with the jealousy of others."

I laughed, and the last bit of tension that had kept me upright faded away.

I was safe. Noctus had come for me, despite my...betrayal? Lies?

It's encouraging—as long as I don't think of how long it will take him to figure out what to do with me, my immunity to magic, and my knowledge of his existence.

The following day—after *two* showers, because I had hygiene practices to catch up on—I snuck outside in the early morning for a little cul-de-sac walk—with Charon's blessing. The quiet elf had nodded his permission when I'd asked—which had pleasantly surprised me.

Now that I could freely walk around as a human, I reveled in the sun on my face and the ability to stretch my legs—though I wasn't inclined to repeat the turf war fun, hence why I stuck to the neighborhood.

I walked at dawn, when I figured no one else would be awake on the street.

That proved to be a tactical error.

I made it up and down the cul-de-sac once before someone called my name.

"Chloe!" Shiloh stood in her driveway, holding her mail and shining a conspiratorial smile at me. "I saw you come out of Noctus's house."

"No," I automatically said. "It's not what you think."

Shiloh wriggled her eyebrows. "Oh? Really?"

I peered up and down the street before I crossed it, joining her on her driveway. "I'm not dating him."

"Okay." Shiloh tapped her mail on her open palm, still grinning.

"I...got kicked out of my apartment," I impulsively blurted out.

Shiloh raised both of her eyebrows. "What for?"

This isn't fair. Why can't she just ignore me like everyone else?

"Oh," I scrambled for a reason. "Remodels. It's just temporary—there's some kind of safety violation that needs to be fixed, so they're going to do some updates to the building while they're at it. I needed a place to crash for a month or two while the work is getting done."

"So handsome-as-an-angel Noctus was your first choice of temporary home?" Shiloh innocently asked.

"Yes," I said. "Wait, no. Uhh..." I wilted under her sharp eye. "How about whatever sounds the least romantic?"

Shiloh laughed. "Hey, I'm the one that suggested you two date. If you want to confess your secret, undying love for my suspiciously handsome neighbor, I'm all for it. He's too awesome a guy to just waste sitting in his house. *Someone* should date him."

"It's not even close to that," I said. "I really do just need a place to stay."

There, at least that's not a total lie. I am a lot more comfortable hiding behind Noctus with the tracker still out there.

Shiloh laid a hand on me. "Hey—I get it. You're both supernaturals, that has to create a unique bond between you two."

You have no idea.

"Yes," I agreed, relaxing under her warm hand.

It wasn't just that her skin was warm, but the touch was somehow infused with warmth—like a hug from Mom.

"As much as I'd like to tease you, it's not that surprising. Noctus is just a great guy." Shiloh squeezed my shoulder then took a step back. "He's had all kinds of people stay with him over the years."

"Oh?" I asked.

"Yeah," Shiloh said. "The place used to be grand central station with folks coming and going at all hours of the day when I was a teenager. That stopped...maybe three or four years ago?"

Probably around the time the Paragon came to town. The "people" Shiloh used to see were most likely the elves from the city. Once the Paragon started showing up, Noctus most likely banished them from using the house, lest the tricky fae realized more elves were alive than him and Charon.

"I hope your apartment gets fixed up all nicely, though," Shiloh said, interrupting my thoughts.

"Thanks. Me too." I awkwardly slid my hands into the pockets of my workout pants. "So...what are you doing up so early?"

"I've got a morning class, and a late night class tonight," Shiloh said. "So I won't be home until late. I got up early to take care of a few houseowner things. I have to keep up on the lawn, or the rabbits try to move in."

"Yeah, rabbits can be surprisingly vicious," I said with feeling.

I'd run into a rabbit on occasion as a kitten. They weren't as bad as geese or ducks, but they could still mess you up!

"Cute, but dangerous." Shiloh groaned as she stretched her arms over her head. "Ugh, no one warned me that ninety percent of home ownership is trying to repair broken things, and keep the local wildlife from moving in."

"It does sound like a battle," I said.

She's talking about house ownership...but mentioned this house was her childhood home. Did her parents move out? Or...?

I felt a brush of elf magic, and I turned around in time to see Noctus ambling out of his Cape Cod house, wearing his glamour that hid the taper of his ears and the swirl of his eyes—though he was also wearing sunglasses.

I was a little puzzled by his presence. Now that I wasn't trying to sneak outside as Ama so I could transform and text my siblings, he didn't really have a reason to come outside like this. Unless...did he think I was going to say something to Shiloh?

"Good morning, Shiloh. Chloe." Noctus nodded to me as he crossed the street, coming to a stop so close to me, I almost automatically leaned into him.

It was all for the sake of my plan, but it seems I was embarrassingly over affectionate with him as Amalourne if my first impulse is to always lean closer.

"Hi, Noctus. I was just telling Shiloh how you're letting me stay with you while my apartment gets remodeled," I chattered, trying to clue him in to the necessary fib.

"Yes," Noctus said. "Remodels are pesky, especially since your landlord is installing a new security system."

Huh? Is that supposed to be a thinly veiled threat?

"Sounds like it," Shiloh agreed. "Oh—but if you're staying with Noctus, that must mean you've gotten the chance to pet Ama! Isn't she the cutest?"

I made a strangled noise in the back of my throat.

Noctus adjusted his sunglasses, and a smile flashed across his lips. "Adorable, affectionate, and perfect. One could almost say Ama is unreal."

Oh, yeah. He's definitely still upset his cat doesn't exist.

I laughed nervously. "Yeah. Yeah she is. Well, I'm hungry. I think I'll go get some breakfast."

"How perfect," Noctus said. "We can eat together. Maybe Ama will join us for the *special* occasion."

I laughed nervously, and I could tell by the way Shiloh flicked her eyes between Noctus and me that she was trying to figure out the strange atmosphere. "Okay. Have a good breakfast."

"Enjoy class, Shiloh," Noctus smoothly said.

I opted to say nothing, and my laugh turned mechanical as I turned on my heel and walked into the street without looking. I almost hoped something would hit me as I crossed to break Noctus's mood.

Noctus followed me all the way to the front porch, where he opened the door for me and ushered me through the house's magical gate that popped us out in the villa.

"I was just going for a walk," I said, feeling guilty for no reason.

"Yes, and I question why given your track record of solo excursions is just *sparkling* these days," Noctus drawled. "Don't leave the villa's premises unless you are taking someone with you. Between the tracker of yours and the fae turf wars, you're guaranteed to get snatched."

"I assumed it was okay if I stuck to the neighborhood since you have it spelled."

"After the ill luck you've brought? It's a risk I don't think all the magic in the world could mitigate," Noctus said. His voice wasn't angry or even snide—which might have made me feel a little bit better. Nope, his voice was a blend of wryness and a complete lack of feeling.

I just can't get a fix on him—isn't he furious about the Amalourne situation?

"Sorry," I glumly said. "I did ask Charon."

"He told me." Noctus removed his sunglasses and shook off his glamour, revealing his pointed ears and spiral shaped pupils. "But I do not share Charon's confidence in the quietness of our neighborhood. You were trouble as a cat. I don't dare to dream you'd be less trouble as a human."

It seemed like I wasn't the only one fighting familiarity as he flicked a piece of my hair out of my face in a way that could have been interpreted as playful.

I blinked rapidly in surprise, but Noctus was already gone, striding down the hallway and disappearing into his study.

Can...am I allowed to be *playful with him? He's an elf king. It feels like I shouldn't, but Ker and Aristide are—they're friends, though.*

Left alone, I stole my way down the hallway, heading to the kitchens.

I still hadn't figured out who prepared the food. It just showed up throughout the day—delicious and ready for consumption. I'd gotten in the bad habit of wandering off to the kitchens whenever I was bored to see what I could eat—especially after one time there were freshly made donuts, and the pitchers of different kinds of milk started showing up.

On my way to the kitchen, I passed a giant painting that was roughly the size of Noctus's enormous bed. It was of an elf dressed in plated armor that glowed with magic. The charred remains of buildings and rubble surrounded the warrior, and he held a massive, jeweled scythe that was flecked with blood.

I knew the portrait was titled "Destruction" thanks to the golden plaque and cursive lettering that was carefully arranged beneath it, but I didn't know who the painting was of since the helm covered the elf's head and only revealed their chin and mouth.

I slowed to a stop in front of the portrait and frowned.

That scythe...it must be like the magical weapon Noctus pulled out when he nearly killed the Unseelie fae that had grabbed me. He almost blew up the neighborhood; it must have been an elven weapon.

I knew the elves had magical weapons they used with their magic. A number of years ago, there had been a fight in the Curia Cloisters that involved an elven holy sword.

This scythe, though...it does not *look holy.*

I shivered at the plaque, but my cat instincts prickled, so I wasn't entirely caught off guard when I heard Ker call out behind me.

"He sure is something, isn't he?" Ker strolled down the hallway, a metal water bottle hanging from the fingers of her left hand.

I guiltily took a step back from the painting, half wondering if I was allowed to look at it. "I'm sorry, what?"

"Noctus. That's him." Ker jutted her chin in the painting's direction. "With the Mors heirloom, Destruction."

I peered at the painting. "Heirloom?"

"The scythe," Ker said. "It's the strongest weapon the Mors have. Or had, as I guess I should say now."

"It was destroyed?"

"No, I'm not sure it could even be destroyed since its very nature is destruction. It's actually cursed—it can't be used. Anyone who touches it will die. So it's considered a lost heirloom. Even if Noctus had kids—which is unlikely given his people skills despite *years* of my tutelage—he couldn't pass it on to them."

"I didn't know elven weapons were inherited," I said.

"It's part inheritance, part selection," Ker said. "The weapons decide who they'll work with."

"They're *sentient*?"

"Sort of—the same way magic is kind of sentient," Ker said. "Or the way wizard Houses are sentient."

"So the weapons don't talk," I said.

Magic had its own way of communicating things, but it was hard to interpret and required a lot of guesswork. That was why things were so messy. Magic was dying, and no one knew why—though there were a few theories that suggested it was because the elves had died out. (Or mostly died out, as I had recently learned.)

Ker made a whining noise, then itched one of her dark

eyebrows. "They *can*, but only really with the elf they choose to wield them. And they don't talk like you and I talk. It's more like they let their wishes be known."

"A weapon with wishes." I stared at the blood-spattered scythe. "That's not terrifying."

Ker chuckled. "Elf magic is pretty frightening in general—"

She was going to go on, but she was interrupted by my stomach, which apparently had decided I'd waited too long to feed it, and complained about the mistreatment with a loud, long grumble that was so fierce I felt it in the back of my throat.

Ker smiled, then beckoned for me to follow her.

We left the painting behind as Ker took me down the side hallway that led to the kitchen.

"The weapons are only a part of elf magic," Ker continued as we walked. "But soldiers and guards were the ones who most often wielded them."

"Which would be the Mors royal family and their people," I said. "Since the Mors specialized in war."

"The other royal families had their own armies, too, but yes. The Mors always had the greatest number of heirloom weapons." Ker opened the kitchen door, and together we stepped inside, the yeasty scent of freshly baked bread embracing us like a hug.

The villa kitchen was a welcoming swirl of centuries and architecture.

Arranged like two squares with joint corners, one of the squares housed a giant fireplace with a fire pit. Fresh herbs hung from the ceiling to dry, and were coiled around the fireplace chimney while glazed, clay containers of spices, syrups, and vinegars lined the wall, giving the lower square a more traditional feel to it.

The upper square had been modernized with two island countertops, a huge range oven, and rows of cabinets that were made from a golden wood that had a polished, warm glow to it.

The island countertops were crowded with covered plates of

food, and sitting on a wooden stool pulled up to one of the islands was Aristide.

Sunlight poured in from a window, highlighting the scant silver in his brown hair. He was peering in our general direction—he'd probably heard our voices as we approached—as he casually poured a blood pouch into a wine glass.

"Up already, Ker? How dreadful of you," Aristide said.

A little box with metal prongs was hooked over the edge of Aristide's wine glass, and when the blood reached a certain spot on the prongs, the little box beeped an alarm. Aristide stopped pouring and set the blood pouch on the counter, upright so it wouldn't spill.

Ker leaned on the counter, surveying the covered food. "I like to rise with the sun—and it seems Chloe agrees with the sentiment. But you can't fool me—you went to bed earlier than I did last night!"

"Nonsense." Aristide swirled his wine glass, then took a sip of blood. "It is merely that I am so quiet, you don't hear me make any noises, so you assume I am asleep."

"Quite the opposite, actually." Ker lifted a silver lid off a tray, revealing still warm donuts dripping with gooey chocolate glaze.

The donuts lured me into motion. I fetched two plates and a glass from the cabinets in the modern half of the kitchen while Ker continued with her food quest.

"You are deafeningly loud when you sleep, because you *snore*." Ker closed the lid and moved a little farther down the counter, smiling when she opened a tray to reveal scrambled eggs and, next to it, a tray of sausages.

"I do not *snore*," Aristide scoffed into his glass before taking another sip.

"You do too. I can hear it through the walls. Thank you, Chloe." Ker took the plate from me, then started loading her plate with sausage and eggs before moving on to freshly cut papaya, bananas, and passion fruit.

"If I snore, you lack *all* tact and decorum," Aristide said. "Which means your Carnegie cult has failed you."

"You're not going to lure me into an argument today," Ker said as she set her loaded plate down next to Aristide, then fetched forks and knives for both of us. "I need to finish explaining elf magic to Chloe."

"Ahh, yes, I did hear part of that discussion." Aristide delicately sipped his glass of blood. "Talking about heirloom weapons, were you?"

"And that they select their wielders, yes." Ker hopped onto a stool. "That's why Noctus has so many of them. He's got a huge cache of weapons that are absolutely besotted with him. It drove his brothers crazy with envy back in the day."

"Noctus has always been a particular favorite of weapons and magic, as displayed by his vast powers," Aristide said. "Though why magic chose to bless him is beyond me. He's clearly lacking in the brain department for agreeing to wear those silly shackles all the time. He should have swatted the Paragon like a bug the minute that buzzard started poking his nose around here."

CHAPTER SIX

Chloe

I limited myself to two donuts, poured myself a giant glass of coconut milk from a pitcher, and made myself take some of the eggs before I sat down on Aristide's other side.

Aristide pointed his face at me as he tapped his finger on the side of his nearly empty wine glass. "You don't have anything to say about that?"

"I already know that Noctus is why everyone is staying in Magiford, even though you'd love to go to Europe," I said. "And I know Noctus must have his reasons for staying here. Since he's letting the Paragon hang around, the Paragon must be serving some kind of purpose."

"I knew I'd like you," Aristide said, his voice thick with smug satisfaction. "Anyone able to convince Noctus that they're a cat deserves him."

"Back to our topic of discussion." Ker scraped her fork on her plate as she finished off the last of her eggs. "Elves have other ways of using magic beyond weapons, of course."

"Like creating magic," I said.

Ker waggled her hand in the air. "Yes and no. They do ooze magic as part of their existence, and they can sense it better than nearly any other supernatural, but I can guess where you're going, and no, even if Noctus and all the elves in Calor Villa teamed up they wouldn't be able to restore magic across the world."

"But are they positively affecting magic in Magiford?" I asked.

"It's safe to assume so," Aristide said. "But, again, not at the amount you're imagining. Magic is dying too swiftly for a general elf population to affect it. It would take an elf from the Vitas family—they specialized in creating and filtering magic—or several colonies of elves."

"So, it's the specialties in elf magic that are really powerful?" I asked.

"They are, yes, but elf magic in general can be powerful. It just also has some very finicky rules," Ker said.

"Like emotions." Aristide toasted me with his wine glass, then drank the last of the blood in it. "If an elf throws an emotional hissy fit, magic won't work for them, at all."

"Their *emotions* can affect magic?" I asked.

"No." Ker started on her sausage while eyeing her fruit—werewolves with their high metabolisms had some perks when it came to food consumption. "Their emotions affect their ability to channel magic. Sadness, fear, anguish—their magic won't flow when they're experiencing anything negative like that."

"What about anger?" I bit into my first donut and had to swallow the hum of appreciation that threatened to burst out of me. The dark chocolate glaze was a rich and smooth taste that perfectly complemented the sweetness of the still warm donut. A sip of my cold coconut milk topped the experience.

I love being human.

"Ah, yes, you caught that, did you?" Aristide placed his three-pronged box back on his wine glass, then found the blood pouch and, using his fingers to make sure the pouch rested on the edge of the glass, poured the rest of the bag in. "Anything like anger, rage, and fury are dangerous, because it can make elf magic explosive."

Was Noctus angry when the fae grabbed me? I couldn't really tell with the armor on. He was just...intense. And terrifying.

"They can still use magic while experiencing anger," Aristide continued. "But there is a very high chance the magic will backfire, or wrestle out of their control."

"Noctus was so feared because he is incredibly powerful—far beyond the rest of his family—but *also* because he is amazingly in tune with his emotions. He can control them with an iron will. I can count the number of times magic has gotten away from him on one hand—with fingers to spare." Ker finished off her fruit, then wiped her fingers off on a napkin. "And that's over *centuries*."

"Really?" I asked skeptically.

"Yep!" Ker uncovered the tray closest to her, revealing hot, steaming biscuits. Next to the biscuit tray was the sausage gravy. She chortled to herself as she grabbed several biscuits, then started ladling the gravy on top of them.

Hmmm. It seems unlikely, then, that he was that mad at the Unseelie fae for grabbing me. He used some pretty extreme magic on my collar, but I'm not vain—or stupid—enough to think that Amalourne could mean that *much to him.*

Thinking of it made me aware of the lacy collar that was still fastened around my throat. The top of it peeked out of my t-shirt collar, but it seemed like Noctus was right, and my magic made it as unimpressive as, well, *me*. No one ever noticed it—though in my usual paranoia I was careful not to touch it or draw any kind of attention to it.

"Noctus's self-control is why his subjects have stayed with him." Aristide removed the little mechanical box he used to judge the liquid levels of his cup and set it on the counter. "It made him absolutely lethal on the battlefield."

"Is that why..." I bit the question off when I realized what I had nearly asked.

I knew Noctus was responsible for killing his family, and that the death of the Mors royal family had turned the tide of the war.

Knowing that, it seemed weird that Noctus had a city of elves who had chosen to follow him. I mean, it was weird Noctus wiped out his family to begin with—he had to have known it was going to affect the war negatively for the elves. *Unless...did he want the other supernaturals to win? But why? He lost his entire existence hiding after the war.*

Ker looked up from her biscuits and gravy. The look she gave me was careful, as if she was reading my soul. "You overheard a lot, Chloe, but did you know that I knew Noctus before the war?"

I finished my second donut and stared at the covered dishes. "I've heard you mention Noctus's family before. I wondered..."

"How that was possible?" Ker asked with a crooked grin.

I hesitated. "Yes..."

Immortality wasn't a thing for most supernaturals.

Wizards were long lived for humans, but still within the range of normal. Fae lived longer and aged more slowly, but werewolves typically didn't make it to old age. Self-preservation didn't run very deep in shifters.

The exception to the shifters were the dragon shifters, who were capable of living for a couple centuries, but there were so few of them they were practically in a category of their own.

Among supernaturals, vampires were the only truly immortal supernatural. Well...vampires and elves.

But I'd seen enough hints to know Ker was a lot older than she looked.

I methodically ate my scrambled eggs, noting with the slightest distraction that they'd been seasoned with fresh parsley as I studied the beautiful werewolf.

"It's a combination of Noctus and Aristide," Ker said. "We have our own little ecosystem at work!"

Aristide made a pained noise in the back of his neck. "Do you have to call it that?"

"Yes," Ker said. "We have a symbiotic relationship of mutualism—I occasionally give Aristide blood, and he uses a nifty and little known vampire power that lets him secrete a compound while feeding that extends my life."

"It is *not* a mutualism relationship," Aristide said. "Your blood tastes like *fur*."

"Does Noctus give you blood, Aristide?" I asked.

"Heavens, *no*," Aristide said. "I'd die before I drank his blood —it would probably be as acidic and salty as his personality." Aristide shuddered. "What Ker was referring to is that I use my vampiric powers to back up the magic Noctus casts on Ker."

"Elves have the ability to share bits of their magic—which he's done with me, channeling it into a regeneration magic like the elves have," Ker said. "I'm still one hundred percent werewolf, but juiced up with his magic I don't age much."

I sat straighter on my stool. "Is that common—for elves to share their magic?"

If Noctus is sharing some of his magic with Ker, that would explain why he was willing to use powerful magic on a cat.

"No," Ker said. "Even before the war it was uncommon, and I suspect Noctus is the only elf alive doing it, given their tiny numbers."

"Elves were too proud and arrogant to share their magic," Aristide said. "Most of them were too convinced in their superiority to seek out friendships with other supernaturals."

"Or they were too paranoid to share their magic," Ker added. "It can be dangerous for them, even the way Noctus does for me where it flows from him to me in a pattern he can control. It's why I still need Aristide's help. Noctus's magic alone isn't enough."

"Noctus has *plenty* of magic," Aristide corrected. "He could outfit an army of shifters. But it's a huge risk for him as the deeper the bond, the deeper the connection is required. Given his emotional baggage packed on him by his psychotic family, he does as much as he can for Ker."

"And I'm very thankful you're willing to stand in the gap for me," Ker laughed.

I smiled a little, warmed by their obvious friendship.

They remind me of Pat and Joy...but this raises more questions than it solves.

In some ways, it explained why Noctus had taken a chance sharing magic with Ama. But it also made me suspect the magic he'd cast on the collar was not the precious thing Ms. Booker thought it was.

Which would be good. Noctus didn't know what I was when he cast the magic. He's an elf king who I've been lying to. Anything involving "special" magic would be a major complication.

I'd only pretended to be his cat. We didn't have an actual relationship. Maybe he'd just put the same life-saving magic on my collar as he'd used on Ker. Knowing what an intense pet owner he was, I'd say it was possible.

I hopped off my stool, and went about investigating the rest of the trays. "How did you end up becoming friends with him? Both of you, I mean. Noctus is elven royalty. And elves..."

Aristide smirked. "Treated the rest of supernatural society like trash? Indeed."

"Yes," I said. "They did horrible things—to *everyone*."

The elves had used the fae like servants, and had frequently used magic to turn shifters into tamed pets. That didn't even touch what they'd done to wizards—oracles specifically.

The only supernaturals they hadn't tangled with had been the dragon shifters. Everyone else...they used and abused. Supernaturals had let it go on because of the elves' connection to magic, but that ended when the elves started considering humans as their next target.

"I would die for Noctus, but that applies to him personally," Ker started. "Before Aristide and I started living with his people, we didn't care for elves." Ker shook her head like a dog shaking its body.

"I *hated* them," Aristide said with great relish.

When I uncovered a dish of grilled fish, Ker pushed her newly emptied plate at me.

I gave her some of the fish, then methodically added steamed rice from the next plate, and some Japanese pickled plums. (Noctus's chefs, I'd learned, were capable of cooking a global variety of human foods.)

"I met Noctus first," Aristide said. "I tried to steal from the Mors in their city fortification in Europe. I was caught on my way out. I almost made it, though!"

"And Noctus took you *in*?" I squeaked as I passed Ker her filled plate.

"No, I was imprisoned," Aristide said. "Originally, I was his brother's prize. Noctus was gone to some battle at the time I attempted my heist—which I had scheduled exactly because he was gone. When he got back, he declared a duel against his brother for me and won."

"Why?" I asked, puzzling over the matter. "Did he want you for something?"

"Of course," Aristide said. "I was the first supernatural—excluding the shadows, of course—to get past the Mors' defenses. Noctus realized I'd be handy to have on staff."

"How did you ever become his friend if he held you prisoner?" I asked.

"Once he won me, he didn't imprison me," Aristide said. "I lived in his estate—he let me wander as I liked after putting enough spells on me to choke a dragon shifter. Normally, I'd call him an idiot for doing so, but he was making a point: he was so powerful that he could afford to let me skulk around without worrying about it. It was a very effective intimidation tactic."

"Wow," I said. "So...what did you do?"

"I tried to kill him," Aristide nonchalantly said.

"You *what?*"

"I wanted my freedom," Aristide casually continued. "It didn't work, obviously. He punished me with subterfuge work—typically against other elves. He publicly declared me his valet, so whenever there was an elven function he dragged me along and I snooped around. Eventually, I came to trust him. I was an Unclaimed vampire—I had no family."

"But he's an elf," I said. "How did you trust him at a time when elves were actively being *horrible?*"

"Because Noctus wasn't," Aristide said. "He was always neutral—horrifically so given his ability to smite. He judges people with actual justice. Which is a miracle. The rest of his family wouldn't have known justice if a judge smacked them upside the head with a gavel."

"Noctus was different from his family," Ker added. "They feared him because of his power and control. But they couldn't get rid of him—though they did try."

I grabbed some bacon, then sat back down. "How did you meet him, Ker?"

"Through my Pack," Ker said. "We worked as foresters for a few of the estates he owned in this world—among the humans, not in the fae realm. My father directly served him as his hunting master. I took over the position and the Pack when he died."

"You voluntarily served him?" I asked.

"Yep. It was an excellent gig. Werewolf hunters were serious threats at the time, but they wouldn't come after anyone connected to Noctus. He rarely visited his properties since he was off to war in the fae realm, but we were never attacked by any elves because the threat of him was enough to make them toe the line," Ker explained.

"History doesn't talk about it much, but as horrible as elves were, they were the one supernatural most capable of standing against all threats—whether that was a war between the various supernatural factions, or something more global like famine and disease. Hiding their true nature, they thrived among humans and actually ruled over some pretty substantial lands," Aristide added. "It wasn't unheard of for other supernaturals to work for the elves, and Noctus was among the richest."

"Were the Mors really that powerful?" I asked.

"Yes, but Noctus took his position as a royal seriously—a stark contrast to his family who mostly lusted for spilled blood," Aristide said. "As a result, his lands flourished, and if he knew something would be advantageous, he'd challenge any family member to claim it."

"It always irritated him to see lands in less than perfect condition," Ker added. "That's why he was the crown prince. It wasn't his power, but that he oversaw the most land—in our realm and the fae realm."

"The truth is he doesn't much care for being a royal, but his sense of responsibility tethered him to the position and thus made him far more reasonable than his peers, which also made him more dangerous," Aristide concluded.

I ate the last of my bacon without tasting it, my brain was working too hard to register it. "So...are you saying Noctus is honorable?"

Aristide hooted. "Hardly!"

"Maybe in a backwards way." Ker ate a forkful of her grilled fish. "He wanted to do right by his lands, which means he would give others the chance to prove themselves—like Aristide and I did—in order to better his lands."

"Don't listen to her, she had an easier time of it," Aristide drawled. "Noctus didn't fully invite me into his circle of trust until I temporarily lost my mind and took on a curse meant for him."

I pulled back from the counter. "Wait, you took a *curse* for Noctus?"

"Indeed," Aristide said. "It was a curse that consumed my eyesight. We'd spent at least a century together by that point, and Noctus and his stupid sense of noblesse oblige had won me over, so I interfered, and got clipped by the curse."

I studied Aristide, but despite his flippant words, I couldn't sense any kind of sadness over the issue. "You don't regret it."

"Not even for a day," Aristide said. "I knew if supernaturals had any hope of changing our future, Noctus was it."

A frown twitched across Ker's lips. "You weren't wrong." She glanced at me, then forced a sunny smile. "But that isn't our story to tell," she said with a firmness that cut off any questions.

I'd better be polite and let it go.

There was no use bothering her when it seemed like she'd only just forgiven me. Besides, I liked Aristide and Ker.

"In that case, if you don't mind my asking, Aristide...could the curse be reversed?" I asked.

"No." Aristide swatted his hand through the air. "Elven curses are horrid things—and besides, the curse is long gone. My lack of eyesight is merely the consequence. It was intolerable at first, but over the centuries I have been able to master what many would assume impossible."

Thinking back on the donut shop excursion, I laid my hands flat on the counter. "Like nailing supernaturals in the heart with a dagger?"

Aristide smiled widely, flashing his elongated fang teeth. "Precisely."

"Your ability to sense heartbeats isn't fair," Ker grumbled.

Aristide scoffed. "That's rich, coming from a wolf who can smell if I walked past someone wearing perfume three hours prior."

That's a lot to digest. I guess I can see Noctus being a dutiful prince. He seems to be a diligent king—although he's distant and stoic. But it sounds like it took Aristide and Ker a while to win him over, so I guess that's no surprise.

I stared at my empty plate for a moment, trying to process everything I'd just learned, then studied the bickering vampire and werewolf.

"You're just jealous of my charisma," Ker said. "I've told you a million times, it's not natural, I learned it. I could teach you, too, if you wanted to become a leader and—"

Aristide cut her off and waggled his wine glass in the air. "For the last time, I'm not interested in your Dale Carnegie propaganda!"

"There are podcasts that dive into the topic—I'm sure that would suit your taste more," Ker said.

"I don't need your Dale Carnegie because I have something you and Noctus lack!"

"What's that?"

"*Common sense*!"

Ker's playful smile and the humorous slant of Aristide's lips betrayed the long-time friends' true feelings. They were playing.

They trust me. Or else they wouldn't have told me all of this, or even shown me the depth of their companionship.

Information was a weapon that could be used by even the weakest of supernaturals.

But I'm not going to do anything to betray their trust. I don't want to be here and risk getting caught up in the business of elves—particularly kings of elves—but I won't hurt them.

"Thank you," I impulsively said.

Ker was in the process of tugging on Aristide's ear, but she let him go and leaned around him so she could peer at me. "For what?"

"For telling me all of this—and for trusting me with it," I said.

Ker's smile was gorgeous, warming her brown eyes. "You've proven that you're worthy of the trust. I know that, now."

"*I* knew it all along," Aristide announced.

"You did," Ker agreed. "I didn't see it—or rather I was too wary to see it. But you did."

"Well. It's no fun when you admit it so easily," Aristide grumbled.

"That's why I do it," Ker mildly said. "Now, let's see what other food is under all these covers, shall we?"

I laughed and watched the werewolf prowl around the island counter, checking on the food.

For the first time since I'd revealed myself, the tightness around my heart eased. *It's going to be okay. Aristide and Ker trust me. Maybe, Noctus will eventually trust me, too. I just have to hope it won't take decades...because I won't be able to hold Pat and Joy off much longer.*

"*AND THAT'S all that's going on with work. Barre class just about murdered me this week. But don't tell Pat—the last time I complained about a workout he told me I needed a refresher course on self-defense. He used my email to sign me up to a bunch of mixed martial arts studios in the area, and now I'm getting a dozen emails a week from them.*" Joy groaned into the phone with all the abhorrence an older sister could muster.

"It's because he cares," I said.

"*It's because he's a brat!*"

I chuckled. "Your secret is safe with me. I haven't talked to him recently." I pinned my cellphone to my ear with my shoulder as I finished putting away the last of my clothes while I chatted.

"*I know. He's been complaining about it. Seriously, you need to call him—my voicemail inbox is getting full.*"

"I will—I finally have some free time."

Now that I'm not prowling around as a cat all the time.

"I had a short call with Mom and Dad. They seem like they're still enjoying camper life." I stepped back, blinking as I studied the shelves.

My bedroom had an enormous, empty walk-in closet, and all the clothes in my suitcase filled exactly one shelf. It looked ridiculous.

"Yep—I'm glad it's working out for them. But how are you doing, Chloe? You've been kind of absent the past few weeks."

"Yeah, life just got crazy for a little bit there." I grabbed my giant glass of milk that I'd almost completely downed—now that I was human, I was going to drink some at every opportunity—and considered going to get more from the kitchen. "I'm getting it sorted."

"Did you ever hear back about that Curia Cloisters secretary position you applied to a month ago?"

I put my glass down. "Nope. They closed applications, so I'm assuming I'm not what they were looking for—it was a bit of a stretch, anyway, since it was in the shifter department, and they typically prefer to have similar supernaturals work with similar supernaturals."

"Hey, you change into an animal just like shifters! That's similar!"

I sighed. "It might seem like that, but we're very different."

A knock rattled the door to my bedroom, and I poked my head out of my closet. "I'm sorry, Joy, but I've gotta go."

"Okay. Love you, little sis. Have a good shift at Book Nookery tonight!"

"Um..." Joy—thankfully—hung up before I could think of a good reply.

I tucked my phone into the pocket of my jean shorts and opened the door.

Charon stood in the hallway, his arms tucked behind his back. "Good afternoon, Miss Chloe," he said.

"Hi, Charon." I tried smiling, but the flinty eyed elf didn't soften at all.

"His Majesty would like a word with you." Charon glanced down at my bare feet. "You'll need shoes appropriate for hiking."

"Okay then." I shuffled back into my room—I left the door open, I didn't want Charon to think I was hiding anything.

I had exactly three pairs of shoes to choose from: flip flops, my black business flats I wore to work—I didn't even know why I'd brought them, I guess it was just in case Noctus had a spontaneous accounting party—and my workout shoes.

I tugged my workout shoes on, then hurried back to Charon, fixing the oversized sweater I was wearing when it fluffed up around my neck. "Okay, I'm ready."

Charon slightly tilted his head. "This way."

He led me down the stairs, but instead of heading off to Noctus's study, or even the library, Charon led me toward the massive hallway that I knew led into the elven city outside.

"Um, where are we going?" I meekly asked.

"To see Noctus work."

CHAPTER SEVEN

Chloe

I clung to my seat as the utility vehicle wildly rocked, and for a second I thought we were going to tip over.

Charon, wearing cream linen pants and his usual hood pulled only partially up over his head, looked out of place behind the wheel of the open-air, all-terrain vehicle.

I didn't know what to expect when he took me to a garage in the elven city, threw a sword and a few daggers in the small cargo area of the vehicle, then sped off with me, flying down the city streets.

Faster than I would choose for safety reasons, we were out of the city and zooming across the vast landscape inside the protective barrier, skirting the lake and entering a forest.

We were almost to an edge of the barrier, which was probably the border closest to the city. The barrier wasn't a perfect circle, but rather seemed to be carved into the land, following mountain lines, rivers, and steep valleys.

My seatbelt strapped me to the seat, but when I glanced at Charon, I couldn't help the worry.

He's not taking me off to a forested area to kill me, is he? But then he wouldn't have cared about what shoes I was wearing.

"We are almost there," Charon announced over the guttural hum of the engine.

"Great," I said.

We followed the dusty trail around a curve, then Charon slammed on the brakes, screeching to a stop.

The hazy barrier stretched across the road, disappearing into the forest that crowded in on it.

I could see through the magic swirling in its surface, to the barren wasteland beyond it.

The barrier—powered by elven magic—kept back the toxic miasma that had eaten away at everything else in the fae realm. Not much could live outside the barriers—only monsters, really. Certainly no plant life or supernatural being.

It was the same in the kingdoms of the other fae Courts—barriers were all that stood between the fae and the annihilation of their homeland.

Charon turned the all-terrain vehicle off and pocketed the keys. "This way." He slipped out of the vehicle and headed into the forest.

I fumbled with my seatbelt then scrambled after him.

When I caught up to him I was able to slow down, watch where he stepped, and copy him. It kept my movements quiet—something Charon must have appreciated, because he glanced back at me and nodded in a way he hadn't since I'd been revealed as Ama.

I heard the crunch of metal slicing through something, and my instincts made me freeze.

Magic.

Even worse, the knife in my ribs sensation was *elven* magic.

"Charon, what did you say Noctus is doing?" I asked.

Charon stopped when he realized I was no longer following him. "Working."

I backed up a step—the pulse of magic that flashed had my instincts screaming that I did *not* want to get any closer. But Charon started off again, and I also disliked the idea of being left alone in a forest in the fae realm.

I have two options: stay back and end up alone in a creepy magical woods, or follow Charon—who might hate me less now than he did yesterday—to an isolated spot that is filled with magic. Okay. Why do both choices sound like the beginning of a horror story?

Figuring it was probably better for my health to be an obedient captive, I hurried after Charon, following him so closely that I almost smacked into his back when he stepped into a meadow and stilled.

Noctus stood in the middle of the clearing, holding a sword that dripped with a thick, tar black liquid.

Directly behind him, huddled on the ground, were two elves. Both were teenagers—or, more correctly, they were that gawky stage of early adulthood. One of them was clutching a book to his chest, the other held a smashed phone. Both of them were absolutely terrified as they gaped at the shadows that scuttled around the meadow.

Shadows—unnatural shapes that moved by their own will and didn't follow anything I could see—circled the meadow. They seemed drawn to an eight-foot stretch of the barrier that cut across the tail end of the clearing.

A loud, sniffing noise filled my ears and made my bones shiver.

One of the shadows went from 2D to 3D, stepping up and filling out into a frightening shape.

It was vaguely humanoid with short, thick arms, clawed hands that had too few fingers, and long, spindly legs with feet that had too many toes. The shadows on its head swirled, as if it couldn't decide between two faces—one that was flat and smashed and looked human enough to make the creature even more eerie, and one smooth and bald with a jagged, bird-like beak.

The entire creature looked incorporeal, and it was an off gray shade—almost a slate color, but more sinister with a swirl of green. I sympathized with the cowering elves who were both sweating and heaving dry, painful sobs as the creature lumbered toward them.

The monster took a swipe at Noctus, who minutely tilted his head back so the creature's clawed fingers missed his face, but passed by so closely it ruffled his golden hair.

Noctus twirled his sword, then stabbed the monster in the chest. He waited a moment before ripping his sword up, slicing through the creature.

Something in the monster snapped, and its chest caved in before its legs and arms smoldered, dissolving into black smoke.

A rock fell from where the creature's chest had been. It fell with a plop, hitting the grassy ground.

The elf clutching the book to his chest exhaled so deeply he almost tipped over. "It's dead. It's really dead. Thank goodness."

Three more of the shadow creatures stopped swirling around the meadow and stepped from their flattened to their full shapes. They glanced at Noctus and his subjects, then headed for the glossy barrier.

"No, no, no!" the elf clutching the book yelled, his voice going higher.

The elf with the busted phone wrapped his arms around his legs and rocked. He was whispering something under his breath, but it was elvish, and I couldn't understand a word of it. It was probably panicked based on the sweat beading on his forehead.

Despite all the fun and excitement, Noctus looked...bored. He tilted his head from side to side as he watched one of the shadows crawl past, his stance relaxed.

He approached the three creatures, his eyes narrowing when one of the monsters slashed at the barrier.

The magic held, but the claw marks were visible on the barrier. They were jagged, gray gashes that seemed to leech color from the magic of the barrier spell.

Wait, they can damage the barrier? How many shadows are there?

Noctus stabbed the first in the chest, ducked under the flailing arm of the second—slashing it in the abdomen as he passed—then popped up in front of the third creature. He head-butted it, and when the creature snapped its head back in obvious pain Noctus cut its throat.

All three creatures dissolved into smoke, and I finished counting eight additional shadows swirling around the meadow. Noctus ignored them and turned around to frown at Charon and me.

"What is she doing here?" he asked.

Charon bowed to Noctus. "You said you wished to speak with her, Your Majesty."

"Not *now*." Noctus sounded only slightly harassed as he strode across the meadow, approaching the young elves.

I glanced up at Charon, trying to get a read on him.

His expression was placid enough, but when he glanced down at me he raised both of his eyebrows.

Yep. He's up to something. But it's Charon, so there's no telling what it is. Of all Noctus's companions, Charon was the sneakiest. And the most doting on his king...so I could at least assume whatever it was, it was for Noctus's sake.

Which doesn't mean it will be good for my health.

Two more of the shadows stepped forward, their forms solidifying. Noctus sliced through the nearest—his sword a metallic flash—spun, then stabbed the second one, downing them both in the blink of an eye.

There was something beautiful and terrifying about it.

Noctus was ripping through these creatures like they were tissue paper, without using any kind of magic. Every movement he made was both brutal and striking—like dark poetry set to iambic pentameter.

I could see how he'd been the pride of the Mors...before he wiped his family out, that was.

Noctus reached the cowering elves and stared imperiously down at them. "Get up."

The trembling elves peered up at him.

Noctus gestured at them with two fingers. "*Stand.*"

Both of the elves scrambled to their feet, their sweat-streaked t-shirts sticking to them.

"Come." Noctus headed back to the barrier as three of the remaining six shadows sprouted, clustering in their incorporeal forms at the spot the previous monsters had slashed at.

Noctus reached the shadows, but this time the monsters tried to attack him first.

One tried to stab him, jabbing its arm at his chest.

Noctus dodged it—striking the monster inside the arm so its jab went wide—then stabbed the creature through with his sword, dissolving it into smoke.

The two other monsters that had manifested jumped him together, each charging him from opposite sides.

Moving like lightning, Noctus grabbed a dagger from his belt and flung it at the first monster. He didn't even wait long enough to make sure the weapon found its mark—it had, digging deep into the first monster's chest so it exploded into smoke—before he turned to the second shadow monster.

This one he kicked into the barrier, which it bounced off like a rag doll before flopping back at him. He speared it with pinpoint precision, and it started to dissolve.

"These are monsters created by an elven spell." Charon spoke, surprising me.

Before the most recently slain monster completely faded away, the last three shadows peeled off the ground, solidifying into forms that were larger than any of the previous creatures.

I started to peer up at him as I registered the deeper meaning of his words. "Wait—you mean they were made? On purpose?"

"Indeed." Charon nodded in the direction of the sweating elves. "The folly of youth."

Noctus watched impassively as the three remaining shadows strode up to the barrier. He briefly sheathed his sword, then reached behind him—grabbing the younger elves by the collars of their t-shirts—and yanked the duo forward.

They choked and fell to their knees. Noctus then placed a hand on the top of each of their heads and pressed their faces into the barrier. "Listen," he ordered when the pair squirmed.

Farther down the line the barrier drew across the meadow. The three large shadow creatures slashed at the barrier, making the magic shudder.

"Do you hear that?" Noctus asked.

One of the elves croaked like a distressed bullfrog.

Noctus leaned over the duo. "That is the sound of magic *dying*."

"There are several varieties of these shadow creatures," Charon translated for me. "This specific type is one of the stronger, evolved types. They are capable of sucking magic into themselves, killing it in the process. As such, they are particularly skilled at breaking through barriers."

"Even *elven* barriers?" I asked.

"Oh yes," Charon said. "The elves frequently warred with one another, so coming up with ways to break elven barriers was necessary for warfare."

Noctus left the duo—who, I assumed, were responsible for the creatures—and sauntered up to the three remaining monsters.

One of the shadow creatures left the barrier and turned toward him, its face continuously shifting from the bird-like skull to the crumpled, humanoid features.

It charged Noctus, picking up speed as it barreled across the meadow, its clawed feet kicking up clods of grass and turf.

Noctus dodged its first strike. He jumped to the left, into the open part of the meadow so the creature couldn't sandwich him against the barrier.

He slashed at its ribcage, but even with his sword, his reach wasn't quite long enough, and he missed.

The monster charged past him, and Noctus pivoted so he stood behind the creature. His expression like stone, Noctus stabbed it through the back.

The monster didn't immediately disappear like its predecessors. It raised its head and opened its mouth, but instead of noise, it felt like everything in the meadow was pulled toward the creature. Air, *magic*, even myself.

Noctus pushed his sword in deeper, and the monster collapsed, dissolving into nothing. Like all the others before it, a rock fell from its chest with a plop.

"Did you see that rock?" Charon asked. "The spell was cast upon it. It serves as an anchor—so to speak."

I only half listened—another one of the overly large monsters had peeled away from the damage it was dealing to the barrier. It silently stalked toward Noctus—whose back was turned to the monster.

My heart beat frantically in my chest as it drew closer and closer to him. "Noctus!" I shouted. "*Behind you!*"

Noctus gave me a curious look—his eyebrows slightly furrowed and his lips slanted—then spun, using his momentum to pull his sword down through the air, slashing the creature across the chest.

Oh. I hunched my shoulders up, feeling like an idiot. *He knew it was there. Obviously*.

As Noctus dealt another blow to the larger shadow monster, pushing it backwards, the last monster crept toward the two younger elves, who hadn't moved from their collapsed position on the ground.

It loomed over them, smiling freakishly with its human face before it lunged.

The pair scrambled to their feet and clambered backwards, dodging the attack. Although they possessed the same elven grace and speed as Charon, their movements were jerkier—roughened by their fear.

Noctus finished with his shadow monster, then watched as the last remaining creature chased the elven boys halfway across the meadow.

The pair were able to keep in front of it, hopping and jumping to avoid it whenever it took a swipe at them with its claws. But they were frantic. Their breaths came in heavy puffs, and their fear made them slip and slide on the grassy ground.

One tripped on his own feet and fell. On his way down he grabbed his friend by the arm, yanking him down so he fell on top of him.

The monster was on them in an instant, towering over them as it drew its clawed hands back.

It lunged down at them, but when its claws were about six inches from the elves' faces, Noctus stabbed it through the back.

The monster heaved upright, and Noctus made a horizontal slash through its torso.

The creature dissolved, and its rock fell on the knee of the elf with the smashed phone.

Sweating so hard their dark hair was streaked, the elf duo peered up at Noctus.

"Up," Noctus ordered.

When the elves kept staring at him, Noctus hauled them upright, then dragged them to the spot where the largest of the shadows had been burrowing into the barrier.

Noctus pointed to the flimsy, colorless section of the barrier. "Do you see that?"

The duo stared dumbly at it.

"They weakened it. Dangerously so. Do you know what

happens when a barrier is weakened like this?" Noctus punched the barrier with his bare hand, shattering the discolored portion.

Toxic miasma swirled in through the plate sized hole, dripping down the side of the barrier and crawling across the grassy meadow.

Wherever it touched, the grass died.

The elves yelped and stumbled backwards, their eyes bulging as the miasma crept closer.

Noctus set his hand on the barrier.

Something tickled my throat, and it took me a moment to realize it was my collar.

He's gathering his magic—or what little bit can get through the shackles.

The sensation of magic thickened around Noctus, and the barrier shimmered, then mended itself, reforming so the sparkling barrier was whole once more.

Cut off, the miasma faded, leaving behind charred streaks of dead grass.

The elf who was clutching the book dropped it and flopped on the ground. His mouth moved, but I didn't hear anything. I think his vocal cords were too weak with relief to produce any noise.

His friend, the one with the busted cellphone, stared at the singed ground.

Noctus turned to the duo, his sword glinting. He didn't point it at them, precisely. Rather, he held it extended with the sharpened tip slanted down at the ground, somewhat near their legs.

The elf with the busted cellphone gulped. He tried to scoot back, but froze when Noctus took a step closer to him.

"We're not done," Noctus said, his words heavy with power.

The elf with the book slowly sat up, his shoulders hunched with fear.

I felt magic dance around Noctus. The elves must have been

able to sense it even better than I could, because even Charon twitched as the air in the meadow grew heavy.

"You two practiced a kind of magic that I outlawed." Noctus said.

"W-we won't do it again," the elf with the book promised.

"We didn't mean any harm," the second elf said. "We were just curious! We used to be so feared, and now—"

"*Feared?*" Noctus's voice was a crack of thunder. "You want to be *feared?* You risked not only the spells harming someone, but the barriers that shelter the city all because you are dissatisfied?"

The young elves sank in on themselves. Noctus must have been hammering at them with some spells—I could feel it, but it brushed past me with barely a whisper.

"I have outlawed certain elven magic because it will always be more harmful than helpful," he said. "But that doesn't seem to matter to you two, so allow me to *enlighten* you." Noctus stabbed his sword into the ground right between the elves, passing so close to them I was pretty sure he must have sliced a hole in their jeans.

"Because you *want* to be feared, I know firsthand that these outlawed spells will *swallow you whole*. Only someone with a weak spirit would wish to be feared, and magic has no use for such a person. It will be your death as it takes over your mind, and destroys everything you love until you are wiped from the face of this planet and the entire world delights in your demise."

The young elves shivered, so frightened their teeth chattered.

"Because you are young and foolish, I'm giving you this *one* opportunity to learn this," Noctus said. "If you break my laws again and attempt outlawed magic, I will put you where you deserve to be: out there." Noctus yanked his sword out of the ground and used it to point beyond the barrier, to the empty wasteland.

"W-we're sorry," the book elf said. "Never—we won't do any magic like this *ever* again. I vow it!"

The elf with the smashed cellphone stared up at Noctus with terror so thick, if I'd been a cat I'd probably feel it in my whiskers. He was white faced and silent until his friend elbowed him. "R-right," he stammered. "We won't touch outlawed magic. Ever."

"Vow it," his friend—his voice brittle with fear—hissed.

"I vow it," the cellphone elf blurted out.

Noctus straightened. "See that you don't."

He stepped around the duo, who cringed. One of them cried out a little.

When Noctus swept past, the two collapsed, gasping for breath and wiping sweat from their foreheads.

I watched their reaction, a frown tugging at my lips.

They're being unfair. They were the ones who created those spells. Noctus just destroyed them. They were the ones who did the stupid—and dangerous—thing. Noctus is merciful for giving them this warning, but they're acting like he's the boogeyman.

Noctus's face was etched in stone, disgust and unflinching power swirling in his eyes as he paused to wipe his sword on the grass, cleansing it of the gross black liquid that coated it before he sheathed it. There was something about his expression that propelled me into motion.

Even though every sense in my body tingled, I approached him, meeting him halfway across the meadow.

I don't know if it was muscle memory, if my brain temporarily flatlined, or what, but when we met, I leaned forward, invading his space with outstretched arms.

It was only when my thoughts caught up with my actions that I realized I was planning to perform my typical cat-hug I usually did whenever I could tell Noctus wanted to pick me up or needed me to purr.

Somehow, Noctus must have gotten swept up in our cat-focused affection swap, because by the time I realized what was going on, he had an arm around my lower back and was ready to sweep me up until our eyes met and we both regained our sanity.

We jolted to a stop and were a confused tangle for a moment.

Woah, I need to get my head out of the clouds. As used to touching him as I am, I'm not his precious Amalourne anymore.

Nothing underlined that more than the quick and efficient way Noctus disentangled himself. Amalourne had been special to him. I was an accidental spy who had brought a lot of complications into his life.

I studied his face as he glanced back at the still-shivering duo. He didn't look hardened anymore, but the brief light I'd seen in his eyes when I'd reached for him—like an *idiot*—was gone.

There was a part of me that was sad I'd had a part in the squelching of the easy affection he'd had for what he thought was his pet. Now we were...something totally different.

Stop moping. He's an elf king!

I cleared my throat and tried to think of something to say. "Those spells were pretty..." I trailed off, mentally kicking myself for my poor topic choice.

Oh, sure. Insult elven magic to his face. That seems like a good way to stay in an elf king's good graces.

"Dark," Noctus said.

"Huh?"

"Those spells are dark and not good for anyone—the spell caster, or their enemy." Noctus glanced back over his shoulder at the shivering friends. "Charon?"

"I'll debrief them," Charon said. "And inform their family. I suspect their parents will have something to say of their offspring's stupidity."

"They're young," Noctus said. "They weren't born until well after the war."

"Their parents, however, were," Charon said. "They know better. All of us who were around then do." Charon offered a flash of a smile. It wasn't warm. In fact it was almost bitter and sad. But Charon's swirled eyes had a knowing look to them, and when he glanced at me...for once he didn't narrow them.

Instead, Charon bowed his head to me, bent at the waist to Noctus, then trotted off to face the spell-casting duo. Judging by the way he was rolling up his sleeves, the young elves were doubly going to regret their actions.

"You don't seem upset," Noctus said.

"Hmmm?" I pulled my attention from Charon and instead peered up at Noctus.

Noctus gestured to the path Charon had led me down, then started for it. "Most would find that display...unsettling."

I scrambled after the elf king. "Well, the monsters were pretty creepy, but you took care of them. Unless...can they respawn from those rocks?"

Noctus slowed so I could walk fast instead of jog at his side. "No," he said.

"Then what is there to be upset about?"

"Most would find the physical display an unsettling reminder of elven capabilities."

"Your Majesty," I said. "My strongest magic is that I turn into a cat. *Everyone* is more powerful than me."

"You are not an elf, so you don't need to use elven titles," Noctus said. "More importantly, it has not escaped my notice that despite being better informed of your past, you still believe that lie."

"Lie? You mean that I believe that I'm weak?"

"Yes. Which brings me to why I wanted to speak to you."

"Okay?" I asked, confused.

"I've decided to have Charon train you in combat."

I stopped walking as my brain digested his words.

Charon is going to train me? But...why?

Noctus slowed to a stop when I didn't rejoin him. "Is something wrong?"

"You said I'm a shadow."

"Yes."

"And shadows were the elves' only natural enemy."

"Yes."

"So *why* would you want Charon to train me?"

"Why wouldn't I?"

"Oh, I don't know, except, maybe, because of *history*?!" I squeaked.

"You know the elves hunted shadows to extinction—or what was believed to be extinction," Noctus said. "And yet you don't seem overly fearful of living in my villa."

"I am plenty scared," I assured him. "I'm scared of getting squashed by living with a league that is so much bigger than my own that by sheer logistics I wouldn't even rate as important enough to be a servant. I'm afraid my human family is somehow going to get dragged into this. I'm afraid of what the tracker guy means for my future, and I'm a little upset that he hasn't popped out because I don't know what he's planning in his murderous skull."

"But you are not afraid of me?" Noctus asked.

I hemmed and hawed at responding, but the truth was I didn't know how much the blasted collar told him about me, so I was better off being honest. "When I first figured out you were an elf I freaked out pretty bad," I said. "There was a reason I was leaving explosions of hair everywhere I went the first few weeks I lived here. The shock of meeting an elf when I'd been taught they didn't exist..."

"But you didn't fear me because of my power?" Noctus added.

Why does he keep asking questions that have dangerous answers? If I start walking back to the vehicle, will this potentially dangerous conversation end?

I tried to edge in the direction I thought the all-terrain vehicle was in. "I was afraid you were going to smite me because I lied about being a cat."

"Your subterfuge remains a problem," Noctus said.

Well, if I wanted proof that I'm not completely forgiven, there we go!

He continued, "But that is the consequence of your actions, not a reflection of my power."

"Yes," I said. "And the consequences *seem* to be that I have to stay in the villa."

"And you're fine with that?" Noctus stepped closer, invading my space. If he meant for it to be intimidating it didn't work—I was so used to him invading my space as Ama that it barely even registered.

"Well, I don't know what I'm going to do when I run out of money and my rent is due, but that's a personal problem," I said. "I'm just grateful you haven't, um, more harshly jailed me. Or taught me a lesson like you did for them." I jerked my thumb back at the meadow. "When you have reason to since there's an entire city you're protecting."

"But you don't fear me because of my power," Noctus repeated.

I awkwardly shuffled my feet. "Um, well, I have more memories of being cuddled by you than anything else, and all of this is just ridiculously bad luck on my end. So...no?"

Pretty sure that's not the answer he's looking for, but—woah.

CHAPTER EIGHT

Chloe

Noctus smiled, and for a moment I stopped breathing.

His strong features were softened by the grin, which was so large it flashed his teeth and gave him smile lines. The spirals of his pupils swirled, and even glittered as his eyes crinkled.

Everything about him seemed warmer—brighter in a way I didn't think was possible for an elf king who was practically flawless.

His smile—more specifically *this* smile, as I'd seen him grin before in a way that was very different from this—wasn't perfect like elves tended to look. Instead...it made him look more real, more *human*.

Woah. I thought he looked amazing in perfection, but this? No comparison!

"Ahhh, yes, Amalourne. You are a rare kind, aren't you?"

Noctus was still smiling when he briefly glanced behind us, then set a hand on my lower back and gently propelled me forward.

"Sorry," I hiccuped. "I went too far."

"Nonsense," Noctus said. "Unless that was your roundabout way of asking to be carried?"

"*No*!"

"Good. Then your training will begin once Charon clears some time in his calendar," Noctus said.

The hand still pressed to my back was gentle, which I didn't know what to think of.

You don't usually touch people you're spitting furious with, right? Does that mean I'm not on the 'dangerous individuals' list anymore?

I could hope—I was generally uninspiring and unintimidating, obviously, or Noctus wouldn't even think about getting me training.

The thought gave me enough daring to clear my throat. "Um, could I ask a question?"

"You may."

"What exactly will he be training me in? Like...is he going to teach me about guns?" That was Charon's weapon when we'd invaded Magiford Donuts.

Noctus steadied the scabbard of his sheathed sword as it tapped his side. "Perhaps, but I don't think a handgun would be the best choice for a shadow. Your stealth is unmatched in the supernatural world, and even the best silencer in the world can't facilitate stealth when dealing with handguns."

A strangled croak made it through my throat. "Good to know."

"Charon will cover the basics of fighting as a shadow and how to use your power to your advantage—including the usage of a variety of bladed weapons. Shadows were excellent poisoners, too, but given the advances of modern-day sciences, that is a subject best ignored for now."

"Yeah, we don't *ever* have to go there." I stepped out of the woods and onto the dirt road where the all-terrain vehicle was parked.

"You'll have fun," Noctus said.

"Fun? With training?"

"You're already well skilled at subterfuge," Noctus mildly pointed out.

"No, I'm just really good at pretending to be a cat," I corrected.

"You are," Noctus said. "You're better at acting like a cat than any of your ancestors that I ever saw."

He's just full of compliments today. That seems...odd. I suspiciously peered up at him, curious, and maybe a tad concerned.

Noctus smiled again—this one more along the lines of what I was used to seeing: sardonic and perfect. "How *did* you get to be so good at pretending to be a cat?"

"Practice," I said. "For self defense. It's the easiest way to shake off other supernaturals when they're chasing after me." I scratched my nose as I climbed into the all-terrain vehicle and buckled my seatbelt. "I watched a lot of nature documentaries on housecats when I was little. That helped."

Noctus shot me a look as he slid into the driver's seat. "*Nature documentaries?*"

"They're really helpful."

Noctus slightly shook his head. "You are unbelievable."

Says the elf king.

I kept my mouth shut as Noctus turned the key to the all-terrain vehicle.

"In case you're wondering," Noctus shouted over the purr of the engine, "Charon does not have plans to show you a *documentary* or give a Power Point presentation when training you."

"That's so sad."

"I doubt he would agree with you."

As I followed Charon down a seemingly endless flight of stairs three days later, I wondered if I had been quick to assume I was safe. Maybe Charon was finally taking me down to the dungeons now that he'd cleared his schedule enough.

The phrase "scaredy cat" isn't a taunt, it's a useful life motto to build on, I thought as I almost slipped down a stair, my palms clammy with my many, many worries.

"There is no need to be anxious, Chloe," Charon said. "We are merely going to the training grounds."

I eyed Charon's back as he nonchalantly continued down the endless, stone spiral staircase. He didn't even stop to look back at me.

"How do you know I'm anxious?" I asked.

"*Everything* made you anxious as a cat," Charon said. "It stands to reason that everything would also make you anxious as a human."

"That is...accurate," I admitted. "Why are the training grounds so deep beneath the villa?"

Charon finally reached the bottom stair, leaving us in a cramped, damp, stone lined landing that edged on inspiring claustrophobia. "We needed the extra space."

"Space?"

Charon pushed against the double doors—the only non-stone part of the dizzying stairwell.

I blinked at the abrupt light and raised a hand to shade my eyes.

Charon stepped inside, so I tottered after him, jumping in surprise when I felt grass beneath my feet. I rapidly blinked, lowering my hand when my eyes finally adjusted, and felt my mouth drop open.

The "training grounds" were enormous—at least the size of two fields, if not larger. And even though we'd walked deep into the mountain, I couldn't quite get a feel for the ceiling—it was blue like the sky, and I swear the *sun* shone on the horizon.

"What is this place?" I asked.

"His Majesty's personal training grounds," Charon said. "The entire area can be shifted with magic to adjust to whatever parameters he wants—cloudy skies, rough terrain, anything."

I took a few steps deeper, turning in a circle as my brain wrestled to accept the sheer size and appearance of the arena.

Charon continued—his voice colored by a rare note of emotion that I recognized as pride. "Snow is possible, but it is quite a mess to clean up, so it is easier to train on one of the nearby mountain tops if one truly wishes to practice fighting in such conditions."

"Why is it so big?" I wondered out loud.

On the far end of the field, something exploded, flattening the green grass with a harsh wind. The ground grumbled beneath my feet.

Whatever had caused the ruckus had similarly raised a cloud of dust, which took a few moments to settle again, revealing Noctus standing on a rock formation.

"Nice try, Ker," he said. "But even you aren't big enough to dislodge these rocks."

Ker—in her wolf body with her dark brown and black undercoat and fiery red overcoat that made her look like a burning coal—stood near the base of one of the large boulders and sneezed.

Aristide—lounging on a bunch of maroon pillows propped up against a much smaller rock a dozen feet away from the pair—raised his teacup. "I don't know what just happened, but that sounds like a point for Noctus."

Ker loudly complained, but Aristide ignored her and flipped the scorekeeping card displayed next to him.

"Don't complain to me," Aristide said. "You're the idiot who thought you stood a chance against him. And welcome, Charon and Chloe, to the bunker." Aristide must have heard us enter, because he raised his teacup in our general direction.

Ker gave a friendly bark, then backed up and aimed herself at the boulders. Noctus mutely watched from his perch.

"I think I get it," I said. "Why it needs to be this big, I mean."

"Indeed," Charon said. "But don't worry. They'll keep an eye out for you. Once you're done with your training, none of them will be able to catch you anyway. Now. You stretched out beforehand as I instructed, yes?"

"Yep." I shuffled a step backwards as Ker made another go at slamming into the boulders, making the ground rumble as the unmovable rocks groaned.

"Then we shall begin—with the basics, of course." Charon started rolling up the sleeves of his moisture-wicking, long-sleeved workout shirt—he wasn't even wearing his regular hood, so he looked weirdly modern. "As vampires are blessed with speed, werewolves with strength, and wizards and fae with their magic, shadows have their own core that works as the center of their abilities, and that is their ability to shift into a cat."

"Wouldn't it just be our stealth *as* a cat?" I asked. "With the side bonus of most magic not working on us?"

"One would think so, but what made the shadows so blasted difficult to fight was that since magic couldn't work on them, you could only face a shadow in physical combat, and that is where their cat shifting abilities gave them the upper hand."

I scratched my head, messing up my ponytail. "Yeah, but *how?*"

"I believe a demonstration would best suit the situation—so you can *learn* the information and not be told it." Charon took up a boxing stance. "I am going to attack you. Prepare yourself."

"Already—wait, prepare how? Charon?" I squawked and started running when Charon sprinted toward me.

I ducked his first punch, frantically trying to look for the best place to run.

In the city it was easy enough—I just had to go high or low as a cat and no one would see me.

But the training grounds were flat—besides the rock formation Noctus had claimed, and I wasn't going anywhere near him.

I dropped to my knees, skidding under Charon's kick and shredding my workout pants in the process.

I swapped to my cat form and put on a burst of speed, getting a lot of space between me and Charon. When I felt my stamina drop, I shifted back to my human shape and looked back.

I didn't see Charon anywhere.

Where did he—

I smacked into what felt like a cloth covered wall and bounced off, falling to the ground in a heap.

Charon crouched over me and tapped my head. "There, you're caught and—for our practice purposes—tagged out. Now, stand."

I obediently stood and dusted off my work out pants—which were probably going to be rags by the end of the session. "What was that supposed to teach me?" I panted. "Because—this isn't a criticism of your teaching skills—but what I got out of that is that I need to always live in a city."

"Next," Charon ignored my question and reset to his boxing stance, "try switching back and forth between cat and human as much as possible, while moving around me. Begin."

Having learned the first time, I took his directions to heart and immediately swapped to a cat. I raced past him, switching into my human form when he tried to kick me.

His kick was aimed low to the ground, so I hopped it with ease, then turned into a cat again when he aimed a punch at me. He had to catch himself so he didn't topple over, and I raced between his legs then turned into a human.

Charon pivoted and—using his momentum—kicked high, aiming at my side.

I turned into a cat, and his foot whisked over my head.

I ran toward him—intending to skirt between his legs again—but he brought his leg in faster than I would have thought possible.

I turned into a human in the hopes of avoiding it, but I was so close to Charon I banged my skull on his chin when I shifted, almost making him wobble for a step.

"Well done," he said. "Now, what was different about that?"

"You moved slower," I said.

"Correct. Why?"

"Because..." I squinted as I mentally compared his movements. "You were having to adjust more. Every time I swapped from cat to human, you had to adjust your fighting movements."

"Yes," Charon said. "Adjusting one's movements is no small thing—it requires adjustments to balance, stance, and even mental calculations for aim. Shadows—with their lightning fast shifting abilities that expend no additional energy—are nearly impossible to track since they move so differently as a human versus a cat. It makes them unpredictable. It's also why the closer the combat, the safer you are. An enemy can't react quickly when you're sitting on their ankles, then suddenly shift at their back and hold a knife to their spine."

I rubbed at a new grass stain in my pants as I mulled over Charon's words.

"Are you starting to see why your ancestors were so feared?" Charon asked.

"I think so," I said. "It just feels...odd. Everything in supernatural society is about how much magic you have. Shadows can just turn into cats."

Charon tsked. "Supernaturals have an unhealthy obsession with magic given its dilapidated state—though I suspect it's also a byproduct of supernaturals living among humans who are obsessed with power."

That's pretty hypocritical coming from an elf, whose entire society is based on power.

Charon raised his eyebrow at me, as if he could guess what I was thinking. "The real question, Chloe, is how much do you value yourself?"

"What do you mean?" I asked.

"As long as you believe you are weaker than other supernaturals, you will continue to allow yourself to be pushed around," Charon said.

"That's not a fair comparison, though. Other supernaturals have backup," I said. "At most, I've got French Fry."

"*French Fry?*"

"The trash griffin that flies around with me sometimes."

Charon furrowed his brow so deeply, I wondered if the deep creases in his forehead would stick. "Fascinating," he said. "Now, do you know how to use any weapons?"

"I know basic self-defense," I said. "And I did gymnastics in high school to help key in my athleticism as a cat. That's about it."

"Very well, then we shall start with throwing daggers and perhaps the short sword. Daggers will give you the opportunity to attack and then get close."

"What about running—"

"Running away is *not* an option."

"Okay, then."

AN HOUR later I thought my arm might fall out of its socket, but I didn't want to face Charon's wrath, so I kept throwing the daggers at the target.

There had been several more...*exciting* sounds at the far end of the arena where Noctus and Ker were, and I heard Aristide squawk a few times before flipping numbers on his score keeper card, but I hadn't paid much attention due to Charon's aforementioned—and feared—wrath.

As a result, I was focused on the bullseye target in front of me, and didn't notice my instincts tugging at me until Noctus was right behind me.

"You have a steady arm."

"Ahh...thank you?" I glanced dubiously at the target. I'd only hit it two out of five times, and both times the daggers had bounced off. "I haven't been improving at all, though."

"I wouldn't expect to see any improvements after practicing with a weapon—for the first time ever—for a mere hour," Noctus said.

"True." I threw another dagger, frowning when it hit the target and bounced harmlessly off instead of sticking.

"Is there a weapon you'd feel more confident with?" Noctus asked.

"Pepper spray," I said. "Joy—my sister—makes me practice every year, so I'm pretty good with it."

"Pepper spray," Noctus repeated.

"Yeah." I adjusted my hold on my last throwing dagger—trying to get my fingers to match the handhold Charon had showed me—and glanced up at Noctus, hoping he would correct me if I was holding it wrong.

Noctus was staring at the paper target, his eyebrows slightly furrowed. "You use pepper spray in combat."

"I have it on my apartment keyring," I said. "Otherwise biting other supernaturals as a cat makes them let me go."

Noctus tilted his head as he studied me.

"Is there a problem, Your Majesty?" Charon asked. He glanced at my hold on the dagger, and I could tell he itched to fix it, but he focused his attention on his adored king.

"Not a problem," Noctus said. "But perhaps you'd be better off training Chloe in a different manner than you would a new recruit?"

"Why?" I asked.

"Of course, Your Majesty," Charon said, forever accepting what his monarch said.

Noctus studied me. "You're a shadow, but you have different skills from those we knew of—like your ability to pass as a cat."

"I thought the ability to turn into a cat was why shadows were stealthy?" I said.

"Yes, because they had the same magic as you and as soon as they became a cat they were less noticeable," Noctus said. "They could pass as cats for a short amount of time, but *never* could they successfully pass as a pet for weeks like you did. Similarly, you are in an entirely different world and landscape."

"What would you have me start her with, Your Majesty?" Charon asked.

Noctus took my hand—the one I used to hold the dagger. His fingers were warm in comparison to the cool touch of the steel dagger, and he rearranged my fingers without thinking.

I, on the other hand, was hardcore blushing.

Suck it up, hormones. I hugged this guy every day *as a cat. Him touching my hand is nothing to get squirrelly about!*

And yet, as his fingers glided across the tops of my fingers, I swear I could hear my own heartbeat.

Is this why Joy was always telling me I need to expand my social life? Because I've been too much of a hermit and now I'm swooning over something like this*? I mean, he* is *keeping me here against my will. Kind of, because I don't really want to go face the tracker myself and I'm safer here. Okay, no, I've got it, he's making me experience financial hardship because he won't let me work!*

Noctus, thankfully, didn't seem to pick up on my embarrassment. He kept his comment directed to Charon. "If she's used to running, why not teach her to use that to her advantage and focus on the physical aspect?"

His words broke the pink-y haze my hermit-induced embarrassment created.

The physical aspect? What is that even supposed to mean?

For the first time ever, Charon looked doubtful at something Noctus had said. "There is merit, Your Majesty...however..." he glanced at me, and for a moment I swear I saw his eyes swirl with the same intensity Noctus's did in the thick of battle. "I don't know that she believes me enough to accept my suggestions in that area. Perhaps, however, she'd trust you more?"

What? No.

Any traces of my embarrassment faded, even though Noctus was still repositioning my fingers.

I cleared my throat. "I'm sorry—please excuse the interruption," I said, trying to be as polite as possible. "But what are you two talking about?"

Satisfied, *finally*, with my grasp on the dagger, Noctus dropped my hand. "No, I don't need to step in. Just carry on with the drills, then."

Charon leaned back a tiny bit, and seemed almost disappointed. "As you wish, Your Majesty."

Noctus nodded to me, then walked off, heading back to Aristide and Ker—who were wrestling in the grass.

"What just happened?" I asked.

"Nothing," Charon said, managing to make the word sound neutral and yet still disappointed. "Return to your drills."

My shoulders curled as I started to withdraw, and Charon glanced at me.

He blinked at me, then said, his voice dry, "The conversation was more about His Majesty than you."

"How?" I asked.

Charon shook his head. "Return to your drills."

I felt marginally better with the explanation—Charon didn't care enough about my feelings to lie to me, so that meant he wanted me to know the conversation was somehow about Noctus.

Does he want Noctus to teach me? But why?

Whatever—I needed to keep to my vow of not meddling in the affairs of kings. Elven or otherwise.

I took a breath, squared my shoulders, then threw the dagger.

It hit the target with a thump, digging into the bullseye for the first time since I'd started practice.

TWO DAYS later I perched on a chair in my lavish bedroom, tapping away on my laptop.

I paused momentarily to rub my arms—the muscles in them burned from all the practice Charon had me clocking in—then adjusted the tilt of my screen to something slightly more ergonomic.

Almost done...

The villa had ridiculously fast Wi-Fi, so after securing Noctus's blessing, I logged in to Book Nookery's software to process payroll for Ms. Booker and to pay a few of the book shop's bills.

I was surprised he let me do it. Maybe all my efforts to be a good captive/repentant liar and show that my greatest ambition was to simply be set free were paying off? More likely, they were tech smart enough that they could log what I was doing. Just in case, I made certain I didn't say *anything* to Ms. Booker about the situation when I emailed her.

I was filing the e-receipts from the latest book order Ms. Booker had made in the shop's email account when I heard a familiar tap in the hallway outside.

The clattering noise of Aristide's walking cane that he used to make sure his path was clear tugged on my ears.

He must have gotten a new podcast and is heading to his room to listen.

The mystery solved, I clicked away on my laptop, logging out of the software.

What should I do next? Maybe email Mom and Dad?

My door swung open so hard it hit the plaster wall, and I jumped in my chair, almost flinging my laptop in surprise.

Aristide tilted his head. "Good," he said. "You're in here."

"W-what?" I asked.

"Don't be surprised—your explosive heartbeat gave you away." Aristide tapped his cane on the ground. "Come on, get hopping."

"Hopping to what?" I stood up and carefully zipped my laptop back up in its bag—since I wasn't working these days I wasn't going to risk breaking any of my stuff. "Charon and I already practiced this morning."

"It's time to earn your keep," Aristide said.

"Earn my keep?" I bewilderedly echoed. "What do you mean by that?"

"I don't hear you walking this way. Why are you not walking this way?" Aristide demanded.

"Sorry. Coming." I hurried across my bedroom, meeting Aristide at the door. "Can you at least tell me where we are going?"

"Downstairs. Come along, now. Keep up!" Aristide called to me as he sailed down the hallway, tapping his walking stick on the ground in a manner so casual it was graceful. "I do not hear the tip tap of little shadow feet!"

I closed my bedroom door, then trotted after him. "Coming."

Just as Aristide reached the staircase, Ker popped up the last few steps, brightening when she saw us.

"Aristide, Chloe, what a perfect coincidence!" Ker said.

Aristide blew past her, starting down the staircase. "It's not a coincidence at all—we had the same idea is all." He held the stair rail on his way down, his pace steady until his hand passed over the fancy banister ending and he reached the last step.

I hurried after him. "Hi, Ker," I said as I passed her.

"Hello!" Ker kept pace with me, an easy smile on her lips.

"Do you know what we're doing?" I asked.

"Yes," Ker said with great satisfaction.

We reached the bottom of the stairs, and before I could ask her anything else, Charon strode down the hallway, heading our way.

"Excellent," he said when he saw us.

"Yes." Aristide started down the hallway, heading in the direction of the front door. “It appears we all had a similar conclusion. Go us, we’re so smart. Chloe?”

“I’m here!” I eased past Charon—who bowed his head to me; apparently I really had resecured a spot in his good graces—and followed after Aristide.

The vampire marched down the hallway, then stopped outside the door to Noctus’s personal study. He tilted his head—listening to something through the door.

“You should knock,” Ker said.

Aristide snorted. “I’ll knock when he stops being such a workaholic that we no longer need to do this.” He pushed the door open and strode inside. “Noctus, what are you doing?”

CHAPTER NINE

Chloe

I peeked inside, wondering what had required the parade.

Noctus was at his desk, a mound of paperwork spread out across the surface in a very unorganized fashion that made me twitch. His eyes flicked from Aristide to the three of us crowded in the hallway. "Apparently, I'm about to talk to you," he dryly said.

Aristide waggled a finger in Noctus's direction. "You're working too much. You need to take a break, and you never do."

When Ker politely cleared her throat, I skulked into the study, stopping at Aristide's side.

It's the first time I've been in here since everyone realized I'm not Ama. It feels...weird.

"I rest," Noctus said.

"I'll believe that when I see it." Aristide cackled, then elbowed me. "Get it? So I'll never believe him. Haha!"

"What are you working on?" Ker leaned against Noctus's desk

and folded her arms across her chest with a frown. "You've got all kinds of maps out."

"It's the Seelie and Unseelie turf wars, isn't it?" Aristide navigated his way to his favorite chair, which had excellent back support and a crosshatch texture. "I knew you'd fixate on those—you're too worried about your people to fully ignore them, particularly since Chloe has showed just how easy it is to get caught up in one."

"With the clocktower's completion, I am less concerned with the turf wars," Noctus said. "The clocktower gate will allow elves to directly enter the downtown area—where many of them work. Even fae of the likes of the Seelie and Unseelie have enough intelligent thoughts in their thick heads to know not to engage in combat downtown."

"That might be an overestimation of their abilities," Aristide grumbled.

"Wait, the clocktower? Did *you* build the clocktower?" I was so intrigued by the idea I stopped awkwardly twisting my fingers together.

I knew the new downtown clocktower had been constructed as a sort of donation for the city to promote tourism and further beautify the area—hence its gorgeous clock face and the beautiful, clear tone it struck. But I would have never guessed that *Noctus* had given it to the city—everyone thought it was from a human!

"I had it built, yes." Noctus leaned back in his chair, pushing away from his desk—which made Ker smile.

I fidgeted for a moment in my curiosity.

I don't think he'll mind answering my question...unless, does it seem like I'm trying to sniff out information? But he knows me by now, he knows there's no one I'd share this with.

"Why?" I finally asked.

"My people cannot use my front door to troop in and out of the city—particularly with the Paragon hanging around like a vulture," Noctus dryly said. "So I've donated various buildings that have gates hidden within them. The clocktower is the newest of the gates, and it was built specifically to give my people easy access to the downtown area."

"That's why there are store spaces in the main floor," Ker added. "So it won't look suspicious for the elves going in and out all the time."

"Wow...and you can have the gates open without anyone picking up on the magic?" I asked.

Noctus stood up, slowly unfolding his long frame from the cramped space of his desk. "Once you cast the initial magic to open it, yes. It doesn't burn magic to maintain the gate, just to open it. The most dangerous part is all the spells cast to hide the gate from those who aren't elves, but it's easy enough to hide by using a human front to hire a few fae to cast some basic safety spells on the tower itself to explain the presence of magic."

"Oh, that's smart." I blinked, trying to digest just how deeply Noctus had infiltrated Magiford.

But all of it really does seem to be for the sake of his people. Ker and Aristide are right, he is a very diligent king.

"If you're not worried about the turf wars, can you explain what is causing this?" Ker leaned across the desk to point at the slight wrinkle between his eyebrows. "He's got his 'thinking line,' Aristide," she added for the vampire's benefit.

"I guessed as much." Aristide settled into his chair. "I swear the air thickens when he's thinking too hard."

Noctus swatted Ker's hand away. "You both worry too much."

"You think we're the only ones worrying?" Aristide snorted. "Charon is going to positively fade away fretting for you. Tell him, Charon."

Noctus and I turned to face Charon—who had his perfect posture and blank face on.

"I am going to positively fade away fretting for you," Charon robotically said.

Aristide groaned. “Charon, you need to practice your delivery more. That wasn’t convincing at all.”

“I apologize for my shortcomings.” Charon checked his watch, then fixed his gaze on *me*.

I instinctively shuffled my feet under his expectant gaze.

What does he want me to do? Everyone dragged me here without explaining anything, and apparently I don’t share the same line of thinking as he, Ker, and Aristide do.

I hunched my shoulders and tried to look apologetic, hoping he’d understand that *I* didn’t understand.

“Anyway.” Ker turned back to the desk and motioned at the mass paper mayhem. “I repeat: what *is* this?”

Noctus slowly circled around the side of his desk. “I’m going over the reports again about the artifacts that were built to break and cause damage.”

For once, Ker, Aristide, and even Charon looked as confused as I felt.

“Why?” Aristide asked. “We found their manufacturing and distribution point and shut it down. Case closed.”

“We found the location,” Noctus said. “But not the leaders who started the operation.”

“You think they’re going to do it again?” I guessed.

“Yes. If the leaders established the location to cause general mayhem among supernaturals and sow distrust with humans, I don’t imagine they’ll just give up and move along because we stopped them once.”

“We don’t even know if the ringleaders are still in Magiford,” Ker pointed out. “It’s most likely they set up the shop and then left—to avoid getting caught.”

“Except Magiford is the magic capital of the Midwest.” Aristide tapped his pointer finger on his walking stick. “If they want to spread distrust, where else would do the most damage but the poster child of the supernatural community?”

“Anywhere with large cities,” Ker said. “Milwaukee, Chicago—

there are plenty of ways to do damage there *without* the threat of the Curia Cloisters' new task force hunting them down or the looming threat of faedom, considering Magiford is the new fae empress's backyard."

"There is a great deal of political clout in Magiford that would make it unwise for any nefarious supernaturals to tarry," Charon agreed. "Unless there was a reason it *had* to be Magiford?"

Ker pursed her lips, and Aristide silently ran his fingers across the fabric of his chair.

They know Noctus insists on staying in Magiford for a specific reason, which he won't share...

I peeked at Noctus, who'd been looking out the window that showed the Cape Cod house's front lawn. He abruptly turned, his eyes meeting my gaze.

There was an intensity to his look, and for one impulsive—and stupid—moment, a part of me wished that I hadn't revealed I was human.

Noctus had always been gentle with Ama. Was there any living supernatural he felt he could be as free with?

And I was the one who stole that from him...

Charon, just a little off to the side, checked his watch again.

I wonder what he's waiting for—

Before I could finish the thought, my stomach erupted in a growl that was so loud I swear I felt my belly twist. It lasted too long. Five seconds at least. And as everyone peered in my direction, my face turned bright red.

Charon, however, had a slight smile of satisfaction. "Shall I fetch some food for you, Chloe?"

"No, no it's fine." I tried to laugh, but it felt like my cheeks were branded with a blush.

"Thank you, Charon," Noctus said.

Charon made his way to the door, then stopped in the threshold to bow to his king. "Shall I bring some tea for you, Your Majesty?"

Noctus frowned, but Ker answered for him. "Yeah, that sounds good. Aristide could probably use a glass of blood, and I'm always starving. I'll come with you and help so you don't have to carry it all by yourself." The werewolf winked at me, then followed Charon through the doorway.

"Make sure to let the blood breathe after you pour it!" Aristide hollered after the pair. "And if you try sticking chocolate in it again, Kerberos, I will shave your head the next time you fall asleep in your wolf form!"

Ker's laughter drifted into the study. "It was a blood cocktail!"

"It was an atrocity!" The volume of Aristide's voice made the chandelier shake, and he made a few disgusted noises as Ker's laughter faded from my hearing range.

I nervously tugged on the hem of my t-shirt as Noctus watched me. "Sorry," I said. "I didn't mean to cause extra work for Charon. I can go with them."

Noctus gestured for me to sit down. "Once Charon has decided upon something, it is remarkably difficult to dissuade him."

When I sat down on the two-person settee, Noctus started to sit down next to me, then paused and arched an eyebrow that had me bracing. "Unless, that is, you wished to go to the kitchens so you could choose your own food? I am aware you have a fondness for roasted chicken."

"No more chicken! Please!" I blurted the words out with a deep desperation, then slapped my hands over my mouth.

Noctus chuckled—a low and raspy sound as he eased himself down, leaving as much space between us as possible. "Yes, I imagine you don't wish to see chicken for a long while considering how much you ate. No wonder you desperately gnawed at the strawberry when that child offered it to you."

I stifled the impulse to shiver. "I don't want chicken," I repeated.

"Now that we're on the subject, it's no small wonder you

turned up your nose to all the raw meat Noctus first tried to feed you." Aristide lounged in his chair, the picture of relaxed elegance as he recalled my early days as a cat. "Though, I must say—Chloe—it does make your cat hugs seem flirtatious now that we know the truth of Ama!"

I shrank in my seat and could feel the incoming blush, even before it hit my cheeks. "Um. Well, it's just that being carried..."

"Yes?" Aristide prompted.

I peered at Noctus, hoping he might save me.

Unfortunately he had both his eyebrows raised. "I find myself siding with Aristide for this issue—a rarity, I assure you."

"Oh. Well. Uhh, being carried or held is..." I smashed my eyes shut. "Really scary."

"Huh?" Aristide said.

"I'm so small as a cat, a regular human walk can feel like a roller coaster. Plus, if someone holding me decided to drop kick me, they could." I rushed to explain. "And I couldn't do anything to save myself if I was dropped—even if it was an accident."

"So you were scared?" The tone to Noctus's voice was enough to make me pop my eyes open. It wasn't disappointment—I was pretty sure Noctus spent his life expecting nothing from the world based on the way he lived his life—but something worse. Something like...regret.

"At first." I waved my hand in the air as if I could wipe Noctus's regret away. "It's just a base instinct for me. But you carried me around so often I knew you'd never drop me—just like how I trust my family when they carry me when I'm in my cat shape. But by the time I knew you were safe, it was just so automatic and, uh, you're really broad shouldered so it was nice to anchor myself so I could look around..."

I could feel the figurative hole I was actively digging, so I snapped my mouth shut as Noctus watched me, his lips slightly curving in his enjoyment of my embarrassed babble.

Aristide was not so easily dissuaded. "But you're a cat," Aristide said. "Cats always land on their feet. Even if someone dropped you, it's not like you'd fall uncontrollably."

"Except—like you said—I'm a cat," I reminded him. "I'm small, and as long as I'm being held I have to trust that person not to harm me, which is hard to accept considering I've spent most of my adult life running from other supernaturals. Plus, while most humans are nice to cats, there are scumbags out there who go out of their way to hurt them."

"A fair point," Aristide said.

I glanced from Noctus, who was staring at one of his bookshelves, to Aristide, who had his head tilted—probably listening for Ker and Charon.

At least I made it through that with some dignity left, I thought far too soon.

"You said you trust me as you trust your family, then?" Noctus asked.

Why, why do I have to babble when I get nervous? I would have pulled on my hair in my exasperation, except I was pretty sure Noctus would find that even more amusing.

"Um," I said. "You were a very diligent pet owner, you know. You gave me a water bowl that costs more than my apartment rent for a year. So. You'd never hurt me. Obviously."

When I peeked at him, Noctus looked more puzzled than anything with his wrinkled forehead. "You trust me," he repeated. "That much."

I only managed to make confused waffled noises that had Aristide cracking up.

"You know she must have trusted you a fair bit, Noctus, since she revealed herself to keep you from blowing up the neighborhood if Charon's observation of that night's security camera footage is anything to go by," Aristide cackled. "I'd call that *stupid* trust. If you were that angry I'd have turned tail and run instead of try to stop you, and I'm your old friend!"

If Aristide meant to embarrass Noctus for his lack of control it didn't work. Noctus's expression shifted from confused to thoughtful.

He watched me, his eyes narrowing as I shifted a little. "You're right, Aristide." Noctus finally turned away from me. "That is very trusting."

Before he could say anything else, Charon and Ker were back, bearing trays of food and tea.

"Did we miss anything fun?" Ker asked. She passed off a goblet to Aristide before she dug into the biggest steak sandwich I'd ever seen in my life while Charon unpacked his tray on the low coffee table in front of our couch.

"Oh, quite a bit," Aristide said. "But if I repeat it, it will just embarrass poor Chloe all over again. Let's just say Noctus has reason to feel smug."

"That was worse than just explaining it!" I yelped. "All he meant is that I give cat hugs because being held is scary!"

"She's glossing over it—it is so much deeper than that." Aristide raised his goblet in the air in a mock toast. "Bottoms up!" He took a sip, then gagged. "*What* did you put in it this time, you terrible wolf?"

Despite Noctus's disinterest, Charon had brought him tea, and some cheeses and mixed fruits as well as some cookies to go with the tea.

"Nothing," Ker innocently said.

Charon put a plate together, which I fully expected him to present to his king. I was surprised when instead he held it out to me.

"Thank you." I awkwardly took it and nibbled on a piece of mango.

"It doesn't *taste* like nothing—it tastes awful!" Aristide complained.

"Well, I did add some extra salt," Ker said.

"*Why would you do that?*"

The next plate Charon made he handed off to Noctus who—

engaged with watching his friends—took it without seemingly noticing.

Charon smiled—but it was so brief and so fast I thought my eyes were playing tricks, until he turned to Ker and nodded slightly.

Ker smiled at him, then tapped the top of Aristide's hand twice before she casually stood, moving so she blocked Noctus's view of his desk.

What are they doing?

"I was trying to do something nice for you, and you said you didn't like it when I added chocolate," Ker said, continuing her conversation with Aristide. "So I attempted to salt the rim. It didn't really work, though, since I didn't think of it until after I'd already poured the glass. I had to try sprinkling it on."

"You could have gotten a new goblet!"

"And make the kitchen staff deal with an extra dish just for you? Nah."

I frowned as I chewed my mango, still puzzled about whatever operation they were running, then nearly jumped out of my skin when Charon put a donut on my plate—which was a bribe if I'd ever seen one.

It had caramel frosting too—which I happened to love as I was sure one of the mysterious chefs knew by now.

But why on earth would Charon bother to give me a donut? He's not the type to butter people up, and I haven't done anything to make him happy...have I?

I was about to take a big bite out of my donut when, next to me, Noctus shifted on his half of the settee and casually dropped his arm over the top of it, laughing at Aristide's angry honks as he sipped his tea, his work momentarily forgotten.

Oh...I'm his distraction.

Aristide, Ker, and Charon had all come to find me in their effort to get Noctus to take a break. Charon *must* have known I was bound to get hungry soon, and Noctus was not the type to send me off to the kitchen alone. (Some pet-owner behaviors die hard.)

But why would I be necessary to get him to take a break? Except...they all came and found me when I was Ama at all hours of the day and insisted on carrying me off to Noctus, too.

I'd assumed they were trying to forcibly get me to love him more, but now that I thought of it, they frequently came and got me when Noctus was deeply immersed in his work and hadn't surfaced in a while.

Does Noctus know? He must.

"Is something wrong?" Noctus asked.

I stared up at his sculpted face and realized no, he did not. So, I smiled. "Everything is great."

Noctus has done a lot to protect his friends, but they love him right back. They're willing to bend over backwards to try to make him a little bit happier—or maybe healthier is a better way to phrase it.

Noctus was still watching me, so I took a massive bite out of my donut to help me keep my mouth shut and accidentally smeared frosting on my chin.

Noctus briefly raised his fingers toward my chin, then apparently thought better of it and handed me a napkin.

"Thanks." I sheepishly wiped the frosting off.

When I glanced up Ker was fondly watching us. She winked at me, then turned her attention to Charon. "How is Chloe progressing on her training, Charon? Will we make a warrior out of her?"

"Are we just going to ignore my suffering, then?" Aristide asked.

Charon shrewdly studied me. "We might if she can muster *any* kind of fighting spirit. She's got excellent aim from her cat reflexes, but the killing instincts of a baby rabbit."

Despite his complaints, Aristide had nearly finished off his glass of blood. "Still can't get the dagger to pierce the target, hmm?"

"No," I said.

"We'll have to change methods," Noctus said.

"That sounds ominous," I said.

Noctus shook his head. "We'll just find something that suits you better. Which reminds me, Ker, I would prefer it if next time you decide to take a nose dive off the rocks in the field, you would *warn* me. I had to fill in a crater this morning."

"Sorry!"

After Ker, Aristide, and Charon used me to break Noctus out of his work drive, I spent less time in my room and more time downstairs at the insistence of the trio. Which was nice—I was starting to get a little stir crazy, despite my room's many luxuries.

Several days later, I finally dragged myself up the last few stairs of the endless spiral staircase that led down to the training grounds.

Charon had put me through an arm-numbing exercise routine to strengthen my muscles, then abruptly ended it when he received a sudden summons upstairs.

Tired as I was, going up all those stairs took a good ten minutes, and once I reached the top I staggered into the hallway, intending to find a furniture piece I could drape myself across and just *breathe*.

Before I found one that I wasn't afraid I would potentially break, Ker slunk down the hallway. "Chloe?"

"Yep. I'm up. Need something?" I tried to nonchalantly wipe sweat off my forehead and pretend I wasn't having a problem breathing after all those steps.

"The Paragon is here," Ker said. "And he's in a mood. You'll need to keep to the upper floor, or change into your cat form."

"Okay." I hesitated, wondering if I should ask why the

Paragon was angry. In the end, it was the worried wrinkles that creased Ker's forehead that did me in. "Is there a problem?"

Ker shook her head. "The Paragon's just mad."

"The Paragon? Mad?" I repeated. The Paragon had the personality of a jolly elderly wizard despite being the fae representative for the USA, and was much more honest than his people. *Of course, he's a fae so that could just be a front, but he's been so perky whenever he visits.*

"Do you want to see? Or rather, hear it?" Ker asked.

For a moment, I hemmed and hawed in indecision.

This was the kind of thing that was none of my business and I should stay out of. It was another way that Noctus and his friends were just so far out of my league politically and magically speaking, there was nothing I'd be able to do to help.

Ker must have sensed my refusal, because she draped her arm across my shoulders—ignoring my sweat—and swept me along. "Come on. It'll be fun."

"I thought you said it was something I should avoid?"

"You should, but that doesn't mean it won't be fun."

With those forbidding words, Ker guided me to the gorgeous room Noctus always received the Paragon in.

Aristide and Charon stood on either side of the door, each settled a few feet away—which seemed odd considering it was just the tiniest bit cracked open. It wasn't enough to see anything, but it let more sound out.

Wouldn't they want to stand closer so they could close the door if the Paragon noticed?

"*Why won't you tell me where she is?*" The shout was so loud and livid, I initially didn't recognize it as the Paragon's voice.

I blinked in surprise, and Ker nodded in agreement at my shock.

"Lower level fae are getting snatched off the streets because of the war between the Unseelie and Seelie Courts, Noctus." His voice grew louder and then quieter in unsteady swings, and I heard heavy footsteps go back and forth across the room—the Paragon was pacing.

"If there is trouble in the fae Courts—particularly the small ones like the Seelie and Unseelie Courts—then *you* should act," Noctus said.

"I can't! I'm just the fae representative—"

"Who possesses enough magic to drop my house on top of me," Noctus said. "You're not helpless, and no one is going to judge you for schooling that unruly king and queen."

"This isn't about the politics, it's that the lower fae Courts are so desperate in their fear of magic dying that they're doing terrible things!" The Paragon's voice roamed closer and then farther away from the door, his tone scoffing.

"The death of magic does not excuse poor behavior," Noctus said, his voice icy. "School them—or get your precious fae empress to handle it. She's half human, she'd do something if you told her about the wars that have torn up human neighborhoods."

"She's still visiting other parts of the USA to solidify her rule. I cannot summon her back when she's already in a precarious situation with the other Courts."

"How convenient," Noctus said.

"All of this is just the symptom, Noctus. We need to restore magic, and we need the lost elven princess to do that!"

My eyes bulged, and I gawked at Ker, Aristide, and Charon.

Based on Ker's dropped jaw, Charon's fast blinks, and Aristide planting his hand over his mouth, I was pretty sure they didn't know the Paragon was after an elven princess, either.

But the Mors elves are all dead besides Noctus, and I don't know if he even had a sister. Is the Paragon referring to another elven royal family?

"You don't *need* anyone." Noctus's voice was low, even, and furious. "You just don't want to extend yourself and handle fading magic—a problem supernaturals made themselves. You want a convenient stooge to imprison and fix the issue so everyone can bullheadedly continue doing what they want!"

Woah, he's really angry. He let the Paragon slap those magic-sucking shackles on him, and yet this is what gets him mad?

I guess it wasn't too shocking. Noctus was obsessed with being a good leader—passing the blame would definitely irk him.

"Look here, you impudent pup!"

"*Impudent pup*?" Noctus's voice lowered an octave, and I swear the crack of light that spilled out from the barely opened door dimmed. "Tell me, Paragon, have you forgotten? I've seen nations rise and fall. I slaughtered my own family when your foolish form of government didn't even exist."

Okay, this is bad.

Ker wildly flapped her hands at Charon, who watched the door. The usually blank faced elf actually furrowed his eyebrows. But when Ker gestured at the doorknob, Charon shook his head.

"I have let you rant and rail at me because at your heart you care for supernatural society. But it seems you need a reminder of just who you're dealing with," Noctus continued.

Ker's right—they need to do something. Maybe they should send in Aristide—he's good at diffusing tension.

Ker made a move toward the door, but Aristide stuck his cane out and Charon grabbed Ker by the shoulder and tugged her back. It seemed like Aristide and Charon—for whatever reason—weren't going to risk it.

When I felt the knife sharp sensation of elf magic in my ribs despite Noctus's cuffs, I knew I had to act.

I was possibly the worst choice to send in, and I was scared to death of facing an enraged Paragon *and* elf king. But...

Noctus had worked too hard, and the Paragon was too good a leader to let them come to blows over a...princess?

Whatever! I don't care—I just need to stop them!

CHAPTER TEN

Chloe

I shifted, going from human to cat in an eye blink. I ducked around Aristide's walking stick, nosed the door open, and was inside before the trio could stop me.

I got two feet in before I felt Noctus's magic wash over me, and I froze.

Noctus was standing, his head raised high as he studied the Paragon through narrowed eyes.

The Paragon bullishly planted his feet and squared his shoulders. For a moment, I saw the glamour everyone saw: an older man with silky white hair and drooping mustache, with stick skinny limbs and a hawkish nose.

And then the magic of the Paragon's glamour swamped my senses, making me sneeze and my eyes water. My own magic unwound like a cat getting up from a nap and set about dismantling the glamour before my eyes.

No, no, no. Stop that—I might be willing to wade into their argument, but I'm not crazy enough to want to see what the Paragon is hiding! I have too many secrets that I'm guarding on behalf of other people the way it is!

I tamped down on my magic, and then snorted/sneezed at the same time, still affected by the magic.

Problem solve with me—what's the situation?

It was easier to push the overwhelming sensation of the Paragon's glamour out of my mind when I peered up at Noctus and tried to read his expression.

He was irritated—as seen by the wrinkles across his brow and the hard swirl of his eyes—but at least he wasn't furious like he'd been the night the Unseelie fae had tried to snatch me. Which was a small consolation prize.

With that thought to bolster me, I did my best to casually trot into the room, even though the feeling of magic was thick enough to pull my whiskers.

I hopped onto the priceless coffee table between the two, wrapped my tail—which was puffed from the stress of the situation—around my paws, then meowed.

Noctus and the Paragon looked down at me.

Even though every hair on my body wanted to stand on end, I made myself purr—or I tried to, it was a little sputtery for a true purr—then licked one of my front paws and scrubbed at my face.

The tension in the room evaporated, and the swirl of magic faded.

"Greetings, beautiful Ama." The Paragon bowed deeply to me. "You are right, I was a poor guest in that I did not greet you, and I dared to raise my voice in such a manner. My deepest apologies."

Since the air no longer crackled, I was able to purr evenly as the Paragon gently patted the top of my head.

I then swiveled to face Noctus, who was staring at me. His brows were still slightly furrowed in the "thinking line" Ker had pointed out in his study.

I meowed at him, but he just kept on staring at me.

Noctus—you gotta work with me! If you don't exhibit even a smidgeon of your usual overly enthusiastic pet owner behavior, this is going to look sketchy!

I knew the collar didn't let him hear my thoughts—thank goodness—but I was hoping it somehow conveyed the emotion of it, because my anxiety was going to spike again if he didn't do anything.

Something must have gotten through, because Noctus scooped me up and propped me against his chest so I could latch my claws into his clothes for my cat hug.

I did that—planting my paws on either side of his neck—and was so pleased with myself that an actual purr leaked out of me before I could stop it.

The amused puff of Noctus's breath on my neck said he'd heard—or felt—the purr. He scratched under my chin and supported my back as he sat down on the couch across from the Paragon.

He didn't sit straight against the back of the couch, but was tilted and almost settled sideways.

When I realized this position let me look at the Paragon without craning my neck, I meowed my approval.

"My poor manners continue, for I didn't think to bring you a toy this time," the Paragon continued. He smiled through his drooping mustache, but there was something about the wrinkles at the corner of his eye. He just seemed...tired.

"What is this about, Paragon?" Noctus asked. "I expect you to plague me for years with your dogged determination, but you aren't prone to outbursts."

The Paragon sighed, and it was like the balloon of air that was keeping him upright emptied, because he flopped back into his chair and stared at the ceiling.

"You remember some time ago I asked you to verify the use of an elven spell?" he asked.

"Yes—it had been used against the Night Queen, your new fae

empress." Noctus adjusted his arms when I moved my back legs, giving me more space to stretch out.

The Paragon tried to massage his eyes, and instead jabbed thumbs on the rims of his spectacles.

Someone doesn't really have to wear glasses, I take it. My magic stirred again, and I felt it tug at my vision. *Stop it! No, I didn't change my mind, I don't want to see the real him!*

The Paragon took his spectacles off with a scowl and flung them onto the coffee table. "There's been proof that whoever used the spell is part of some sort of shadowy group. They've been behind the worst of the trouble that has hit Magiford recently—several attacks on the Night Queen, they supported a wizard House coup that nearly tore the wizarding community apart, and so on."

Noctus listened to the Paragon, but I could feel my fur puff in fear.

Wait, there's a group that's purposely *doing all of this?! How—why?* My brain couldn't even process the idea. Although supernaturals weren't particularly great at working together, there at least had always been a basic understanding that attacking one another would only bring about the death of magic even faster.

I tucked myself even closer to Noctus, trying to mask my puffing fur, and make it look like I wasn't listening.

Noctus hitched me higher up his chest, so I could rest my furry head against his neck.

"I cannot discern the group's motive, except to say they appear to enjoy wanton destruction," the Paragon continued, "and that the group is made up of diverse members—vampires, werewolves, fae—but I have never managed to pin down any of the leaders, who seem to have a suspiciously deep arsenal of elf magic."

"You think they're elves?" Noctus guessed.

"It's possible," the Paragon grimly said. "I'm aware several family heirs escaped, but I haven't been able to track anyone down besides you, your butler, and the offshoot of the Vitas royal family."

Wait, Noctus isn't the only royal elven survivor?

Noctus didn't seemed surprised by the declaration, and I didn't sense any shock radiating through the door, so the others must have known as well.

"I'm terrified the shadowy group will realize the princess exists," the Paragon continued.

"*If* she exists," Noctus corrected.

The Paragon rubbed his large nose. "She does, and I know you know where she is!" He smoothed his fingers over his mustache, then frowned. "Once they realize she exists, it will be a race to see who finds her first."

"Why would they want her?" Noctus asked.

The Paragon picked up his glasses and studied them. "I'm not certain. But I'm half afraid that—given their inclination to cause harm—they'll eliminate her."

"Ah," Noctus said. "That would ruin all your plans for hope, wouldn't it?"

The Paragon scowled. "I know you believe I'd use her, but, Noctus—surely you must see how hopeless things are?"

"No." Noctus peeled me off his chest and gave me his full attention, making a show of scratching me under my chin before tickling my cheeks. "I'd say Magiford is doing better now than it was the day the Curia Cloisters were built. The vampires are held in check by the Eminence, who is finally taking an interest in other types of supernaturals thanks to his wizard wife. The fae have a decent leader who punishes them for their propensity toward murder, and it looks like even the werewolves are going to be forced to heel by the Pre-Dominant's protégé and his mate."

"You're right," the Paragon agreed. "But that is only true in—as you said—Magiford, and the Midwest. The other regions aren't faring half as well."

"Your precious Night Queen has only recently been recognized as the fae empress. Give her time, and the fae will fall in line, which will model things for the rest," Noctus said.

"Even as magic continues to die?" the Paragon sourly asked.

"Is it, though?" Noctus calmly asked.

"I now get why people tell me how annoying I get when I'm being cagey," the Paragon grumbled. He sighed again—but this one didn't sound soul deep or weary. "So. Are you going to call for snacks?"

"I was not inclined to during your temper tantrum," Noctus said.

"Yes, but that's over, and I'm hungry now," the Paragon said. "I planned on eating lunch with my bestie, but he kicked me out of his house before I got to eat."

"Then leave so you can eat in your own home."

"No, I'd like to play with Ama—oh! I've got it!" The Paragon sprang to his feet so fast his robes twisted around him and he knocked his chair back a few inches. "I'll be right back—just give me a few minutes!"

He tottered from the room—Ker and Aristide must have heard, because I only heard Charon's calm murmurs when the Paragon banged his way into the hallway.

Immediately, I could breathe easier without the weight of his glamour that my magic itched to strip.

Noctus glanced down at me. "Thank you."

I meowed. *You're welcome. Please don't do that again—I don't think my heart could handle it.*

Even now that it was over, I was surprised that I'd jumped in during the heat of the moment, but I didn't regret it. It would have been bad if Noctus and the Paragon fought.

Now that the situation was over, my heart had finally settled back into its correct place. I started to wriggle, planning to jump down and escape before the Paragon got back, but Noctus stood up, still cradling me in his arms.

He tilted his head as he walked across the room. "You must have seen through his glamour?"

Nope! We are not going to discuss that! I growled in the back of my throat, then sneezed just thinking about the power of the Paragon's spell.

Noctus raised an eyebrow as he stared down at me. "You seriously refused to see through it?"

I nodded.

Noctus held eye contact with me long enough to make me hunker down on his arms. "I can't decide whether you shame your lineage with your unique usage of your powers, or whether you have exceeded them all."

Thinking of all the times Pat, Joy, and I had submitted posed photos of my cat form to pet photo contests for the sake of winning prizes, I guiltily gulped. *Shame. It's definitely shame.*

Noctus paused in front of a painting—this one was a beautiful mountain landscape with a blue lake and birds in the sky.

We stood in front of it for a moment, and I relaxed enough that I yawned.

"I'll make sure you won't have to interfere between the Paragon and me again," Noctus abruptly said.

His expression was stony as he studied the painting, the thinking line between his eyebrows deepening.

He's condemning himself for not being the perfect king he's convinced he must be, isn't he? Ugh. Books describe how terrifying elves were, but they never mentioned how they're so self-critical it's exhausting. Though that's probably a Noctus-only trait.

Feeling bold—whether it was because I was back in Ama's form, or because Noctus had chosen to carry me around instead of setting me down—I raised one black furry paw, and softly tapped Noctus on the lips a couple of times, keeping my claws in so he just felt the fluff of my fur and my soft paw pads.

Noctus raised an eyebrow. "You disagree with me?"

I tapped his lips twice more, then slumped against him and rested my chin on his shoulder.

Noctus chuckled and kept studying the painting, which was why I was facing the door for the Paragon's grand re-entrance.

The Paragon—wearing a pair of aviator shades and sipping the paper straw of an iced coffee drink—kicked the door in. "I brought a friend!" He hefted a baby car seat up to his skinny shoulders, then marched into the room, rattling the ice in his drink.

He set his drink down on the coffee table—Charon was possibly going to deck him because he didn't use coasters—then bent over the car seat and picked something bald and pink out of the contraption.

"Behold!" The Paragon held the egg-like shape over his head for a moment, and a head with two large triangular ears popped out, revealing the object was an overweight, hairless sphinx cat.

The sheer sight was enough that my magic even reacted when the obnoxious magic brushed at my senses.

Woah, I'm impressed he can haul that cat around with those skinny arms. She's huge!

"*Mmert*," the cat purred/meowed.

"You left so you could bring your cat here?" Noctus asked.

"And snacks!" The Paragon clutched his cat to his chest in one arm, then plucked a white pastry bag from the car seat and shook it. "Since you're a bad host and refuse to offer me food—though you do get points for noting Aphrodite and not calling her any names. Well done—I knew you were a fellow feline appreciator."

The rapidly multiplying wrinkles on Noctus's forehead told me he wasn't sure how he felt about being a "fellow feline appreciator."

"But where are my manners? Ama, please let me introduce you to the most beautiful and magnificent of cat specimens, Aphrodite." The Paragon—still supporting his cat with one arm—used his free hand to pick up one of her pink paws and wave it.

"*Mmert,*" the cat—Aphrodite—said.

This cat has all the patience in the world, I realized as I stared at her. *Like...ALL of it.*

"Aphrodite, this is the very royal and kinder-than-Noctus-deserves Ama," the Paragon continued, treating the conversation with the severity of a loon. "She plays very nicely, so you can finally have a friend!"

The Paragon put her down on the ground.

I looked up at Noctus, and Noctus looked down at me, both of us confused.

I don't know what I'm supposed to do.

Noctus peered down at Aphrodite, who had extended herself enough to pad two steps toward the coffee table so she could lean against it. "Is Aphrodite friendly with other cats?"

"They are below her, naturally, given her great beauty and wisdom. But she deigns to play with them." The Paragon beamed. "I'm sure Ama shall be her near equal in play—so this is an exciting occasion for her!"

I guess you should put me down. I don't think he's going to leave until I meet his cat.

Noctus must have come to a similar conclusion, because he stared at the Paragon—who had plunked back down in his chair and was noisily sipping his coffee drink—then crouched down and reluctantly set me on the ground.

The second my paw pads touched the flooring, I realized a massive problem with this plan.

Regular cats might love me, but I was betting a hairless cat owned by the Paragon couldn't possibly be a regular cat. In fact, it was quickly occurring to me that she might be able to tell I was *not* a cat.

Noctus, I changed my mind. Please pick me up, I have regrets.

I stood on Noctus's boots, facing out so I could watch Aphrodite's slow approach.

The copious wrinkles on her face weren't enough to wash out her big eyes, which were wide with curiosity.

She delicately touched noses with me, then instantly started purring.

I peered up at Noctus—who had an eyebrow cocked in amusement—as Aphrodite attempted to climb onto his boots, too, still purring as she rubbed her head into my cheek.

Okay, I guess I was worried about nothing?

The Paragon set his coffee down. "Fantastic—I knew they'd be great friends! Look, Aphrodite even likes *you*—that's something I didn't expect! Want an egg, bacon, and cheese bagel? I recently swapped my coffee patronage to the Queen's Court to see if it's up to all the hype it's been getting, and it has made me a convert!"

"No, thank you," Noctus said.

The Paragon shrugged. "Suit yourself. So, what do you do around here for fun? You seem crusty, I bet it's boring."

"Were you always this querulous, or is it a fae thing to lose wisdom as you age?"

The Paragon laughed. "I deserve that—though I won't apologize. It shocks me that a member of the Mors family is so even tempered."

Aphrodite succeeded in hefting herself onto Noctus's boots and almost body slammed me off.

I felt brave enough to climb off them, then jumped up onto the couch. Aphrodite followed, still purring.

I flicked my tail, then positioned myself next to a pillow, giving Aphrodite enough space to crawl in between me and the pillow.

She did exactly that, her purr still deep like a motorboat.

Settled in, I watched the King of the Mors elves and the Paragon exchange insults while the Paragon ate.

How did my life get to be this *weird?*

Cat of the day pic incoming! Pat, this one looks like you on rainy days.

I LAUGHED when I opened Joy's text and was treated to the picture of a long-haired cat that was soaked to the bone so its wet fur was plastered to its body and its eyes were bulging in displeasure.

I leaned against the staircase's banister as I tapped out a reply.

He has your eyes, Pat.

Joy's string of laughing emojis was about five deep before Pat finally deigned to respond.

Ur both twerps.

I adjusted my balance, which made my running shoes squeak on the polished floor. I guiltily looked up, but Charon was most likely to care, and he'd left suddenly with Noctus on an errand within the city—that was why I was standing here in my training clothes with my belt of daggers.

He was supposed to take me downstairs for a training session before the interruption. I wasn't sure if I was thankful for the break, or disappointed.

I was slowly getting better with the knives, and even with the short sword he'd started drilling me in more recently. Even better, the running drills and strength training Charon was putting me through were really starting to pay off.

The next time I was getting chased, I'd have an easier time of scaling a wall to get away!

My phone chimed.

Chloe, how's Book Nookery?

I grimaced at Pat's text and carefully worded my reply.

It's great—lots of books coming in.

It was the truth—I could tell from all the receipts I'd processed over the last few days.

My phone chirped when Pat responded to my text.

I'll come visit you soon.

"No, no, no, no, no," I muttered under my breath. This called for the emergency response.

That would be fun, but maybe I should come visit you! It's been forever since Joy and I have crashed at your apartment.

I waited, holding my breath, to see if my siblings would take the bait.

That's because he lives like a pig in a pigpen. If you're visiting someone, it should be me.

I relaxed as Joy picked up right where I wanted her to.

If my place is a pigpen, your apartment has the personality of burnt toast, Pat texted. *You don't even have any of Chloe's kitten pictures hanging up!*

I heaved a sigh of relief—I was out of the danger zone, but it did raise a point. Sooner or later my overprotective siblings would insist on visiting me.

I thought avoiding the topic of how long I'd be "staying" here was the safest thing to do, but so much time has passed I can't avoid it much longer. I have too many loose ends between my siblings, my apartment, and my job.

I wasn't looking forward to it because I suspected I wasn't

going to like Noctus's answer, but, hey. A difficult future was still a future! A month ago I would have thought for sure my life would be over if Noctus found out I was Ama.

I never did find out why he called me Amalourne when it was just the two of us...

I looked up from my phone when I heard confident strides—only one person in Noctus's villa walked like that.

Sure enough, Ker turned a corner and beamed when she saw me. "Chloe, just the person I was looking for!"

"If you intend to foist me onto Noctus to get him to take a break it's not going to work," I said. "He and Charon left and are in the city."

"Yeah, Charon texted me to see if I'd have a go at training you," Ker said.

"Okay." I reluctantly pointed myself at the splitting off hallway that led to the horrible, never-ending staircase.

"Except I had a different kind of exercise in mind," Ker said. "I thought we could venture outside the barriers Noctus has on the neighborhood and see if the tracker is out."

I gulped at the thought. "Is that really...wise?"

"I don't think we're actually going to find him, because I don't think he intends to confront you face to face anymore, but I'd like to confirm it."

"So should I leave my daggers here?"

"*No*! Never go out unarmed. Mind you, I don't think we're going to run into trouble. We'll stick to the human neighborhoods just outside ours, and I'll make sure we're within running distance. Plus, I'm armed!" Ker winked as she swung her side at me, flashing the holster that was well disguised as a purse. "Let's go!" She trotted off to the front door.

"Wait, you're going as a human?"

"Yeah, I can risk it when we're sticking this close to home. No supernaturals live in this area. I'm pretty sure that's why Noctus insisted on the place years ago," Ker said. "And it's not the end of the world if a stray fae sees me. It's mostly the vamps—who are long lived and way more likely to realize I've been around for a suspiciously long time—and the werewolves—who'd be able to tell I've got a different kind of magic on me—that I must avoid."

We reached the golden gate that acted as a passageway between Noctus's villa and the Cape Cod house. Ker opened it and stepped through. I gave her a moment to open the Cape Cod home's front door so I didn't slam into her, then followed her out.

Power crackled through my body. Darkness cradled me, making it impossible to tell up from down until I got through and stepped onto the front porch as Ker held the front door open for me.

"Thank you," I said.

"Yep!" Ker closed the door behind me, then hopped off the front porch.

"Going back to what you said inside." I glanced around, my experience-gifted paranoia riding me hard, but Shiloh and the uncles were the only neighbors outside, and Shiloh was mowing her lawn while the uncles shouted to one another over the putter of her hand lawn mower.

"Yeah?" Ker prompted as she strolled across the lawn to the driveway.

"So, you basically are just trying to keep supernaturals from having a record of your existence?" I paused long enough to wave to Shiloh—who smiled at me and waggled a foot in greeting since she couldn't let go of the mower—then hurried to catch up to Ker who'd reached the sidewalk and was setting off down the street.

"Yep." Ker's inner wolf showed as she marched up the sidewalk with a dogged determination only werewolves seemed to have. "Because it will lead straight back to Noctus, and once more people than the Paragon realize he's an elf, it's game over. If I get discovered, I'd have to split from him for a few years—probably a decade—and disappear again."

"Wouldn't Noctus help you get out of it?"

"Nope."

I felt my eyes bulge in shock as I gaped up at Ker. "But...you and Aristide are his only friends!"

"And he'd abandon us both in a flash if it meant people realized who and what he was," Ker said.

We'd reached the end of the cul-de-sac by that point. Ker picked a direction and trotted off. When she realized I was slower to follow—still trying to process what she'd just told me about Noctus—she continued. "Don't get me wrong—it's not that he doesn't care about us. He's loyal. But he's also a king, and he'd never risk his people like that. He could survive being discovered as an elf—he's too strong not to. But his people?" Ker shook her head. "They're not warriors. At least half of the original families he took in didn't even live under the Mors rule and are just scattered survivors."

"So what you're saying is...being a monarch is the worst," I said.

Ker laughed from deep in her belly. "Now you've got it!"

"And other werewolves...they'd be able to smell his magic on you?" I asked.

"Not quite," Ker said. "Elf magic is too subtle for it—no fae or wizard would even be able to tell I had the magic on me, it only hits their radar if it's actively pulling magic. But a werewolf could smell that I'm different since I'm so much older."

I thought I sensed something so I stopped, spun around, then peered down the street. A car rolled down the road, and two kids were playing in their driveway, jumping through a sprinkler even though it was *barely* summer and the water had to be icy cold judging by their shrieks.

But I didn't feel any magic, or see anyone who looked like a supernatural.

"Everything okay?" Ker asked.

"Yeah, I just thought I felt something." I rejoined her, keeping pace as we turned up a block. "But—if you don't mind me asking

—does Noctus's magic and the compound Aristide gives you…do they really change you that much?"

Ker tilted her head back and scented the air. She must not have smelled anything because she walked on—though at a slightly slower pace. "Not really," she said. "Noctus uses regenerative magic, so it just keeps me from aging, and I rarely get sick. The effects of Aristide drinking from me are similar, even if he does complain about the way I taste. The real problem is that I was born so long ago, *and* I've got elf magic in me, so while I'm fundamentally the same, there's enough differences you can scent it out. The big concern is that if someone realized what kept me this way, they could single out the scent of Noctus's magic—which, as I said, can't happen."

"But do people even *know* this kind of elf magic exists?" I asked.

"Not really—that's why I feel comfortable walking around like this," Ker said. "Elves didn't typically use their magic in a positive way on any supernaturals—they had too much of a superiority complex for that. Mind you, vampires have been hiding their ability to retain a blood donor's youth for centuries, but Noctus's regenerative magic requires him to siphon off some of his most powerful magic. There's a lot of danger associated with it—and only an elf as powerful as Noctus would be able to keep it going—but the biggest issue is since it's something so close to his true self, it would be a cinch for a werewolf to smell him out once they knew to search for it."

"You must have been really important to Noctus for him to cast that kind of magic on you," I said.

"Noctus doesn't have many friends. Those that he does, he cherishes." She gave me a side eye. "I know things are a little weird between you two, but I think you're one of the few on his list."

I shook my head. "After lying as long as I did? No way."

Ker laughed. "Hiding your identity is quite tame, believe me.

Aristide tried to kill Noctus a couple of times before they settled into friendship!"

"Aristide had centuries to befriend him," I said. "It's been just a few weeks for me." I couldn't say why, but there was something about the conversation that made me uncomfortable. Maybe it was the guilt? That I'd been so close to Noctus as Amalourne, and then I'd ruined that. I'd broken one of the few ways Noctus was able to relax.

Ahh yes, that's guilt inducing for sure.

I cleared my throat, and decided now was the perfect time to change topics. "You became friends with Noctus while working with your Pack as a forester, right?"

"No, actually. My Pack left Noctus's employ as foresters for his summer villa because we knew the elf war was coming. We fought in the war—against the elves. My entire Pack was wiped out in an attack."

"I'm sorry," I said. "That must have been...traumatic."

Ker's smile was sad, but she patted my back like she was soothing a wolf pup. "It was hard to lose my Pack, yes. It took a lot of work to come back from it. But Aristide and I have both healed from those long ago times."

There was something about her eyes. They were soft with warmth and wisdom as she continued. "Healing is the only way any being can live so long, or eventually the trauma will crush you. And I wasn't without Pack very long. Aristide found me after the attack—barely alive. He dragged me back to Noctus. By the time I recovered, Noctus...er...the war had shifted. Eventually, I regained my will to live, and I chose to stay. Noctus, Charon, and Aristide became my new Pack. We were on the run—Noctus had to hide, obviously—and that tends to build trust fast. About a year or two later, he and Aristide cooked up our 'ecosystem of friendship, magic, and blood' as I like to call it. If I'm remembering correctly, that was when the elves seeking sanctuary began finding us. Do you sense the tracker?"

It took me a moment to realize she was breaking from her story as we rounded the corner of the block and turned. We were following a rectangular path, so the cul-de-sac wasn't that far away. If we cut through two backyards we'd be within eye sight of it. "No—he's hard to miss. His presence inspires dread." I turned in a tight circle, but I didn't see any shadowy areas. "It's a good sign we haven't seen him, because that means he's not just sitting here waiting to jump me, right?"

"Maybe," Ker said. "But I doubt he's just given up, which means he's got some other sneaky plan, and I'd rather know what he's up to."

I grimaced. "Yeah, that's true—" I felt a spark of magic behind me—so fleeting and so fast I couldn't even identify the sensation. I whirled around and rubbed my elbow.

"Did you sense something?" Ker lifted her nose and sniffed.

"Yeah, but it was so fast I couldn't tell what it was."

Ker turned in a circle, her warm eyes hardening into something deadly. "I don't smell anything, but that doesn't mean there's no one out there."

I pressed my lips together as my belly did acrobatics in my gut. "I don't think the tracker is here, but..."

It felt insane to say someone else could be when Ker didn't smell anyone and I couldn't sense them, but my gut was telling me something was off.

No humans were out and about on this block—which was probably a good thing, though it was another possible indication that something was wrong. Humans might not be magical, but something in them knew better than to wander into potentially dangerous situations.

"If your instincts are telling you something, we should listen," Ker said. "Aristide told me shadows are sensitive."

I could feel the hairs on the back of my neck prickle. "Yeah, maybe we should head back."

"We'll cut through the backyards," Ker said. "We'll be fast—

the neighbors won't notice. We'll go...there." She pointed about two houses up, to a small two-story home that didn't have a fence, unlike its neighbors.

We could see into the backyard even from here. It only had a shady tree—no fence from the property behind it. It'd be perfect to run through.

"Okay." I started sprinting for it, Ker right with me. We turned off into the house's lawn—avoiding the landscaping beds of petunias and flowering mint. We weren't parallel with the house yet, when I felt silky fae magic on my elbow, and an explosion went off behind us. Something sharp pelted my back, slicing through my clothes and digging into my skin.

I gaped at the burning pain, and then the shockwave of the explosion threw us to the ground.

CHAPTER ELEVEN

Chloe

"W-what?" I gasped, trying to make sense as my ears rang.

"That was a fae spell," Ker growled. She bared her teeth as she climbed to her feet, and I could briefly see blood speckled her back—whatever had sliced into me had gotten her, too. She hauled me to my feet, then dragged me behind an overgrown lilac bush.

My back still felt like it was on fire from whatever shrapnel we'd been sprayed with, but my body was already prepping me for flight mode. The impulse to turn into a cat flooded me, but I checked my belt to make sure all my daggers were still securely strapped into place.

"There—that's the spell." Ker pointed to a spindly legged fae who clutched two glowing glass canning jars while he peered up and down the street. "It's an explosive spell packed with metal shrapnel—not deadly, but nasty and *dangerous*. I can't believe they set it off in a human neighborhood!"

The spindly legged fae scowled up and down the street, then nearly face planted when a beautiful woman—a siren, probably—smacked him upside the head.

"Be more *careful*!" the siren snarled.

"But the outsider said she was somewhere on this street." The much shorter fae brushed out his shirt, which had the flower insignia of King Harel of the Seelie fae sewn over his heart. "If we don't retrieve her, King Harel is going to make us approach *him* again!"

They're here looking for someone? That's weird, Ker said supernaturals don't live in this area. The "him" must be Noctus, though. There's no way the fae could be skulking this close to his house, referring to a "he" that isn't Noctus.

The siren swiped the jars from the apparently over-zealous fae. "Maybe so, but carelessly throwing spells around is a good way to get the humans' attentions—or give away our location to the Unseelie fae! We don't want them to know our plan."

A fae noble, a troll, and a leprechaun emerged from the shadows, bringing the party up to five. I didn't like those numbers.

Ker could take them without a problem, except she's in her human form, and it will take her half a minute to shift. If the fae recognize her...

Ker had said if one or two fae saw her it wasn't terrible, but I was willing to bet an entire scouting party out on a mission wasn't what she had in mind.

I peered around the bush, looking up and down the street. No one was incoming—I only felt fae magic. "We need to run," I said.

Ker was staring at the fae, her eyes hard. "This has something to do with Noctus."

"Maybe, but do you think we can risk hanging around to find out?" I asked.

Ker glanced at me. "Not in this form—and definitely not you. Aristide and Charon would skin me if I risked you. Come on—let's get back to the cul-de-sac. I can change there and come back."

I watched the leprechaun draw on the sidewalk with purple chalk, making the flower symbol of the Seelie Court. "Maybe we're wrong? They're tagging the sidewalk. Maybe they're just reclaiming this area for the Seelie Court."

"I'd love it if that were true," Ker said. "But experience has taught me that we never have that kind of luck."

"Same," I agreed with feeling despite the seriousness of the situation.

Ker flashed me a brief, thin smile. "Turn into a cat, would you?"

I instantly swapped shapes, and followed Ker, who crawled from shadow to shadow, heading toward the backyard of the house we were creeping along.

My fur was puffed up to the maximum, but Ker made sure she used the house's landscape so the fae didn't notice us.

Feeling encouraged, I flicked my tail as we ran past a bedroom window of the house, and then the dogs started barking.

A German Shepherd, a collie, and a beagle crowded the window, barking so much they fogged it up. The German Shepherd's fierce growls, the collie's warning barks, and the beagle's wailing howl were easy to hear through the walls of the house.

Ker—hidden behind a bush—growled at the dogs. I think she meant to startle them into silence, but apparently she'd misread them, because their volume hitched up, and they wagged their tails so hard the beagle almost fell off from where he'd planted his paws on the edge of the window.

I risked glancing back, and met the eyes of the siren.

"There's something over there—we should check it out," the siren said—her voice musical.

"Aw, they're just barking at that cat." The spindly fae kicked a pebble.

"But we're looking for a cat," the siren pointed out.

I'd started to move, but at her words I stopped again. *Wait, what?*

"A human who can turn *into* a cat," the spindly fae said. "Not the same thing."

No, no, no, no. The refusal became a chant in my brain. *This can't be happening. Why would the Seelie fae be looking for me?*

The siren stared at me for a moment, and my heart thudded in my chest as I waited for my magic to kick in. The longest moment of my life passed, and she shrugged, turning back to her companions.

"*You're* looking for the human," the fae noble declared. "I'm here for our territory, and I'll not tell King Harel we recovered this neighborhood, only for some Unseelie stooge to be waiting in the shadows to turn it back once we leave!"

Time to move!

I ran when they started in our direction, reaching the house's backyard.

Ker edged along the side of the house so the fae didn't see her, batting her hand at me to keep going. Unfortunately, the dogs ran from the bedroom to the back door and were still howling at Ker.

I paused at the property line that divided the dogs' house from their back neighbor's, twitching my tail.

Ker motioned for me to keep going, then raced across the patio—making the dogs go crazy.

Instead of running across the backyard with me, which had absolutely no cover, she kept to the side of the house.

She wants us to split up—she's going to go a different way...because if she's out in the open like I am, the fae will see her.

I crossed the property line into the other house's backyard, taking refuge behind the trunk of the shady tree—which was again the only shelter in the backyard.

Why don't these homeowners have messy children who leave bikes and toys out to hide behind?

I felt too open from my position at the tree, but it'd have to do.

The fae crossed the dog house's front yard, passing along the side as we had.

"What were we following again?" the spindly legged fae asked.

"Was it...a cat? I thought?" The siren sounded uncertain—that was my magic at work.

"The dogs were barking," the leprechaun said. "They're still barking—at that window." He pointed to the far side of the house, where Ker was crouched behind an air conditioning unit.

The dogs had moved from peering out the back door to what looked like the dining room, still barking at her.

My back arched with anxiety, and I watched the fae shuffle off in Ker's direction.

No, no. They can't see her—what if they tell King Harel? If we call up the Curia Cloisters to take care of them, they might complain about a lone werewolf, and that would probably launch an investigation...

This was why I didn't like playing with leagues above me. Everything was complicated. But I couldn't just run and leave Ker to deal with it.

They were almost on her, and she didn't have anything else she could hide behind—there were no more bushes or landscaping.

My heartbeat was so rapid in my furry chest it was hard to breathe.

Dang it.

I skittered out from behind my tree and meowed.

The siren glanced at me for only a second—my occasionally inconvenient magic—so I meowed again, then shape shifted.

This time the fae noble saw the change. He stopped and stared at me for several long moments—his cohorts stopping around him when they realized he was frozen.

Ker also saw, and looked murderous—unhappy with my snap decision.

Then at least take advantage of it—I can only buy you so much time! I waved at the fae as I scuttled farther away.

If I give myself enough of a head start, they won't be able to reach me before I get to the Cape Cod house. I have my daggers, but there's no way I could use them against so many targets. Running is my best option.

"Is that...she was the cat, wasn't she?" the fae noble said.

"The one we're supposed to get?" the leprechaun asked.

Ker bared her teeth at me, then slipped around the side of the house, heading to the front.

"Nope, definitely not," I said. "Goodbye!"

I sidestepped my way along the new house. I cut across the front yard, to the road it was built on. The turn off for our cul-de-sac was just a block up. My back burned from the shards of whatever was in the canning jar, but I had the determination of a cockroach scuttling to safety and was able to ignore it.

"That's the cat girl we need to capture?" That was the troll—his voice deep and rumbling. "So we can use her to bait *him*?"

Oh, yeah, whatever their little scheme is, I'm not a fan. I scurried faster—I was almost to the front yard now.

I heard the tap of something touching glass. "We can't take the risk if it is her. King Harel will be upset." The fae noble grunted in effort.

What is he—

Glass shattered behind me.

Another explosion rippled—this one close enough that I could feel the heat it produced. The magic harmlessly washed over me, but the spell had been in one of the glass jars packed with metal bits. The shards of shrapnel shredded my back, producing a wave of hot, wet pain. The fae noble had chucked the jar close to my heels, so the metal even hit the backs of my thighs and my skull, slicing through my clothes and burrowing into my skin.

I gasped in pain before the shockwave of noise the spell produced threw me to the ground. My ears rang, and for a moment my vision swirled.

Holy buckets—that hurt way worse. If they do that again, I need to dodge!

"*We got her!*" one of the fae shouted—their voice oddly muffled by the ringing noise in my ears.

The furry sensation of werewolf power brushed at me, and my dazed senses barely noticed it. Ker was probably shifting, but werewolves took half a minute to shift. Would she get to me in time?

The fae noble strolled up to me as I internally screamed at my body to move—to get up.

I flexed my fingers, and I was able to push myself up to my knees. I sucked in a deep gulp of air, which made the skin on my back tighten so I felt every bit of shrapnel stuck in me.

"Do you really think *he* can be flushed out if she's the bait?" he asked.

"The Unseelie supposedly tried to snatch her. The entire party came back so hyped up on fae realm magic they didn't make sense for a week," the leprechaun said. "I'd say that's proof he will at least respond to threats involving her."

Wait...are they after me to get to Noctus?

I was just barely strong enough to brace against the pain with one arm on the ground, so I used my free hand to grapple at the daggers on my belt. I found one, held it by the blade, then flung it up.

The hilt of the dagger hit the fae noble in the nose with a magnificent crack, and he shouted as he backed up, holding his nose.

I got a hit—Charon will be happy.

"Are you sure we've got the right person? Cat girl never used weapons." The siren's musical voice was off to my side.

I pulled another dagger from the front of my belt—using my own body to hide my movements—then threw the weapon at the siren's legs.

She screamed as the dagger dug into her calf.

That one stuck—Charon will really *be happy.*

The leprechaun learned from his cohorts. He approached me

from behind and kicked me in the back, nearly toppling me over. "She's not so tough!" he declared.

I heard the other fae grumbling as they closed around me in a ring.

I need to run!

I took a breath, intending to tap my magic and switch to my cat form.

"I thought I made myself clear that you are to *stay away* from this area?" Noctus's voice was low and menacing.

It felt like my heart stopped in my chest just from hearing it.

Together, the fae and I looked back.

CHAPTER TWELVE

Chloe

Noctus stood behind them, wearing his utilitarian clothing of black pants, boots, and shirt, and holding a sword.

His aviator sunglasses hid his eyes, and he had a glamour that I could sense but couldn't see, but it must have been enough to fool the fae, who were now hemming and hawing.

"Hello, sir. Um."

"We apologize. We didn't mean to...disturb you."

"That is, we are quite far from your home, so..."

"*I'll* decide what is *far enough* from my home." Noctus rotated his hold on his sword so the blade gleamed in the sunlight.

The fae noble whimpered.

"Tell that intolerable king of yours to *stop eyeing up what's mine*," Noctus said. "Next time I won't leave any messengers alive."

A cloud passed over the sun, and Noctus moved.

His sword was a blur, and he moved from target to target,

striking like lightning. His movements weren't just fast and precise, they *flowed*—like the unforgiving surge of a flood.

The troll toppled first. Noctus threw his sword's scabbard at the troll's neck, hitting him with enough force to make him choke.

The leprechaun was next. Noctus kicked the back of his leg so he collapsed, then picked him up by the shirt and threw him at the troll's head.

The fae noble yelled and tried to flee, but wherever he turned, Noctus was there.

Assured I was safe, I tuned out the one-sided slaughter and looked at the ground while I breathed. The burning pain was agony on my back, and I had to figure out how I was going to get up.

Hot breath lapped at my arm.

"It's fine, Ker. I couldn't let them see you." I glanced to the side and attempted to smile at the shifted werewolf.

She whined and stuck her nose in my ear, then looked past me and backed up.

"Were you only injured on your back?" Noctus asked.

Oh, the shouting stopped. He's done.

I worked to swallow the metallic tasting spit in my mouth. "Yeah, it only got my back." I finally managed to stand up, but I wobbled and couldn't straighten up, so I was bent over at the waist.

Noctus ducked under me, and hoisted me like a bag of cat food. My stomach was pressed into his shoulder, and my arms draped over his back. My left hand brushed the hilt of his sword that was sheathed and fastened to his belt.

"Um?" I said.

"I'm picking you up—I'll try not to touch your injuries, but it's still going to hurt," he warned. He gripped the sides of my knees, then stood up, easing me into a fireman's carry position so only my front side was splayed over him.

I exhaled through the pain, then braced my arms on his back so I wouldn't flop around. "Thanks."

He walked through the yard, heading to the street, Ker trotting at his side.

I tried to look around, but the view was too wobbly. "What about the fae?"

"They ran," he said. "I didn't want to knock them out and get the Curia Cloisters involved, but they'll have learned their lesson. They'll leave you alone now."

"Thank you." My eyes fluttered shut. "Oh—but they were looking for me, to get to you...they had a plan. Ask Ker, please."

Noctus was silent—with anger, I was pretty sure.

Pretty sure I'm going to get yelled at once I'm no longer in pain. But this isn't so bad. Usually I have to get myself out of scrapes like this.

Scared by my own thoughts, I shut my eyes and focused on ignoring the pain.

I STARED GLOOMILY at the navy blue couch my face was pressed into, peeling my cheek off the surface just long enough to take another swig of a tasteless potion Charon had forced into my hand as soon as Noctus stepped into the villa.

It was some kind of pain potion; I could tell by the cooling effect it had on my back. But it wasn't fae manufactured—fae potions had flavors.

It's probably an elven potion. The lack of flavors matches up with their personality.

The potion was fizzy, and little bubbles popped on my tongue and tickled my nose.

"Her wounds aren't grievous, but pulling out all the shrapnel will be painful for her," Charon said. "The potion she's drinking now will take her pain away, but she'll need at least one more in her to endure the removal."

"Not a healing potion?" This question came from Aristide, who stood in the middle of the open study doorway.

"If she starts healing with these metal bits still stuck in her, her skin will heal over them. That would be far worse," Charon said.

"Then get another numbing potion," Noctus said.

"Very well—I will also fetch her something to eat—that much magic on an empty stomach will likely make her sick, otherwise."

I heard Charon's steps as he crossed Noctus's study.

"I'll come with," Aristide said. "I bought some new potions—I might have something useful for the occasion." He tapped his walking stick on the ground as he moved.

"Could you also get a sheet to spread over the couch?" I called. "I have to be bleeding on it."

"*Lie still*," Noctus ordered.

"Moving you will only cause you more harm," Charon said. "It's best to leave you as you are."

"What about the couch?" I asked.

"Do you really think there is a stain magic can't remove?" Charon asked.

"Or we'll just throw out the couch," Aristide volunteered. "Something we might have to do anyway if Noctus gets angry every time he sees it."

I laboriously turned my head so my face was pointed out to the rest of Noctus's study, cringing when the movement made some of the metal bits stuck in the back of my neck move. "But why would he—"

"Finish your potion." Noctus pulled the potion from my left hand—which I couldn't see anymore since I'd turned my head—and pushed it into my right.

I obediently went back to swigging it.

"What a charmingly domestic exchange. Don't worry, Chloe, you'll tame him yet!" Aristide laughed as he stepped into the hallway, his voice getting quieter once he was out of the room.

"I will take my leave for now and be back with the potion and food," Charon said.

"Hey, Charon," I called before he could disappear through the door. "Did Ker tell you how I used my daggers?"

As soon as we'd gotten back to the villa, Ker had changed into her human form to tell Charon and Noctus everything we'd overheard. Maybe she'd mentioned that I had managed to fight back against the fae?

Charon raised an eyebrow as he peered at me.

"Didn't I do good?" I asked.

Charon switched his gaze to Noctus. "It should be noted the numbing effect of the potion also slightly affects her mind, so as to protect her from the mental effects of the pain." He turned his back to me.

I sniffed, hurt that he didn't respond, then shook my mostly-empty potion bottle.

Charon started to close the door. When there was only a tiny space left, he added, "You did admirably well."

It clicked shut before I could say anything, but I smiled widely, and might have even giggled a little.

Woah, yeah he's definitely right about this drink.

Noctus had been pacing back and forth in front of the couch I was steadily ruining. At my giggle he stopped next to my head. "Finish it."

I downed the last of the potion, almost snorting on bubbles before I fixed the angle I was drinking it at, then gave Noctus the glass vial when he held out his hand. "Thanks."

He took the bottle and set it on his desk.

Someone—Noctus, probably—had started a fire of glowing white and blue flames in the fireplace. The flames were silent, but they cast a warm white glow on the room that I found soothing.

I focused on not moving—I didn't want to shove any of the shrapnel deeper into my skin, but I also didn't want to get more blood on the couch than I already had. Unfortunately, either the shock from the fight was starting to set in, or I was getting cold from all the holes in me, because my teeth were starting to chatter. "You know, it's interesting that most forms of magic don't work on me since I'm a shadow, and yet healing potions work great."

"It's a side effect of being human," Noctus said. "Magic has favorites—though I'd say shadows are the favorite among favorites."

I scoffed. "Me? Magic's favorite? Yeah, right." I pressed my cheek into the couch pillow.

"You think elves are?" Noctus leaned against his desk.

"Well, elves have the strongest magic."

Noctus rubbed at the cuffs on his wrists. "The strength of one's magic has very little to do with all around abilities and how they can be applied. I'm the strongest elf in the Calor Villa, and yet you were able to successfully pose as my pet. For weeks."

I snapped my mouth shut so hard my teeth audibly clicked.

Ahh yes, he wants to go there. I guess it's better to get it out in the open. I've been scuttling around like a guilty cockroach for weeks.

"I'm sorry about that," I said. "Pretending to be your pet, I mean."

"Are you?" Noctus asked, his voice flat.

Aw, crud. Just how well can he read me now?

"No, not at all." I anxiously hiccupped as I spilled the truth. "I was scared, and I didn't know who or what the tracker was, and then when I realized what you were—what the Villa was—I was in too deep. Being honest is important, but I *really* like living."

Woah, I did not mean to spill all of that. This potion is dangerous!

I peered up at Noctus, desperately trying to read his stony expression. He stared at me, the dim lighting of the room casting shadows across his face.

An oppressive silence filled the room. It was so smothering, it was hard to breathe.

"I can understand why you did it." Noctus pushed off his desk and approached me and the unsanitary couch. "I would not have taken it well if you had immediately revealed yourself."

Something deep within me—so deep I hadn't recognized it was anything besides my usual paranoid anxiety—relaxed.

I hadn't realized that—somewhere between near panic attacks, him saving me so many times from the tracker, and all the gentleness he'd shown Amalourne—I had come to respect and like Noctus. I didn't *want* him to be irked with me—not because he was a powerful elf king, but because he was Noctus.

"I wanted to tell you," I said. "I should have told you earlier, but, the fear..."

Noctus shrugged as he loomed over me and the couch. "You did what you had to. I'd be a hypocrite for holding it against you as I am also doing what I must in keeping you here."

"Is that the consequence of my actions?" I asked, half afraid to hear his answer.

"Limited captivity? Yes. I can't afford to set you free, particularly since the Seelie and Unseelie know you are connected to me. They knew you lived with me when *I* didn't," Noctus said.

"Soon—not in the next few weeks, but for certain by the end of summer—my family will want to see me," I said.

"It will be a problem then," Noctus said. "But it doesn't matter now, particularly since this tracker of yours is proving to be smarter than originally estimated."

"Yeah," I quietly said as I tried to pick through his words. My shivers were getting worse, and it was getting harder to keep my teeth from chattering—I had to bite my tongue to cushion them.

That will be a problem then? Does that mean he really does intend to keep me all summer? There's no way I can afford that. There's no way Ms. Booker can go that long without me working.

Noctus set a knee on the edge of the couch, then braced his left arm on the back of it so he could lean over me and look at my bleeding back. "You're upset," he said factually.

"No. Well. Sort of?" He was so close, he made the room feel

small. Which was weird—I'd sat on his shoulders as a cat. This shouldn't bother me. I scrunched my eyes shut, but even then I could feel his closeness. "I know I only have myself to blame, but staying here does cause some financial problems for me."

"Your rent is paid for," Noctus said.

I popped my eyes open. "What?"

Noctus's fingers were gentle on my back as he peered through the holes in my shirt, trying to get a look at my injuries. "I contacted your landlord. While you remain here, I will pay for your rent," Noctus said.

I stared up at him, two sides of me—my finance minded self and my whatever it was that made his closeness feel...close—warring against each other.

Finances won with logic prevailing.

"But wouldn't this be considered a consequence to my actions?" I asked.

"Perhaps." Noctus frowned as he straightened up, but I think it was because he was irritated with my injuries. When he glanced at my face, his expression smoothed. "In this case, I am free to select the consequences at my discretion."

I thought over his words for several seconds, then exhaled. "Thank you. I was so afraid—thanks, Noctus. I mean it."

How can someone be so brutal and powerful, yet thoughtful? I mean, he just told me I wasn't going home for months, then seconds later takes my biggest worry of rent off my mind.

I didn't like the juxtaposition. It wasn't that he was untrustworthy. No, it killed me to admit it, but it was that I didn't like how attentive he was to everything involving me. As if I mattered to him, when he was the elf king involved in politics that would shift supernatural society, and I had perfected how to act like a cat to avoid getting beat up.

Noctus watched me for a moment, then chose to sit down. Not on a separate chair, which would have made me a lot less flighty, no, my luck as terrible as ever. Instead he chose to plant himself on the edge of my couch. Even worse, his presence felt *soothing*. My nerves actually settled down.

I don't like where this is going for me, so it's time to say something. Anything!

"I'm not going to tell anyone about Calor Villa," I blurted out.

Noctus cocked his head. "You specified Calor Villa, but not me?"

It took everything in me not to react. *Okay. Okay. This is okay. I can keep Ms. Booker hidden—I will keep Ms. Booker hidden. I don't like keeping the truth from him, but—respect or not—I'm not going to let Noctus imprison Ms. Booker here with me. This place might be close to a vacation resort, but Ms. Booker has a business to run, and I'm not going to ruin her life because she was willing to help me.*

"You are already outed." I dug my fingers under the pillow my head was cushioned on, and drew my arms closer to my chest as I tried to retain my heat. "Between the Paragon and the Seelie and Unseelie Courts. If you don't do something soon, your cover is going to get blown."

Noctus nodded. "I'm aware. I also have reason to believe we will be moving soon, which will end this nonsense."

Believe we will be moving soon? That's a weird phrasing considering he's totally in control of moving or not moving.

A piece of my hair fell across my face, getting in my eyes. I tried to brush it away, but it hurt to raise my hand.

Noctus moved it for me, the pads of his fingers gently sliding across my cheek before he tucked the wayward strand behind my ear.

Weirdly, when I should have been in seventh heaven because I had been officially forgiven, my guts felt like they were tied in knots.

It's because of his expression.

Although Noctus's fingers were gentle, his expression was blank. Nothing showed in the swirl of his eyes or the tilt of his mouth. He was stony faced.

If I'd been Ama, he'd be smiling at me.

I saw things as Ama...she was his pet, and he was freer with her. I took that away. I don't regret my actions, except for that.

"Noctus, I—" I tried to move, which sent a jolt of pain through my numb back. On the plus side, it stopped the impulse to shiver.

Somehow, Noctus's face grew even more expressionless. "It still hurts."

"A little." I tried not to shift, but the back of my calf had an itch that was really starting to get to me. "The potion took the sting away. It's more like my body knows it's in pain, so I don't feel very good." I opened my eyes and tried to muster a smile.

Noctus, still seated on the edge of my couch, narrowed his eyes.

"I'll be fine," I said. "Charon said the wounds aren't terrible. Once the shrapnel is removed and I can take an actual healing potion, I'll be back to training in a few days."

Although, I suspect the shrapnel removal isn't going to be fun. I don't know how badly my back is torn up, but every piece will have to be individually removed. Yuck.

"There's another way." Noctus's deep voice invaded my thoughts.

"Hm?" I didn't say anything because my teeth were finally chattering so hard I couldn't hide it.

Noctus clenched his jaw and looked away. He was silent for several heartbeats, then spoke. "There's another way to heal you. With the collar."

"The collar," I repeated, the words draining the glossy feeling the numbing potion had left on my brain. I opened and closed my mouth a few times. "Wouldn't it have the same downside and heal over the shrapnel like a potion?"

"Not necessarily." Noctus's dark, golden hair glinted when it caught the white light from the fire. "Elves are capable of healing magic, but it has limitations—like requiring the shrapnel to be removed. The collar can bypass that as it has an added, personal conduit onto the magic—something regular healing magic doesn't have." He peeled off the utility vest he was wearing.

"So..." I spoke very slowly—I didn't want to mess this up. "That means...it would be *your* magic?"

A muscle jumped on Noctus's cheek—I couldn't tell what that meant—and he laid his vest over me, instantly warming me up. *Is he reluctant to use it?*

"Thanks," I said as I pulled his vest up against my chin. "The collar...isn't it just a connection between us?" I asked. Ms. Booker had told me it had an old and powerful spell on it, and that there was a possibility it contained a part of Noctus himself in it. But that seemed unlikely after he had me keep wearing it since discovering me.

His gaze swiveled back to me, and in the light of the fire his hazel eyes seemed brighter than usual. "You researched it?"

"A little."

"What do you know?"

I licked my lips, and my pillow slipped a little. "That the jewels might possibly be a tie to...you."

Noctus studied me for several long moments. "They are," he said. "It's a special sort of magic elves do with those they trust above all as it gives them a pathway to their inner selves, and essentially allows you to carry a part of me. It's somewhat like a werewolf mate bond, except it allows you to potentially use my magic as well," he said. "It's called binding magic. It wasn't done often—which I'm sure comes as a surprise to you with how *trusting* we elves are—though usually it's in the form of an exchange."

"Which is why you didn't want anyone to know about it." When I spoke, the silky material of my pillow slipped, and it almost slid off the side of the couch. "But you could have just taken the collar off me?"

Noctus shrugged. "You don't know how to use it, and it serves as an excellent way to track you and lets me tell when you are in trouble—as you were today."

I grimaced. "Sorry. We should have known better."

Noctus stretched over me, his nearness again affecting me in weird ways that made my spine want to shiver—and not from the cold.

Thankfully, he didn't notice my weird expression as he eased my pillow back into position under my head. "As irked as I am about the situation, I cannot fault you. None of us—myself included—thought the fae would venture so close. Shockingly, it turns out the Paragon is correct and the Unseelie-Seelie conflict is worse than I was aware of if they're desperate enough to listen to the tracker and attempt to snatch you."

That's right, Ker told him what happened when she shifted after we got back.

I blinked again as I tried to organize my thoughts. "You think the outsider the fae mentioned was the tracker?"

"I highly doubt there is anyone else capable of tracking your movements so precisely. Though it seems we'll have to cleanse the neighborhood as he *must* have some spells laid outside the cul-de-sac if he was able to notify the fae so swiftly of your presence."

"They said they wanted to use me to get to you." I groaned when I shifted on my couch, but I kept Noctus's vest wrapped tightly around me. "They're really desperate to recruit you."

"They're desperate for *power*," Noctus corrected. "Because they mistakenly believe power will save them, when if they focused on finding a way to revive their Court they would flourish. And while I might have been their target, I highly doubt the tracker intended to turn you over to the fae. He was likely using them to do his dirty work and retrieve you—a classic elf tactic, so it would seem even though he's only a half blood he was raised in our ways. But. We return to the current issue: your back. Using the collar I can heal you much faster—and without removing the shrapnel."

"Will it actually work on me?" I asked.

Noctus snorted. "Due to magic's rampant favoritism, yes, it will."

"But then you'd have to explain it to everyone, wouldn't you?" I asked. "Because Charon would see that I'm better."

Noctus looked away from me again, the expression that almost looked *angry* slipping back over his face. "Yes."

CHAPTER THIRTEEN

Chloe

I waited a few moments, but he didn't say anything else. "Didn't you want to keep it a secret?"

"Realistically, I'm not sure it can be hidden much longer," he said. "Sooner or later they'll realize you're wearing your collar, despite your magic. If discovery is inevitable, I may as well spare you the pain of the shrapnel removal."

I pressed my lips together—not because my back was hurting, the numbing potion was still working—but because of Noctus's words.

Stop it, I internally warned myself. *"I may as well spare you pain" is barely polite, much less than affectionate.*

But it was, in the context of what Noctus was going to do for it.

Noctus—still seated on the edge of my couch—watched me, waiting for my reply. He was going to let me choose.

I can see it...not his dutiful king persona, but whatever it is in him that made him save Ker and Aristide. He's not soft—or really he's as soft as a thunderstorm. But there's something in him that will reach out...when he knows.

But how did he know I was like Ker and Aristide? I certainly wasn't brave or good at fighting like them. I hadn't done anything remarkable. For most of the time he'd known me, he thought I was a *cat*!

But he was willing to take the risk.

What's going to happen when it's time for me to leave? Will he just take the collar, and it will be like none of this happened?

The thought pricked me like a needle, so I ran from it, focusing on the issue at hand.

"Okay." Feeling weirdly shy, I pulled his vest up so it covered my mouth. "If you don't mind, can you heal me?"

He nodded, then stood up, and went to his desk.

"Noctus?" I called.

He stopped, his back to me. "Yes?"

"Thank you."

Noctus grabbed something off his desk, then was back at my side. "Of course." He reached out to touch my shoulder, his fingers warm on my skin. "It's easier if we touch."

"Go for it," I said. "Remember how many naps I took on you as Ama? It's fine."

Noctus gently lifted my upper body off the couch. He bumped the pillow so it fell off, then took its vacated position, carefully arranging me across his lap.

He used the item he'd swiped off the desk—a bejeweled dagger—and pressed it to the shackle on his right hand. Something in the shackle clicked, and it broke in half. Noctus leaned sideways and dropped the shackle over the side of the couch arm.

When he saw me peering up at him, he held the dagger out for my inspection. "It cancels magic," he said. "Specifically fae spells."

"The Paragon would squawk if he knew," I said.

"The Paragon would know such a thing existed if he was as old as he pretends to be," Noctus said. "And the dagger is a much easier way to deal with the shackles than ripping the spell apart and putting it back together."

I yawned. "Will Charon and the others be able to tell you took it off?"

"Not until after I blast half the villa with the magic needed to heal you," he dryly said.

I laughed. "Won't that be exciting?"

Noctus gently combed my hair away from my body so it spilled over his lap, carefully untangling it from any of the metal shards the Seelie fae had packed in their magic bomb.

"Do I need to do anything?" I asked.

"No—the magic will do the work." Noctus leaned over me, tugging his vest down so it was spread over my legs, giving him a view of the holes in my clothes from my injuries. "Just stay still."

I exhaled, and waited for Noctus's magic.

I could feel when it flared with the familiar knife-in-the-ribs sensation, but it still brushed past me, unable to affect me.

The collar started to warm at my throat, and the pomegranate red gems started to glow.

I held my breath for several moments.

"Relax." Noctus tapped the collar.

"That's kind of hard to do," I said. "I can tell magic is coming."

I braced myself when his magic started to trickle through the collar, giving me a warm, ticklish sensation in my entire body that chased away the last of my shivers.

"This is nice," I said after a few moments. "Is this how it—" I snapped my mouth shut when I looked up and saw Noctus frown.

"It's not enough," he said.

"You can't get enough magic because of the cuffs?" I guessed. "That's okay. Thanks for trying." I smiled, trying to show him I didn't mind.

Noctus eyed me. "I have *more* than enough magic."

"Okay?"

He set his jaw again. "It's the...touching. It's not enough."

"Huh. Well. Wanna put your hand on my face or something?" I asked.

Noctus ignored my suggestion. "Might I shift you?"

"Yeah, I'm feeling pretty good between the potion and your mag—" I cut myself off with a sharp inhale when Noctus slipped his hands under my shoulder and elevated me so I was almost sitting upright. It didn't hurt because of the potion, but I could feel the metal in my back dig deeper.

"Sorry." He tugged me closer, gingerly turning me so I turned toward him.

Once I realized what he wanted, I twisted in his direction, clenching my teeth. I stretched to reach the arm of the couch, but it was hard to brace myself at that angle.

Noctus hooked his arms around my sides—being careful not to touch any of my injuries—then tipped me so I fell against his chest with an ungainly thump.

"Well," I said into his shoulder.

Noctus fixed his hold on me so he was supporting me with one arm snug against my side. I didn't have to do any work, just greedily suck up his magic.

For a moment, it felt awkward. Then, I relaxed my clenched hands and smoothed my fingers over a wrinkle in his shirt, flattening it against his chest, and Noctus rested his chin on top of my head.

This is a lot nicer hug than anything I got as a cat.

I was warmer, supported, and the pain from turning faded away into nothing from the sheer comfort Noctus radiated.

I briefly closed my eyes. "How will you know if this is enough—wow." Words failed me when Noctus's magic gushed through the collar.

The ticklish sensation solidified to a stronger tingling feeling, sweeping from the top of my head to my toes. But that wasn't what had me captivated. His magic *sang.*

Like the crescendo of a choir, Noctus's magic sank into my body—each particle forming a harmonious note.

The crackling of the sterile white and blue flames of the fireplace grew muffled as the world took on a golden hue. Noctus's magic hummed, settling deeper into my skin.

I awkwardly turned my head, craning my neck so I could peer up over my own shoulder and look at him. "Your magic sings?"

Noctus had been studying my back, but at my question he flicked his eyes to my face. "You can hear it?"

I closed my eyes as I listened to his magic croon in a sound that was like a human voice, except it was too crystalline and pure. "Oh yeah."

"Interesting. And yes, my magic is a noise. Elves hear all magic as sounds," Noctus said. "Can you hear anything besides my spell?"

"No. I don't think I'd want to even if I could," I said, dazed.

"Why?" Noctus asked.

"Because it's so beautiful." I was so enraptured by the sound—which soared high and then twined low—I was having a hard time keeping my mouth shut.

Noctus chuckled—a deep, baritone sound that harmonized with the crescendo of his magic.

The cool, numb feeling from the potion retreated, and my whole body warmed. The tightness of my muscles eased. I could feel the pinpoints where shrapnel had buried into my skin disappear as my insides felt bubbly.

"What's happening?" I asked.

"My magic is disintegrating the shrapnel," Noctus said. "Since we are connected, it can identify what is part of you and what isn't. It's getting rid of what shouldn't be there."

My inner book-nerd perked up. "Wait, it's weighing things out and making decisions? That's fascinating—can you do this for yourself?"

"No," Noctus said. "It requires the ability to pump magic through a connection like ours." His voice was a lot cooler, and I got the general sense he didn't want me to ask anything else.

Remember the goal: I don't want to learn more than I need to. Except...this is so interesting! I mean, he said it requires a connection like ours. Does that mean I could technically do this for him?

His magic hit me with another surge—bringing another song with it.

"How do you get anything done? If my magic sang I'd just sit around and listen to it all day." I hummed in appreciation as his magic settled bone deep into me.

I was getting sleepy, and his magic sounded like how looking at stars and mountains felt.

"I'm glad you find it soothing—it makes the healing process easier." Noctus's fingers glided up the back of my neck, which made his magic trill. He tugged on my hole-y shirt, inspecting my skin—although he was very respectful in that he didn't try to touch me, and I only felt the twitch of my clothes.

I barely noticed; I was still giddy from the feeling of magic. "Is this what it's like to actually have wieldable magic?" I asked. "I can feel spells externally, but my shifting magic is so instantaneous, it's barely a twinge. I can feel my magic, and clamp down on it, but I can't direct it. I just have to pray it's working, which maybe is a good thing because, wow, this is better than getting Book Nookery's accounts to balance. It's even better than buying a new book!"

"Your high praise is noted." Noctus combed his fingers through my hair as he tried to inspect my scalp, searching for any wayward injuries. "And no, this isn't quite an accurate representation. My magic would not be nearly as soft to anyone else."

I forced my fingers to cooperate so I could give him two

thumbs up. "In that case, tell your magic this is five star treatment, would do again."

There was that chuckle again—which sent his magic chiming through my body.

"You are healed now," he continued after his inspection. "But you'll want to move carefully for the rest of today. The magic closed all your wounds, but there still needs to be some minor healing of your muscles—my residual magic that's floating around you will be enough to handle it. It just needs a little more time."

"Mmhmm," I said.

The only thing I was aware of was that if I relaxed any more, I was going to start drooling.

The song of his magic quieted, but it didn't fade entirely. I could still feel it in my bones. I was so enraptured by it, I missed the sound of footsteps outside.

The door banged open, and Aristide strode in. "Noctus, *what* are you doing? Ker said she could smell your magic all the way down the hallway."

"I was healing Chloe." Noctus shifted slightly so he could pick up his abandoned shackle, but he didn't try to move me. I was too addled to care that I was draped across his chest, so I stayed where I was, soaking up the last bit of his magic.

"Okay, that makes sense. You must have taken off at least one of your shackles—wait, *what*?" Aristide said.

"I thought I made it clear she needed the debris removed, Your Majesty," Charon said.

I cracked an eye open and watched the elf and vampire storm the room.

Ker was behind them, back in her human body with her nose twitching and her brow furrowed.

"I thought about it, and decided waiting was unnecessary given that there was an alternative way to heal her that got rid of the shrapnel," Noctus said.

"*What* alternative way would that be?" Charon asked, his voice tightening like my nerves when I could sense another supernatural in the area.

Noctus rolled me onto my side and nudged my upper body so I peeled myself off him, supported by his hands on my shoulders. "Binding magic."

He stood up and let go of me. I think he thought I'd bear my own weight, but I didn't, so I bonelessly flopped back onto the couch and hit it with a loud "womph!"

Ker started laughing—the sound so loud and joyous it was close to a howl. Aristide had been in the process of sitting down in his favorite chair, but with Noctus's words he snapped back up into standing. "*Binding magic?*"

"Yes," Noctus said.

The room was silent—except for Ker, who was still laughing. She was actually bent over, and I was pretty sure she was starting to cry.

Charon's mask was still impressively impassive. "When?"

"Shortly after I brought her into the villa as Ama," Noctus said.

"That's sweet," Ker declared, her voice shaking as she got her laughter under control and brushed moisture from her eyes.

"Hmm," was all Charon said as he studied me. "The collar?"

"Yes," Noctus said.

I still hadn't shaken the fuzzy warmth of Noctus's magic, and so when I sat up I yanked the neckline of my t-shirt farther down to show the collar was still there. "I can't take it off," I told Charon since he was still staring at me. "I tried."

"I imagine so," Charon said.

I'm not sure how to take his reaction...or Aristide's...

I briefly scrunched my eyes shut and tried to rally my brain cells together for coherent thinking.

"I want to know *why*," Aristide demanded. "Why would you perform *binding magic*—which you elves rarely do, because you're a paranoid bunch for all your arrogance."

"She was my cat," Noctus said.

"Yeah, well she's *definitely* not anymore!" Aristide said. "Why does she still have it on?"

Noctus studied me, seemingly bemused. "Just because she's not a cat doesn't mean she stopped being mine."

Ker pressed both of her hands to her mouth, and I thought she might be crying—for real this time, not because of laughter.

"Ker?" I asked. "Are you okay?"

"I'm trying to decide," Ker slowly said.

"Decide what?" I asked.

"Whether I should take a picture to preserve this big moment of personal growth for Noctus, or use this as a teaching lesson so he learns how to rephrase things so he can actually make friends," Ker said.

Aristide groaned. "Please tell me you aren't going to drag your Dale Carnegie obsession into this?"

"He needs to learn," Ker insisted.

"Whatever." Aristide pointed himself in Noctus's direction and scowled. "I'm more concerned that you used *that* kind of magic...*on a cat*!"

"As you pointed out, she is no longer a cat," Noctus said.

"Except she was when you put it on her! Why would you forge an eternal connection *with a cat*?!"

"She was important to me," Noctus said.

Aristide made strangled noises and collapsed in his chair.

My brain was finally running well enough that it occurred to me Noctus's obtuse answers were maybe designed to inspire emotions in his friends. *But what does he have to hide? I was just a cat. There couldn't have been a deeper reason for it.*

"Understood." Charon set down the tray and covered platter he was carrying on an end table, though he grabbed a glass vial with a cork stopper off it. "If that is so, I am glad you were able to use the binding magic to heal Chloe's back. Since the potion is no longer necessary, I will take it back—though I do advise you,

Chloe, to eat. Even though magic healed your body, you will still need nutrients to replace blood and for general recovery." He slightly bowed to me then left, carrying on as if nothing out of the ordinary had happened.

Ker sat down next to me and patted my knee. "I knew you were on the list," she said.

"As a cat," I reminded her.

"Sure," Ker chirped.

Aristide still looked a little stormy with a scowl on his face. "You should have told us, Noctus, when we found out she was human. That was dangerous."

Noctus shrugged. "You would have lectured me, and I would have refused to take the collar off since it's an excellent way to track her."

"Maybe, but the heads up would have been nice. If you don't knock that kind of behavior off I'll unleash Ker on you, and she'll make you attend one of her silly 'make friends' classes," Aristide said.

"I take it, then, that the next time I decide to do something emotional you want me to inform you?" Noctus asked.

"*Yes!*" Aristide hissed.

"If you say so," Noctus said.

"The circle of trust has been established," Ker declared.

"Um, I think you might be missing the reason why Noctus has decided to keep the collar on me," I said.

"Nonsense," Ker said. "You'll see! Now—let us eat!"

CHAPTER FOURTEEN

Noctus

The mantel clock nestled onto one of my bookshelves struck the hour—six o'clock in the evening.

I looked up from the pile of my paperwork and stood. *It's time to leave, or I'll be late.*

I was meeting with the representatives of the city tiers tonight. Officially it was to give them time to air any grievances, but my people were so terrified of me they never dared complain, so it usually became a session of me prying words out of the representatives who only babbled positive things.

I shrugged my black suitcoat over my gray button up shirt as I weaved around the furniture that cluttered my office. When I passed by the couch I slowed down, noticing my utility vest—which Chloe had burrowed in before I'd healed her—was still there.

I'll put it away when I get back.

I tilted my head from one side to the other as I tried to catch sight of any stain on the newly cleaned couch.

It looked fine, though staring at it made me want to light it on fire.

Which irritates me more: the couch bothering me because Chloe bled all over it and thinking of that puts me in a foul mood, or knowing that Aristide was right about me hating it?

Regardless, the couch was getting dumped, and I didn't want one of its identical replacements. We'd have to get something entirely new.

Now I'm holding grudges against furniture. Fantastic. I've been alive so long that I'm no longer maturing, I'm regressing into a juvenile state.

Sensing my weakness, the wild magic in the air hummed, surrounding me in an aggressive chorus.

I shook my head as I headed for the door, tugging the sleeves of my suitcoat down—they'd bunched awkwardly over the metal cuffs that cut off my magic. "Whatever it is you want, the answer is *no*."

The wild magic didn't have the decency to quiet itself. Instead, the musical notes followed me out of my study and down the hallway.

I walked past the central staircase, heading for one of the back doors to the city that would allow a less conspicuous entry than the giant double doors. When I heard laughter float from the short hallway that led to the kitchens, I paused.

That's Chloe.

She didn't laugh often—a side effect of near constant anxiety.

Aristide's low voice was barely audible before it spiked louder, nearly covering Ker's yapping cackles.

For a moment I considered canceling the meeting and going to the kitchens.

But while I never intended to be king, I was. With that came the duties of keeping order. Besides, when Chloe spoke again, the wild magic around me once again crooned its happiness. That alone was enough to prod me into walking on.

I might have bound Chloe to me because I'm an idiot who was too distracted by magic finally speaking to me again that I let it cloud all logic and reason, but I refuse to let it use me for whatever other plans it has for Chloe.

I was certain if Chloe knew magic was taking an interest in her, her heart would explode in fright, but it wasn't that surprising.

Shadows—with their ability to walk through any barrier, survive fouled magic, and be unaffected by any negative magic cast by a supernatural—were always magic's favorites. It was only natural that wild magic would be pleased to have a shadow around.

But, this time, I wasn't going to side with it.

This, however, was very different from the occasion with the war. I had my people to think of, and Chloe's future was all that magic was concerned with, not the future of supernaturals in general.

The only problem with that plan was Chloe.

I was almost down the hallway when I heard Chloe call.

"Noctus?"

I exhaled and turned around and watched her jog down the hallway.

She'd changed into new clothes since I'd healed her and wrapped her brown hair—which I now personally knew was as silky as her fur had been as Amalourne—in a bun that I was sure she did only to make herself look taller. "I know you've got a thing to go to, but I just wanted to say thanks. Again. For healing me."

I slipped my hands into my pockets. "Of course. But next time don't act as the bait. Shadows are better suited for ambushes and stealth work."

She smiled, and the beauty mark below her left eye somehow

made her eyes warmer. "Let's be honest, I'm best suited for running away."

"If Charon hears you say that he's going to increase your drills," I warned her. "He has dreams of molding you into an elite fighter."

"Why is it that everyone here are the only supernaturals I've ever met who have high expectations for me?" Chloe asked.

I allowed myself a slight smile. "Because we know what you're capable of. Good evening, Chloe."

Chloe wavered awkwardly on her feet, barely avoiding falling into old patterns of getting physically close to me, most likely. (The only reason why I didn't was because I—expecting magic's excessive fangirling over her—had firmly planted myself so I wouldn't do something stupid, like reach out for her.)

When she fixed her stagger, Chloe flashed a smile at me, turned on her heel, then trotted back to the kitchens.

I watched her go with a frown.

Yes, I'm aware magic wants to use me for her sake, and it makes me furious. But knowing that isn't any help when I don't really mind *aiding her, as I did in healing her.*

I made myself walk on, splitting off from the main hallway.

Earlier in the day, wild magic had practically sung a human opera at me until I offered to heal her. I'd been reluctant to do it, firstly because the wild magic wanted it so badly, and secondly because I *knew* we'd have to have a great deal more bodily contact, and I suspected that once I'd sat with Chloe in an embrace, it was going to be difficult to let her go.

Regardless, I wasn't going to let her remain in pain just because I had poor self-control and magic was pushy.

The end of the tiny hallway I'd entered ended with a tight, spiral staircase made of stone and rotting wood—Charon's lack of upkeeping the area was his passive aggressive attempt to keep me from using the side entrances. I started down the staircase as I absently checked that my hidden knives and daggers were tucked into place—a habit that hung on from my days as the Mors family death-dealer.

If I was at all egotistical I would blame Chloe for my weakness in desiring to help her, and try to avoid her. But I am no fool. Magic is the problem, not her.

Approximately two flights down I reached the bottom of the staircase, which ended with a battered wooden door that had seen better days. I pushed it open, grimacing when the hinges creaked.

I'm also not stupid enough to blame my unexpected affection for Chloe on her time spent as my pet.

Amalourne had been a warmth to me I hadn't experienced, as she gave a selfless, unconditional kind of love that only pets could represent.

Chloe, however...

I stepped outside into the humid night air, unsurprised to see the tier-leaders waiting for me by a phoenix fountain.

They bowed immediately, folding themselves in half so I couldn't see their faces or expressions. Even from this distance I could see the white in their clenched hands and hear the whistle of the uneven breaths of air they took in.

They still feared me, even after all this time.

And I couldn't blame them—not after spending much of my life in bloodshed that culminated with the elimination of my entire family.

This is how Chloe, as a person, has swiftly come to mean so much during our complicated and short history. Despite all her personal fears and anxiety, she still reaches for me. She doesn't flinch when she touches me, she doesn't care if she must lean against my chest.

If Amalourne was a pet's love—warm but focused only on affection as a comfort and moment of peace—Chloe was the dangerous and alluring hint of a binding love—something that lasted through death, pain...and power. Something far deeper, far rarer, and far more precious.

And yet, it is something I still can't have. I doubt it's what wild magic has in mind for her, but—more importantly—that's the kind of love that is dangerous for me to have when my sole purpose in life is to fulfill my duties. It would distract me and keep me from it.

That knowledge, though, didn't stop the knife of regret that twisted in my heart as I walked up to my quivering people, cursed with knowing fear was all that awaited me for the entirety of my remaining life.

CHAPTER FIFTEEN

Chloe

"This is a really bad idea," I said.

I stood on one of the steps that overlooked the elven city and led down to the topmost tier. As I stared at the bustling city, every nerve in my body burned. "It's a city of elves, they couldn't possibly be thrilled to learn I'm a shadow."

"It won't matter one bit," Ker assured me as she held Aristide's arm, guiding him down the steps.

I stayed where I was, my knees shaking. "I'm a *shadow*—the enemy they hunted down and killed."

"Centuries ago," Ker said. "Many of the elves here weren't even alive for those times."

"Please excuse me if I'm not convinced," I said.

"For crying out loud!" Aristide stopped on a step so he could shuffle around and call back to me where I was at least six stairs up. "Chloe, Noctus *told* us to bring you down to the city. He made the announcement that you exist and were

Ama, and he wants at least some of the elves to see you to drive the point home. You think they fear you, but—here's the hot take—they are *way* more terrified of Noctus and his reaction!"

"They respect him," Ker protested.

"If you'd rather phrase it that way, sure," Aristide grumbled. "The point is, they'll never move against him. You'll be *fine*."

I still wasn't convinced, but the duo was starting back down the stairs, and I didn't want to be left alone in the city, so I hurried after them.

"You've got about ten steps until we reach the next level spot," Ker said.

"Got it," Aristide said.

"Now eight steps."

"Please don't tell me you intend to tell me every two steps?"

"Now six—and why not? You *are* getting old."

"As if you aren't?!"

I smiled at the duo—calmed by their easy friendship, though even their bickering couldn't stop the avalanche of my thoughts.

Noctus told his people, so doesn't that mean he really does intend for me to stay here for a long time?

He'd said as much the day he healed me. I was still hoping he might let me go sooner than expected, but I wasn't sure how the binding magic would play into that.

Does that mean we'll stay friends once this is over and I do leave?

I'd always assumed eventually Noctus would drop me off at the doorstop of my apartment building, and I'd never hear from him again.

I wouldn't have wanted to hear from him—he was an *elf king*—but I was starting to suspect if that was what happened, I'd feel...sad.

Feeling embarrassed, I glanced at Aristide and Ker, who were still arguing as they strode across the platform, heading for the next level of stairs.

I'd miss Ker and Aristide—and even Charon, too. They care—and they believe in me in a way no one besides my family has.

My heart metaphorically tapped me on the shoulder, and I was *deeply* aware that although I really prized the new friendships I'd made, and their willingness to invest in me like Charon had in trying to teach me daggers, I would miss Noctus most of all.

And that is a dangerous thought pattern.

"Chloe, are you coming?" Ker called to me. "You're falling pretty far behind."

"Sorry—I got lost in thought!" I squared my shoulders, then darted after the two.

I followed them past the top three tiers of the city, which were carved into the sides of the mountain so the entire city resembled an enormous staircase.

We got off at the fourth level, following a wide platform that opened into a plaza that took over a good chunk of this level of the city.

The plaza was constructed of shining white stone, and a stone walkway from the third tier of the city spanned across it with a gigantic half-moon bridge. Colorful flags hung from the bridge, and a food stall selling some variation of fried dough—something I would recognize with my love of donuts no matter the culture, especially with the fried sugar scent it wafted invitingly to me—was set by the base of a giant fountain, or rather the remnants of one.

Water still bubbled in the enormous fountain—which was at least as big as my luxurious room in Noctus's villa. But at the center of the pool was a platform of chipped stone, and one statue.

The statue was about eight feet tall, and was of an armored warrior holding a scythe. It took me a moment to recognize the scythe and armor from the portrait inside the villa.

That must be Noctus with...what did Ker call it? Destruction.

The weapon was pretty distinctive with all its deadliness. Even as a statue the thing looked dangerously sharp.

Yeesh, I can't say I'm sad it's cursed and no longer useable. Noctus must have been terrifying when wielding it.

It seemed like previously there'd been several figures in the fountain—I could spy a set of chipped boots and a set of sandaled feet carved into the ruined stone. But now, Noctus was the only figure that remained.

That must have been their choice, I realized as I watched the elves bustle through the plaza. *Because Noctus would have torn the whole thing down.*

The plaza was busier than I would have expected for a weekday, but it seemed like people were passing through it to get out to the large stairway so they could access the other levels of the city. Maybe they were going home for lunch?

"Chloe."

I defensively pushed my shoulders up, but it was just Noctus, standing with Charon and an elf—it took me a moment to recognize Valaria.

She was a beautiful young elf who'd gifted Noctus with a pink ribbon embroidered with black cats for me.

Noctus motioned for me to approach.

I glanced at all the elves, but no one had noticed me, so I scooted my way to Noctus, stopping next to him.

He glanced down at me, then shifted his gaze to Valaria. "Chloe, allow me to officially introduce you to Valaria. Valaria, you remember Chloe—formerly Ama?"

"Of course, Your Majesty. It's an honor, Chloe." Valaria bobbed a curtsey to me.

Is that a thing? Oh gosh.

I also curtseyed—which wasn't as pretty since I was wearing jean shorts and not a skirt like she was. "The honor is mine—you do beautiful embroidery work," I blurted out before I could think of anything better to say.

"You're too kind." Valaria curtseyed again. "But I am highly gratified that you remember my work, and I am delighted to see you standing beside our king."

I curtseyed back—because if I didn't curtsey back, wouldn't that be bad manners? Ms. Booker would know. "Thank you. But I don't know about that."

Valaria swished her skirts as she curtseyed again—the movement graceful. "But of course it is a delight—as a shadow you are his equal, and all elves know what the gravity of a binding ceremony means."

I started to curtsey again, until my brain caught up with what Valaria had said. My eyes bulged, and I stared up at Noctus. "You *told* people that?"

Noctus was too busy opening a paper bag to look at me. "Of course. I told them everything."

I meant to say something, but all I could do was wheeze.

"Breathe," Noctus advised me as he pulled something out of his bag. "Then eat this."

I took it without thinking and ate a chunk, realizing, belatedly, it was a piece of fried dough from the stand.

It was roughly the length of a french fry, but as thick as my thumb. It had a crispier exterior than a donut, but it had been soaked in a sticky sweet syrup that exploded with flavor in my mouth.

"Now then, you are certain you have *not* seen this man?" Charon held out a photograph of the tracker—a still shot taken from the security footage when he'd tried breaking the house's barrier.

"Correct," Valaria said.

"Understood." Charon slid the photograph into his small notebook and made a notation. "Thank you for your cooperation."

"It is always my honor." Valaria curtseyed again, first to Noctus, then—bafflingly—to me.

With my hands full of donuts, my curtsey looked more like a bob, but it made Valaria smile and shake her head.

"You don't need to curtsey to me," she said as she curtseyed again.

"That would be rude." My social awareness kicked me in the gut, so I curtseyed again.

"I assure you it is not." Valaria curtseyed one last time, and before I could curtsey back Noctus slipped a thumb through a belt loop on my jean shorts, keeping me standing since I didn't want a mega wedgie.

"Elven customs dictate you don't need to curtsey as you have been bound to me," Noctus said as Valaria took the moment to escape our curtsey battle.

I ate another piece of my not-quite-a-donut-but-same-vibe dessert. "I can see how that would make sense—since I'm connected to you that puts me on a different social level even though normally I wouldn't be there, right?"

"Something like that," Noctus said.

"Got it. She seemed to take me pretty well," I said.

"You think anyone would dare object to His Majesty using binding magic?" Charon asked, conveniently forgetting Aristide had done exactly that.

"I thought she'd hate me for being..." I looked around, then lowered my voice. "A shadow."

Noctus shrugged. "The elves who live in this city might physically be the same type of elf who lived before the war, but much has changed. They're from different regions, not just the Mors—Vitas, Auron, and others. Before the war they never would have lived in the same city due to the bad blood between the elven royals. Now they've been forced to adjust to a world that hasn't been theirs in centuries. What would it matter to them if you're a shadow or not?"

Charon made another note in his notebook; from the way he

glanced at me I knew he was thinking something else, but he'd never naysay Noctus.

"So you're confirming the tracker isn't working with the artifacts manufacturer?" I asked.

"Indeed," Charon said.

"Normally we'd believe they are two separate issues." Noctus let go of my shorts and rested his hand on the hilt of the sword that was strapped to his belt. "But since it appears he's willing to mess with fae politics, and we haven't physically seen him since the night of the artifacts raid, it is best to confirm that he was not involved."

Charon glanced up as his hood slipped off his head. "We also recovered footage of the supposed human that attempted to sell magical artifacts to non-supernaturals."

"The one the Queen's Court barista told you about?" I asked, stretching my memory of everything we'd learned when Noctus and the others had visited the coffee shop when they were first searching for signs of the artifacts manufacturer. "He was trying to sell them outside of supernatural markets and wasn't a very convincing human, right?"

"Correct," Noctus said. "One of my people works in a shop whose storefront overlooks the market. He was able to retrieve security footage."

"Thus far no one has recognized him either," Charon said. "So it is possible he is working with the tracker. Although it seems most likely the tracker's goal continues to be you, and his involvement in fae politics is an attempt to get you from Noctus without having to confront him, and the artifact seller is entirely unrelated."

"Do you think the tracker knows who Noctus is?" I asked.

"No," Noctus said. "He wouldn't have approached the house if he did. But his willingness to involve others means tighter security is necessary. I expect he will try another tactic soon if he cannot use the Seelie and Unseelie fae to snatch you."

Judging by the stony looks on Noctus and Charon, they were still displeased about the attack on Ker and me, so it was better not to comment. I shoved another piece of bread into my mouth. "This is delicious," I said as Aristide and Ker joined us.

"It's elven paneum," Charon said. "A fried confectionary food typically sold from street carts."

I'd finished my paneum, but that left me with sticky fingers—because I absolutely wasn't going to lick them in front of *elves*.

Before I got a chance to ponder the problem, Noctus placed a moist towelette in my hand.

"Thank you." I wiped my hands clean, and the towelette left my fingers smelling like lavender.

Before I could look for a trash can—if elven cities even had trash cans?—Noctus plucked the towelette from my hands and gave me a canteen of water.

I automatically opened it and took a sip, which was when it hit me.

He's still treating me like I'm a cat.

Our heart to heart that we'd had while he healed me must have restored me to his good graces, and he was falling back into old patterns. He'd fed me, watered me, and was tracking me like he had when I was Ama.

Still, I was feeling better than when I'd first entered the city, though it did occur to me that the fact I felt *better* after the pet treatment was a worrying sign.

"We've checked with three of the elves to confirm they don't recognize the tracker. Would you like me to make appointments with anyone else?" Charon asked.

"Yes—ask Prydwen. I wish to be certain and not assume things," Noctus said.

"Of course, Your Majesty." Charon checked his notebook again.

I took another sip of water, when there was an explosion of feathers above me. I looked up, and a striped raccoon tail with glossy pigeon wings almost dropped into my face. It was French Fry.

How did he find me here?

French Fry course-corrected and made a wobbly landing on the ground, where he frantically flapped his wings and tripped on my shoes.

"Hi, French Fry." I capped Noctus's canteen, then crouched down and held my hand out to the trash griffin.

French Fry waddled so he was under my hand, then cooed in delight when I stroked his head and back.

"You know this..." Noctus clicked his mouth shut, and I could tell he'd narrowly avoided calling French Fry vermin.

"Yes. I see him all around Magiford. He's my friend."

"I do recall you mentioning him." Charon's normally serene expression briefly crusted over with distaste as French Fry peered up at him with one orange eye, then swiveled his head and looked at him out of the other eye. "But..."

"You didn't believe me?" I asked.

"No," Charon slowly said. "It is merely that trash griffins—er... the species that your...French Fry...belongs to are not typically seen outside of the Night Court."

Noctus frowned and glanced at the glowing barrier that spanned the city for miles around. "Nor should one have been able to follow you into my realm. There are spells against it."

"He doesn't mean any harm, and he's not attached to anyone. I don't think he spends much time in the realm of the Night Court based on how often I see him," I said.

"Do you think there is a security risk?" Charon asked.

Noctus shook his head. "I would have felt a disturbance in the spells."

I scratched French Fry on the top of the head, and he was so excited he whacked me with his wings. "What did you do, French Fry?"

Noctus crouched down next to me. He briefly held out his

hand to French Fry—who nibbled on the pads of his fingers—then checked over the little guy. "Perhaps it is not that surprising he was able to enter here. He found you—a supposedly dead race." Noctus opened both of French Fry's wings—I was pretty sure he was checking for spells based on the way he stared at him.

"It's said trash griffins used to be smarter creatures," Charon said. "But I never interacted much with them in my life."

"Nor did I," Noctus agreed.

"He's cute!" Ker called as she and Aristide joined our group. She patted Aristide's hand, then knelt next to me. "He's got a raccoon tail and rear feet with a gray pigeon head and wings," she described for Aristide.

"Do you want to pet him, Aristide?" I asked.

French Fry pecked at the ground, then choked and made a hacking noise.

"No, hearing him—and his description—is more than enough," Aristide shuddered. "I am perfectly capable of recalling what trash griffins look like—though they were not called that back in the day."

"What were they called?" I asked.

"Something not suitable for the present company," Aristide said.

Noctus stood up, his hands falling to the sword strapped at his side as he did a visual sweep of the area. "Why does a creature of the Night Court follow you around?"

"I'm not sure." I stood up and tugged my shorts straight as French Fry hopped onto one of my shoes, promptly lost his balance, and pitched over the side. "He just started following me around Magiford when I moved here. I usually see him at least once or twice a week."

"Interesting," Noctus said.

"That explains why we saw a drastic increase in the number of trash griffins we ran into around Magiford," Aristide said.

"Mmm." Charon had checked out of the conversation and was

staring at my blue jean shorts with narrowed eyes. "Is this a typical sample of your wardrobe, Chloe?"

I looked down at my plain cotton t-shirt and shorts. "Uh, for summer, yes?"

"I see." Charon cleared his throat. "If there are no objections to...*French Fry's* presence, I believe now would be an excellent moment to check with the armorer to see if they finished with the commission of the short sword and daggers I asked for."

Noctus glanced at me. "They are finished. They sent word to me since I also had a specialty harness made for her—she can't have her daggers falling out."

I had to disentangle French Fry from my shoelaces. "Why would they fall out?"

"In your new training it's very unlikely they'd stay in place with what you're going to do," Noctus said.

"New training?" I parroted.

"Yes. Given your poor luck despite your inclination to avoid fighting, it's high time you learn how a shadow really operates," Noctus said.

"Ooh." Aristide whistled. "Am I the only one who thought that sounded ominous?"

"Probably because besides Noctus and Charon, you're the only one old enough to know what that means," Ker said.

"How is it that despite being a lover of self-affirmations and leadership classes, you are utterly uncharismatic?" Aristide asked.

Ker positioned herself so she was slightly in front of Aristide. "The self-affirmations are to boost *my* confidence, not yours."

Aristide snorted as he tucked his hand around her upper arm. "How generous. To the armorer?"

"To the armorer," Ker agreed, and the two set out across the plaza.

"I'll go ahead," Charon said. "And inform the armory."

Noctus nodded, and Charon disappeared into the crowd.

Noctus and I followed Ker and Aristide—who were bickering.

French Fry tripped a few elves before he also took off, landing on the stone bridge and almost falling over the side.

I awkwardly cleared my throat in the silence. "Thank you for the paneum." I stumbled over the unfamiliar word, but Noctus didn't seem offended.

"I'm glad you enjoyed it," he said.

I twitched my shoulders, then leaned in and whispered. "Is it really okay for me to just...*walk* around like this?" I asked.

Noctus scanned the crowd, nodding whenever anyone stopped to bow or curtsey to him. "What are you referring to?"

"I'm a shadow," I said. "Isn't it bad for me—as your enemy—to see all of this?"

Noctus stared at me as if I'd just publicly lowered my IQ. "You didn't even *know* you were a shadow. Somehow I doubt you have nefarious plans to carry this information off to your studio-apartment lair and start plotting our demise."

"I'm glad you realize that." I nervously scratched my arm as we passed under the stone bridge and the plaza narrowed into a city street. "But I thought everyone would be...upset by me—or by my existence."

"*I* was upset because I realized Amalourne was magic, and that she was connected to Chloe of Book Nookery, but I hadn't realized you were one and the same. That you are a shadow is irrelevant," Noctus said. "Except for the fact that it should have occurred to me that some of them survived. As they could match us elves, it stands to reason that they would have been capable of out-planning us."

"So does everyone in the city know? That I'm Ama—and a shadow—I mean." A woody scent grabbed my nose, and I saw a stall—shoved between two stone buildings—stocked with freshly chopped wood of all different types. I couldn't tell what kind of trees they were, but I smelled cedar and pine, and the different shades of the chopped logs were fascinating.

"Yes," Noctus said. "I sent an email out two days ago, along with a realm-wide text announcement."

I'd been watching a teenager in a leather jacket haggle for a log, and then load it onto his scooter, but at that tidbit of info I had to gape up at Noctus. "You guys have email and text messages?"

"Yes. It's the easiest method of communication." Noctus frowned. "That *surprises* you?"

"No, well, yes. It's just supernaturals like fae and even vampires aren't always on top of human technology. I assumed elves would be similar," I said. We passed what looked like a mechanic shop based on the smell of oil and gasoline that wafted from it. When I glanced inside I saw a couple of elves gawking at me—they hastily bowed.

"We had to adapt," Noctus said. "Because we needed humans to survive, and we couldn't let other supernaturals learn of our existence."

"I see." I instinctively ducked, barely avoiding French Fry when he glided overhead. He found an elaborately arched lamp post to perch on, which he sat on for a moment before he started sliding to the side and had to fly again or fall off his perch.

"And everyone's fine with the binding magic?" I asked.

"Why wouldn't they be?" Noctus's voice was dark.

"Well..." I tried to carefully pick my words as I saw—out of the corner of my eye—a little boy point at me and say something to his mother, who forced his arm down. "Aristide didn't seem thrilled when he heard about it, and I don't think Charon was exactly giddy with the realization, either."

"Aristide wasn't thrilled because he has the personality of a moldy blanket that has been left to soak in a swamp for several centuries," Noctus said.

Aristide—with his vampire hearing—stopped long enough to turn around and scowl in our direction. "I heard that," he snapped. "And I hope that trash griffin of hers poops on you!"

Noctus held out his hand toward Aristide. "A very fine example."

I cracked a smile as Ker and Aristide stopped outside a store that smelled like coal, hot metal, and leather.

"Here it is—the armory," Ker announced.

The building was made of the same white stone as the rest of the city, but dark timbers marked out the edges of the structure's walls, and the glass door and neon "open" sign were mind-breakingly modern.

It was two stories, but the second floor was an open-air shelter with practice dummies and targets set up in orderly rows that I could see from the street.

Noctus opened the door and motioned me inside, where I discovered another mixture of modern human tech with ancient elven lore.

The armory had display cases—*glass* display cases—and each one was fixed with at least three LED lights pointed at the weapon encased in it to make it glitter.

The displays were filled with metal weapons—swords, daggers, that kind of thing—no polearms or axes. But there were some leather armor, scabbards, and gauntlets on display, too.

Charon stood at the back of the store with two elves. One of the elves leaned against a counter and clutched a computer tablet with one of those credit-card reading accessories plugged into it.

"Your Majesty." Charon bowed, then swiveled his attention to me. "Chloe, this is Rodaric and Kestya. They own and run the armory." Charon indicated first the male then the female elf.

CHAPTER SIXTEEN

Chloe

Rodaric was tall and slender, with long, elegant fingers, a monocle over his right eye, and hair that was more gray than black.

Kestya's silvery blond hair was pulled back in a bun, and had biceps that would make Pat green with envy.

"I believe—in addition to the original order—there are a few pieces I'd like to show you, Your Majesty, to gain your opinion on whether they'd be suitable for Chloe," Charon said.

"Lead on," Noctus said.

Charon headed back to the front of the store, Noctus going with him.

"We're going too," Aristide said.

"Why?" Ker asked.

"Because I intend to make a case that Charon should teach her how to use poisons, so she'll need vials and a holster for them, too," Aristide said. "Don't you know poisons were traditionally used by shadows?"

Ker opened her mouth, and Aristide held up his hand. "Wait —don't answer that. I can tell you're just going to call me old. Off we go!"

Ker laughed. "We'll be back, Chloe. Enjoy your new gear!"

I nervously waved, then grimaced when I realized Aristide wouldn't see it. "Yeah...thanks."

The duo headed out, and Rodaric and Kestya bowed deeply to their backs.

By the time my friends had intermingled with the display cases again, the elven pair turned their curious gazes to me.

"You are Chloe, who was once Ama?" Kestya asked.

I tried not to blush as I bowed to them. "Yes."

The pair exchanged looks. Something must have passed between them, because both turned to me with quiet grins that made the spirals in their eyes swirl.

"She's perfect," Kestya murmured.

"An excellent fit." Rodaric nodded his approval as he ducked behind the counter.

I fidgeted nervously. "I'm sorry...what?"

Kestya bowed. "I beg your pardon, Chloe. It is merely that you are exquisite."

I stared at Kestya with her perfect skin, frizz-free hair, and enchanting spiral eyes. "What?" I repeated.

Rodaric re-emerged from behind the counter, holding an armload of leather. "Here is your new harness—designed so your weapons won't slide out during acrobatics."

"Acrobatics?" I echoed, feeling more like a parrot than a cat.

"Flips, climbing—anything that would have you hanging upside down," Rodaric explained.

Acrobatics? What were the original shadows like that I have to be worried about my weapons sliding out due to being suspended upside down? Although I have done a lot of scrambling across rooftops in my life...

"Here is your short sword—though to be correct it is actually a large dagger for an average elf given your shorter size," Kestya explained, unknowingly rubbing salt in my wounds.

"It's to be your primary weapon, so we have specially designed a back scabbard for it, to make it easy to pull and use," Rodaric explained as he fitted a scabbard to the back of a leather harness. "This is how you wear it."

For the next few minutes, Rodaric and Kestya taught me how to assemble my new getup.

The base design was a belt that hooked into my pants, and a secondary specialty belt that buckled diagonally across my front, then hooked diagonally across my back and buckled into my pants belt.

The scabbard—made of leather with beautiful designs stamped into it—was threaded through the back buckle. The left side of the scabbard had a few inches of extra leather that sat across my back, creating a ramp for my new weapon—which was necessary because the left side of the scabbard had an open slit.

The slit made it easy to pull my short sword from my back with a single hand since I could angle it out—exposing the blade much more quickly than if I had to pull the full thing free.

"It's also quieter," Rodaric—the unusual scabbard's artist—explained. "And the decorative work on the crossguard here," he pointed to two tiny triangular pieces of the crossguard that settled over the two flat sides of the short sword, "they hook onto the scabbard. But for extra security, you need to use this leather strap to secure it." He showed me the strap that hooked over the crossguard, pinning the sword into the scabbard. "I built the scabbard for the short sword, so it's a tight fit, but you needed to be able to pull the dagger free with a tug, and the momentum from the acrobatics you'll likely employ will heft a similar pull, so you *need* to have your weapons strapped if you aren't actively fighting."

It was still murky to me what acrobatics they expected me to do, but that was a question for Noctus and Charon, so I focused on sucking in all the information the pair was offering me.

"To counterbalance the weight of your short sword, there are three small daggers that hook into your chest strap." Kestya showed me the weapons before sliding them into place now that the various straps were properly buckled. "You will have additional daggers hooked to your pants belt, but Lord Charon said he will add those into your routine over time."

"For now you'll need to practice sheathing your short sword on your back," Rodaric said. "Muscle memory will make it easier over time."

"Thank you." I rubbed my nose as the smell of conditioned leather filled my senses.

Rodaric bowed his head. "It was our honor to receive a commission from His Majesty."

Kestya probably would have bowed as well—it seemed like a gesture elves used as often as nodding—but she was narrowing her eyes at my daggers, pursing her lips as she scrutinized their placement.

I looked back over my shoulder, momentarily distracted by the new weight on my chest and shoulders from my new get up, and peered at the front of the store. I didn't see Noctus anywhere, but Charon, Aristide, and Ker were gathered around a display case.

They seem distracted...I'll risk it.

I sucked in a breath of air and screwed up what little bit of courage I possessed before asking, "Does it bother you—to be asked to make weapons for a shadow?"

"Hm?" Kestya finally looked up from her glaring match with my new daggers.

"Shadows and elves are technically enemies...aren't they?" I asked.

Kestya wrinkled her forehead before she shifted to look at her business partner for guidance.

Rodaric smiled and adjusted his monocle so it glinted in the light. "Elves tend to be our own worst enemies," he said, his voice calm and practical. "No help is needed in that area."

"But the history with shadows..." I trailed off, not certain where to go.

"Is history," Kestya gently said. "Rodaric and I were alive when there were more shadows...but what most humans never ponder about immortal lives is how much you *forget*."

"Kestya and I have forgotten more history than the USA has made since it became a country," Rodaric mused. "But, then again, it's easy for us to forget. Shadows typically went after the leaders of the elves and the various royal families. We never fought a shadow. So perhaps we should ask you, Chloe, are you fine with receiving weapons made by elves?"

Kestya popped off a nod as she leaned back and propped her elbows up on the counter.

"I..." I looked back and forth between the two of them, surprised by their question. "I didn't even know what I was until recently."

I paused, and the air was achingly quiet. The faint tick-tock of the cuckoo clock that hung on the wall sounded like drums in my ears, whereas Aristide's soured voice was the faintest murmur as he hissed something at Ker.

"There's been trouble," I said, thinking of the tracker, "so I guess I assumed it would be that way with everyone here."

Kestya shook her head. "Those of us who came to His Majesty to survive, we had to be different. Our mindset had to be different. No one in this city will make trouble with you."

"You came to Noctus so you could survive?" I asked. "When he—" I cut myself off from blurting out that Noctus had killed his entire family.

Rodaric glanced to the front of the store, where Charon and

the others were. "His Majesty was the surest way of survival," he said. "Provided you agreed with his...actions."

I stared blankly at the pair. *You agreed with his actions? You agreed with him being a...what did he call it? A kingslayer? Unless...was there more to it?*

There must have been. Noctus obviously hadn't done it to become king—he clearly found the position annoying and would have been happy to ghost the entire city if he thought he could get away with it.

"What do you think of your new gear, Chloe?" Ker called to me as she and Aristide walked arm in arm toward us.

"It's beautiful," I said.

"It will do," Charon said. "We shall see how serviceable it is during practice."

"I think I'll adjust pretty fast," I said. "The daggers felt like they were made for my grip."

"That's because they were," Charon said. "And I wasn't referring to our practice sessions."

I squinted up at the elf. "Huh?"

"I'M GOING TO DIE." I had my arms wrapped around a stone statue of a lion. I was clinging to it like a leech, so I could feel its rough, stony texture through the thin jersey fabric of my black, long-sleeved shirt. "I'm going to die. Tonight. Right now."

"We're up here because you're a shadow, which means you *won't* die, or even get injured if you jump from here." Noctus fearlessly strode past me, casually strolling around the edge of the platform, ignoring the winds that tugged at the black hood he had pulled up over his golden hair.

"Genetically I might be a shadow, but I don't have their training. I can't really be called a shadow." I squirmed as my clutching grasp of the statue smashed my three new daggers into my chest so their scabbards uncomfortably poked at me.

We were on top of the newly constructed clocktower in Magiford. The *clocktower*. The little walkway/platform we were on served as a slight overhang above the actual clock on the tower, and the shiny copper roof of the tower sloped down into the walkway, making it the highest point you could reach unless you wanted to scale the steeply slanted roof and maybe go impale yourself on the vane on the tippy top.

I didn't even want to know how many stories we were up. The whistling wind and the twinkling lights of the buildings below were enough to assure me we were *too high*.

"That's why we're here—to get you the training and experience so you can properly begin using the advantages of your birthright." Noctus turned away from the edge and approached me, fixing his gray-black gloves.

He was clothed head to toe in a gray-ish black—I'd already received a lecture that pitch black was actually bad for night camouflage because it stuck out in the grays and shadows of the city.

With a mask covering the lower portion of his face and his hood up, he looked...different. I'd say more intense, except there was an unmistakable glimmer of amusement in his eyes as he studied me. He was...more free. His movements always had a careless grace to them, but everything he did was measured. That wasn't the feeling I got now.

"This can't be legal," I said.

"It is my property," Moneybags Noctus pointed out.

"*I know*."

"I promise, Chloe, you'll be safe falling at this height," Noctus said. "If you're scared, jump as a cat."

"So I can shed fur the whole way down and so my yowling will be less notable than the frantic screams I'd have as a human?" I asked.

Noctus's eyes swirled—at least he found me funny? "No," he chuckled. "Because cats have a thing called 'the righting reflex,' which allows them to land on their feet. Cat legs are formed in a way that makes it easier to reduce impact and absorb shock. Surely you've experienced that before?"

I reluctantly unhooked my leg off the front of the statue. "Yeah. I've jumped off a house or three in my lifetime. But then I'd only be jumping one or two stories down. This is..." I glanced out at the city. Almost all the buildings—with a few exceptions like Magiford's fanciest hotel, *Luxe Sejour*—were shorter than the clocktower, treating me to the sight of rooftops, small streetlights, and sputtering neon signs that stayed on all night long.

That's terrifying. Look away—look away!

I craned my neck so I stared at the copper roofing of the tower spire next to me. "It's too high," I concluded, my voice cracking.

"It's a good height, yes," Noctus said. "But heights like this are safer for you than something that's only a few stories up. As a cat you can increase your drag force if you stretch your legs out. A cat's terminal velocity is much smaller than a human's. Combine that with the increased drag and your natural magic, and a fall like this will feel like nothing."

"Look, I want to learn how to protect myself," I said. "But I don't think I'm going to have many rooftop fights."

"No, but a shadow's acrobatic abilities are a huge leverage that no other supernatural—werewolves and vampires included—can match," Noctus countered. "If you can use it to get distance between yourself and your opponent, it will make it that much easier to defeat them."

I considered hooking my leg over the statue again.

Noctus must have guessed what I was thinking because he added—slowly, as if it pained him to even think the words much less utter them, "It will also make escaping any supernaturals much easier."

I froze, considering his words.

He's right. No fae would jump off a building after me. If I get better about falling—and climbing—no supernatural will be able to snatch me anymore.

I peeled myself off the statue. "You're *positive* I can survive this?" I asked.

"Yes." Noctus rolled his shoulders in a shrug. "It's far more dangerous for me to be jumping off. Come on." He walked up to the edge of the platform and casually leaned against the brickwork that made a hip high barrier.

"I feel like we should make a public service announcement." I shuffled across the platform, dragging my feet. "So any humans happening to watch us know, 'do not attempt this professional—well, one idiot and one professional—stunt.'"

Noctus set a booted foot on the barrier and then stepped up. "We're out here at three in the morning precisely so we *won't* be seen. An announcement isn't necessary."

"Yeah." I glumly peered over the side of the tower.

I didn't see anyone—or even a moving car—out on the streets, but the world tilted alarmingly as I heard a roaring in my ears. "I changed my mind," I gulped. "I don't want to do this."

I started to rapidly back up, but Noctus caught me by the hand. "Amalourne," he said. "I *know* you can do this. I would never ask you to risk yourself."

I hunched my shoulders up, my nerves flopping around in my gut despite his use of my old nickname.

"If you are so unwilling to trust yourself, then trust me," Noctus said. "With my increased terminal velocity, I'll land much faster than you. If it appears you won't land correctly, I'll catch you with my magic."

It would be stupid not to trust him. He's an elf king. There's no way he's not capable of catching me, and he's proven I can trust him with my life.

I sucked in a breath, then scrambled onto the wall with him before I could second guess myself.

Noctus squeezed my fingers, then released my hand. "Due to the inherent magic you have as a shadow, you can survive a jump like this, but I still recommend you change into a cat for your first jump. Your brain will have an easier time accepting it since cats *can* survive a leap like this."

I twitched my new harness into place and then checked to make sure the leather straps were secured over my short sword and my daggers. I'd like to say it was because I was responsible and I didn't want them falling out, but really it was just to give my twitchy fingers something to do. "Okay."

"Push off the building as a human to give yourself the force to move away from the walls, and then transform," he said.

My belly gurgled, and I slapped my arms around my stomach so I was effectively clutching it. "Okay."

"Amalourne."

"Huh?" I finally peered up at Noctus, and felt like I was speared through the heart. I couldn't see his mouth because of his mask, but his eyes definitely weren't laughing now.

They blaze. Like fire. Consuming and yet...beautiful.

"You're bound to me." Noctus brushed a piece of my brunette hair that had escaped the tight bun I'd yanked it back into. "You have a piece of me. I won't let anything happen to you." He peeled my right hand off my belly, engulfing it in his much larger hand, before he raised my fingers, pressing them against his mask. I couldn't feel his skin through the mesh of his mask, but my fingers traced the curve of his lips.

For a second I forgot about the height and all my fears. I just felt Noctus's eyes on mine, and it was hard to breathe.

Noctus's eyes softened. He rubbed his thumb over the top of my hand, released it, then casually tipped over the side of the clocktower, plummeting to the ground.

I gurgled. "That crazy, insane, lunatic!"

Before I lost my nerve—before I had enough time to think about it—I jumped off the clocktower after him.

I felt a scream claw at my throat when I started to free-fall—my brain panicked at the feeling of *nothing*—so I tapped my magic and switched to my cat form.

As a cat, my body was easier to maneuver with magical spurred instincts kicking in.

I arched my back, and my front half twisted on an entirely different axis from my back half, so my front end flipped around, followed by my back feet so I'd land feet first. I then stretched my little legs out as Noctus had suggested.

Despite my best efforts, I yowled. The whistling air, the rapidly flashing floors of the clocktower, it was just a little too much to keep me quiet.

This isn't training—it's insanity!

It seemed like the ground was rushing up, but I landed, my legs taking the brunt of it by touching down first with my paws, and then I rolled my body into it.

I wheezed, and as I had predicted some of my fur fell out from the surge of anxiety I'd just experienced, but nothing hurt.

The landing—which was on the cement sidewalk—hadn't been hard or painful. It sent a jolt through my joints, but I was shaky from the leftover anxiety, not injuries.

"See?"

I puffed up and flipped around, calming a little when I realized it was just Noctus.

"You're fine," he said.

I tapped my magic, shifting from cat to human in less time than it took to blink. "It didn't hurt, but I'm not sure about being *fine*." I shivered as my heart frantically beat in my chest.

"You're adjusting." Noctus turned away from me and walked through one of the brick arches that made up the base of the clocktower. "After enough repetitions, you'll no longer react. Particularly once you learn how to do it in your human form."

"Wait...I have to do that again?" I tottered after him, lurching to one side as my stress was still strong enough to mess with my coordination skills.

"Of course." Noctus punched in the keycode at a door labeled "employees only," then set his hand on the door.

The area must have been spelled to recognize him, because the door clicked open, revealing a staircase.

Noctus propped the door open, then glanced back at me. "You have to learn how to safely fall, first, before all else."

I VAULTED over the brick ledge of the clocktower and turned into a cat as I started my free-fall.

I fell more slowly as a cat, and it was easier to position my body correctly for landing, so it was my preferred jumping shape after the countless jumps Noctus had made me practice.

He hadn't been wrong, though. I was a lot calmer about falling now. In fact, the worst part was probably the endless stairs I had to haul my carcass up to get to the top of the clocktower after jumping over the side.

What's up with elves and stairs? Did no one tell them about elevators?

I had fallen almost to the bottom of the clocktower—it was time to get ready to change back into my human shape.

A shadow fluttered beneath me. I saw the feathers, and realized who it was.

French Fry—you idiot! You're going to get us both killed!

I wailed, but thankfully French Fry either got distracted or lost his balance—maybe both—because he wheeled aside just in time to avoid colliding with me midair.

I almost missed turning into a human, but I pulled it off, landing lightly as my magic rolled through me.

I turned on my heels and scowled at the sky. "French Fry—get out of the way!" I called in a hissing whisper.

French Fry—who had shown up about half an hour ago—cooed at me before he crash landed onto one of the ground level clocktower lights, which looked like a lantern to match the cathedral-esque feel to the clocktower.

I shook my head at the trash griffin, but couldn't help my grin.

I'd been practicing for at least an hour. The horizon was still dark, but the moon no longer hung in the sky, and I was starting to see the occasional car.

Thankfully, I wasn't dragging like I thought I would since I slept most nights now—thank you late night shifts at Book Nookery!

I propped my arms up on my side, supporting myself as I craned my neck to peer up at the top of the clocktower.

Noctus—a dark shape—leaped off the side of the tower.

He fell considerably faster than me and had to cushion his landing with magic.

Even then, he made a lot of noise. The sound of his magic hitting the sidewalk was like a muted thunderstrike, and he had to roll when he hit the ground to help dissipate some of the extra force, so he needed more space for his landing than I did.

I glanced at French Fry as I approached Noctus, checking to make sure the trash griffin wasn't getting into trouble—he'd already gotten into the clocktower twice, and I'd had to chase him out both times. "We should probably stop soon. I think the early morning shift is starting to show up for work, and someone is bound to see us tower jumping—why are you kneeling?"

Noctus had popped out of his roll into a kneeling position—where he stayed as he rubbed the back of his neck.

He tugged down his black mask so I could see his sardonic grin. "In case you didn't know, we can't *all* fall from such heights so effortlessly. I told you that I have far more terminal velocity, too."

"But you're an elf," I said.

"Elves have physical limitations." He stood, rolling his shoulders back with the motion.

I blinked. "No. There's no way I can do something that's harder for you."

"*All* of your abilities make things that are hard for me easy for you," Noctus said. "Why else would we elves have feared shadows so greatly?"

"I thought it was the sneaking around and our immunity to magic," I said.

"It is that, too." Noctus reached out and tugged my harness straight for me. "But even your ability to fall is beyond most elves. I had to be the one to teach you this falling strategy because Charon and any member of my Court would not survive it without sustaining injuries."

"I see..." I leaned forward on the tips of my toes, and the black, shin-high boots Charon had given me bent with the movement, conforming to my muscles and the bottoms of my feet.

Living with Noctus and Charon has challenged the historic picture I had of elves. In a lot of ways, he's more powerful, but it's kind of weird to think that they have limits. Well, all other elves have limits. I'm not so convinced Noctus shares those limits.

"Thank you—for helping me find my limits." I stared up at the clocktower—it was easier to look at than Noctus with its illuminated clock face. "It never occurred to me I could do something like this."

"You had no way of knowing," Noctus said. "You were adopted, weren't you?"

"Yeah. I was found at the emergency entrance of a hospital with a note that said my name was Chloe." I looked away from the clock face and instead glanced up and down the street, glancing at the many traffic lights—which blinked yellow. "The hospital cameras only picked up a figure wearing all black—they never saw a face, and no one saw them drop me off. Mom was a nurse at the hospital, so she and Dad asked to adopt me." I nervously plucked at my shirt. I had sweated through it after my first few jumps off the clocktower in my anxiety, but I had long since dried off.

Noctus tilted his head so his face wasn't quite so shadowed by his hood. "Your adopted family are regular humans, yes?"

"Yeah, they're humans, but there's nothing regular about them," I said. "They're amazing—Dad, Mom, my brother and my sister." I smiled at the thought of Pat and Joy, until I heard French Fry when he launched himself off the light.

He landed on the sidewalk a few feet away and started pecking.

"It's impressive that with a human family you're as skilled at your powers as you are—in ways even shadows weren't." Noctus scratched his jaw. "Although perhaps it's because you were raised by humans that you are the way you are."

"My sister and brother helped me a lot with learning to act like a cat, and my parents took me to all the offered magic classes they could find." I knelt and held out my hand to French Fry, but the greedy creature must have seen something he wanted to eat, because he hotfooted it in the opposite direction, his head bobbing as he narrowed in on a garbage can.

I shook my head at the griffin, then brushed my knees off as I stood up again. "My family did everything they could to help me figure out what I was," I said. "It wasn't their fault the Curia Cloisters didn't have a classification for me."

French Fry cooed when he got to the trash can, then flung himself inside. A moment passed, and one of his hoot-like coos wafted out of the can.

"No, only the oldest of vampires would be able to recall what you are," Noctus agreed. "And I doubt any of them are active enough to trouble themselves with something like the Curia Cloisters."

Noctus approached the employees only door we'd been using all night, entered the keycode, and opened it for me.

I slipped past him, and sighed at the endless stairs.

Maybe I *should talk to them about elevators. Because even with the endless stairs to get to the basement training room...this is so much worse.*

Instead of starting up the stairs, Noctus slipped through a door on the opposite side of the stairwell.

"We're done?" I asked.

"Yes. You're right, we'll soon be spotted. The eatery and the flower shop will begin opening processes in approximately an hour." Noctus pointed to the two different gated store fronts that were closest to us. "Unless—are you worried about your pet?" He had started to stroll down the tomb-silent aisle that stretched between the small shops that made up the lower floor of the clocktower—which had opened up approximately a week or two prior—but he stopped to look back at me.

"French Fry? Nah," I said. "He's eating, and he never stays with me. He just visits."

My phone chimed with a text message notification. I undid the snap over my pocket that kept my phone safe.

"Is that Charon?" Noctus pulled his own cellphone from his pocket and checked it.

I smiled when I unlocked my screen and saw the message.

Wut's the family alfredo sauce recipe? Joy knows it, but if i ask her 4 it again she'll be annoying.

"No, it's a text from my brother, Pat." I typed out a reply that I'd get him the recipe later.

"He's awake now?" Noctus slipped down a narrow passageway between the flower shop and the next-door store—a small boutique clothing store.

A floral scent tickled my nose—compliments of the flower shop. I didn't know enough about flowers to be able to tell what specific scents they were, but they were so full and ripe smelling it made me rub my nose.

"He's a detective in a police force." I followed after Noctus, our voices echoing in the silence of the clocktower. "He gets a lot of weird shifts."

"I see." Noctus opened another "employees only" door. This one opened to...more stairs.

I smashed my lips together and worked on not groaning as Noctus closed the door behind me.

"Coming?" he asked.

I put my foot on the lowest stair, then paused. "I wanted to ask, have you ever used an elevator?"

Noctus paused two steps up from me. "Of course. Why?"

"No reason," I glumly said.

Something cracked, and then a thunderous toll rang loud enough that I felt it buzz in the molars of my teeth.

I swapped to my cat form and hissed, jumping up two stairs and pressing myself against Noctus's leg before I realized it was just the bell in the clocktower.

It's a pretty noise, but it's a lot louder than I realized when it's directly overhead.

Noctus wasn't surprised at all, in fact I was pretty sure he was laughing—though I couldn't hear him over the toll of the bell.

CHAPTER SEVENTEEN

Chloe

I flattened my ears to my skull as the remaining three tolls sounded. When the sound finally cleared, Noctus was still laughing.

It was a pleasant, low sound that would have made my spine tingle as a human, if I hadn't been the cause of the laughter.

I flicked my tail as I climbed up a stair—feeling too embarrassed to turn back into a human.

"I'm not laughing because the sound frightened you, I'm laughing because you're so capable. There's not much that can take you out," Noctus said. "And yet...a bell...." He laughed again, and I swear the area *brightened*. His laugh was so genuine and infectious, I found it hard not to purr even though I was determinedly climbing up the despicable stairs it seemed Noctus was fond of including in his architecture.

Elves. It's not enough to be so superior, they also have to be charming enough to bend the rules of nature, I glumly thought.

I looked back at him over my shoulder in disgust.

Noctus had an elbow resting on the stair railing, and his posture was sloped and relaxed as he leaned over.

It was a different side to him I'd only seen as "Amalourne," and it was a thousand times more captivating. Kingly Noctus was powerful and intimidating. Relaxed Noctus was irresistibly warm.

I could feel pure wild magic coming off him, but it blew past me like the wind—unable to stick thanks to my magic resistance.

Good riddance.

"You really hate stairs, don't you?" Noctus tugged his hood down. He was still smiling—with his eyes, even. They almost glowed as they swirled.

At least he's not laughing.

"Here," Noctus said. "I'll just carry you."

Before I realized what was happening, Noctus bent over and scooped me up, propping me on his chest.

Just like old times, I automatically placed my paws on either side of the neckline of his shirt, hooking my claws into the fabric. Noctus tucked me against his arm so I was half cradled, and his hand supported my rear legs.

Woah, I didn't think he'd ever pick me up again—outside of acting for the Paragon anyway.

Surprised by the turn of events, I meowed.

"No, I'm not putting you down," Noctus correctly guessed my thoughts.

He took the stairs two at a time. Although I felt a lot more comfortable in his arms than when he first unwittingly cat-napped me, I still didn't like the out-of-control feeling.

I better change back. Then he'll let me go!

When he reached the top stair of the floor I made the switch, popping into my human shape.

Noctus didn't even *react* to the sudden increase in his armload —I'd give a lot to have strength like that considering that stairs made me wheeze. Maybe I needed to increase my practice time with Charon after all.

He just shifted his arms, tilting my weight so I was splayed against his chest.

"What, what—excuse me?" I sputtered as I threw my arms around his shoulders for balance.

"I assumed you'd prefer this position," Noctus said. "Given how little you liked your rear being touched—much less looked at —as Amalourne."

Slightly concerned for my own powers of observation, I peered down at the lower half of my body. Noctus was so disgustingly tall, my legs dangled, except for the arm he had wrapped around my lower thighs. When I'd first changed his arm had been...higher.

"You could just put me down," I said. "Carrying extra weight like this on a staircase can't be safe."

Noctus didn't even blink. "Safety concern? You barely weigh as much as half of the weapons I use."

I clung to his shoulders, which made each bounding step he took—he was still going up the stairs two at a time—more of a smooth rocking motion. But that meant being close to him, and there was something distinctly embarrassing about the ordeal that made my cheeks burn.

I didn't get close to people outside my family too much. I'd dealt with it out of necessity when Noctus and the others thought I was a cat, but besides Ker's tendency to snuggle up, they hadn't invaded my personal space in my human shape. It felt *weird* to have an arm thrown around Noctus's neck. I could feel every shift in his muscles, and every nerve in my body blazed with awareness so my skin felt like pins and needles were prickling me.

My cheeks burned with bashfulness, and I cleared my throat. "Please allow me to rephrase that: might I suggest you put me down?"

"You can suggest," Noctus said with regal approval.

"*Why* won't you put me down?" I asked, hastily changing tactics.

"The enjoyment factor." Noctus turned a corner in the staircase.

After almost biting my tongue when Noctus jumped another stair, I glumly rested my chin on his shoulder and stared backwards. "Fine, go ahead and laugh at the shy cat."

"Am I laughing?"

"You said you were enjoying this."

"I never said it's because I found the situation amusing."

I pushed off Noctus's shoulder so I could gawk at his face, but Noctus reached the gate at that exact moment and stepped through it.

Magic surged through my body. It washed through my system so I couldn't see, hear, or feel anything else, until Noctus cleared the gate, stepping into the elven city.

This particular gate spat us out on a platform by the arched bridge that crossed the plaza we'd visited on the way to the armorer.

The horizon line was starting to lighten in the elf realm from the inky black of night to a velvety purple, but it was still so dark you needed all the streetlights—which were lit by the white/blue flames that burned in Noctus's villa.

A few elves were out and about, but the roads were empty and the plaza was silent except for the gurgle of the fountain.

Noctus still didn't release me as he shifted his weight, snagging the iron gate—this one had floral swirls and a leaf pattern—with his foot and kicking it shut.

His expression was as casual as the motion—though I noticed he didn't have the usual hardness in his face. His laughing session from the bell seemed to have lasting effects.

On the other hand, the longer he was holding on to me, the more my intelligence seemed to leak out of my ears.

It wasn't that he was heart-stoppingly handsome. That's something you can get used to. For heaven's sake, I'd seen his sleeping face enough as a cat.

No, it was that it was *Noctus*, and he was being playful.

"Okay," I babbled, trying to make sense of the situation which had my brain doing flops in my skull. "I learned my lesson. You can put me down."

Noctus paused and studied my face, the slant of his eyebrows curious. "Lesson?"

"Uh-huh," I said.

Noctus kept on holding me as he took a few steps, slowly approaching the arched bridge. "What lesson, pray tell, are you referring to?"

"I...don't know," I said. "But I learned it." Yep, there went the last of my intelligence, floating off in the cool morning breeze.

Maybe I should just turn back into a cat. If I can't talk and keep putting my foot in my mouth, this would probably be thirty percent less embarrassing.

My cat instincts screamed at me that I was in *so much* danger, so I risked peeking at Noctus again.

He was grinning, and the light in his swirling eyes said he'd thought of something that *he* thought was fun, which probably meant I wasn't going to like it one bit.

"Lesson, you say," he said. "Let's test that out."

Noctus—still holding me—jumped onto the bridge's stone railing, then stepped off. Like a lunatic!

I shrieked as we started to free-fall. My strangled shouts were barely audible over Noctus's laughter—just another sign he was bananas.

Instinct kicked in, and I turned into a cat, slipping through Noctus's arms. Free, I switched into a human so I could push off Noctus—unapologetically kneeing him in the gut. I immediately turned back into a cat, manipulating my legs so I turned in time to land paws first.

Noctus didn't manage quite as well. He also landed feet first, but he was still laughing, so he missed rolling like he usually did and instead staggered before falling to his knees.

I stared at him for a moment, my ears flat against my skull as he got himself under control.

"You're right." His voice was low but warm with mischief. "You did learn the lesson."

I'm done with him for tonight.

I turned my back to him and started to pick my way across the plaza. I glanced up at the few elves who had stopped to see what the commotion was.

An elf who was headed for the gate was hanging off the side of the bridge, gaping at his laughing monarch. Another elf standing on the steps that acted as one of the ways up and down the various tiers of the city and ended at Noctus's villa, stared at me with wide eyes as I passed her.

"You cannot deny it was a proper test, Chloe," Noctus called after me, ignoring our audience.

His voice was closing in on me, so I hurried, narrowly avoiding him when he tried to grab me.

"I see you learned that lesson, too," he said. "What a pity."

I swapped to my human form in hopes that he wouldn't get any ideas. "I think you fell off the clocktower too many times."

"Why would you say that?" Noctus asked—thank you, elf ears.

"Because you're acting crazy," I said.

"I am," Noctus agreed. "I'm afraid the thrill of it all has gotten to me." He bumped my shoulder as he caught up with me so we climbed the stairs together—he didn't even take them two at a time.

"The *thrill*?" I repeated. "The thrill of what?"

Noctus held his hand out, palm up.

I didn't even think about it, didn't even pause. After *weeks* of being drilled as a cat, I automatically reached out and clapped my hand against his in a high five.

Wait—but I'm not a cat anymore?

Before my brain could self-correct, Noctus used the opportunity to intertwine his fingers with mine, and he held my hand, swinging it slightly.

Huh? I stared at our joint hands, surprised by the open affection but also shocked that I *liked* it.

His palm was calloused—from his weapons, probably, which somehow surprised me because he was a *king* after all—and his fingers were pleasantly warm. But what really had me was that I could feel it—the binding magic.

Whatever was in my collar warmed at his prolonged touch. I could feel his magic flowing from him to me, just like when he'd used it to heal me.

"The thrill," Noctus began while I was still half distracted, "is having someone who can match me. Effortlessly."

I jolted out of the day-dreamy feeling his magic inspired in me. "Match you? I nearly died climbing all those stairs."

"That wasn't what I was referring to—but even Charon would have some fatigue by the end of our tower-jumping practice from all those stairs," Noctus said.

"Then what *were* you referring to?" I asked.

"Your ability to survive," Noctus said. "No one else alive could have jumped off the tower like that with me. Rather, I was struggling to keep up with you."

I was quiet as we climbed a few stairs, thinking. "I'm starting to see what you mean about being a shadow," I said. "I can do a lot more than I ever assumed was possible."

Noctus squeezed my hand. "You had no way of knowing."

"You're right," I said. "But you said something that I think is wrong."

"Oh?"

"Yes. I don't think I'm the only one alive that could have done that," I said.

Noctus shrugged. "Perhaps. There are some powerful supernaturals that still live."

"Yeah, but that's not what I'm talking about." I cleared my throat, and even the warm bubbling sensation of Noctus's magic couldn't entirely clear my worry. "I meant I'm positive there are others who can do it...Because I'm pretty sure I wasn't born—and dropped off at a human hospital with no supernaturals around for miles—by accident," I grimly said.

"I DON'T THINK I'll be able to pick up your next round of bills until tomorrow, but I can process payroll today." I pinched my phone between the side of my head and my shoulder as I struggled with the fabric shorts I was wearing, tugging them higher up my hips.

"Unless you needed me to wait on payroll for something?" I had to do a little shimmy dance to keep from getting a wedgie as I pulled, but my phone stayed in place.

"*That's fine, Chloe dear,*" Ms. Booker said on the other end of the phone. "*Today is the scheduled payroll day. I'll have the hours to you by noon.*"

"Great." I finished my dance and hesitated, wondering if I should say the words that burned in my brain.

I need to. Ms. Booker has been amazingly understanding, but it's summer now. I've been gone for months.

"And, I wanted to again say, that if you want to hire someone to take my position I completely understand, and I'd be happy to train the person if you do decide to bring someone new on board—not that I want to be fired, but I don't know how much longer I won't be able to come in and..." I trailed off with a grimace, preparing myself for the worst.

"*Have you finished?*" Ms. Booker asked with her usual sheen of politeness.

"Yeah. I mean, yes." I swiveled to face the golden gate that barred the entrance/exit to the front lawn of the Cape Cod house.

"Good. Thank you for completing payroll this evening."

"Does that mean you aren't firing me?" I nervously hooked my fingers into a fleur in the gate, clinging to it so tightly my knuckles turned white.

"Of course I'm not firing you. Who would do payroll?"

"But I haven't been able to come in for my night shift for weeks," I said, feeling honor bound to at least attempt to convince her—this had to be inconvenient for everyone at Book Nookery.

"Yes, dear, but the schedule was about to change for summer, regardless of your absence. We'll deal with it until you finish things with that elf of yours," Ms. Booker said.

"Thank you, Ms. Booker," I said. "Thank you *so* much."

"You're a good employee, Chloe. I'd be loath to lose you," Ms. Booker said, her voice softening for a moment. *"But!"* She tsked through the phone, her politeness back in full force. *"I am disappointed you don't think I'd have the good manners to inform you if I was firing you."*

"Sorry." I smiled and let go of the gate so I could trace the fleur with my pointer finger.

"Indeed," Ms. Booker said. *"Good afternoon, Chloe dear."*

"Good afternoon, Ms. Booker," I said.

I ended the phone conversation and heaved a sigh of relief.

I still have my job, good. Even with Noctus covering my rent, I would be in deep trouble if I didn't have a job to go back to once we figure everything out about the tracker.

Giddy with relief, I did a one-handed cartwheel—one handed because I didn't want to crack my phone—in the hallway. *Maybe Noctus will let me go back to work soon, even if I can't move out of the villa. We're friends, now. I think his main concern is safety.*

I felt a presence far down the hallway so I swung around and waved. "Hi, Charon. Thanks for helping me with this!"

Charon ignored my greeting and stared at my shorts as he strode closer. "Is that what you're wearing?"

"Yes?" I peered down at my athletic shorts—which were a

plain black color—and wondered what he found offensive about them. "But I'll be acting as Ama, so no one will see them."

Charon blinked. "Hmm."

"What, are you turning into the fashion police?" Aristide yelled as he ambled down the hallway, holding the handle of Ker's harness.

Ker "*awoo*-ed" a greeting at me and wagged her tail.

I waved to the pair, but my eyebrows puckered as I looked back and forth between the vampire and werewolf. "Are you two going somewhere?"

"Outside." Aristide used his free hands to adjust his sunglasses. "With you. Because you might do something interesting."

"Oh." I double checked my phone was safe. "Okay then."

With that, I stepped from human to cat, then waited at the gate for Charon to open it for me.

I'd concluded I needed to make an appearance as Ama, or Noctus's neighbors might start to question why Noctus's cat switched from daily walks to disappearing entirely, so I'd recruited Charon to go outside with me (because I wasn't going to have a repeat of the fun Ker and I had) and stroll around for a bit.

Apparently, Aristide and Ker were coming too.

Charon opened the golden gate, then stepped through the portal.

I gave him a few seconds to open the Cape Cod's door, then hustled through after him. The wonky feeling the portal gave me buzzed through my small body, but I hopped out, emerging on the cement porch.

I meowed my thanks at Charon, then trotted across the lawn, flicking my tail as I did my best to imitate a cat that had things to do.

Despite Aristide's interest, I planned to just do cat things—nothing that would be entertaining, though now that I pondered it, maybe that was just his excuse and he was actually coming with to act as even more backup.

Isn't this street spelled to the gills? Are they that concerned about the tracker and the fae, or is it just sheer nosiness? You couldn't tell with Aristide involved.

I sat next to the mailbox and licked a paw, waiting until Aristide and Ker emerged.

Ker carefully led Aristide down the step and across the lawn. Charon fetched a lawn chair—one of those aluminum ones with the nylon fabric strips that you would have assumed went out of style in the 80s but could still be found in dusty garages and, apparently, in the possession of immortal supernaturals.

He unfolded it and set it out on the front lawn for Aristide. Once seated, Aristide unleashed Ker, who promptly rolled in the grass.

Aristide fixed his sunglasses again, then folded his hands in his lap while Charon inspected the house's landscaping and bushes.

I decided to press on, following the sidewalk down the end of the cul-de-sac so I circled around to the other side.

Shiloh was outside, watering her beds of flowers. "Hi, Ama!" She waved to me as she moved to the next flower bed. "I haven't seen you in a while."

I'm sorry. I wanted to say hello as Chloe, but it's more important you see me as Ama because I haven't gone on my morning walks in a while.

I purred—though I wasn't sure she could hear me over the bubble of her hose.

"Are you taking a walk?" Shiloh set the hose down, then trotted back to her house where she cranked the squeaky spigot, turning the water off. She slapped her hands on her thighs as she made her way over to me, kneeling down to pet me. "Are you here to take a break? Seriously, Mr. Shade must have that house stuffed with people all the time—I see so many people going in and out."

Well, this could be trouble. Shiloh is more observant than I guessed.

I'd suspected she was the neighbor I needed to watch. The

night the tracker tried to break inside, she'd woken up and turned on the lights in her house, and she'd realized I was a supernatural when she met me in my human form.

Shiloh scratched me under my chin, and I deepened my purr.

Maybe I should get going. Who knows what else she'll realize if I stick around too long? Besides, I need to let the uncles see me.

I backed up, rubbed my face one last time on Shiloh's hand, then picked my way up the sidewalk, heading to Shiloh's next-door neighbors—a trio of elderly gentlemen who had the tendency to cackle and sit out on the porch all day long drinking sweet tea.

Shiloh followed after me—which I had half expected. She slipped her hands into the pockets of her jean shorts. "Hello, uncles!" she called to her neighbors.

I meowed and flicked my fluffy tail back and forth, making sure they noticed me.

"If it isn't little Shiloh," one of the men declared.

"And Noctus's overly loved pet," the second man chortled.

The third and last of the elderly men—he had a thick mustache—squinted at us. "Finish watering your flowers, Shiloh?"

Shiloh rocked forward and backward from the balls to the heels of her feet. "For now!"

I heard the garage door open, and I peered back at the Cape Cod house in time to see Charon and Ker disappear inside the garage while Noctus himself stepped through the front door.

Now everyone is outside? Are we just being cautious, or is this really necessary? I'd like to think it's just caution, but the tracker did manipulate the Seelie fae into trying to grab me...

I considered going home, but Shiloh scratched behind my ear, so I had no choice but to melt into her hand. "It's a lovely day, isn't it?" Shiloh asked.

The uncles bobbed their heads, but one of the trio rattled their nearly empty pitcher of sweet tea. "It's warm," he announced. "We're going through tea faster!"

Noctus ambled across the street, coming in our direction.

Perfect! A rescue!

I meowed to him and left Shiloh, stepping into the gutter to join Noctus in the road.

He scooped me up in his arms and propped me against his chest so I could hook my claws into the v-neck of his t-shirt. "Ama, don't cross the street without supervision. It's too dangerous."

He's just doing that for effect. He can't be serious.

I meowed as I scooted into my regular position with his arm supporting me.

Noctus tickled my chest, which made me look up at him. "Don't try it again without me," he said.

I couldn't see his eyes—he was wearing his aviator sunglasses and a glamour like he usually did whenever he was out of his house—but his voice was serious.

Nah, he's just playing it up. Right?

"Hello Mr. Shade!" Shiloh called in a sing-song voice.

"Hello, Shiloh." Noctus stepped onto the sidewalk while I—still coping with Noctus's ridiculous order—peered over his shoulder. "How has your summer been so far?"

Across the street, Ker emerged from the garage with a ball—one of those thick ones that were supposed to be safe for dogs to chew that also had a chewable rubber handle. She held the handle in her mouth, then whipped her head back and forth.

"Good! I'm struggling to keep the landscape in order, but that's nothing new," Shiloh said. "How are you?"

"Fine." Noctus petted me, then took a moment to straighten my jeweled collar.

I barely noticed. I watched in fascination as Ker let go of her ball, sending it flying across the lawn. She ran after it, picked it up by the handle, and started shaking it again.

"I am enduring in the incoming summer heat," Noctus continued, engaging in human social niceties with a patience that still surprised me.

"It's only going to get worse." Shiloh shuffled her feet, then peered up at Noctus. "So...Chloe is still staying with you?"

"Yes." Noctus patted one of my paws latched on to the neckline of his shirt as if I were an upset baby.

"Her apartment still hasn't finished getting remodeled?" Shiloh asked.

"Her landlord is a very unhurried individual," Noctus smoothly said.

"You can't fool us, you young pup!" the first uncle shouted.

"You just don't *want* her to go back to her apartment," the second chimed in before all three of them cackled and toasted each other with their nearly-empty glasses.

I rested my chin on Noctus's shoulder, content to watch our friends while he was grilled.

Back on our lawn, Ker launched her ball again, and it smacked Aristide on the shoulder.

The werewolf sat on her rear and pitched her head back as she made a barking-whine noise that was clearly her wolf version of a laugh.

"Ker, stop that." Aristide picked the ball off his lap—making a face when he touched the drool coated handle—then threw the ball.

Ker raced after it, kicking up grass in her exuberance.

"That must be fun," Shiloh said.

"Chloe staying with me?" Noctus asked.

"Yeah."

Noctus cocked his head in a way. "It is," he said. "She is...comfortable."

Shiloh made a humming noise in the back of her throat.

Noctus rocked back and forth slightly. I wasn't sure if it was to soothe me or...some other reason? "You seem like you have something else to say," Noctus said.

"I do."

"Then say it."

I still find it funny she calls him "Mr. Shade" when they clearly have an excellent friendship, I mused as I listened to the exchange.

On the Cape Cod's lawn, Ker had her ball again and was once again whipping it back and forth. She launched it at Aristide. This time the vampire caught it, then chucked it back at the fleeing Ker, smacking her in her rear with enough force to knock her off course so she nearly sprawled over.

Ker released another round of her barking-laugh as she flopped into the grass.

"You're sick, you know that?" Aristide asked, sounding disgusted.

Heartbeat, I thought to myself. *He was definitely tracking her by her heartbeat.*

"Well," Shiloh said. "Are you and Chloe dating?"

CHAPTER EIGHTEEN

Chloe

Three things happened in very short succession.

1) Aristide grabbed the arms of his folding chair and turned to us so fast he almost flipped his chair over. 2) Ker stood up so fast she stepped on her own tail in the process and fell down again. 3) Something loud crashed in the garage—Charon had obviously heard Shiloh's question as well thanks to his elf hearing.

I remained perfectly still—not because I wasn't shocked by the question. No. It was only because of years of practice at passing as a normal cat that made me remain in Noctus's arms. Well, practice, and maybe I was paralyzed in my shock.

Noctus didn't bat an eye, didn't react to any of us, he didn't even hesitate. "Yes," he said.

This time Aristide *did* tip over, but that was all I had time to see before I bonelessly slid off Noctus's shoulder and pooled into his arms like goo, gazing up at him in horror.

Have you lost your mind!? What could possibly inspire you to say that?

"I knew it!" Shiloh grinned widely as she clapped her hands. "I knew you had your eye on her!"

"Way to go, sonny!" an uncle shouted as he tossed what bit of ice was left in his cup onto the lawn. "Getting romance at your age—now that's a surprise!"

Noctus ignored the elderly neighbor and smiled angelically at Shiloh. "She is a captivating woman."

"Ooh—that's high praise coming from you," Shiloh said. "But congratulations! I'm glad you found someone." She lost the sheepish edge she'd had before her off-base question, and casually stretched her arms out in front of her. "Dad always said he worried you'd be forever alone. When you got Ama I thought maybe you were going to become one of those bachelor-pet-owner types. Not that there's anything wrong with that, but I think Chloe will be good for you!" Shiloh winked and made a heart shape with her fingers.

I lay in Noctus's arms, deeply traumatized by the conversation.

She thought Noctus was going to become an old cat lady? Noctus. The elf king?!

Noctus took advantage of my shock to ease me onto my back so he cradled me like a baby.

"Oh yes, Chloe saved me from myself," he agreed with enough innocence to make my fur puff up in fear. "It's quite romantic. I dare say it's almost like she has a piece of me that she carries around with her."

That jolted me out of my shock enough to make me growl.

Careful! She's smart! If you give her too much information who knows what she'll figure out?

Noctus mildly smiled in a way that I was willing to bet would have dazzled the crabbiest of cats, but his fancy animal magic didn't work on me, so I squirmed in his arms, desperately trying to flee before I had to witness more of this embarrassing conversation.

"I'm so happy for you," Shiloh said. "I mean it, Mr. Shade."

"The neighborhood is!" one of the uncles shouted.

"Thank you," Noctus said. "Now, if you'll excuse me, I believe Ama wishes to go inside."

What I wish, I thought savagely as I sank my claws into his shirt and dragged myself up to his shoulder, *is for you to stop saying stuff that's going to get us into trouble!*

"Sure, sure! Have a great day—tell the girlfriend I say hi!" Shiloh backed down the sidewalk, inching her way back to her house.

"I will. Farewell." Noctus turned from Shiloh, pausing long enough to raise his eyebrows at the cackling uncles, then stepped down into the street.

I growled and flicked my tail.

"I know you don't like it," Noctus murmured, his lips barely moving as he closed in on his front yard. "But saying we're in a relationship is a reason more humans will understand and accept than 'Chloe is being stalked by a supernatural because she's a shadow.'"

I licked my chops as I considered his argument. *I guess he has a point, and we can only say my apartment is getting remodeled for so long—plus everyone knows Aristide and Charon live in the house, too. Hopefully that means Shiloh will chalk it up to a supernatural thing and won't think too deeply about any of this.*

Judging by her excited reaction, she hadn't been lying at all when she told me previously—as Chloe—that she had zero interest in Noctus. She'd said he'd been around forever so she saw him as more of an uncle or something.

It's interesting that he chooses to socialize with his neighbors. I assumed it was just to solidify his cover, but Shiloh and the uncles seem pretty invested in his life.

Charon emerged from the garage as Noctus stepped onto the

curb. "Your Majesty." Charon nodded to Noctus before he continued on.

Are you seriously not going to question him after this? Yeah, I'm still on the fence because it kind of makes sense. But really. Dating?! How could he just casually say that? He's an elf king!

Aristide set his chair upright with some help from Charon, then gingerly sat down again. "What was that about?" he asked in a lowered tone.

"Believability," Noctus said.

"Hah!" Aristide snorted so loudly his voice echoed. "Yeah, right. Because you dating anyone at all is more believable than Chloe becoming a temporary roommate or some other reasonable explanation. Sure, that seems on target for your personality—you have a history of being cuddly. Not!"

Ker howled her agreement as she sat down next to Charon.

"In His Majesty's defense," Charon murmured, keeping his voice lowered, "he was remarkably cuddly with Ama."

"This and that are two entirely different situations," Aristide declared. "Chloe, are you upset about it?"

No, but thank you for asking. That's very emotionally responsible of you. I purred my approval.

Aristide must have heard because he held his hand out, and Noctus bent over so Aristide could pat my back.

Charon frowned during the entire interaction. "Why would Chloe be upset?"

"Because despite what you think, Charon, not everyone would want to date Noctus," Aristide said.

Noctus held me up so I was eye to eye with him, pointed at his face and dangling from his hands.

It was a precarious position that I didn't like. The only reason I wasn't clawing him was because it was Noctus.

"Did my excuse upset you that much?" he asked.

My ears twitched as I tried to weigh it out. *I was shocked, and I think we could have come up with a better excuse, but I'd say it makes you look worse than me, so I guess it's okay.*

The nagging thought that having Noctus as a boyfriend would be an experience tugged on the tips of my proverbial whiskers. That bothered me more than Noctus's terrible lying skills.

"It's not like she can tell you." Aristide leaned back in his chair with a huff as Noctus finally held me against his chest again. "Unless you suddenly sprouted powers no other elf alive has and can now directly communicate with animals?"

"Why are you so concerned how she feels about this?" Charon asked. "It's a mere excuse, it has no real bearing."

"I care because," Aristide paused and made a show of folding one leg over the other, "this could reflect poorly on her reputation."

I couldn't see Noctus's eyes through his sunglasses, but I could still feel the weight of his stare at Aristide. "...Nostalgia vampire."

Aristide popped up out of his chair, reminding me of a hissing, spitting cat. "Reputation is a perfectly reasonable word to use in modern language!"

Ker howled her amusement, then trotted off and grabbed her ball.

I wriggled in Noctus's arms until he let me go and I hopped from him to the lawn.

Noctus ignored Aristide's temper tantrum. "I'll ask Chloe later—when she can answer."

"That would be wise, Your Majesty," Charon said.

"Oh, so *now* you support my ideas?" Aristide demanded.

Noctus tilted his head up to point at the sky. "Our street has gotten remarkably louder these days, has it not, Charon?"

"It's the bats, Your Majesty."

"Oh, that's it," Aristide said. "Next time you do something stupid involving Chloe, I'm not going to tell you, and then you can pay for it yourself!"

"I'm trembling, I assure you."

"Twerp!"

I sauntered across the lawn, enjoying the springy feeling of the grass under my paws. *It's fun, having friends to laugh with,* I thought as Ker raced past me with her ball. *Except, all of this is temporary, isn't it? Eventually I'll have to return to normal life.*

Thinking the question made me a little more somber, so the hot sun on my black fur didn't feel quite so luxurious, and more stifling. A corner of my soul—one that I hoped Noctus couldn't feel through our binding—rebelled at the thought.

But...maybe, normal will include them?

CHAPTER NINETEEN

Noctus

I tugged at the shackles fastened around my wrist as I climbed the last staircase and pointed my body to the door of my room.

I was chafing under the shackles' restraint even more than I usually did.

Previously it was little more than an irritation, but since I'd started teaching Chloe, I found the crippling of my magic a lot more offensive. The *fun* we could have if I was able to freely draw out my weapons...

Maybe it's about time I tell the Paragon to bugger off. He'd still come around to whine at me and ask for information, anyway. I'm nearly certain that he trusts me enough that he wouldn't tell anyone even if I refused to wear them anymore—especially since he's so worried.

I paused in front of the door, considering the matter.

The Paragon is a fae—shrewd to the bone. If I offer to help in other ways, he'd keep my secret forever. Though I don't like the idea of being indebted to him even through a fair exchange. Perhaps what I should really focus on is why *I'd like to be rid of these shackles.*

I reached for the doorknob, when I heard a muffled shriek.

Chloe.

I was at her door before I could finish taking a breath, nearly ripping it off its hinges. "Chloe?"

"Sorry! I'm sorry—I'm fine!" Chloe called, her voice still muffled.

I took an uneasy step into her room—it was elven custom to respect one's personal space until a close relationship was reached. I wasn't entirely certain Chloe and I were there—though I suppose there were fewer closer than us, given her collar.

Chloe popped out of her walk-in closet, still wearing the workout clothes she'd donned for her practice session with Charon downstairs. "You can come in. I'm fine, it's just...what's this?"

She pressed herself against the wall like a frightened animal, then pointed into the depths of her closet.

"A walk-in closet," I supplied.

"No—I mean, yes—but what are these?" Chloe slunk into her closet and picked up a maroon cocktail dress hanging off a padded hanger and shook it at me, then turned to the other side of the closet where she removed a thin summer shirt that was reminiscent of the silken tunics elves used to wear with the embroidery on the sleeve cuffs and the neckline.

Looks like Charon's work. I did ask him to expand Chloe's wardrobe about two weeks ago. He must have gotten all the orders in.

It had been remarkably easy to convince Charon to make the purchases—he'd been despairing over Chloe's wardrobe since the day he'd found out she and I were bound together.

The stray thought that Chloe would look *very* good in elven designed clothes threatened to distract me, but I stayed focused. "Clothes," I said.

"Yes, clothes, but they're not *my* clothes," Chloe said.

"They're in your closet," I said.

"Yes." Chloe shook the hem of the tunic styled shirt. "But they're not from my apartment, and I didn't buy them. I don't think I've owned these many clothes my entire life!" Chloe turned in a circle, her shoulders hunching as she eyed her new wardrobe.

If she were in her cat form, she'd be shedding fur like crazy.

I didn't try to hide my smile as Chloe peered in my direction.

"No." She puffed up, her dark eyes large and moon-like. "No, this is not going to be Ama version 2.0!"

"I'm certain I don't know what you mean," I said, my voice admirably free of any falsities.

"You spoiled Ama to a *ridiculous* degree," Chloe said. "You can't do the same to me!"

"Why not?" I asked. "You *are* Ama, after all."

Chloe opened and closed her mouth a few times in a way I found very charming—her shifting emotions were a reflection of what I'd seen in her as Amalourne, which went a long way in telling me how genuine a person she really was.

She may be a shadow, but she doesn't hide herself—at least not emotionally. If it was possible to use magic to make the floor swallow her, I'm sure she'd be giddy, but she's as open as a book in her expressions.

Chloe blinked a few times and studied her closet once more before she turned to me. "How?"

"Charon," I said.

As if he was waiting for the perfect entrance—which, given his sly intelligence, was entirely possible—Charon stepped into the doorframe of Chloe's bedroom. "You called for me, Your Majesty?"

"Charon," Chloe called, her voice halfway to a wail.

I stepped to the side as Charon padded across the room and joined me.

"Your Majesty. Chloe." Charon bowed—first to me, then to Chloe. His mask was perfectly in place—though I could tell by the way his eyes swirled that he was enjoying every moment of this. "Is your new wardrobe to your liking?"

Chloe puffed up again. "No, it's too excessive."

Charon joined Chloe in the closet and mournfully studied a rack of new belts. "You do not like the clothes chosen for you?"

"No, it's not that, I mean, I *do* like them." Chloe sucked her arms close to her chest and eyed the full closet with suspicion.

"Then what's the problem?"

"You can't just buy a new wardrobe for me!"

"It was necessary, I assure you," Charon said. "In order for you to stand by His Majesty's side, you required a larger wardrobe."

A tiny wrinkle spread across Chloe's forehead. "Are you saying I have bad taste in clothes?"

"Not at all," Charon said. "Just that your wardrobe needed to be expanded given the new situations you will be exposed to."

Charon must have been able to tell he wasn't winning her over, because he slipped past her, disappearing into the depths of the closet. "See? I purchased more training clothes for you. Some of them even have special sheaths for your knives built into the outfit."

Chloe had been giving me her best glare—the human version of the scolding look she used to give me as a cat when I tried petting her belly. But at Charon's temptation she reluctantly followed him deeper. "More training clothes?"

"Yes. Some of them are reinforced with special padding—to limit the chance of injury if you're forced to roll across a stony surface and whatnot." I couldn't even see Charon, but his voice was warm—for Charon, anyway—and tempting.

Chloe looked back at me—her eyes briefly straying to the maroon dress she'd pointed out earlier, before she snapped her gaze back to me.

I smiled at her—which seemed to frighten her more because she turned bright red, then jumped past a layer of clothes so she, too, was no longer visible. "That would be nice—can I see them?"

I chuckled. My voice was low, but Chloe must have heard it, because she made some kind of wheezing sound in retort.

Even more amused, I slipped my hands into my hidden pockets, briefly touching the reassuring coolness of the daggers hidden there before I sat down on a chair and waited.

Charon will win her over, however…

She'd been spooked by the clothes. I didn't think it made her afraid of me or Charon—at least not that I could sense. Was it just that she thought it was too opulent? But I frequently gifted things to Aristide and Ker in a similar manner.

Maybe I really am as out of touch with human reality as Aristide likes to accuse me of being.

"Noctus," Chloe hissed, lingering in the entrance to her closet.

"Yes?" I draped my arms over the sides of the chair, relaxing.

"Is this really okay?" Chloe asked.

I blinked. "I don't know what you're asking."

Chloe motioned behind her. "All of this. It's beautiful, but considering *I* was the one skulking around without telling you what I was, and that you're still protecting me from whatever the tracker is planning…is this really okay?" She shifted nervously from foot to foot, and the red gemstones in her collar gleamed in the daylight that flooded her room.

"If we're going by those metrics, technically I'm a brute who has imprisoned you in my villa against your will," I pointed out.

"That's not what I meant." Chloe's voice was tight—not with fear, but something closer to distress. Her eyebrows were pushed together, and she fidgeted—in constant nervous motion. This really was bothering her.

I stood up from my chair and cautiously approached her.

I need to be careful in the way I approach this, or she'll just see herself as a pet project.

"It's a gift, Chloe." I held my hand out, palm up, in the same way I used to ask Amalourne for a high five.

Chloe unthinkingly reached out and tapped her hand against

mine. I used the contact to my advantage and intertwined my fingers with hers.

I waited a moment, but she didn't protest, so I squeezed her hand. "You've become important to me—*you*, as yourself. Not a cat," I said. "Those who are important to me, I treat accordingly."

I took another step closer to her.

She relaxed when I slid an arm around her upper back, and leaned into me. She raised her free hand and lightly grasped the neck of my shirt in a gesture that I was sure had to be automatic, and seemed quite comfortable.

I, on the other hand, found myself rendered stupid.

Ker, Aristide, and Charon had been my companions for centuries. They knew my soul. But I'd never been a particularly demonstrative person—something that had been drilled into me as a child raised for war.

But even though centuries had passed, it was something I hadn't been able to shake. Until I'd gotten a cat, that was, and realized just how soothing a kind touch could be.

Now, with Chloe tilted against me, I was coming to a new realization: as much as Amalourne had meant to me, human Chloe freely hugging me was like magic.

Even better, the effect was multiplied by my magic that tied me to her, giving me the feedback of her contentment.

She didn't fear me—intellectually she had no reason to. As a shadow, she'd be extraordinarily dangerous once she was sufficiently trained—already she was reaching a skill level that would make her feared by most supernaturals. But Chloe lived in fear. For her to willingly embrace me, with no reluctance...

I was right in thinking I needed to bring her in.

"If you're sure..." Chloe said, jarring me from my thoughts. She backed up a step, breaking our embrace apart so she could peer up at my face. "About the wardrobe, I mean."

"I am. Besides." I swung our joint hands to break the tension in the moment. "Charon was days away from turning to embezzling funds and stealth delivering you clothes anyway. Once he has decided he likes a person, he has *ideas* about how one should dress."

"Yeah, I noticed that," Chloe admitted. She peered back over her shoulder, into the depths of her closet, and once again the gemstones on her collar gleamed, and I felt the swirl of my magic that tied me to her.

"Ask Charon to show you the dresses," I advised. "All of them were designed with the idea of hiding daggers."

Chloe's eyes grew moon-wide again. "Really?"

"Really."

My odd conduct forgotten, Chloe gleefully pounced on her wardrobe again. "Charon? Can I hide daggers in my dresses?"

"Of course," Charon said. "I taught you to use daggers. What kind of teacher do you take me to be that I wouldn't think my pupil would need to carry some at all times?"

"I thought maybe I'd have to put them in a purse."

"No, no, no—a purse can be taken from you," Charon said. "Please allow me to instruct you on the advantages of carefully arranged clothes, and thicker fabrics."

I headed back to my chair—still feeling warm from Chloe's embrace, until I remembered the way the jewels of her collar twinkled at her throat.

It's not too far off to say I hold her imprisoned. If she wears the collar, I'm not giving her a choice to live in my world.

Before I'd known her character, it made sense to keep the collar—with its superior tracking spell—on her. Wild magic had supported the idea, anyway—though that wasn't necessarily good news for me.

But I'd continued to hide behind that excuse well after Chloe had proven herself trustworthy.

I'm being cowardly. There are dozens of other spells we could use—magic she could toggle herself if the tracker found her. But, selfishly, I haven't. Because the collar keeps her close.

If I really cared about Chloe, I'd give her a choice to take or reject the collar, and not force my lifestyle upon her.

Besides...much of my life I hadn't been given a choice—or rather it was a choice between terrible options. I wanted to give Chloe what I hadn't had.

Wild magic silently stirred around me, oppressively silent.

So it doesn't want me to give her the option? It must have an end game in mind for her.

That alone made it a good idea to take the collar off—I wasn't interested in wild magic using me for its purposes again. Besides, this time it wasn't just me it would potentially sacrifice, but everyone in Calor Villa.

Since the war, I'd dedicated my life to keeping the remnant elves that chose to stay with me safe. Nothing—not wild magic, not even Chloe—could change that.

But Chloe wouldn't knowingly risk my people. She cares.

Caring or not, while living in Calor Villa was not a trial, the need for secrecy—of the city itself, of my own heritage, of so much—required isolation.

Chloe didn't have many connections here in Magiford, which was why she hadn't yet fought her situation. But her family...

Her siblings, especially. They're close in a way I don't understand. But I don't think she could part with them, much less stand to lie to them. If she stayed with me, she'd have to.

And that was the crux of the situation, and why I was reluctant to take the collar off Chloe despite the potential dangers.

I didn't think I'd win against her siblings. In fact, I *obviously* wouldn't win against her siblings, and it would be a completely justified choice for Chloe.

But I was selfish.

Or at least I'd been acting selfish—and stupid since wild magic was so obviously taken with her, and this entire façade was a danger to Calor Villa.

But if she chose to stay, I was powerful enough to keep

everyone—Chloe *and* the elves—safe, despite whatever plans wild magic had for her.

It would potentially mean I'd have to pick up weapons, heirlooms, that I hadn't touched since the war and tap into powers I hated. But duty came before everything—if I could just manage to keep Chloe somehow as well...

Chloe briefly popped out of the closet, holding a dress with a delicate grasp as if it could be ruined through simple touch. "Noctus, do you have black tie occasions a lot here in the villa?"

I readjusted my sitting position in the chair so one of my daggers stopped digging into my gut. "Not really, why?"

"Then why did Charon get me so many dresses?"

"Because Charon's definition for what requires dressing up is vastly different from yours or mine."

"Ah. Okay." Chloe blinked at me, flashing her large doe eyes in a way that conveyed horror and the need for help. But she rolled her shoulders back, and marched into the closet with a grim sort of resignation.

I grinned at her back, but my humor fell away now that I was left to my own thoughts again.

I must give her the choice—because I can't force this on her. Or I'll be more like the tyrants my family had been.

CHAPTER TWENTY

Chloe

I sprinted across a rooftop, my short sword smacking my back. I stuck close to the edge of the building, but the footsteps echoing behind me sounded louder than they had a few moments ago.

He's catching up!

A stitch in my side made breathing painful, but he was close enough that I could hear him exhale.

I need to escape!

I made a sharp left turn, switched to a cat, and leaped off the building's roof, twisting my body so I would land on my paws.

The second I landed I shifted into a human and was off, running before he could pop out of the roll he'd had to take.

I was so much faster than when I'd first learned how to jump, and the motions were now automatic.

I hurtled down the street, mentally tracking my progress through the city. When I reached the end of the block I turned right, and there it was: the clocktower, rising high above the surrounding buildings.

The safe zone!

I heard him behind me, so I turned into a cat and darted up an alleyway, scooting around a trash bin.

I found what I was looking for: a fire escape. It was barely more than a ladder with a safety cage wrapped around it, and it didn't go all the way to the ground, it stopped at roughly the ceiling of the first floor.

I turned human, then ran at the wall and leaped. My gloved fingers scraped the wall, but I managed to secure a grip on the fingertip wide brick outcropping that marked out a door. I planted a foot on the door handle to push up, then wobbled for a moment, balancing without anything to support me until my fingers caught on the ladder.

My arms burned as I pulled myself up, until I was able to plant my knees on the side of the building and push off it, sucking myself into the tube.

I focused on stealth over speed as I climbed up the ladder, trying to be as noiseless as possible.

Stealth scared the tar out of me and went against every instinct I had—which said I was better off being as far away from danger as possible.

But he hadn't found me by the time I climbed onto the roof. I kept my footsteps quiet as I trekked across the building. I had to hop a narrow alleyway to get to the next building, but once I crossed it, the clocktower was just across the street.

I swapped to a cat and stuck to the shadows, staying low to the ground until I reached the wall of the building. Then I stood on my hind paws and peered over the side.

Nothing moved on the street—not even a car. I strained my ears, but I only heard the distant squeak of a mouse—not unusual considering it had to be about three in the morning.

I eyed the distance—I was three stories up—then scrambled

over the side, swinging my cat body so I landed paws first, right behind a garbage can.

I peered around it—looking up and down the street.

I couldn't see anyone, but I could feel the tug of his magic.

Staying so low my belly brushed the asphalt, I scurried from the trash can to a car parked on the street. I tucked myself behind a tire and again peered out.

His magic was still there, despite the silence of the street.

I could try to circle the building to see if I can reach it from a different angle...but I don't think I'll shake him. I should just go for it—or try to, at least.

My ears twitched as I listened for cars—there were none—and opted to keep my cat body. The burst of speed I could use as a cat was ideal since I just needed to sprint across the street.

I edged out from under the car, then ran.

I made it across the right lane of traffic no problem, but as I hit the center of the road I heard footsteps.

He's here!

Noctus emerged from behind one of the support columns of the clocktower. He was on me faster than I could breathe, getting so close his fingers brushed my fur.

Rather than run away from him, I ran toward him, darting between his feet.

I turned human before I'd entirely cleared his body, colliding into him with the unstoppable force of my body-swapping magic.

He wobbled, and I pushed off his back, using him like a springboard to fling myself at the sidewalk.

Noctus swung around, slicing at me with a *sword.* Not a sheathed one, a *bare blade* that gleamed in the dim glow of the streetlights.

I immediately turned back into a cat so his swipe passed high over my head, leaped onto the sidewalk, and smacked into the building before I turned human again.

"You tried to *stab* me!" I yipped, my voice high with anxiety.

Noctus stood on the edge of the road, a tuft of black fur —*mine*, no doubt—pinched between his fingers. "You avoided it."

"You said you'd keep your sword sheathed!"

"Yes, but you've improved so much," Noctus said. "It would be a disservice not to level up my attacks. Improvement is what we're after, not a comfortable practice session."

I wrapped my arms around one of the clocktower's support pillars and suspiciously peered out at him. "Practice has *never* been comfortable."

"Good." Noctus sheathed his sword as he stepped onto the sidewalk. "But you did well—you're drastically improving. It's quite impressive that you got past me."

I released the support column. "It's not that impressive—you aren't at full strength."

"Correct." Noctus motioned for me to follow him as we approached a side door of the clocktower. "But you could still outpace an elf. Possibly even Charon."

"There's not a chance I could beat Charon," I said. "Escape him? Maybe in, like, a year. But no way could I fight him on even ground."

Noctus held the door open so I could step in—it was the greatly hated staircase that took us to the top floor of the clocktower. I breathed a sigh of relief when Noctus passed the stairs and opened the door to the lobby for me.

"You could escape him now—you escaped me, and even with using his magic Charon is slower than I am, and his magic wouldn't affect you anyway," Noctus said. "I wouldn't be so sure that you are unable to fight him on even ground."

"No, I'm very sure." I naturally hushed my voice as we walked across the empty lobby, our footsteps echoing in the smothering silence. "Charon has had centuries to practice with weapons. Bootcamp—even with Charon as my teacher—cannot make up for that kind of practice." I shivered a little even just *thinking* of

Charon's easy skills with daggers, handguns, swords, spears, and the long list of weapons I'd seen him handle.

"Raw power could bridge the gap—and surpass it," Noctus said.

I peered up at Noctus, confused. *That must be a joke. He and Charon tower over me—even with my magic influenced abilities, there's no way I could match them in sheer strength.*

"Raw power?" I echoed.

Noctus glanced down at me. "Yes. From magic."

Okay, now I know he must be joking. All my magic is innate. I can't channel any of it.

"What magic are you referring to?" I asked.

"Mine."

I was so confused, my body couldn't handle the work of propelling myself forward in a walk and thinking, so I stopped in the middle of the lobby. "*What*?"

Noctus glanced down at me, then did a sweeping inspection of the lower level.

It was just the two of us, but something about it wasn't satisfactory, because he motioned for me to follow him. We went through a set of glass doors, popping out by an elevator.

Noctus activated it, then stepped inside when the doors dinged.

He hit the button for the top floor as I stuck my head in. "Wait—that says rooftop. There was an elevator to the rooftop this whole time?"

Noctus caught my hand in his and pulled me inside. "Stairs can be excellent for physical conditioning."

I fish mouthed the whole trip up, caught halfway between fury—a rare experience for me—and disbelief.

When the door dinged open, Noctus towed me out—I hadn't realized he had yet to drop my hand.

Apparently the rooftop level was the clock face. The elevator dropped us off on a wide walkway that wound snug against the exterior of the building, cutting just beneath the giant, glowing clock face and its fancy hour and minute hands.

Noctus tugged me along, stopping directly beneath the clock face to study me. "It's possible for you to use my magic," he said.

I blinked, then shook my head. "No."

"Yes," he countered. "Because of the collar."

"You mean the connection the collar creates?"

Noctus nodded. "It gives you access to my magic. It's partially why the bond isn't just used for romantic relationships—it can be a boon in war."

"But I'm a shadow, not an elf," I said. "Do you really think the connection would work the same way?"

"We can try it," Noctus suggested.

I fidgeted. "Okay, except would it be weird for *you* to have me using your magic? That's a pretty personal thing."

"Considering the bond? You have no idea," Noctus dryly said.

I squirmed. "Look, you made the connection with Ama, not human me. You don't *have* to let me do stuff like this."

Noctus tilted his head. "You don't want to try using my magic?"

"Yes. No." I was pretty sure my hand was starting to sweat, but I couldn't tell for sure since Noctus was still in possession of it. "Noctus, you're an *elf*. Any supernatural would like to try using your magic."

"Except for those with strong self-preservation instincts, like you," Noctus said. His eyes definitely weren't swirling.

Oof, that must have hurt. But it's not what he thinks!

"It's not that I'm scared, it's just...magic is so *personal*," I scrambled, trying to find a way to put my feelings into words. "I don't know—it's just—I was your *cat*. I'm used to getting carried around by you—I still give you high fives without thinking! You did this because you believed I was your cat. Are you really okay doing this when we haven't known each other for long?"

Noctus had decades with Ker, Aristide, and Charon. He'd had

weeks with me. I knew I had meant something to him as Ama, and I suspected I meant something to him as Chloe, but was this raw curiosity on his end, or...?

"It has only been weeks," Noctus acknowledged. "But it's been weeks in which I've felt your heart."

Woah. That's enough to make me blush. I would have wobbled if Noctus still wasn't holding my hand.

"You're trustworthy, Chloe. And I've...wondered."

"About the magic?"

"Partially, yes."

I stared up at him, still not quite satisfied with his answer.

"Wild magic approves of you," he finally said.

If I was in my cat form, I'd be twitching my tail like crazy. "What's that supposed to mean?"

Noctus shrugged. "It's an explanation."

Maybe, but not a very good one. I narrowed my eyes, and I felt my mouth tighten as if I'd been sucking on lemons.

"If you are willing, I'd like to try," Noctus said.

"I have zero experience casting magic," I said.

"I'm aware," Noctus said. "Which is why we'll start with seeing if you can call any of my weapons."

I'd been nodding, until I realized what he was saying. "Wait. You're referring to your regular weapons that you just carry around, right, not your magical—"

"I was referring to my magical weapons, the heirlooms passed through generations."

I gulped. "Of course you were. But, um, problem."

"Yes?"

"Aren't those kinds of...weapons...really, really powerful? And dangerous?"

I'd known vaguely of the existence of elven heirloom weapons, and Ker had given me a little bit of a crash course when she'd started warming up to me after the realization that I was a human. But I didn't have to know much to be aware that the magic embedded weapons were *the* most powerful tools in supernatural society.

The night Noctus had put down the fae who had tried to steal me back, he was wielding enough power to turn the neighborhood into a crater.

Elven weapons were *deadly*, and I highly doubted a weapon that was sort-of-alive and able to express its own opinions was going to take kindly to *me*.

"They are meant to be dangerous," Noctus said. "They're designed to be an elf's strongest resource in battle. That's why they're weapons."

I didn't know if Noctus had too much confidence in me, or if he was so powerful he couldn't comprehend why this was a bad idea. It was probably a combination of both.

I finally pulled my hand from Noctus's—a situation this ridiculous meant a possible headache, so I started rubbing my temples. "And you think we should start there. With the strongest resource." The urge to run shook my gut.

"Yes," Noctus said. "Because they don't require magic to use them, you just need my magic to create the connection with the weapon."

I stared at Noctus, completely unconvinced.

"Stretch out your hand," Noctus said.

I mulishly sucked my head into my shoulders.

He must have been able to tell I wasn't going to give in, because Noctus slipped his fingers under my chin, trailed them along my jawline, and combed his fingers through my hair so his hand rested on the back of my head.

I couldn't resist looking up into his enchanting eyes.

"Please," he said. "I'd like to know if this could work."

Then—because I'm an idiot—I nodded. "Okay," my mouth said without permission.

Noctus smiled before I could take the words back, and there was something about the expression...it wasn't his unearthly beauty. I'd been around him enough that I could handle *that*. It was the sentiment behind his smile—the genuine delight—that kept me from taking my agreement back.

"Stretch out your hand," he repeated.

I reluctantly did so.

"Can you feel the collar at your neck?" he asked.

"Yes."

"Focus on that feeling—shut everything else out."

I shut my eyes as I immersed myself in the collar. It was a constant warm presence in the back of my mind—like the heat given off by the beautiful blue and white flames that appeared in every fireplace in the villa.

When I focused in on it, I could feel the steady burn of magic—which was seductive beyond my imagination.

I didn't experience magic the way other supernaturals did. It either passed through me, or it did its own thing—like my magic that made me unnoticeable. But Noctus's magic...it responded to me.

It stayed with me like a bonfire, warming me from the inside out. When I focused on it, it seemed to take that as an invitation, and it grew around me. My body felt pleasantly tingly and warm, and my usual jittery nerves were lulled into a calmness by the heat.

"Follow the flow of my magic back to me," Noctus instructed.

Figuring it'd be just as pleasant as what I was experiencing with the collar, I followed the burning trail of his magic, stopping when I felt it meld back into Noctus.

If the connection was a warm bonfire, Noctus's being was a burning inferno. His magic was so concentrated, so *pure*, it was a wonder he didn't burn the ground he stood on.

In that moment, I had a stark realization: Noctus had let supernaturals win the war of the elves. Because there was no way any supernatural could have defeated him, there was no way anyone could have waged a war against him and won.

"Have you followed my magic?" Noctus asked.

"Hm? What—yes." I snapped my eyes open, then squirmed because I could still sense Noctus and his magic. "You are...uh..."

"Through me, you should be able to access my weapon storage," Noctus said, ignoring my embarrassed stammers.

"Are you talking about your closet back in the villa?" I asked, thinking of the many weapons he had around his room.

"No," Noctus said. "Those are non-magical weapons that I use since my access to my magic is mostly blocked. The heirlooms we're trying to access are all stored in a sort of pocket realm that can be reached only with a gate made by my magic."

"You expect me to make a *gate*?"

"No—the connection is always forged. I just can't access it because of these." Noctus held up a wrist, showing off his metal cuff. "You just need to find it and reach into it—as I did the night the fae tried to take you and I retrieved one of my weapons, Rioten."

"And how am I supposed to find it?"

"It's the only gate that is infused with magic besides my own," Noctus said. "The weapons' powers leak through the gate. Therefore, it will be the only thing that feels different."

I squeezed my eyes shut as I focused again, and the fiery power that was Noctus blazed bright in my mind.

I'd say I let his powers circle me, but the truth was he was so powerful they just kind of...swooped around me regardless of my wishes, like a wildfire spreading across a forest.

But the engulfing method did make it *very* easy to find the magic link to his gate. It was the only thing that was solid and unmoving, and to say it felt different from the rest of his magic was an understatement.

Noctus's magic was overwhelming. The presence that gate to his weapons had? It was something sharper and focused—like a thousand needles prickling my skin.

"I found it," I said.

"Reach for it—mentally and physically," Noctus coached.

I shivered. "Are you sure? This is setting off every self-preservation instinct I have."

"That's a mere mental hurdle," Noctus said. "Even if one of my weapons grew angry and blew up, it couldn't harm you—the magic would wash right over you."

I snapped my eyes open. "Wait, *it could blow up*?"

Noctus tilted his head, making a few strands of his golden hair fan across his forehead. "Did you fail to hear the part where I mentioned it wouldn't hurt you?"

"Yeah, but what about the tower—and the city?" I nodded out at the city spread below us, glowing from the streetlights.

Noctus chuckled. "It won't happen—you have a connection with me, it's the only reason why you can access my storage. They wouldn't harm you. Most likely, they simply won't answer you."

"Well, I guess not answering is better than expressing their opinions about the situation," I said.

"They may do that, too," Noctus said blandly, as if expressive, magic infused weapons were something that could be discussed over one of Ms. Booker's cups of tea. "Except you have a piece of me. They're not going to dislike you. Now, reach."

With that idea to cheer me, I shuffled in my boots, but mentally reached for the needle-like door, physically reaching my hand out at the same time.

I yelped when hazy white colored magic formed around my hand, and I could *feel* the upside-down sensation of reaching into a different realm. There was even a little space around my wrist where I could see—it was misty in Noctus's realm, but I could make out shadowy shapes that loosely looked like weapons.

"Now call them," Noctus said.

"I don't know their names—don't they have names?"

"Yes, but you don't need to know their names to call them."

"Really? Because it seems like it would be rude to not use their names."

Noctus stared at me. "Are you truly considering if an heirloom—a weapon created for blood and battle—can have feelings that can be *hurt*?"

I swirled my hand through the pocket realm's mist. "Well. Politeness doesn't cost anything."

And it's entirely possible Ms. Booker has rubbed off on me...

Noctus's expression didn't change, but the spiral in his eyes swirled—in either amusement or...yeah, no, probably just amusement. "After a weapon accepts you, yes, you need to call it by its name," he said. "But you won't know its name until it accepts your call and materializes for you. Then you are partners and working together."

"So there *are* rules of politeness for this. Got it. So how do I call?"

"You request their presence," Noctus said. "and their partnership."

"Out loud?" I asked. "They'll hear me in the pocket realm?"

"You can use magic, but in this case out loud is the easiest way, so yes, that's how you should ask," Noctus said.

"Okay." I rolled my shoulders back and took in a deep breath. "My name is Chloe Anderson, and I respectfully request the pleasure of your presence."

Noctus exploded into laughter.

My ears started to burn with embarrassment—I thought the heirlooms, being ancient and powerful, would be less...deadly if I used my best manners to appeal to them. Apparently that wasn't necessary.

Before I could ask Noctus how I was *supposed* to ask them, I felt something—like unwound cotton swabs or cobwebs trailing across my hand. "Um, Noctus?"

Noctus was still laughing. "You sound like you're inviting them for tea."

I peered into the pocket realm, watching as black shadows passed through my fingers. "Noctus—they're moving. Your weapons, or heirlooms—whatever you call them—are moving."

Noctus pushed his hair back and exhaled, his posture relaxed and casual. "Good."

"They're just passing through my fingers, though—is that normal? Are they getting mad?" I swapped my weight from my right foot to my left foot and contemplated yanking my hand out.

"They're considering your call. If they decide to answer it, you'll feel the weapon materialize in your hand, and then you can pull it out."

Watching through what little space I could see around my wrist, I saw the shadowy shape of a spear, then a sword, followed by a bow pass.

Soon, nothing passed by my hand. I could still see shadows moving around inside the realm—I even caught sight of a sword that had a metallic glint to it unlike the rest of the weapons covered in fog—but nothing came close.

"They're not passing by anymore," I said.

"I see." Noctus rubbed his jaw.

"Does that mean they aren't going to respond?" I asked, caught between glee and a twisted sense of disappointment.

"Not necessarily," Noctus said. "I have a very large collection. It would take some time for each weapon to decide if they want to respond to you."

"How many weapons do you have?" I asked.

Noctus peered up at the sky, a rare line slithering across his forehead as he contemplated the question.

Ah, that probably means it's several dozen at least—it's probably as many, if not more than, his closet back in the villa.

"Well over two hundred," Noctus concluded.

My shoulders shot up and I puffed up like a cat. "*Over* two hundred?"

"Maybe three hundred," Noctus said. "Keep in mind, at least half of those came into my possession after the war. I didn't particularly want them, but—more importantly—I didn't want anyone else taking them and using them for ill purposes."

He had to have attacked his family for a good reason. He's too conscious of danger and the abuse of power for him to have done it out of sheer bloodlust. But of course, that was obvious when I was still Ama.

"You can take your hand out," Noctus said. "The weapons at least heard you. Next time we try, perhaps one of them will respond after being given the chance to ponder you."

I shivered. "The more you explain weapons, the more weirded out I get."

I started to pull my hand out of the storage realm. When my palm passed through the threshold—leaving just my fingers in the pocket realm—I heard something echo in my mind.

Truck.

CHAPTER TWENTY-ONE

Chloe

I hadn't thought of the word, and I hadn't exactly *heard* it—at least, not with my ears. The word bloomed in my chest, spoken by a foreign, unrecognizable voice.

"Is something wrong?" Noctus asked.

"I thought I heard something."

Noctus straightened up. "What did you hear?"

"Truck."

"Truck?" Noctus repeated.

"Yeah. Truck."

Noctus scratched his neck. "I don't have any weapons named truck—all of them were forged well before the invention of the human car, anyway."

"I must have misheard it," I said. "Or was just having an auditory hallucination."

"It could be a weapon," Noctus said. "Perhaps it's trying to tell you something, but you didn't catch it all."

I paused—my fingertips still in the realm—then shook my head. "I don't think so. I can't hear anything else."

"I see. Regardless, it's encouraging. We should attempt this again," Noctus said.

I only half listened as I pulled my fingers free from the storage realm and watched with freaked-out interest as the mist faded.

That was an experience. It wasn't as terrifying as I thought it would be, but only because nothing actually answered me.

Aloud, I said, "I think I'll stick to my daggers and short sword."

"Once you're skilled with them, you'll get bored." Noctus looked out at the glowing city. "Then you'll want to try something else."

"I doubt it'll ever come to that," I said. "I won't have the centuries you've had to get bored."

Noctus yanked his gaze from the city to me. I could tell by the furrow to his eyebrows that the thought hadn't occurred to him.

"Because shadows aren't immortal—we're humans," I reminded him. "Right?"

"Right," Noctus said slowly—as if he didn't agree but couldn't find a way to counter the laws of nature.

I watched him for a moment, but he stared at the ground, thinking.

I turned, and leaned against the railing. I could see the building that used to house Magiford Donuts—until Noctus, Charon, Ker, and Aristide had busted the place up, anyway.

I wonder if a new bakery will move in there...

Thinking of the donut shop—of everything that had happened in the past few weeks, my shoulders fell. "Thank you, Noctus."

Noctus was silent as he joined me at the railing. He waited for a moment or two, staring out at the twin lakes that were black puddles outlined by the city's streetlights. "For what?"

When I shifted, our shoulders touched. "For the training, for keeping me safe, for outfitting me with weapons—for everything."

"You've thanked me multiple times," Noctus said. "It's not necessary."

"You've done so much for me."

"Including keeping you as a captive," Noctus dryly said.

I winced—it was easy to forget that while I was here voluntarily due to the tracker creeper, Noctus still wasn't going to let me just waltz off into the sunset when everything was finished.

"Isn't it just that everything is complicated?" I asked him. "I betrayed you, you're a king so you can't let loose ends wander around..." I felt Noctus's eyes on me, so I smiled up at him.

"You have an incredible ability to forgive," he said.

"Technically, you forgave me first," I said. "I was the one who lied to you."

Noctus shook his head. "Except you've proven yourself trustworthy—or Charon would never have agreed to train you in the first place."

"It's been interesting—the training I mean." I tugged at my short sword that was strapped to my back. "I can tell my reactions are getting faster, and more automatic."

"Soon you'll be able to face the tracker on your own," Noctus predicted. "If we could flush him out, that is."

"No way—he's too terrifying, and I've only been training for, what, a month? Maybe two?"

"You are a shadow," Noctus pointed out. "A *full blooded* shadow. Taking on a single half elf is easy work."

I shook my head. "Maybe after years of training—"

"And that's why you're not ready yet," Noctus informed me. "Because your first instinct is still to deny your own abilities and to run. Once you are confident enough to face the tracker on your own, you will be safe enough to live where you like."

There was something about Noctus's near lecture that made me relax.

•

I'd said we had a complicated relationship, but that was understating it.

It didn't matter, though. Noctus had come at me openly, from the beginning. Whatever weirdness there was in the future, we'd figure it out. He wasn't going to lock me up and throw away the key, and I would make sure I *died* before breathing a word about the existence of the elves.

It'll work. Because Noctus is how people in positions of power are supposed *to be.*

"Do you think the tracker gave up on using the Seelie and Unseelie Courts?" I asked.

"Doubtful," Noctus said.

"What makes you say that?"

"Because both Seelie and Unseelie fae still skirt around the neighborhood. If *they* haven't given up on trying to recruit me, the tracker still has a shot at manipulating them to do as he wishes, particularly since everything that has happened can only support the claim that you're important to me."

I winced. "I was hoping I'd be able to start working for Ms. Booker soon. Do you think I could get a few shifts, maybe see if he shows up?"

Noctus stared up at the bright moon. "Someone would have to accompany you as backup—against both the tracker, and to keep watch on you."

A knife twisted in my gut. *I thought he trusted me? Did I overestimate how close we are?*

"I'm not going to tell anyone about Calor Villa," I said.

Noctus glanced down at me. "I know."

I relaxed. "Really?"

"The problem isn't that you aren't trustworthy, it's that all my people depend upon this secret staying hidden. The smallest mistake could ruin everything. For now, I must be overly cautious."

Ohhh, I really need to tell him about Ms. Booker. But then he'll surely want to bring her here, and she only knows about him, and she's helped me so much—plus it was my fault she learned about it to begin with.

This was one of my worst nightmares: two people I cared deeply about needing opposing things. Guilt gnawed at my insides.

It's a complication I'll have to figure out. Eventually I'll need to tell him, but I refuse to risk Ms. Booker because of my problems.

Noctus slightly narrowed his eyes. "Chloe."

"Yeah?" I asked when he didn't go on.

Noctus turned toward me. Slowly—giving me plenty of time to move away—he reached out and rubbed the jewels on my necklace/collar with his thumb. "I never gave you a choice."

He was studying me with such an intense and personal expression, I had to clear my throat twice before I could speak. "A choice in what?"

"Having a connection with me," Noctus said.

"You thought I was a cat," I said. "You wanted to protect your pet."

"But I didn't ask you after you revealed yourself," Noctus said.

"Yeah, because you only knew me as the clerk at Book Nookery who'd been pretending to *be* your pet," I said.

Noctus narrowed his eyes. "Why are you defending me?"

I would have fidgeted, but Noctus's fingers were still resting on my collar. "Because your actions are logical considering your career and how sketchy I appeared to be. It makes sense you'd want a very precise tracking spell that wouldn't wear out on a potential information leak."

Noctus frowned at me, so I smiled. "I would have done the same thing in your position," I said. "In fact, I was totally prepared for you to throw me into a dungeon."

Noctus shifted his gaze back to my collar. "I wouldn't do that—to you."

"And you didn't," I agreed—though I had caught his stipulation.

So he'd do that to others, hmm?

Noctus stared at me for a few long moments that were starting to make me feel a little self-conscious. Sure, his hair looked perfect, but mine was probably a sweaty, frizzy mess at this point from all the running.

"Something wrong?" I asked.

He shook his head. "It's time I give you the choice."

Lost, I sifted back through our conversation for anything I'd missed. "The choice of what?"

Noctus slid a finger under my collar, the pad of his finger scraping my neck. He slipped another finger on the opposite side, then tugged my collar upwards.

The sensation of his magic grazed not just my neck, but also my *mind* as the fabric of the collar stretched and Noctus slipped it over my head.

He pulled it free, and I staggered as I felt...loss.

It took me a moment to realize that the steady invasion of his magic was gone. It had become so familiar—almost like a pet—that its absence was a gaping hole in my mind.

"W-what?" I blinked up at him.

Noctus put the collar in my hand, then gently pushed my fingers shut over the material. "You must choose whether you'd like to be bound to me." He took a step back, putting space between us. "It isn't something that should be forced. It wasn't meant for that, and in the end it wouldn't help either of us."

I opened my fingers and stared at the collar. "But...tracking?"

"We can use another spell. It's unlikely, anyway, that Aristide or Ker will let you out of the house on your own." Noctus's voice was wry.

Ms. Booker said the magic that goes into this spell is very powerful, and I knew he did it because he adored Amalourne, then kept it on me for convenience. But...

I carefully folded the collar in half so it better fit my palm, then gazed up at Noctus. "What does this mean?"

"It means," Noctus was slow to begin, his voice even deeper than usual, "that I am not often in a position where I know a person has made a choice—a true, free choice."

Because he's a king, and because he's powerful. Even if he offered, he'd never really know if they genuinely wanted their choice, or if it's because they fear him or need him.

He leaned against the stone wall and rested his hands on the metal railing that shot out of the stone. "And an elven binding is something I would offer only if it was freely accepted."

"Would it be like Ker?" I asked.

Noctus glanced at me. "She told you her past?"

"Yeah."

He nodded. "The collar is...far more advanced than what I do for Ker. It's more personal and reveals much more of your inner self. It's called binding for good reason."

That makes sense, given that I could use his magic with the collar on. But, if I accepted, what would that mean for my life?

My automatic reaction was to give Noctus the collar back and thank him for the choice.

I did not need to be tied to an elf king—that was going to not only complicate my life here in Magiford, but my family life.

I'd have to lie to my parents, and it would mean changing my entire life. No more dreams of working at the Curia Cloisters—there was no way I could risk that if I were tied to Noctus.

But I don't have *to work at the Curia Cloisters to be safe anymore. I've been trained up; I can defend myself. I don't need that kind of protection.*

I scratched my arm with my free hand, desperately trying to give my body something to do as my nerves cranked into high gear under Noctus's stare.

What really kept me from handing the collar over, though, was Charon, Ker, Aristide, and—most importantly—Noctus himself.

They had come to mean the world to me. Despite everything,

they were my friends. Not only were they kind to me, they'd gone out of their way to train me up and teach me about my abilities. I trusted them on a completely different level from what I'd experienced before.

And that didn't even count all the head busting Noctus had done for my sake.

Ms. Booker was unbelievably kind and understanding, but besides my family I'd never had anyone *fight* for me before. I'd been too weak, and not worth protecting by supernatural standards.

I risked sneaking a glance at Noctus. His expression was blank, which I knew meant caution. He was waiting for my reaction.

Maybe that's why I want to think it over.

I would never admit it out loud, but I trusted Noctus the most. He was the only one I would have followed over the side of the clocktower, because he was the only one who had nothing to gain in befriending me.

Don't get me wrong, Aristide, Ker, and Charon were amazing friends, but they also unapologetically used me to get Noctus to adopt healthier patterns.

Noctus...just wanted friendship.

And as a supernatural who'd spent my life excluded from the supernatural community, that was something I understood all too well.

But my family—I'd have to lie to them! This could even endanger them.

With that in mind, I took a deep breath. "Can I think about it for a little while?" I peered up at Noctus as I nervously fidgeted.

His eyes softened. "Of course. It's not a decision to be made lightly."

"It's not," I agreed. "But, thank you—for the choice, and even for offering the binding. I really—it's just my family."

Noctus pushed off the wall with a shrug. "I can't say I understand, but family is a very foreign thing to me."

"They're important to me," I said. "They're amazing."

"Chloe." Noctus's voice was deep and tinged with amusement. "You don't have to defend yourself. This is an important decision. Think it over carefully."

I deflated. "Thank you for—"

"If you say 'for everything' I will toss you over the side of the clocktower and make you take the stairs up," Noctus said.

I made a face at him. "I was going to say for understanding, and for offering this to me in the first place. I'm...I'm..." I struggled to try to find words to explain just what I was feeling.

Noctus watched with a raised eyebrow.

He doesn't think this means as much to me as it does, I realized, disappointed for him and myself.

Before I could lose my nerve, I leaned into him. Noctus froze, staying motionless as I did my best to hug him. I had to stand on my tip toes so I could wrap my arms around his neck. I was familiar enough with him that the intensity of his harnessed magic didn't bother me. I didn't even feel uncomfortable...at least not until he *remained* frozen.

I hope he hugs me back soon, or this is going to get awkward, fast. Maybe I smell ripe from our practice session and he—

Noctus swept me up in his arms, picking me up off my feet.

I was so relieved he understood what I was trying to say, that I laughed a little as I clung to his neck, and my heart thumped in my chest in a *good* way.

When he set me down, he had to bend, slightly, so I could keep on hugging him.

I briefly rested my forehead on his shoulder, enjoying the contact.

There's just one question I have about all of this, and it should probably factor big time into my decision.

"But, Noctus, why would you—" I started. I kept my arms

around his neck, but leaned back a little so I could look up at him. "—want to be bound to…" I trailed off when I looked up into his clear, hazel eyes, and saw the spirals of his pupils were swirling.

The light from the clock face behind us cast a golden glow on him that felt like magic, but it was the absolute attention he was giving me that made my belly flop in my gut with a weird, giddy feeling.

"Why would I want to be bound to you?" Noctus asked. "Do you *really* have to wonder, Amalourne?"

"Maybe I wouldn't." I swallowed, my mouth suddenly dry. "If I knew what Amalourne meant in Elvish."

Noctus's laugh was low, but he was so close I could feel it through my arms draped on his shoulders. "So you're bargaining now, are you? You've come so far."

For some reason, I went up on my tip toes again, and Noctus simultaneously slanted his head down.

We were so close, his hair brushed my forehead.

When I moved my lips to say something, my lips brushed his, and it felt like a fire erupted in my heart.

"Noctus," I said, my brain shockingly silent for once.

Noctus's lips curved into a teasing smile. "Yes?"

He tilted his head closer, and it felt like we were magnets, pulling each other closer.

My eyes fluttered shut, and I again felt the soft brush of his lips on mine. The pressure increased from a brush of our lips to the start of a kiss, and—

DING-DONG!

CHAPTER TWENTY-TWO

Chloe

The clocktower bell tolled, making me scream and shoot out of Noctus's arms like the scaredy cat I was.

I teleported about six feet away and latched on to the railing, puffed up and on high alert. The bell was so loud it made the stone reverberate under my feet, and as the minute hand moved above us so it pointed to twelve, the hour hand dropped down a notch to the three. Both of the hands made a loud, cranking noise.

After tolling three times, the clock fell silent—at least, I think it did. My ears were ringing, and my heart was pounding so hard I don't think I could have heard anything else over it.

I turned back to Noctus, my heart stopping when I saw he was watching me, laughing so hard he had to lean up against the clocktower.

I was not nearly so amused—my heart was still frantically beating from the fright.

"We have the worst timing," he said.

I froze, wide-eyed. "Uhhh."

Noctus shook his head, and pulled out his cellphone. He checked it, then typed out a message. "Come on. Charon's starting to fret." He held out his hand.

So...I guess that's it?

The thought both disappointed and relieved me. I mean, I almost got to kiss *Noctus*.

But! I almost kissed *Noctus*. I liked to think I was logical and smart, but kissing *Noctus* was a big flashing sign of "here there be danger" if I wanted to make a good, unbiased choice about the collar.

Besides, if he was able to shrug it off so fast...does that mean something?

Probably not, I was probably over-analyzing. But, retreating for the day sounded like a good plan. So I hurried after him and slapped my hand in his for our traditional high five. Once again, he caught my hand and threaded his fingers through mine as he led the way to the elevator.

I knew I'd go tomato red from just holding his hand if I didn't do anything to distract myself, so I scrambled for conversation. "Are we going home?"

"Yes." Noctus pressed the button for the elevator, and it opened with a ding. "After we stop by the flower shop. Ker wanted me to check on it."

I stepped into the elevator and pressed the button for the ground floor. "Why?"

Noctus twitched our joint hands as the elevator rocked into motion. "Because it's her store."

I straightened in surprise. "Really?"

"Yes. She opens a new business whenever she gets bored, but since she can't appear openly in public, she relies on elven staff members—it's why she's so obsessed with Dale Carnegie."

"Wow. I never knew."

"Only because she was waiting to tell you—she was probably hoping she could send you to the shop and then get your personal opinion on it."

"Is it okay that you told me?"

"After all the crap she's given me over not realizing Ama was a shadow? Yes," Noctus said.

I laughed as the elevator stopped and the doors opened.

What an amazing and perfect night!

AROUND NOON THE FOLLOWING DAY, I dragged my human butt outside to make myself wake up.

I was pretty used to night life from my shifts at Book Nookery, but I also knew that I needed to get up and move or I'd sleep all day. So I went for a walk—just around the cul-de-sac.

I waved to Charon—he was washing the car in the driveway—as I finished my third cul-de-sac loop, ending outside Shiloh's house.

"Chloe!" Shiloh threw open her front door and charged outside. "Hey—you want to try some cheese?"

I stopped by her mailbox and wondered if I'd heard her right. "Cheese?"

Shiloh brandished the wooden tray she was carrying in the air. "Yes, cheese! My best friend from high school sent me some—she's going to college up in Wisconsin and knows I *love* cheese." Shiloh presented the wooden tray—which was filled with organized rows of creamy white and orange cheeses—to me with a bow. "I was born in the Wisconsin half of Magiford, so I have to be loyal to my state! Here—try this one. It's ten-year aged cheddar!"

Shiloh pointed to an orange piece of cheese on the end.

"Thank you." I took a piece and ate it. It had a nutty, sharp flavor that I felt in my cheeks, weirdly enough.

"Did you get a piece with salt crystals? Those are the best." Shiloh nibbled on a slice.

"It's really good," I said. "Thanks for sharing."

"Of course! Cheese is meant to be shared—or else I'd just get sad!" Shiloh laughed.

"Because you miss your friend, or because you don't live in cheeseland like her?" I laughed.

"Both." Shiloh sighed morosely. "I mean, we can get good cheese here, and Wisconsin is literally half of the city. But originally we were going to go to Wisconsin for college together."

"What kept you here?" I asked.

"The house, really." Shiloh looked back at her well-kept home —which looked storybook perfect. "If I followed the plan of moving north, I would have had to sell the house—there's no way I could have afforded to pay for college *and* the expenses of a home."

"Your parents..." I trailed off, thinking of what Shiloh had mentioned of them, and realizing I'd been as dense as a dog.

Her dad...she's referred to him in past tense this entire time...

"My mom died when I was little, and Dad passed away when I was nineteen," Shiloh said. "He was diagnosed with cancer, so I took a gap year to spend time with him before he passed." Her smile was sad.

"Shiloh...I'm so sorry," I said.

Shiloh shrugged. "You didn't know. And it's been a few years, now."

"But I didn't need to make you talk about it."

"Grief is a funny thing—it sticks around like a bad smell in the fridge, but if I didn't have it, I'd be worse off since it's proof that I loved them. But I can grieve them and still have happiness. They'd want that for me."

I slowly set my hand on her shoulder. "I know I never met them, but I can promise you they'd want your happiness."

Shiloh flashed me a smile. "Thanks. I just don't know what

I'm going to do about this house. I'm about at the end of the classes I can take at the local community college. If I want to get a degree in the career field that I'd like, I'll have to switch to a state college."

She glanced down at her cheese tray and made a face. "But that's a worry for later. For now, there's cheese."

Sensing she wanted to change the topic, I peered down at her tray. "What other kinds of cheese do you have?"

Shiloh immediately perked up. "*So* many! This is a cave aged sheep's milk cheese, this is a cranberry cheddar—this one with the herbs in it is fontina. It's *amazing*!"

We chatted about cheese as Shiloh talked me into sampling every flavor her friend had sent and Charon made steady progress on the car.

We'd relocated to the chairs on Shiloh's front porch, when my cellphone started frantically beeping as I apparently got an influx of texts.

"Sorry." I stood up as I struggled to pull my phone out of my exercise shorts.

"No trouble. I should actually get back inside and get ready—I have to leave for class in about ten minutes." Shiloh stood up, retrieving her cheese tray from the coffee table she'd put it on.

"Thanks for the cheese, and have a great class." I retreated down the sidewalk as I finally started to swipe my phone open.

"Thanks! Tell your boyfriend I say hello!" Shiloh wriggled her eyebrows and disappeared inside before I could correct her.

I started to groan, but the noise died in my throat when I finally read my incoming text messages.

We have your siblings

That message had come from Pat's number.

If you wish for them to be safely released, surrender for judgment.

That message had come from Joy.

Interrupting the messages was a picture of Pat and Joy. Both of them were seated in rickety metal chairs, their legs zip tied to the chair and their hands bound to their sides with duct tape.

The background looked industrial—cement floor with metal siding behind them. There were two figures on either side of the photo, but only their shoulders were visible—the rest had been sliced off.

My heart froze in my chest as I stared at the chat.

Is it some kind of sick joke? No—we'd never joke about something like this. Not with Pat's background in law enforcement. But how did it happen?

Joy hadn't sent her morning cat picture in our group text, but that wasn't too unusual. She missed the occasional day when she was pulling long hours for work as a lawyer.

But was that a clue that she'd already been taken? Who would do this—the tracker? But one guy isn't a "we"!

I finally scrolled past the photo, my fingers tingling with my nerves so I couldn't even feel the screen.

If you notify the Curia Cloisters, they will be eliminated.
If you try to fight, the wrath of the Seelie and the Unseelie shall rain down upon you.

When I read that final message, I looked back at the photo.

Those were guards on either side of the picture, and thanks to the text, I could see one of the guards—the one on the right who wore a green tunic—was a Seelie dryad. He had the Seelie flower patch on his pauldron. The other was a faun of some kind—he was probably Unseelie.

I clutched my phone in my hand and raced across the road without looking for traffic—which earned me a shout from Charon.

I ignored him and raced past, throwing open the door of the

house. I barely noticed when I ramrodded through the magic portal. My chest was tight, and it felt like I couldn't breathe, so the usual strange sensation didn't even register.

I leaped out of the portal and almost smacked into the fancy gate. And as my world crumbled, I gave in to a gut instinct I'd never had before.

I screamed for help.

"*Noctus!*"

CHAPTER TWENTY-THREE

Chloe

Noctus prowled back and forth across his study, his phone held up to his ear. He didn't say anything, but he oozed a seething sort of fury as he listened. He'd been trying to reach the Paragon for the past twenty minutes, but the fae representative wasn't picking his phone up.

I sat on the couch, swinging from feeling numb and empty to worry in which my brain overheated with out-of-my-mind anxiety.

Ker was perched next to me, an arm thrown across my shoulders. "They're going to be okay," she said. "King Harel and Queen Darina aren't going to do anything to them—they know better than to harm humans."

"But do they really?" I asked. I felt so *cold*, even with Ker pressing her side against mine. "Some of their battles have ripped up human neighborhoods."

"Maybe, but if they bothered to take your siblings, they care too much about the outcome of this to impulsively get rid of them," Ker said.

I shook my head, and glanced at Aristide.

He was sitting on his favorite chair, his fingers pressed together like a church steeple.

His intense silence frightened me more than anything else. If Aristide wasn't attempting to break the moment with a complaint or sarcastic statement, things were *really* bad.

The door clicked shut when Charon entered the study, easing the door shut behind him. "I beg your pardon, Chloe?"

"Y-yes?" I tried to swallow around the lump in my throat.

"You said your siblings had location sharing enabled?" Charon asked.

"Just for the family, yeah." I held my phone out—I'd checked as soon as I'd explained everything to Noctus and the others.

Both Pat's and Joy's phones were located in the same spot in an industrial part of Magiford. I'd marked the spots on my maps app.

Charon took my phone and zoomed in and out on the app as he surveyed the surrounding area.

I wiped my watery eyes. "But just because their phones are there, doesn't mean they are."

Charon bowed his head after he handed me my phone back. "I am aware, although I suspect the chances are better than you'd think. Fae reluctantly use technology, but by no means do they understand all possible applications."

Noctus stopped pacing, and his phone blared loudly enough for me to recognize the Paragon's jolly-sounding voicemail message. "Check your messages and get back to me, *immediately*," Noctus growled into his phone. He hung up, then turned to Charon. "Send someone to the area to check—someone who blends in with humans and knows Magiford."

Charon bowed deeper. "Of course, Your Majesty."

"If you can get a visual of fae hanging around that spot, you think it means they're there?" Aristide asked.

"Possibly," Noctus said.

"Hey, Charon?" I called after the elf, who paused at the door. "Is that part of town neutral?" I asked. "Because if the Seelie and Unseelie are working together, there's no way they'd keep them in one territory."

Charon's brow puckered. "I believe that particular area was indeed neutral as of earlier this week—there's a supernatural restaurant that maintains the area instead. But with the increase in the fights between the Unseelie and Seelie, I am not certain if that is still the case. I will look into it."

"Okay, thank you," I said.

Charon slipped away like a ghost, while Noctus tossed his phone on his desk.

I miserably clenched my hands into fists. "This is my fault—I should have warned Pat and Joy about the tracker and that the fae were after me."

"You had no reason to think they needed warning," Noctus said. "As your siblings live solidly outside of Harel's and Darina's territories, I can't believe they managed to retrieve your siblings. The local Seelie and Unseelie fae from their cities would take their presence as an act of war."

"Why would they even think grabbing them was a good idea?" Ker asked. "The risk is way too big for the payout. *All* supernatural society will come down hard on them for endangering humans."

"I don't know that they thought of this idea," Aristide said, his voice chilly.

"What do you mean?" I asked, dread turning my fingers cold.

"This reeks of a larger political ploy," Aristide said. "Possibly it's all a ruse to drag Noctus out. You and Ker did hear that they had determined you were a good way to get to him."

I licked my dry, cracked lips. "Do you think the tracker told them to do this? In the last few times he chased me, he proved he was willing to endanger humans to get to me."

"This does seem more his style," Ker said. "And we already know he's been whispering into the fae's ears."

Noctus frowned. "Regardless, they did their homework. Queen Leila of the Night Court—the new fae empress—is currently gone visiting other Courts. The Paragon could possibly contact her to ask for her return so she could handle the situation, but he's not picking up."

"Then what do we do?" I asked. "Notify the Curia Cloisters—" I shut my mouth when Noctus and Ker exchanged looks. "What? What is it?"

"While the Curia Cloisters would surely spring into action considering your siblings are human," Ker slowly said, "bringing them into the situation is...risky."

I shook my head. "I know the text said not to tell them, but the Curia Cloisters is powerful enough—wait." My heart twisted painfully in my chest as I studied Noctus's closed expression. "You don't mean it's risky for Pat and Joy, but it's risky for *you*."

"The Curia Cloisters will undoubtedly wonder why the Seelie and Unseelie chose to kidnap your brother and sister," Ker said, her voice soft. "The Paragon could *possibly* be reasoned with—Noctus could make him a bargain so he wouldn't ask questions. The Curia Cloisters would uncover your connection to Noctus."

I wanted to say something, but my mouth wouldn't work.

She's not wrong, but it's Pat and Joy *on the line. My family is my everything!*

"If Charon confirms that the fae are where my siblings' phones are, couldn't we attack them and get them back like you did when you busted up Magiford Donuts?" I asked, my voice shaking.

"It's a very different situation," Noctus said. "Since we know two fae Courts are involved. It was easy to overwhelm the illegal artifact set up because it was one isolated situation."

"We cannot risk tipping off Harel and Darina to what Noctus

really is," Aristide said. "And if we took them out, both Courts would be certain of what he is, and there's no telling who they'd inform."

I stared at my clenched hands, an unpleasant ringing filling my ears.

This is it, I realized, faintly. *This is what I've been paranoidly worrying about—a clash between everything Noctus is protecting, and what I hold dearest: my family.*

"There's a possibility we can handle it," Noctus said. "For now, our best option is to wait until we hear back from the scout. Perhaps your siblings are being held by only a few guards, in which case we could get them back ourselves."

I woodenly nodded. "Yeah," I agreed. "Rushing in is a terrible battle tactic," I acknowledged, even though I wanted to race to my siblings, screaming and howling.

"There's still a chance the Paragon will get back to us." Ker squeezed my shoulders. "Don't despair, Chloe. You'll get your siblings back."

Despite Ker's assurances, Noctus's distance hadn't escaped me.

It was like a wall had gone up between us.

He knows it, too, I realized as I watched Noctus turn back to his desk and retrieve his cellphone. *He knows that I'd give up anything for my siblings, just as he would sacrifice anything for his people.*

HOURS TICKED by in what felt like years. I spent the time pacing my bedroom, my palms clammy with worry.

Ker stayed with me for most of it, and Aristide checked in a few times, but by the time night fell, neither could put off eating any longer, and they left for the kitchens.

I couldn't even think of eating—my stomach rolled at the

idea. So I headed to Noctus's study, hoping something had changed.

I knocked, then timidly stuck my head inside. My heartbeat doubled when I saw Charon. "Any news?" I asked.

"Yes." Charon held up his signature tiny notebook. "The scout has reported back."

I staggered into the room. "Are they there? Are they okay?"

"The scout didn't see your siblings, but he confirmed a fae presence at the address," Charon said. "Guards from both the Seelie and Unseelie Court were present. Additionally, the scout heard some of the guards reporting in that Harel and Darina wanted an update on the prisoners' status."

"That's Pat and Joy," I said. "It has to be them."

"It does seem so," Charon agreed. "The area is in neutral territory, and the guard updates had to be given on speaker phone so both monarchs could be assured they were receiving the same information."

"It seems Harel and Darina are able to work together quite well when properly incentivized," Noctus dryly said. "Any word of the tracker?"

"None," Charon said. "But the scout couldn't infiltrate the address—there were too many guards."

Too many guards? That's not a good sign; if it's a large force, Noctus won't move because it'll be too flashy.

"Did he get a count of the guards?" Noctus asked.

"An estimated fifty—probably more," Charon said.

Noctus's expression stayed emotionless, and any hope I had that he would head a rescue effort crumbled.

Charon could tell, too. He actually *stopped* looking at Noctus and glanced at me, his eyebrows bunching together in a look that could have been called concern, before he dropped his gaze to his notebook.

"A frontal attack, then, isn't possible," Noctus said.

"It would be," Charon bluntly said. "The Unseelie and Seelie fae would fall before you, Aristide, and Ker like bits of rubbish. But it would also undoubtedly reveal who—and what—you are, putting Calor Villa and everyone in it at risk."

I closed my eyes against the news I didn't want to hear. "Any word back from the Paragon?" I asked.

"None." Noctus's chair creaked as he leaned back in it.

I struggled to maintain even breathing and ignore the burning in my eyes from the tears that wanted to fall.

I can't fall apart. Pat and Joy need to be rescued. They're my top priority. I must hold it together, for their sakes.

Slowly, I opened my eyes once I knew I wasn't going to cry.

"Thank you, Charon. If there's nothing more, that will be all," Noctus said.

"Your Majesty." Charon bowed to Noctus, then turned to leave the room. He paused next to me and spoke in a lowered tone. "While a full front assault is not recommended, ambush and subterfuge tactics, on the other hand, would take better advantage of the situation and likely be more successful."

Is he saying I could handle it, with my particular kind of magic?

Charon slipped out of the study before I could ask, the door closing behind him.

I bit my cheek as I approached Noctus's desk. "So you're going to do nothing?"

Noctus was silent.

He doesn't want to say it.

"As soon as political movements are involved, I'm not free to move as I wish," Noctus said. "I have a city that *must* remain hidden."

I stared at a pink sparkly ball—an errant cat toy—that was stuck under a pile of paperwork.

"I could survive being ousted, but they cannot." Noctus rubbed his forehead—the first sign of emotion, though his face was still expressionless. "I wish it was different, but I have a duty—"

"I get it." My voice was soft, and far too fragile with my mixed emotions. "Ker told me you'd abandon her and Aristide without hesitation to save the city, and I know it's not personal, it's because you take your role seriously."

He looked away, and the white light of the white and blue flames in the fireplace highlighted the sharpness of his features.

"But, Noctus, *I* won't leave my family hanging any longer," I said, my voice gaining strength. "I'm going after them."

"And if I try to stop you?"

"You can't," I said. "Because I'll get out. Even if you throw me in a dungeon."

Noctus's stone mask cracked, and he frowned at me. "I'd never do that to you."

I pressed my lips together, but couldn't think of a response.

"I said I'd give you a choice," he continued. "Is this, then, your answer?"

I reached into my pocket, pulling out my lace collar. "Yes. No matter what happens, I promise I won't tell anyone about Calor Villa, and all your people." I set the collar on Noctus's desk, but my fingers wouldn't let go.

Noctus pushed back from his desk and stood up. I was aware of him moving around his desk, but I couldn't seem to look away from the collar, clenched in my hand.

Then Noctus put his hand on my shoulder. "And is there nothing I can say, nothing I can offer, that would convince you to stay?"

My vow to keep from crying was deeply rattled as I tried to smile at him, still clutching the collar. "I can't wait any longer, Noctus. Pat and Joy mean too much to me, just like your people mean too much to you."

Noctus stared at me, and while his face was blank, his hazel brown eyes were less warm than usual. They were clearer, and cold with regret. His hand skated down the length of my arm until he slid it around my waist, tugging me closer. "Anything, Chloe. Just name it."

I pressed my face into his shoulder and scrunched my eyes shut, losing the battle when I still shed a tear or two. "We can't. There's no way for us to coexist based on what we want—what we each must protect." The collar was twisted around my fingers by this point. "You *knew* this would one day happen."

"I did," Noctus agreed. "But I hoped it wouldn't." He scooped me up in a hug, once again lifting me off my feet.

I wrapped my arms around his chest and clung to him, trying to ingrain the moment in my memory: the softness of the worn fabric of his shirt on my cheek as I pressed it against his shoulder, him holding me up with one arm wrapped securely around my waist while the other snaked up my back, as if he could pull me any closer.

A salty taste flooded my mouth—probably from all the unshed tears—and my heart twisted in my chest.

He kissed my temple—a sensation so soft I barely felt it, but it made me grab a fistful of his shirt to keep breathing, because I knew he was saying goodbye.

When he set me down, the air between us was ripe with what-could-have-beens, and deep regret.

I grabbed his hand, set the collar on his palm, and made myself let go. Turning, I fled without looking back, rushing out of the room.

I bolted to my room—intent on getting out of the villa as quickly as possible. If Ker or Aristide saw me, I wouldn't be able to hold it together.

For once, luck was on my side. I stuffed my laptop and necessities in my backpack, and my clothes in my suitcase.

I hauled them downstairs, ramming my heels with my suitcase so hard I would have cut myself if I wasn't wearing the boots I wore when playing around the clocktower.

I opened the golden gate with a shaking hand.

"Amalourne."

I paused, then—despite my better judgment—looked back.

Noctus, carrying my leather harness, short sword, and daggers, stalked down the hallway. "Take these."

I might need them if I follow Charon's advice and try an ambush, but it seems wrong. I squeezed the gate so hard I could feel the flourishes etched into the metal press into the palm of my hand. "I can't," I said. "They're elven made. Someone could realize it and—"

"With your magic to escape attention, no one will even notice," Noctus said. "Take them." Whatever emotion he'd shown in the study was gone. He was back to being the perfect ruler—the way he looked at me was almost as if we were strangers.

"T-thank you," I said.

"Here." Noctus offered the short sword, holding it by the scabbard so we wouldn't touch.

"I'll have to put something in my suitcase," I said. "I can't really hold all of this."

"I'll put it in your backpack." Noctus grabbed my backpack, rotating me—and still being careful not to touch me. I heard him unzip a pocket and rummage around my bag. "Be careful of the tracker. Notify the Curia Cloisters immediately. You can safely tell them what you are—just don't say where you learned it from."

"Okay," I said.

"Don't be stupid about rescuing your siblings. Good luck." Noctus zipped the pocket back up.

I turned around, but he was already stalking off, his back to me.

The moment felt so final it was hard to tear my eyes off Noctus's back. It felt like the last time I'd ever see him. *Probably because it is.* My heart twisted in my chest. I clutched my sword to my chest, then forced myself to pull the golden gate open and step into the portal. *I must move—for Pat and Joy.*

CHAPTER TWENTY-FOUR

Chloe

Several hours later, in the coolness of the night, I stood in the shadows and watched the three warehouses I'd tracked my siblings' phones to.

The warehouses were owned by a human company—the owners probably had no idea this was going on—and were used as boat and car storage in the fall/winter/early spring. Now, in the middle of summer, they were mostly empty.

Charon was right; they must have chosen this area because the industrial part of Magiford is neutral ground, but I bet it was also because it was easier to find an empty location to store Pat and Joy in.

I double checked the buckles of my harness and made sure the strap that held my short sword in its scabbard for any of my upside-down moments was in place as I studied the area.

The three warehouses were unevenly arranged on either side of the road that split the lot in half. Two warehouses were on one side, with the third warehouse by itself, on the opposite side of the road, pushed toward the back of the lot.

The problem is that I don't know which of the warehouses Pat and Joy are in.

I was safely positioned across the street, leaning next to a commercial printing factory that was closed for the night. It reopened at six in the morning, but that was fine. I planned to act in the dark, when I had the greatest advantage with my powers. As it was barely midnight, I had plenty of time to act. The question was how.

The area was swarming with fae—Unseelie and Seelie alike. As Charon's scout had confirmed, I'd counted twenty-five fae from each Court, so fifty total, but already I'd seen guards go in and out of the buildings, so there were probably more stationed inside the warehouses.

Each warehouse had two doors—a large garage door used to pull the boats and cars in and out, and a human-sized side door. Four guards were stationed at every one of the side doors, and six were by the rolling garage doors.

The rest of the guards milled around, patrolling the well-lit paved road that rolled between the buildings.

That was a lot of fae for holding two humans, but I was pretty sure it was actually a continuation of the Seelie/Unseelie competition—that's why there were even numbers of guards everywhere. Because there had to be at least one member of each Court present.

I checked to make sure my cellphone was silenced and secure, then nervously checked the daggers strapped across my front for the third time as I scanned the area.

They must have disabled the human security system, I thought as I studied the cameras pointed at the warehouses. *Unless they really are that ignorant of human tech? I mean, they didn't think to turn off location tracking on Pat's and Joy's phones.*

Regardless, I wasn't going to worry about it. I was more upset about the warehouses.

Normal, industrial warehouses had more entrances and exits, or ventilation systems that I—as a cat—could exploit. These storage warehouses? They didn't even have windows. There was an external office out by the road that had windows, so I already knew Pat and Joy weren't being held there—I could see through the windows of the darkened office. No one was in there.

Charon was right. An outright war would either mean you'd need superior fighting power—like Noctus and the others—or large numbers, like the Curia Cloisters. I can't just take on fifty fae, particularly when I don't know how many reinforcements are inside the warehouses.

There was Charon's idea: subterfuge and stealth attacks. But I wondered if stealthily sneaking around the compound would accomplish anything. So on my trek over to this place I'd come up with a plan I had hoped to avoid: to go in boldly as a cat, and pray my magic meant they took me for a stray.

It meant trusting in my magic that I really had no way of knowing would work on so many fae at once. But I wasn't skilled enough to pick off the fae one by one, and I didn't have the power to face them all at once, so for now this was my best shot.

It's a risk, but this isn't about me, it's about Pat and Joy. If they catch me, there's a pretty good chance they'd release Pat and Joy anyway since they're humans.

With that thought to cheer me on, I took a deep breath, checked my short sword one last time, then changed into a cat.

In my cat form I was black as night, so it was easy to pick my way across the street without getting noticed.

The warehouses were penned in with a chain link fence—which would hardly have stopped me—but I went in the front entrance because I wanted to double check the office.

I hopped up on a windowsill to peer inside. Yep, there wasn't a sign of life—no Pat and Joy. Although I did feel a strong confusion charm that settled over the lot—it brushed past me, unable to stick to me thanks to my immunity to magic.

I was pretty sure the charm was an effort to keep humans out more than a true defensive maneuver, but it did surprise me they didn't have anything else in place. Although, since this was a joint effort between the Seelie and Unseelie, maybe they couldn't have anything else in place without breaking the unlikely truce they'd made to snatch Pat and Joy.

It doesn't matter—it won't stop us from leaving. I'll just have to keep an eye on Pat and Joy when we get out of here. However we get out of here.

I hopped off the windowsill and headed for the chain link fence.

I'll start by checking the furthest warehouse. It'll be easier to circle around that one since it's by itself.

Sticking closer to the chain link fence—which was shadowed by night, unlike the rest of the brilliantly lit up complex—and the weeds that sprouted around the border, it was easy enough to get down to the warehouse without being noticed.

I couldn't hear Pat or Joy, but that was maybe a good thing as it implied at least the fae weren't hurting them.

Or maybe the deafening thud of my heartbeat was covering any sounds they made. It echoed in my cat ears as I finally broke off from the fence and approached the third warehouse that sat alone on its side of the road.

I aimed for the side door first, as it had fewer guards I'd have to fool.

I stepped into the light and padded past them—as if I was more interested in cutting across the warehouse yard.

The guards—a leprechaun who was arguing with a pixie, and two naiads—didn't even notice me, which suited me fine. The door was shut, so I'd have to look through the big, open garage doors to find my siblings.

When I slipped around the building I again tried to act like a cat that was just passing through. I kept my tail up, but casually twitched it back and forth. I didn't look at the guards—although they certainly noticed me.

"Hey. Look." A goblin pointed a long, green finger at me. "A cat."

The five fae standing guard with him, stared at me.

"Think it could be cat girl?" the goblin asked.

I very purposefully stopped to sniff the ground.

"She does have a black cat form..." Another guard—this one a selkie, going by the melodic timber of her voice—narrowed her eyes as she watched me.

Although my instincts screamed at me to run, I made myself drop to the ground and roll in the dirt. By the time I stood up and shook myself off, the guards were losing interest in me.

"There's no way," the goblin declared. "Must be a stray."

The thing about cats was they didn't give a rip about what others thought. I'd learned over time that the best way to make my magic work—or to straight up fool people—was to be bold and *appear* to be totally unconcerned about them.

My heart beat furiously in my chest as I made myself wander a little closer to the guards—for appearances, and so I could peer into the warehouse.

It was empty—not a soul stood inside it. Weirdly, though, there was a wooden table covered with a white tablecloth. Vases of fresh flowers, a copper tea set, and a copper tray covered with tiny raspberry tarts, blueberry scones, and tiny finger sandwiches crowded the table's surface.

That can't be good—I doubt the guards are given a tea break...

I twitched my tail, then padded off, leaving the ring of light the open door cast into the night, rejoining the safety of darkness.

I better hurry. A fancy tea set up like that means they're expecting someone important. Important probably means backup.

Covered by the shadows, I easily avoided a patrol as I made my way to the warehouse directly across the paved driveway.

I couldn't see in—the guards were bunched up, blocking most of the view. I'd have to get closer.

Gravel prickled my paws as I drew closer. This time, I opted for the coy approach. I meowed while I was still in the shadows.

"What was that?" One of the fae brandished a bracelet—her magical artifact—high over her head, casting a tiny bit of extra light.

I meowed again, then stepped into the light shed by the open door.

"It's just a cat," a troll rumbled.

"Wait—a cat!" A centaur guard wearing leather armor emblazoned with the Seelie flower brandished a spear at me, scraping the ground with his front hoof.

I meowed again, then sat down and licked a paw, using it to scrub at my face.

It was hard to breathe normally, and it still felt like my heart might pop out of my chest—forget my lineage, I was so not cut out for all this cloak and dagger stuff.

"We're supposed to watch for cats," the centaur said, unmoved by my act.

A pixie broke off from the group and fluttered over to me, her wings beating like a hummingbird's. "Hello there," she said in a tiny, musical voice.

I sniffed at her, then sneezed three times when I accidentally inhaled a tiny piece of pixie dust.

The pixie tried to pet me, but like any good cat I leaned back, avoiding the uninvited touch. "She's a normal cat," the pixie declared.

"You can't know." The centaur took two clopping steps forward and changed the hold of his spear into one I recognized from seeing Charon fight as an attack stance.

Oh gosh, oh gosh. Is my magic not working on him? Come on—work!

"Surely it's not cat girl," the troll stated in such a confident way I knew my magic was working on him, at least. "It's too normal, and cat girl is not that skilled." He scratched the patch sewn into his shirt over his heart. It was an inky black droplet, marking him as a member of the Unseelie Court.

The centaur took another step closer to me, ignoring the pixie that buzzed around his head. "Is she not skilled, or is that what she wants us to think?"

Internally, I hyperventilated, unable to think of any thoughts that made sense. My hair was starting to puff up from my anxiety, but I stayed sitting and meowed again.

The centaur narrowed his eyes, and I saw his fingers tighten on his spear.

Magic, what are you doing?! Get him!

I thought I might throw up, when a high-pitched meow broke through the hysterical screams of my brain.

I—and all the guards—peered behind me, into the darkness of night.

A calico cat that was even smaller than me emerged from the shadows. She had to be a stray—she was rail thin, and the white fur on her chest and paws was closer to a shade of gray, while the orange and black patches of fur that covered her back and the top of her head were crusty.

She ignored the guards and approached me—my cat magic calling out to her.

We touched noses, then she immediately butted her head into my chest and crowded me, purring so deeply she made *my* bones vibrate.

Meanwhile, the pixie did a circle over us. "See? They must be lost!"

"No." The troll shifted his weight from foot to foot, then leaned against the wall of the warehouse, making it groan. "They're strays. I seen the little one hanging around here during the day."

"They're probably hoping we have food—woah!" The pixie dropped closer to the stray cat and I, but the calico was not as patient as I was, and she batted at her—claws extended.

The centaur relaxed his grasp on his spear. "That sounds like an understandable assumption." He swished his black horse tail as he returned to his place in the lineup.

The troll scoffed. "Getting all worked up over two crusty strays."

With danger backing a few safer steps away, I allowed myself a moment of outrage. *Crusty? Both of us are crusty? I am not! Noctus would have started pouring vitamins down my throat or looked for potions for fur if I looked crusty!*

When I stalked closer to the guards—I needed to look past them and see in the warehouse—the kitten followed me, chasing my tail. She didn't even notice when we were about a foot or two away.

The troll crouched down and offered his hand out to me—which was as big as I was. I sniffed it, but played coy so whenever he or the other guards tried to pet me, I darted just out of reach.

"They're very friendly for strays," the pixie said. She seemed especially determined to pet me as she landed on the ground and stopped beating her wings—a dangerous position for the pixie to put herself in.

"Agreed," the troll said as I ducked his hand. "Normally animals are scared of me."

The calico kitten wasn't as fast as me, so the troll managed to rub the top of her head with a single fingertip.

The kitten purred, but my magic was a stronger draw, so she left the troll and romped after me.

The centaur rested the butt of his spear on the ground. "Domestic animals fear most fae who lack animal taming magic. Even horses reject centaurs."

It's because you all are so bloodthirsty!

The troll stood up. "You encounter many horses as a member of the Seelie Court?"

The centaur shrugged. "On occasion."

"The Night Court has lots of animals," the pixie said.

One of the guards—a dryad, who'd been quiet this whole time—snorted. "Yeah, right. Good luck getting accepted into there. Your Seelie King will order you crushed before you even make it to their territory."

The pixie scowled and put her hands on her hips. "As if your Unseelie Queen would be any better!"

"We do what we must to survive," the troll said. "Same as everyone else here."

The guards all shifted in place and looked out into the shadowy night.

I thought the most dangerous thing would be convincing everyone I'm a cat, but no. It's encountering unexpectedly soft-hearted guards with sob stories. But, I'm here for my siblings. Not to change the Courts.

I took advantage of their sudden renewed interest in the yard to dart between the centaur's legs.

Behind them, in the middle of the warehouse, were Pat and Joy, zip tied and duct taped to their chairs, with four guards watching them.

Pat had his eyes closed and was sagging in the chair.

My heart clenched, but I didn't see any wounds on him.

Next to him, Joy was awake and alert. Her eyes were sharp, but her usually perfect blond curls were crushed from the manhandling, and the blank set of her face told me she was *ticked.*

She saw me, but she didn't react. Instead she looked at the guards.

She doesn't seem concerned about Pat. Maybe he's sleeping?

Joy fidgeted in her chair, and Pat's eyes shot open. He glanced in my direction, and—like Joy—immediately looked away.

Normally I'd say it was a sign my magic was working, but my distraction magic rarely worked on Joy and Pat—which was good because I would have spent a lot more time in animal shelters as a kid if they hadn't been able to get over it.

A faun guard who stood in front of my siblings lowered his sword to Joy's throat. "Stop moving."

My fur puffed up as I watched, and I wanted to tear across the warehouse, yowling, but that would hardly have stopped the fae.

Joy's forehead wrinkled, and I saw the glaze of fear in her eyes, but she did as he ordered.

I twitched my tail and forced myself to look away from my family. I needed to investigate the warehouse.

It didn't have any magic spells on it—no magical sensations besides the ticklish feeling in my elbow that I got from the fae in general.

How do I get Pat and Joy out of here with so many guards?

"Cat."

I looked back and realized I was somewhat standing underneath the centaur.

"Move," he said.

"Kick it," another Seelie guard suggested. "That'll teach it."

The centaur didn't answer—I didn't give him a chance to before I scurried out of the warehouse—I needed to check the last building before I came up with a plan. I didn't want any unpleasant surprises during my rescue attempt.

I did take a brief moment to rub against the troll's boots, then I trotted away, my tail high in the air.

The kitten meowed, and I waited for her to catch up.

She also ran past the troll—who smiled, his great craggy face puckering into a grin.

The Seelie guard who had suggested kicking me threw a rock at the kitten, nailing her on the back.

The kitten squeaked in pain, and I tore back to her, getting between her and the guards as I puffed up and hissed.

"Hey!" The troll took a step toward him. "How about I knock you one—see how *you* like it!"

"You're welcome to try!"

"*Enough*." The centaur thumped his spear on the ground. "No fighting—we vowed it. And leave the cats alone."

"Why? They're mangy fleabags."

"*I said*, leave it alone!" the centaur growled.

Crouched low to the ground, I slipped out of the circle of light the open door shed on the ground, the kitten following me.

The pixie followed, buzzing over our heads. "It's okay—I don't think the kitten was hurt," she shouted before she returned to the other guards.

I waited until we were able to hide behind a scrubby bush thing that had sprouted in a crack in the cement before I stopped to check the kitten.

She purred as she rubbed her head on my shoulder, so the rock couldn't have hurt her too badly.

Well, at least now I can comfortably go back to hating them, I thought as the kitten curled up next to me. *I should check this third warehouse, and then begin planning.*

I used the same tactics on the last warehouse—this one I didn't even have to get very close to see inside because the guards were clumped to one side. It was totally empty with no extra guards inside—which was good, because these guards were a lot more proactive and threw a spear, an empty water canteen, and a rock at the kitten and me.

I twitched my tail behind me as I stalked back to my scrubby bush—the kitten still trailing after me—barely registering the faint purr of high-powered engines. *At least they don't have hidden forces that will come pouring out if an alarm is raised—woah.*

Two cars crawled down the street, slowing just outside the warehouse compound.

They turned—without using a turn signal—and pulled into the yard. They glided past the first warehouse, the kitten, and me, and along the side of the third warehouse—the lone one that stood across from the second warehouse where Pat and Joy were.

I don't know cars, but both vehicles screamed expensive with that over engineered/robotic look found in only the gaudiest of luxury cars. I wasn't surprised when the doors opened upwards—because, again, overly engineered—and Queen Darina slipped out of the silver-colored car while King Harel got out of the red one.

CHAPTER TWENTY-FIVE

Chloe

Mom always told me you could tell how desperate a person was to impress others by how far their car was from the price range they could actually afford. Between the cars and all the battles they'd been in, the Unseelie Queen Darina and the Seelie King Harel *reeked* of desperation.

Queen Darina was dressed in a black dress liberally studded with glittering crystals, and a crown of black gems was tucked into her red hair.

King Harel was dressed more traditionally, wearing a fae tunic that looked like it had been embroidered with real gold. A cape with his insignia—a glowing purple flower—fell from his shoulders, and a golden circlet with a giant diamond emblazoned in the center was pressed against his forehead.

"I greet you, Queen Darina," King Harel boomed.

Queen Darina smiled cruelly. "And I greet you, King Harel."

Greetings observed, the pair eyed each other with open animosity.

"How is the Seelie Queen of Landford doing? I heard you recently saw her," King Harel said, naming a city made of mostly suburbs that was a short fifteen minutes away from Magiford.

"She shares your greed for territory that isn't yours," Queen Darina declared.

"Territory is won, thus it belongs to the victor," King Harel said.

"Oh, is *that* why your territory to the north shrank? The Seelie Queen of Lakeside is that much more of a victor than you are?" Queen Darina asked sweetly.

King Harel's lips formed what was supposed to be a smile, but was too toothy and not quite right, and he chuckled like a maniac.

Yikes, yes, they are desperate.

Since Seelie and Unseelie Courts were local, there were Seelie and Unseelie Courts all over the states. Cities like Chicago and Milwaukee had more than one Seelie and Unseelie Court.

But what if Harel and Darina were fighting not only with each other, but with monarchs from neighboring Courts? No wonder they didn't care if humans got caught in the crossfire. They were probably months away from losing their thrones if they didn't manage to defeat each other.

Two Unseelie guards stepped away from the third warehouse —the one set up with food—to flank Queen Darina, while two Seelie fae joined King Harel.

"Report in," Queen Darina demanded.

"No movement," an Unseelie Guard said.

"No magical presences or intruders," a Seelie guard said.

"Any magic at all?" Queen Darina asked. "Elven magic is advanced—he need not be here for his spells to be present."

So they're after Noctus as we guessed. But why did they decide to drag my family into it—how did they even find *them?*

"No magic at all," the guard confirmed.

"Any cats?" King Harel asked.

"Yes," the Seelie guard said. "Two. A black one, and a calico."

"A black cat?" Queen Darina's voice was as grating as shattered glass. "Chloe Anderson can turn into a black cat!"

"It wasn't her, Your Majesty," said the Unseelie guard.

"How do you *know* it wasn't her?" King Harel asked.

The guards blinked at each other, and my hair puffed up.

Oh no—my own magic might give me away if they can't make any logic out of this!

"It had a kitten—the calico," the Unseelie guard said.

"Yes," the Seelie guard backed them up with absolute certainty. "Chloe Anderson doesn't have any pets—or children."

The two monarchs glanced at each other—not to exchange looks of disbelief like I'd imagine, but rather to peer at each other with jaded suspicion.

"Five of you, search the area," King Harel ordered his people.

"Gather six soldiers and send them with," Queen Darina told her bodyguards.

"Six of you," King Harel barked at his guards.

For a moment it seemed like Queen Darina might scream at him, but she kept her emotions in check with a brittle smile.

Their distrust of each other is going to make this...not easier, but possible? They're so competitive, and since they can't trust each other, they need their people everywhere the other Court goes. But how do I use that?

Queen Darina watched her soldiers summon glowing globes of light before they—and the six Seelie guards—strode off, starting a circuit around the fenced compound.

Once she was satisfied, she marched toward the second warehouse, casually studying her nails. "It surprises me the elf hasn't moved yet, given how dear he seems to hold Chloe Anderson."

"Having some kind of attachment to Chloe Anderson hardly equates to caring if her family is threatened," King Harel growled.

That's a fae sentiment, but it's not wrong—though only because Noctus has way more he's protecting than they know.

"I knew it was a mistake to trust the words of that no name, mixed mutt supernatural," King Harel added. "Why would an *elf* move because of two humans?"

Wait, what? I stirred from my spot behind the bush, waking the kitten—who had started to doze off while snuggled against me. *Who told you what?*

"It's not like it matters," Queen Darina said. "You weren't getting anywhere recruiting him."

"Neither were you!"

A part of me was relieved it really was Noctus they were after. I'd spent my life trying to avoid this kind of attention. But there was something deep within my gut that boiled with fury.

They'd taken my *brother* and my *sister* because they were upset Noctus kept rejecting them? They were that petty—no, they were such terrible monarchs that *this* was the best solution they'd come up with?

Except, they said another supernatural had suggested it...that must be the tracker. We already knew he was advising Harel, but I wonder how he got Darina to listen to him too. He must have been the one to find Pat and Joy.

Queen Darina and King Harel entered the second warehouse —the one my siblings were being held in—as the guards parted for them.

I left my bush, but stuck to the shadows—I didn't need anyone seeing me since the king and queen had raised suspicions again.

The kitten bounded along next to me, occasionally pouncing on my tail before I pulled it from her tiny paws.

We skirted around to the side of the building, approaching it from an angle. I took us as close as I could because I wanted to hear whatever the king and queen said, but we stopped short of the light the open warehouse door cast on the ground, and watched Queen Darina and King Harel walk the last few steps to reach my siblings.

Most of the guards at the large rolling door had gone with them. Only the troll and centaur remained behind.

Fear lodged itself in my throat as the guards removed my siblings' gags.

Don't hurt them. Please, for once, don't be bloodthirsty!

"Where is Chloe Anderson?" King Harel demanded.

Naturally, my siblings ignored the king.

"The Magiford Seelie King, I reckon?" Pat said to Joy.

"Yeah," Joy confirmed. "I never bothered to remember his name—too unimportant—but I recognize his flower thing on his back when I read up on the city for Chloe. Pretty lame in person, isn't he?"

King Harel sputtered. "*Unimportant*?"

Queen Darina smirked, but my siblings weren't done yet.

Pat glanced at the Unseelie Queen. "Think she's a courtier, or is that too important a role for her?"

Joy shrugged. "Maybe his queen?"

Queen Darina inflated with her anger and shrieked.

Stop it, you two!

I recognized what they were doing. Pat and Joy were pushing the pair's buttons to get them to lose control, most likely in the hope that Darina and Harel would let some useful, important information drop.

But unhinged fae were the *last* thing you wanted coming at you when you were tied up, because they'd definitely—

CRACK!

Pat's head whipped backwards after Darina slapped him across the face, her hand leaving a red imprint and a cut from one of her rings.

She grabbed Pat's hair and yanked his head forward. "You lowly, *miserable* human! Learn your place and mind your tongue!"

King Harel grabbed a spear from one of his people—making every hair on my body puff up and stand on end. He rotated the spear so the blunt, wooden end pointed at Joy, then slammed it into her ankle.

No—stop! Stop it! My desperation and anger overrode my fear, and I nearly ran into the warehouse howling and spitting. My entire body tingled, but I fought to think clearly. *Get them out, I need to get the monarchs out of there. But how?*

I struggled to think while sounds of the assault echoed in my ears.

Pat was silent as Darina slapped him, and Joy whimpered as King Harel hammered at her ankle again.

The guards stirred and exchanged glances, but none of them moved to stop the monarchs—none of them *could* or they'd probably suffer a worse fate.

King Harel eventually tossed the spear away and turned to the guards. "Did Chloe Anderson ever respond to the text messages?"

"N-no," a leprechaun said.

"Queen Darina," King Harel snapped.

The queen let go of Pat and stepped back. "If you do not cease your disrespect, you will endure further treatment."

My brother spat, his spit pink with blood, and raised an eyebrow at her.

He exchanged a look with Joy. "Unimportant," they said simultaneously.

Queen Darina looked ready to strangle them, until King Harel shoved Joy's cellphone into her hands.

"No contact," King Harel said flatly. "From Chloe Anderson or otherwise. Have your men fetch that mixed mutt from your Court. He has some questions to answer considering he *guaranteed* this plot would work."

Queen Darina scowled. "He isn't staying with my Court, he's staying with *yours*!"

"No, he isn't," King Harel said. "He left with *your* retinue!"

"He isn't staying in Unseelie territory!"

"Well he certainly isn't in Seelie land!"

I filed away their comments to ponder later, but now wasn't the time to analyze their motives. Instead, I restlessly paced in the shadows, constructing a plan as fast as I could.

I need a fast out. A stealth operation would mean waiting until Harel and Darina left, and who knows how long that will be—or what they'll do to Pat and Joy in the meantime? But with magic that's only good for stealth, what else can I do?

My eyes landed on the expensive cars, and the beginning of a plan clicked into place. My magic was made for stealth, but that wasn't its only use.

It was risky, and possibly terrifying, but my whiskers didn't even quiver with fear—Pat and Joy were in danger. I needed to get them out. *Now*.

The kitten purred into my ear.

But first, I need to get this little guy to safety.

I purred as I stepped out of the shadows and trotted up to my chosen target: the troll.

The centaur frowned at me, but I ignored him, doing my best to charm the troll.

"Shh," the troll cautioned. "Shoo—they don't like cats here."

I ignored him, and purred louder as I sat down.

The kitten came running out of the shadows—chasing after me. It was young enough that it was still clumsy, so the kitten tripped on its own paws, fell, and smacked against the troll's boots.

The troll peered down at the kitten.

Yes, isn't it cute? Don't you want to pick it up? I purred—I didn't dare meow, or the monarchs might hear it.

The troll stooped over and rubbed the kitten on the top of its head before he helped it stand.

"Careful," the centaur warned.

"They're strays," the troll said. "They're not gonna hurt nobody."

"Softhearted," the centaur said, though he pointedly looked away from us and kept his back to the monarchs.

I waited until the kitten was practically falling over it was so excited by the troll's fingertip pats on the head, then I ran into the shadows, disappearing.

The kitten mewled its distress.

"What was that?" someone—Darina, I think—said in the warehouse.

The centaur hissed an oath. "Push it away!"

"If it comes back, they'll kill it," the troll said. He picked up the tiny kitten—his hand was so large he cradled it with ease—then dumped it in a pocket of his pants.

I saw the kitten move in the pocket, but it didn't complain. When the troll casually rested his hand over the pocket, I actually heard it purr.

The kitten is safe, time to execute the rescue mission. Hopefully.

If the worst happened, at least I knew Noctus would eventually get through to the Paragon, and if I was captured Harel and Darina would stop abusing my siblings—though I'd probably pay a price once they realized Noctus wasn't coming...

No, I'm going to be optimistic. I may, possibly make it—

Joy's scream ripped through the air.

I took off running. *I'll succeed. Or die.*

I skirted a patrol group—who didn't even notice me—and approached Darina's and Harel's expensive wheels.

Let's see...I didn't see either of them pocket the keys—are they still in the ignition?

I hopped on the trunk of the red car—Harel's. I slid a little because it had been polished with too much wax, which had left a slippery film on it that probably would have upset a car enthusiast. I managed to crawl up to the back windshield and peer inside the car.

A sparkle of silver dangled from the ignition.

Bingo—of course he'd assume no one would touch his *car. How about Darina?*

I hopped off and trotted toward Darina's car when a patrol group abruptly veered off their usual path and headed for the vehicles.

I had to wedge myself under Darina's car because it rode so low, and I barely managed to tuck my tail under, too, before one of the guards shone a light on the vehicle.

I crouched next to a tire, and my heart thumped painfully in my chest as the guards did a circuit around the vehicles.

One of the guards—a pixie, darted around the car, then landed on the ground, near to my wheel.

I held my breath as he walked under the car, until he stood next to my tire.

I pushed against the wheel, the smell of grease and car fumes overwhelming my nose, even though I still wasn't breathing. *If he comes in even a step farther, he's going to see me.*

"Under the car is clear," the pixie called before he ducked out, the shine that engulfed his body retreating until he launched into the air and disappeared.

I didn't breathe until the guards left—making the area darker as they carried their globes of light away with them.

Finally safe, I sucked in a gulp of air that was almost a wheeze. *I didn't know the Seelie and Unseelie guards were that competent! Wha—stress!*

I shook my head, but—remembering Joy's scream of pain—wriggled out from under the car, and shakily inspected Darina's car.

Hers was an even better choice than Harel's, because she'd not only left her keys in the ignition, but her driver and passenger windows were open.

Not that Harel had locked his door, but me opening and closing a door was more likely to catch attention before I was ready, and the car had those cab lights that came on with the doors, which was another dead giveaway.

Staying in my cat form, I leaped onto the frame of the passenger window and did a glancing inspection of the car.

There was some kind of spell, but it glossed over my fur like nothing as I hopped onto the passenger seat.

I climbed into the driver's seat, then maneuvered myself so I was sitting on my butt before I tapped my magic.

For once, being average height worked to my advantage, because when I swapped to my human body, my feet didn't slam into the pedals, and I didn't hit my head on the roof.

I slumped in the chair—leather interior, of course—to make sure I was out of sight. Next, I twisted around so I could peer through the back windshield, solidifying my plan.

My head and brain were shouting at me to stop—that busting my siblings out was *not* the way to stay unnoticed by supernatural society, and I was going to regret this, or get myself caught and it wouldn't help Pat or Joy.

But my gut?

My gut instinct, which had led me to Noctus, seethed.

Save them.

I took a breath, and turned on the car.

The engine roared to life, and I sat up straight so I'd be visible. All the lights came on immediately, so I pressed down on the brake, shifted to reverse, then watched through the open window, waiting.

The guards standing outside the third warehouse leaned forward so they could see me, but that was it.

Okay. I best get me some attention.

I laid on the horn, holding a long blasting note until all the moving patrols and the guards standing outside the warehouses swiveled in my direction.

I stuck my hand out of the window and waved. "Good evening!" I yelled at the top of my lungs. "This is a *very* nice car!"

"It's Chloe Anderson," the centaur guard outside warehouse two yelled. "Seize her!"

The guards bolted, abandoning their posts as they ran at me in unorganized mobs.

That's the problem with the fae—disorganization. Organization was what made Noctus, Aristide, Ker, and Charon so terrifying as a group.

I slammed on the gas, and the car roared backwards, bouncing and groaning when it ran over scrubby bushes that poked out of the ground.

I almost rammed into the centaur guard and a naiad, but I slammed on the brakes at the last second.

"Come on, come on," I hissed as I switched from reverse to drive, sweating while the centaur tried the door handle. "Go!"

I ground my heel on the gas, shrieking when it lurched forward.

Tires squealed as I made a hard right turn, circling around the unmowed backside of the third warehouse.

I hit a giant rock when I swerved to avoid a naiad. The rock sounded like it tore up the underside, and the entire car shook.

"Sorry." I patted the car's dashboard with a sweaty hand. "But it's only going to get worse from here."

I turned left, and we shot along the long side of the third warehouse as lights from pursuing fae started to cut around the corner.

My cat-like agility kicked in, and I cranked left again, turning up the road between warehouse three and two.

The luxury car wasn't made for off-roading, so when it switched from dirt to cement, the car sprayed the loose gravel that lined the road and skidded sideways. I drove on ice every winter, so fishtailing was a way of life for me, and the swerve was possibly the only thing about the event that didn't worry me. I let the car slide into the turn and slowed a bit before I corrected and went zipping up the road.

A dryad lobbed a ball of magic at me with amazing accuracy. It flew through the open window and smacked me. The accuracy didn't matter, however. It bounced off me—unable to stick thanks to my abilities—and landed on the passenger's seat, rolling with the car's movements.

A smart thinking goblin who had been guarding the first warehouse tried chucking a spear at a tire, but I cranked the steering wheel, whipping so hard to the left that I almost gave myself a neck injury.

The car roared to the end of the driveway/gravel road faster than I was prepared for. I got a few inches of air when it screeched over the smoothed curb and hit the city street. I was pretty sure it dented the front bumper because I heard a horrible crunch before I slammed on the brakes.

I looked back—the guards were racing after me, but I still had enough time to execute what was supposed to be a three-point turn to make a 180 degree turn.

I slammed the car's gear into reverse and backed up, peering out the window instead of watching where I was going—it wasn't like I was worried about damaging the car.

There's Harel and Darina. They were standing outside the second warehouse. I could hear Darina's high pitched, angry voice even over the hum of the engine.

I shifted to drive and turned, but I hit the gas too hard, so it didn't turn very well and just lurched and squealed its tires.

"Come on, come on, come on," I chanted.

I did my second attempt to turn the car. By the third attempt to turn—it still didn't turn enough, but that was my fault, not the car's, as the car handled well but I was not made for high stress situations—the fastest of the guards were almost to the property line.

I could hear their hurried footsteps on the gravel road.

By the time my three-point turn morphed into a five-point turn, a naiad took a shot at me. *Literally.*

A bullet dinged off the side of the car.

I sank lower in my seat and screamed, but by then I'd managed to turn the car entirely around. "Go, go, *go!*"

The car lurched its way back onto the warehouse property. I drove past the office, then slammed on the brakes, waiting.

I double checked that both the driver and passenger window were down, my breathing and heartbeat staying remarkably normal—though hearing your siblings scream in pain will do that I suppose.

I consulted my mirrors to see that the guards who had followed me to the road had almost caught up.

Darina and Harel were still by the second warehouse, but all the guards who had been posted outside the warehouses or moving around on patrols were trying to intercept me.

Perfect.

The pursuing guards were almost on me again. A faun led the charge; he was so close that when he stretched out his arm his fingertips brushed the back of the car.

So I floored it.

The car went from zero to *too fast* in a second. I was thrown back against my seat, but I gritted my teeth and kept my hands on the wheel.

The car roared down the short lane. I turned off it, pointing Darina's car directly at Harel's red car.

"*Stop her!*" Harel shouted.

I revved the engine one last time by slamming my foot on the gas pedal, then pulled my legs up and made the switch to my cat body.

I scrambled across the seats, ignoring the still active spell that had fallen into the leg space of the passenger seat, jumped onto the passenger window, and leaped out into the cover of darkness.

The car careened on and barreled into Harel's.

There was a tremendous screech of tires, then the groan of bending metal and the crunch of shattering glass.

I landed on the ground with an oomph, and dashed off,

keeping to the shadows as I ran back toward the entrance of the compound, avoiding the guards who were hot footing it to the car wreckage. Not like they could do anything—the front end of Darina's car was so crumpled, it wasn't even half the length it should have been. Even more gloriously, it had flattened the entire left side of Harel's car and slammed it against the warehouse.

"My car!" Darina shouted.

"*Your* car?" Harel yelled. "What about *my*—"

Something ignited in the wreckage, and the shockwave wrenched the two cars apart, smashing them both through the side of the warehouse.

The spell the naiad had tossed at me must have been activated.

The spell, combined with all the panicked shouting, made it easy for me to cut across the road, aiming for the second warehouse without being noticed.

The centaur and the troll were gone—they stood with Darina and Harel, who were sputtering over the damage to their cars—because of course they valued their vehicles over my siblings' lives.

They're fae, I reminded myself. *They don't value* anybody's *life.*

I ran into the warehouse, using a burst of speed, and crept around the inner wall.

Pat and Joy didn't make a noise. They had to have noticed me, but they were pointedly looking away as the two guards who remained with them nervously fidgeted.

The first guard, a faun, I took out by shifting to human and kicking him in the back of the head—self defense lesson from Pat: never use your fists when your foot can take the brunt *and* can do more damage.

The guard crumpled with a groan and fell to the ground. The second guard, a goblin, whipped around at the sound.

His eyes widened, and he sucked in a breath. "SHE'S—" He broke off, coughing, when I popped him in the windpipe.

I wedged my arm around his throat in a stranglehold and

clung to him. He scratched at my arm, and his pointed nails were sharp enough to leave gouges, but I held on despite the pain. I needed him out of it, but I wasn't desperate enough that I was willing to stab him with my daggers or sword.

He gurgled, his struggles weakened, and eventually he drooped over.

I felt for his heartbeat, then cautiously let him go, slowly releasing him so he didn't crack his head on the ground.

My siblings were smartly trying to wriggle free of their duct tape and zip tie bonds, though they froze when I pulled a dagger from my harness and made quick work of their restraints.

"Thanks," Joy whispered as she sprang out of her chair, rubbing at her wrists. "We should—" She trailed off when she swung around and saw what I was wearing—and my many weapons.

"Something you want to tell us, Chloe?" Pat mildly asked as I started cutting through his bonds. "Maybe that you've taken up a vigilante lifestyle?"

"You're worried about my clothes when you were—and technically still are—kidnapped by the Seelie and Unseelie monarchs of Magiford?" I whisper-hissed.

Pat shook his legs out, then stood when I cut through the last of the duct tape. "Yes, because it seems to be a symptom of a problem we didn't know about."

"I *told* you we should have moved to Magiford with her," Joy said. "But no, you *insisted* we had to wait until we were further in our careers."

"Yeah, because I didn't think she had a secret wish to become Batman!"

"She's a *cat*, she'd be *Catwoman*!"

"Both of you, keep *quiet*! We've still got to get out of here..." It was my turn to trail off when I finally got a look at my siblings.

Pat had bruises all over his face, and Joy had a cut that sliced across her arm. Her hair was so mussed, I was pretty sure a patch of it had to be missing.

"Hey, Chloe, it's fine." Pat set his hands on my shoulders and squeezed. "We're okay. Don't blame yourself for this. You didn't do this."

"I didn't," I agreed. "But I should have stopped it before it got to this point."

"You couldn't have done anything," Joy said. "It's fine. Let's go."

Except it wasn't fine.

The monarchs did this because they were convinced they could get to Noctus through me. This could happen again. Someone could hurt them again. And I'm finally strong enough to stop it.

"Chloe Grace Anderson," Joy said in a warning tone—she must have seen something in my face. "Don't—*Chloe*!"

CHAPTER TWENTY-SIX

Chloe

I shifted to cat and ran, using a boost of cat speed to get me out of the warehouse before my siblings could respond.

It took a moment for my eyes to adjust from the dim lighting of the warehouse to the outdoors—which was admittedly brighter than normal given the flaming torches that were the burning cars.

I saw the monarchs; they were starting to rally their guards to search, shouting orders at their grim troops.

They took Pat and Joy. They've been ripping apart human neighborhoods. Their own people don't want to do this, and they don't care.

I didn't know if it was all the training Charon and Noctus had invested in me, my gut instinct, or what, but something deep within me shifted.

Take them down. Now.

Keeping my cat shape, I surged up behind them, moving faster than a whisper.

I switched to my human shape when I reached Harel, pulled a

dagger from my harness, and had it at his throat with my left hand.

"Don't move," I said.

Darina swung her artifact—a wooden staff with the carving of a hawk on the top—at me.

I caught the glowing staff with my right hand. Whatever spell she'd prepared ghosted across my skin and fizzled out.

Keeping my left hand and dagger anchored at Harel's throat, I thrust Darina's staff back at her, then popped the tethers off my short sword and yanked it free.

Darina tried to hit me with her staff. That was a mistake, because I had elven steel.

I raised my sword to block her strike, and the edge of my blade cut straight through the body of the wooden hawk, and the glowing magic that surrounded her was snuffed out.

"No." Darina gaped at her now top-less—and magic-less—staff. "No—how?"

I didn't want to move in on her—I needed to keep my dagger at Harel's throat—but, lucky me, she was within kicking range!

I savagely kicked her on the side, which made her stagger and brought her head down a few inches, so I delivered a high kick to the side of her head.

That dropped her like a load of bricks, and gave me the chance to turn my attention to Harel.

He'd learned from my encounter with Darina, so while I was paying attention to the Unseelie queen, he'd carefully pulled his sword.

Darn it—I was hoping he'd go for his magic. I'll have to get out of this fast.

Charon was a good teacher, but he wasn't good enough to get me to the point of going head-to-head with a fae king after just a few weeks.

Harel roared as he tried to stab me. With his arms raised up, his tunic fell differently, and I could see the gray links of chain-mail under his pushed-up sleeves.

I dodged to the left, so he rushed past me.

He used a broadsword, which was so large and heavy he had to use both hands to wield it. It was a longer blade, so he'd have not only a strength advantage, but a reach advantage as well since my short sword was much smaller.

How do I counter it? Unlike Darina, he's got chainmail on under his tunic.

I skirted past a guard—the centaur who'd guarded the entrance to the second warehouse. He was still carrying his spear and shield—wait, shield!

"Shield!" I shouted as I circled around him. "Give it! Please!"

It didn't occur to me until after I'd spoken that I was asking a *fae* to hand over a potential weapon to beat a *fae monarch* with.

But, to my shock, he slipped his arm from the bands and passed it over when I sprinted past him.

"Thank you!" I took the shield, holding it by one of the two arm bands—I had to bide my time.

Harel tried to stab me again. I turned into a cat and ducked under him, then turned into a human again.

Smashing into existence underneath him, I knocked him over, then turned into a cat again so I didn't get tangled with him.

Once free of his legs, I turned back into a human and stabbed my short sword through his cloak, driving it into the ground.

As Harel struggled like a turtle tossed on his back, I raised the shield with both arms, then brought it down over his head with a tremendous clang.

The shield vibrated so badly from the impact it instantly numbed my hands.

Harel groaned.

He can still make noises—AGAIN!

I smashed the shield down on his head, and this time he

slumped over, either completely unconscious, or addled with a concussion.

I fixed my grip on the shield, then flung it like a frisbee.

Darina had recovered and was staggering toward me with an evil looking dagger, but the frisbee-shield caught her in the temple, and she fell with a thump.

I stood over the bodies of the unconscious monarchs, panting as my brain caught up with the adrenaline surging through my body.

I yanked my sword out of the ground and turned around. Every fae guard—Seelie and Unseelie—in the area immediately backed up.

Pat and Joy were fine. They were standing at the entrance to the warehouse, slack mouthed and wide eyed.

None of the fae looked inclined to attack either me or my siblings since I'd downed their leaders. *This is my chance*, I realized. *I can change things now—for me, but also for them. I can end their stupid fights.*

"Chloe," Joy started. "You just..."

I glanced down at Harel and Darina. "Yeah." I flicked my gaze to the fae guards. "And I'll do it again to anyone who *dares* to even think of harming you two."

The troll—who was holding the calico kitten in his hands—happened to be closest to Pat and Joy. He took a giant step away from them.

I fixed my grip on my short sword and screwed up what little courage I had. "Harel and Darina are no longer your rulers," I said. "In taking my siblings, they challenged me. *I won*."

The compound was silent, though I heard the faint sound of police sirens echo across the city. None of the fae protested.

"As soon as we're done here, you will all report in to the Curia Cloisters to settle the matter of who rules over you now," I said. "*Vow it*."

All the fae—fauns, centaurs, goblins, trolls—kneeled. Even the pixies landed so they could kneel. "We vow to follow your orders," they said, taking on a fae vow.

In addition to being unable to lie, fae had to follow the vows they made. They'd do as they said, or else magic would see that they paid.

I wanted to relax, but there was one more thing I needed to do.

"There is one more vow you must take," I started, then broke off.

My heart twisted in my chest—not because of the watchful stares of the fae, but because I didn't want to do this. This would cut my last tie to Noctus.

I owe him this much—for the training, for shielding me from the tracker, and most of all for telling me what I am.

I sucked in a breath. "You must vow not to speak of the supernatural whose house I stayed at," I said. "You *know* who I'm referring to, yes?"

The kneeling fae blanched.

"Yes," they murmured.

Joy straightened up. "Wait, who are you talking about?"

"Then vow—you will not speak of him, or venture to his neighborhood and house without his permission. If asked about tonight, all you must say is Darina and Harel took my siblings to lure me out. Promise it, now." My voice cracked, but none of the fae seemed to notice.

They started to repeat the vow back to me.

It's not a full fix, but if Noctus doesn't tell the Paragon about my siblings, he might be able to get through this without more of Magiford learning about him. Since that's what he needs, that's what I want for him. No matter how sad it makes me.

Joy elbowed Pat, who was bent over his cellphone. "Pat—are you getting this?"

Pat, thankfully, ignored her.

When the fae finished this vow, I relaxed. "Good." I paused, then added. "If clashes continue between you—if *anyone* fights over the Unseelie and Seelie thrones—I will come find your new monarchs. In the dark. They won't even have the chance to scream for help."

A few of the guards nearest to me audibly gulped.

I glanced down at the brained monarchs at my feet. "The Curia Cloisters will deal with these two. Keep them under control until then."

The fae, still kneeling, bowed to me.

I sheathed my short sword and replaced the leather straps to hold it in place, then walked out of the circle the fae had formed around their monarchs.

I better call the Cloisters as soon as Pat, Joy, and I are out of the area.

I marched toward my siblings, slowing down when I was about halfway to them. Something stirred around me, and I felt the claws of fear dig into my heart.

No.

I whirled around, scanning the area, all while the oppressive, terror-inspiring sensation of the tracker scraped at my back.

He's here! He must have thought Harel and Darina had heard from me! I bet he really was planning to grab me once they lured me here.

I unsheathed my sword, which sent alarm spiraling through the fae guards as they wobbled to their feet while simultaneously trying to back away from me. I ignored them, as I frantically tried to tell which direction the horrible fear was drifting from.

The area was well lit between the warehouse lights and all the fae toting their globes of light, but darkness and shadows sprawled outside the compound.

He could be anywhere.

"Chloe, cat up," Pat called from where he stood at the warehouse entrance.

I barely heard him. "Why?" I tried to tamp down on the direction the tracker's magic was coming from, but it was starting to grow fainter.

Pat jerked this thumb toward the street, which was starting to glow red and blue as cop cars rolled onto the street, sirens blaring. "Because the cavalry is here, and I'm getting you and Joy out."

Just as quickly as it had arrived, the horrible sensation of the tracker's presence retreated. I blinked in surprise as I felt the last wisp of his terrible magic disappear.

He left? Why—wait.

"What cavalry?" I asked.

Pat held up his cellphone—he must have grabbed it off the fallen guards. "I got a text message out to my squad before these goons nabbed me."

"Oh." I relaxed and put my sword back in its scabbard.

That makes sense, then, that the tracker left. He might not care about bystanders but a police car or two, combined with fifty fae guards? He wouldn't risk it. Thank goodness for Pat's connections!

I shifted into my cat form and jumped into Joy's outstretched arms.

Pat continued, "My squad's been trying to save us, but they had to work with the Magiford Police Department since the area is out of our jurisdiction."

"Good," Joy said. "That will make things easier to clean up."

What do you mean, that will make things easier—WOAH!

The Magiford police cars with the familiar insignias pulled up on the street, but a large, unmarked SUV barreled into the warehouse yard, with red lights flashing on the dashboard.

"Fae, put your hands in the air so the officers can see them." Pat roughly petted the top of my head, then meandered toward the anxious fae guards.

He waved when three officers in swat gear piled out of the unmarked SUV...along with an enormous gray and brown mottled wolf, and a bouncing ball of glowing light that had to be a pixie.

I stared at the wolf, my fur puffing up. *That...that's a werewolf.*

"Yes, he is a werewolf," Joy said, guessing my thoughts. "And that's a pixie. They're both part of Pat's squad."

But…he's on a human city police force. How—and why didn't he tell me?

The werewolf and pixie trotted up and down the lines Pat made the fae guards form—the wolf appeared to be sniffing them, while I was pretty sure the pixie was tracing through the magic in the area.

"Pat got his department to hire the werewolf last winter—apparently there's a werewolf in the police department of some tiny Wisconsin town, Timber Ridge. He argued that set a precedent. But the pixie's been with his department for three years now."

Joy hesitated, then added, "He was determined to get supernaturals in the department for the sake of the police force, and because he's been preparing—we've been preparing—to make the move to Magiford, and we wanted to get positions that would put enough force behind our names to protect you."

…What?

One of the officers dressed in swat gear waved to Joy. She shifted me to one arm to wave back. They knew her. But I didn't know anything about it—whatever this was.

I have too many questions—I need answers.

I wriggled out of Joy's arms, then tucked myself behind a warehouse wall—where I wouldn't be seen with my admittedly intimidating array of weaponry—and turned human.

"What are you talking about, Joy?" I asked. "You're humans, when it comes to supernaturals—"

"We're nothing, unless we're useful, we know," Joy said. "We figured out quickly the only way we'd ever be able to help you was to be part of the bridge that spans the gap between supernaturals and humans."

I fussed with my harness, trying to give my nervous fingers something to do. "So Pat is working with supernaturals?"

"With the intent of building his resume and skills, so when he transferred to Magiford he could start a similar program here, which would give him some clout in the supernatural world," Joy said.

He was planning to move here? But he never said anything to me...

"Wait, you said 'we'. What have *you* been doing that you didn't tell me about?" I snapped my shoulders back as I frowned at my older sister.

Joy held her hands up. "I've been working as a city attorney, as I always have."

"But?" I suspiciously asked.

"But...I have a nonprofit where I teach supernatural clients how city systems work—how to get a permit, local ordinances, that kind of thing," Joy said. "I have a lot of fae clients—they want to know how to get IDs, how to use the library, any of them getting human employment need social security numbers, and so on. Though I've also helped a few vampires get some of their personal letters and belongings back from museums."

Oh my gosh, my siblings are poster children for "How to Win Friends and Influence People" I realized. *Ker would die laughing if she knew.*

"You did all of this without telling me?" I asked.

"Because you refused to tell us how bad things were," Joy said. "We knew you were getting messed with, but you'd never tell us. If we'd known things had escalated to the point where a Seelie King and Unseelie Queen were bothering you, we would have done something much sooner."

"Things...changed this spring," I said evasively.

Joy stared hard at the hilt of my short sword that poked up over my shoulder. "Yeah, I can see that."

I studied Joy; the lights on her face constantly switched from blue to red and back thanks to the police lights, and I could hear Pat's familiar, sarcastic, lecturing tone.

"It's not that I feel betrayed," I said, struggling to put my feelings into words. "It's just...why didn't you tell me? I would have just left Magiford—"

"Which is exactly why we didn't tell you," Joy said. "You would have settled somewhere just because you wanted us to be safe, and that's not fair to you. You *deserve* to have a place in supernatural society. We want to help you fight for it."

"Because you don't think I could do it by myself?"

"Because we're family. Family means you don't *have* to do it by yourself," Joy said.

She's right. That's why I had to leave Noct—

I ruthlessly cut the thought off, and cracked a smile. "Thanks, Joy."

"Of course." Joy—several inches taller than me—stooped over so she could hug me. "Although you owe us an explanation about the sword, and how you suddenly came to have spy-class abilities."

I weakly laughed. "Yeah, it's not as impressive as it seems. The whole time I was anxious, and I only didn't get caught because the kitten—the kitten!"

I poked my head out of the warehouse.

"The little calico kitten?" Joy asked.

"Yeah, I dumped her off on the troll to keep her safe—but I can't just leave her here as a stray," I said.

"Okay, I get it. Turn back into a cat, and we can go out there."

"Thanks, Joy." I swapped to my cat body, then butted my head against her leg.

"Yeah, you're charming, I know. Let's go rescue a kitten." Joy picked me up, and walked out of the warehouse.

I purred loudly in her arms and started to automatically set my paws on either side of her neck, then froze. *No, I don't do that with her...only with Noctus.*

That one realization cast a bittersweet shade on a triumphant night.

I'd been able to save my siblings because of Noctus, Ker, Aristide, and Charon.

And I'd never see any of them again.

CHAPTER TWENTY-SEVEN

Noctus

"—Eventually the Curia Cloisters' task force was called onto the scene. The fae guards were released, but Darina and Harel were taken in for medical attention due to severe concussions and possible brain damage. Both are awake and have been informed by the Paragon that they've been stripped of their titles and ranks." Charon looked up from his notebook. He'd pulled his hood high over his head, so the shadows made him appear gloomy even though his expression hadn't changed.

How fascinating that Chloe's exit has him emoting this much.

I rubbed the metal cuffs on my wrists as I stared at the fake sky painted in the practice arena by magic. "The Paragon hasn't made a connection between Chloe and myself?"

Since the Paragon hadn't returned my phone call until after Chloe had saved her siblings, I'd fed him some ridiculous question about owning cats to explain my need to speak to him. He'd been positively giddy and had yakked for a good hour until I felt I was beyond suspicion and hung up on him.

"It appears so," Charon said. "While he was brought in to deal with Darina and Harel, he hasn't interacted with any of the fae involved in the kidnapping of Chloe's siblings."

"What of the Seelie and Unseelie Courts?" I asked.

"They appear to be most concerned with survival." Charon flipped to a different page in his tiny notebook. "Both the Seelie and Unseelie Courts already sent representatives to Queen Leila of the Night Court. She's temporarily sent some of her people to reinforce them until new rulers are selected, or until her people finish processing all the requests she received from the fae eager to join her Court."

"I was referring to their silence."

"Ah. Yes. The fae who were at the warehouses and made the vow Chloe required of them have, as expected given the nature of fae vows, kept the promise and have spoken not a word of your connection."

"Excellent. We'd better use this opportunity to our advantage," I said. "I want Darina's and Harel's memories wiped."

Charon looked up from his notebook. "With memory charms?"

"Yes."

Ker frowned deeply. "Why wipe them? Someone is going to find out about the connection between you and Chloe eventually. Forget the possibility of Harel and Darina blabbing, there were fae not present at the warehouses who knew 'cat girl' was staying at your house. They'll talk."

"Not necessarily." Charon narrowed his eyes as he thought. "Chloe's disposal of Darina and Harel has inspired a great deal of...*respect* for her among the lower fae Courts. I imagine they keenly remember their history of picking on her prior to her time with us. With her newly trained powers, they are going to do everything they can to avoid stirring her wrath given that she'd be perfectly justified in attacking them."

"Exactly," I said. "With Chloe having cowed most of the fae, we have the possibility to emerge from this without anyone else learning of our existence—if we take care of Harel and Darina."

Ker folded her arms across her chest. "You weren't thinking about this when Chloe first told you about her siblings getting kidnapped."

"No, but that was when she was still one of us," I answered. "She isn't anymore, which means now is the time to cover our tracks and stop anyone else from learning of us." I shifted my gaze back to Charon. "I'll lead the team you assemble. We do this tonight."

"Understood, Your Majesty," Charon said.

"Good." I flexed my fingers, warming them up. "No further questions."

"Now that's a lie," Aristide shouted from the rock he was lounging on. "You haven't asked the most important question that we *all* want to know: how is Chloe?"

"She's fine, obviously," I said. "Or Charon would have led with that."

"Yeah, but how about her siblings?" Ker asked. "Is she back in her apartment? What's going on?"

Charon stared at me as he clutched his notebook so hard I thought I heard a paper rip. He wouldn't say a word until I asked, even though he was obviously burning to tell me.

"You are all aware that she's gone, correct?" I asked. "Continuing to inquire after her is only going to drag out the separation."

"Oh, pooh." Aristide grabbed his white-tipped walking stick and slid off his rock. "Just because you've given up all hope doesn't mean we have to."

"Yeah," Ker echoed like a bad sidekick.

Charon only communicated the intensity of his desire to speak by staring harder at me.

"Fine," I capitulated. "How is Chloe?"

"She's returned to her studio apartment—both of her siblings went with her. She's called her boss, Ms. Booker, and it seems she is back on the schedule for work. She has an appointment with the Curia Cloisters next week. I believe she intends to tell them she's a shadow," Charon blurted out.

I shot Aristide a look he couldn't see. "See? Fine." I made sure to layer my sarcasm on extra thick for his benefit.

"What's she going to do about the tracker?" Ker asked. "Didn't the scout report someone encouraged Harel and Darina to nab her siblings as a way to get to Noctus? I'd bet my signed copy of *How to Win Friends and Influence People* that the creep tracking her is behind that."

Charon gave me another wordless stare.

I sighed—I hadn't wanted to admit this. "I've assigned additional warriors to watch Chloe's apartment and place of employment."

"If the tracker comes after her again, we'll know," Charon said. "And I flatter myself to say I trained her well enough to be able to beat him."

"Probably," Aristide said, sounding unconvinced. "Unless he messes with her siblings again."

"Except she beat the snot out of Harel and Darina for doing exactly that," Ker said. "Sounds like she's werewolf-fierce when her family is involved."

"I would agree with that conclusion," Charon said.

I felt the magic in me swirl—so eager to find a release it felt like it was burning me from the inside out. "The point is, she's fine. Now, everyone out."

"Ah, if I might—one last thing, Your Majesty." Charon flipped to a new page in his notebook. "Early this morning—while the Curia Cloisters were busy dealing with the fae—the security system on the clocktower got a visual of the fae selling illegal artifacts that we learned of from the Queen's Court Café. He walked past the clocktower, keeping to the sidewalk."

"He's back in town, then?" Aristide tapped his way across the arena. "I wonder if that means they're planning to set up another operation."

"If so, it is an indication that there are larger games at play," Charon said.

It was a worrisome statement, but in a way it was excellent timing.

I can throw myself into catching this fae—that will distract me from... other things.

"Spread his information out among the elves who work in Magiford, as well as among the scouts," I said. "I want to know this fae's every movement."

"Understood, your Majesty."

"Now, *leave*." It came out as more of a growl than I wanted—I didn't need everyone to realize just how much Chloe's leaving affected me.

Aristide tilted his head. I thought he'd argue, but he must have realized something was off, because he tapped his walking stick on the ground, then made his way toward the exit.

Ker frowned. "Are you okay, Noctus?"

I attempted a smile. "Fine, but thanks for your concern."

Ker also tilted her head—though she tipped from side to side like a wolf. "Noctus...are you sure about letting Chloe go—"

"Positive," I said. "She wouldn't have been happy here. Eventually she would have wanted her family."

"But couldn't they have moved in with us?" Ker asked.

"Her *human* family?" I asked. "Including her brother and sister who have both been very publicly pursuing human-supernatural relations? They couldn't slip into obscurity, Ker. Neither could Chloe, for that matter. She's a shadow. Someone obviously knew that when they gave her to the humans to safekeep. Whether she knows it or not, she's destined to play a larger role in the future of supernaturals,"

"But you bonded with her."

"Because I thought she was a *cat*." I made my voice as flat and emotionless as possible.

"But—"

"*Ker*," I warned her, my voice deepening.

Ker watched me with sad brown eyes. Slowly, carefully, she stepped closer to me and patted my back. "I'm sorry," she said.

As am I.

I kept my mouth shut.

One last pat, and Ker trotted after Aristide, disappearing into the main staircase.

Charon flipped his tiny notebook shut, then bowed.

"Thank you for the report, Charon," I said.

"Of course, Your Majesty." Charon silently padded after our friends, and he too entered the staircase, the door swinging shut behind him.

I stretched for a few minutes, giving my friends the chance to get higher before I unleashed my bloodthirsty magic.

The metal cuffs on my wrists shattered, breaking into a thousand tiny pieces.

I held the shards suspended in the air with my magic—I'd need to piece them together before I went upstairs.

The rest of my magic rampaged, expelling from me so forcefully that it flung the giant boulders at the sides of the arena, leaving craters in the painted walls.

Sighing in irritation, I exerted control over my powers, reigning them in. I needed to release my magic, but I was not going to be so incompetent as to lose control. Loss of control was for overly emotional and feeble elves, like my brothers had been.

My magic raged under my firm hand, howling in anger.

"Enough." I squeezed down on it, cutting it off so it stopped flowing from me. Despite how desperate my magic was for a release, I had perfect control over it. I held back enough magic to bring down the mountain my villa was built into.

It was then that I realized it wasn't *my* magic that was wailing. It was wild magic.

The pleasant hum it had produced in Chloe's presence was gone. Now, it was keening—an unpleasant, high-pitched noise that sounded like profound loss.

Wild magic was mourning Chloe's absence.

"Oh *shut up*!" I snapped at it, a flicker of anger burning in my soul. "Do you really think I'm going to feel bad about this? I killed my own family because of *you*. I ended a dynasty to save your precious humans. I'm not sacrificing more. Whatever you wanted Chloe for, I don't care. You will not play with her life!"

I released my magic, which roared with my anger, burning the wild magic in an inferno.

I took half a breath, before it hit me.

What am I doing? I regained control, tamping down on my magic once again. I didn't hold it all in, I let a steady river flow from me, but I shifted to control myself.

Feel nothing, think nothing. Perfect control.

I exhaled as my magic went from wildfire to pliant and calm.

This...this is another reason why it's just as well Chloe left. I can't let my feelings control me, because everyone except me would pay the price.

EPILOGUE

Chloe

When I stepped out of my bathroom and into my studio apartment, Pat was kicking his shoes off at the door with a sour expression, while Joy was filling her water bottle at my kitchen sink and humming happily.

"Hey, Pat." I smiled, and was only slightly distracted when I noticed the lengthening shadows out the one window in my studio apartment.

*It's almost evening...*I automatically checked my watch, but it was Friday—I didn't have a shift at Book Nookery until tomorrow.

Pat grunted a greeting as he rifled through the pockets of his jeans—he must have changed at his new place before coming over.

"Was your first day that rough?" I asked.

"What?" Pat's forehead smoothed over so it was wrinkle free. "No. It was good—though the task force is so loosely cobbled together that it needs some serious restructuring. And—though I *hate* to admit it—I'll need Joy to look at some of their procedures. The only reason they haven't gotten their butts sued yet is because supernaturals are terrified of the squad. As they start dealing with more humans, they'll need to learn about police procedures. It's a good team, though. Some of them are scary strong, but that's fun to see."

"If you like the new job, why do you look so upset?" I asked.

Pat narrowed his eyes. "Because coming to your building is a reminder that I'm related to a low-bellied *thief*," he growled.

Joy screwed on the lid of her water bottle, her makeup and clothes perfect despite the drive she'd had to get here. "You're just upset because you didn't think to check with Chloe's apartment manager first. It's not my fault they only had one apartment available right now."

"You aren't even living in it because you don't have a job in Magiford yet!" Pat said. "You should have just let me have it!"

Joy tapped her chin and looked thoughtful. "Mmm, no."

"It's a security thing," Pat argued. "What if that creep who's stalking her comes sniffing around some more?"

For maybe the sixth time since reuniting with my siblings, I wondered if it was truly wise to fess up about the whole tracker drama to my family, given that Pat and Joy loved to use him as an excuse for corralling me into doing what they wanted.

No, they needed to know in case he tries to go after one of them. Again.

There was no doubt in my mind—after sensing his presence at the warehouses—that the tracker was behind the entire kidnapping plot, and that he'd hung around, waiting for a chance to take me out.

It was a good thing Pat's department and the Magiford police showed up when they did.

I hadn't sensed the tracker since that night, but I doubted he'd given up. He'd probably temporarily retreated now that the Curia

Cloisters knew about him and were actively combing the city for him.

But while I'd told my family about the tracker, I hadn't said a word about Noctus and the others. When Joy asked me about the vow I made the fae take, I explained that some supernaturals had taken me in to keep me safe from the tracker, and I wanted to make sure they weren't endangered because of me.

Joy's expression shifted from smug to worried, and she glanced over at me. "I've got some job interviews lined up," she said. "I promise I'll be living in Magiford in under a month."

"The building has new, updated security, and the Curia Cloisters are trying to track him down," I said. "Since lots of witnesses from the Seelie and Unseelie Courts saw him meeting with Darina and Harel, they know what he looks like. He can't slink around undetected like he did previously. I'm safe."

"But—" Joy started.

I unrelentingly continued. "Pat, stop trying to use me to guilt trip Joy. Your condo is perfect for you since it's close to the Curia Cloisters. You'll want to be close in case of emergencies."

Pat made a noise at the back of his throat that said he wasn't convinced, until his eyes strayed to the sword harness I was still wearing—I'd temporarily adapted my wardrobe to include slacks and suspenders, which made my leather harness look like more of a fashion choice.

He sighed, rolled his shoulders back, then forced a smile. "So are we going to go out for dinner, or what?"

"Of course!" Joy crossed from my kitchen to the front door in a step and pinched Pat's cheek. "We've got to celebrate your new job!"

"Ow—stop that." Pat swatted her hand away. "Then let's go. I'm starving, and pretty much every place is going to have a waiting time since it's Friday night."

Pat put his shoes back on, then banged his way out of the apartment.

Joy started to follow him, then paused. "Chloe? Do you have a backpack or something I can use?" She held her water bottle and purse up. "I'd rather carry my stuff around on my back."

"You know they'll have water at the restaurant, right?" Pat called from the hallway. "It's not like you're a fish who is going to die without it."

"Hydration is key to a healthy and long life, as well as good skin and the glow of beauty," Joy declared.

"Oh," Pat said. "In that case, I've got news for you: it's not working."

"Yeah, I've got a backpack," I said before they could start another fight. "Just give me a minute, and I'll grab it."

"Perfect," Joy said. "We'll wait for you at *my* parking spot, that I have because *I* have an apartment here."

"You're the worst," Pat said.

Joy laughed maniacally as she shut my apartment door.

I grabbed my cellphone, then darted around the screen that partitioned off my bed from the rest of my apartment. Kneeling, I pushed aside the suitcase I still hadn't unpacked, and grabbed my backpack.

I haven't opened this since the night I left Noctus.

When I'd stopped by my apartment the night of the kidnapping, I'd yanked my daggers, laptop, cellphone, and wallet out, and then abandoned the backpack in the corner with my suitcase.

It'd been a week since then. I'd already had three shifts at Book Nookery, and Pat had moved in two days ago.

Life had returned to normal shockingly fast.

Well, maybe not normal. I didn't know Joy and Pat had plans to move to Magiford.

I picked at one of the zippers of the backpack and glanced at my cellphone again.

I'd been hoping that maybe Noctus—or Charon, Aristide, or Ker for that matter—would reach out. That maybe they'd want to know that I was safe and my siblings were fine. I'd gone so far as to plan how I'd tell them that I'd trashed the Seelie King and Unseelie Queen, because that was bound to make Charon happy.

But I hadn't gotten any texts or calls. And when I'd tried to call Charon the night everything went down to let him know how I'd done, a mechanical voice had told me the number no longer existed.

It really is over. We can't even be friends from a distance.

Yesterday, I'd "happened" to wander through Magiford so I was only a block or two away from the Cape Cod's cul-de-sac, and I could feel several new spells on it—including what I was certain was a powerful confusion charm. If he was that determined to stay hidden...

I'd rather let it end like this, with some sadness and regret, particularly since I know it's all just to protect them. I told Noctus this was it. I agreed to cutting ties—I had to.

None of this was our fault—not mine, and not Noctus's.

It was the product of what had to happen. I needed and wanted to be there for my family. Noctus needed to protect his people.

All the laughter and fun from the past few months was the very short timeframe in which our contending desires could survive. But that was over now.

I can still miss it, though. I unzipped my backpack with more force than necessary and scooped out my clothes that I'd brought back home. *And I can be sad it's over. It's proof that we had fun and we were friends—*

My thoughts stopped when I unzipped a different pocket, and I found my black collar with its three pomegranate red gems.

I rubbed my thumb over the gems, and my throat squeezed tight. Noctus must have put it in my backpack when he'd given me my weapons.

It's not an invitation to come back—the collar will only rebind us if Noctus puts it on me. But it's an acknowledgment. Of what happened...and maybe what could have been.

Tears burned my eyes, and I hiccupped a little.

Who am I kidding? I'm not sad about this, I'm broken hearted. But, this is the way things have to be. Supernaturals wouldn't accept elves—they'd never accept Noctus as the last King of the Mors elves. But it's not fair, and it's not what I want.

I gave in and sobbed as I clutched the collar to my heart. In a minute I'd make myself stop, and go eat with my siblings with a grateful heart.

But for now, for this moment, I could let my heart break.

To be Continued in The King's Queen: Gate of Myth and Power Book 3

For free short stories and more information about the Gate of Myth and Power Series, visit kmshea.com!

OTHER SERIES BY K. M. SHEA

The Snow Queen

Timeless Fairy Tales

The Fairy Tale Enchantress

The Elves of Lessa

Hall of Blood and Mercy

Court of Midnight and Deception

Pack of Dawn and Destiny

Gate of Myth and Power

King Arthur and Her Knights

Robyn Hood

The Magical Beings' Rehabilitation Center

Second Age of Retha: Written under pen name A. M. Sohma

ADDITIONAL NOVELS

Life Reader

Princess Ahira

A Goose Girl

ABOUT THE AUTHOR

K. M. Shea is a fantasy-romance author who never quite grew out of adventure books or fairy tales, and still searches closets in hopes of stumbling into Narnia. She is addicted to sweet romances, witty characters, and happy endings. She also writes LitRPG and GameLit under the pen name, A. M. Sohma.

Hang out with the K. M. Shea Community at...
kmshea.com

Printed in Great Britain
by Amazon

38967030R00195